Legends of Good Women

Sandra Adickes

Castalia Bookmakers, Inc.
Long Lake, Minnesota

All of the characters in this book are fictitious, and any resemblance to actual persons, living or dead, is purely coincidental.

All rights reserved.
Copyright © *1992 by Sandra Adickes.*
Cover art copyright © *1992 by Mary Manning.*
No part of this book may be reproduced or transmitted in any form or by any means, electronic or mechanical, including photocopying, recording, or by any information storage and retrieval system; without permission in writing from the publisher. For information address: Castalia Bookmakers, Inc. 770 Tonkawa Road, Long Lake, Minnesota 55356

ISBN 1-878723-01-4

First Edition, First Printing

*I want to dedicate this book
to all the good women in my life,
but especially
Anna, Edith, Joanne, and Delores*

CHAPTER

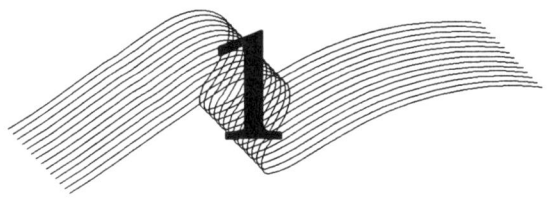

May, 1980

When the car would not start, when only end-of-the-world silence followed the turn of the key in the ignition, I went back to the house, grabbed the telephone directory, turned to the automotive services section, skipped past five names, most of them closer to my home than the name I fingered, *Ritter's Auto Center: Family Business — Over Thirty-Six Years of Experience*, and dialed the number, wondering if the family business was now owned by the prince of my adolescent fantasies, wondering if the prince had become a frog, wondering if the encounter I had wanted yet avoided in the year since I had returned to my home town was about to happen. I must have unconsciously set it up, I thought; that must have been the reason why I, a maternal car owner, had neglected my six-year-old Volvo so badly the battery had died.

To the unfamiliar voice that answered, I identified myself and explained that my battery was dead, I did not have access to booster cables, and needed towing. He asked my address; I told him, and he promised me "the kid" would be at my home with the tow truck in less than a half hour.

And indeed he was. I walked onto my front porch as a tall male dismounted from the tow truck cab; he was about seventeen or eighteen, a well-built, blond-haired, regular featured, good looking, polite-faced midwesterner my ex-husband would describe as a "real *goyische* kopf" and my daughter Janey would say was "neat." Because of the startling resemblance, I knew instantly whose "kid" he was. He looked at me and then down at the name on his call slip; the blonde woman in the cotton plaid shirt, blue jeans, and running shoes was obviously not the person he was expecting to see.

"Dr. Schaefer?"

"That's right."

I went back to the car and released the hood; after a brief examination he confirmed that my battery was dead.

"I could charge you up," he offered, "but it would only die on you again. You really need a new one."

"Take her into the garage," I told him.

He quickly hooked up my beloved elderly Volvo; we both climbed into the cab of the tow truck; then Mike—the name was on the pocket of his olive drab coverall—drove from my house on the east side of town a few blocks from the Great River, which curves at this point so the town is to its north. Star Lake, once a brawling river town, boomed when the bars and brothels gave way after the Civil War to a lumber industry, then became less prosperous when the lumber industry was replaced by production line industries.

Mike drove over to Broadway, past the center of town with its mix of business and professional offices, churches, and the large Victorian homes built by the town's early entrepreneurs, through the better residential side of town, and past the high school at the western edge of the artificial lake which gives the town its name. The big sign which usually honored the student named "Warrior of the Week" was draped in black.

"Did you know the students who were killed?" I asked.

"Yes. They weren't close friends, but they were classmates."

On the previous Saturday, a car with six Star Lake High School seniors on their prom night had gone into a ravine. Their bodies had not been found until late Sunday afternoon. This week a memorial service had been held at the high school, and the *Star Lake Daily News* declared the town in mourning. One of my reasons for returning here to live was to shelter my daughter from the New York drug scene; I had forgotten how strongly the culture of alcohol prevailed in the midwest, and how, each spring, young lives were claimed by it.

"That was a dreadful accident. Their parents must just be heartbroken. I can't imagine anything worse than to lose a child." I looked at Mike. "And your school, your classmates especially, must be devastated."

"Yeah. Everyone's down about it."

"When do you graduate?"

"Next week. I'm finished with classes, everything except exams." He kept his eyes on the road.

"I graduated from Star Lake High School."

"Really," he said, polite enough to try to pretend he was interested."

"Yes, class of '63."

"Where did you go to college?" He made a left.

"UW, Madison."

"I'm planning to go stay close to home and go to UW, LaCrosse. Where'd you go to medical school?" He turned around to check the Volvo.

"I'm not an M.D., I'm a PH.D. I teach at Fontbonne College."

"Oh."

Sensing I had dropped in Mike's esteem, I dropped the conversation. But Mike had a question.

"When you were at Madison, were you involved in the anti-war protests and stuff?"

"Yes, I was."

"Wow. I've heard people talk about what Madison was like in those days. Huge demonstrations, students taking over buildings, and of course the bombing."

"The bombing was in 1970, after my time."

"Well, it was part of the same thing."

I was ready to argue that in 1970, when Karlton Armstrong planted a bomb in the Math Research building that exploded and killed a graduate student, Robert Fassnacht, I had separated myself from the male-dominated Left that could justify such actions, but sensing that I would sound self-serving and unconvincing, I answered simply, "Not in my mind, it wasn't."

"I bet the girls at Fontbonne are different from the way you were." I could hear the smirk in his voice.

"Indeed they are."

"What are they like?"

"They are pretty, nice girls from good, affluent Catholic families. They look forward to having it all: careers, good marriages, happy, healthy children. They think life is just peachy right now." I knew Mike would not hear the irony in my voice.

"I can't complain. Except for the tragedy, of course. But I've had a great time in high school. I was on the football team, and we won conference and regional, and made it to state. And I was on the softball team, and we made it to regional."

You're your father's son, I thought.

"But," Mike continued, "I don't think college will be as exciting for me as it was for you when you were young."

Mike turned from Broadway to the highway service road, and then pulled into Ritter's Auto Service. He parked the truck on the side of the service station lot and fitted my Volvo into a space among other cars under repair. I got out of the truck and waited while Mike detached the car and then I walked with him toward the service station office.

"My dad will give you the bad news officially," he said, nodding toward the office. I looked expectantly through the office window, my pulse racing a bit, but I did not recognize the man Mike indicated, a stocky, brown-haired man in a coverall like Mike's who was talking to a man in a business suit.

"Hi, Dad; hi, Uncle Ted," Mike said as we entered the office.

"Uncle Ted" turned around, and I immediately adjusted the characters in my fantasy. Ted Ritter, whom Mike resembled even more than he did his own father, had been the object of my almost obsessive infatuation through four years of high school. He had started out at Madison when I did, but had not completed his sophomore year. I had concluded that when he left college, he had gone into his father's business, where he had worked part-time during his high school years. But obviously Ted's brother had taken over the family business, while Ted had gone on to a white collar career.

Facing him at last, I remembered myself as I had been, a giddily anxious teenager standing in the high school corridor, pretending to look for books in my hall locker, daily risking being marked late to class, just to see him as he walked by, surrounded by his friends like a prince among courtiers. If he was aware of me – and he must have been, I was so crudely obvious – he had the grace to ignore me. But his friends noticed me. One day, seeing me gawk after Ted, one of his followers had called out in the hallway, "There she is again, Ted, waiting for just one glimpse of you." Ted had not turned around, but his friends stopped to laugh at me. The boy who pointed me out to them widened his eyes and dropped his jaw, mocking my love-lorn stare. Each time he saw me after that day, he made a jeering comment like "Teddy's girl, don't you wish." I stopped waiting in the hall, but I did not abandon my vigil. All through high school and even after, I knew, with that entranced concentration so many adolescent girls have (but not, I fervently hope, my Janey) what Ted was doing and whom he was dating. Only after I had pitched myself headlong into civil rights and anti-war activism, and, of course, after meeting my husband, had I managed to purge him from my memory. But during the early days in Star Lake after my return, seeing the service station sign as I drove to K-Mart had brought the memory of him back.

"I know you," the man he had become was saying. "You're Claire Schaefer. I'm Ted Ritter. We were in the same class in high school."

If he recognized me, he must have remembered the lonely, esteemless girl I had been. Was he being kind or had I, as I wanted to think, improved so much that he could be pleased to see me?

Ted introduced me to his brother, who also had his name, 'Jack' hand- embroidered on his coverall pocket.

"Why don't you catch up with my brother on old times while I check out your car, Dr. Schaefer?" Jack suggested and then left us.

As I faced Ted, I suddenly remembered a meeting of my consciousness-raising group nearly ten years before. We had gone around the circle indulging in a fantasy many women probably have: a triumphant reunion with the men who had been the boys we had adored. "He'll be fat, bald, and loud," I had predicted of Ted, but the man standing before me had kept his hair, fitness, and good looks, seemed confident but not boorish. He looked like a successful, well-married business man. I hoped he would ask me why his brother had called me 'Dr. Schaefer.'

"How do you like living in Star Lake again?"

I gave Ted an edited version of the answer I have prepared for this inquiry. I liked having a house, the house I had grown up in and taken for granted, but now appreciated after living in a small New York apartment. I had renewed appreciation for the natural beauty of this region, the Driftless Area, which the ice age never reached, leaving untouched the ancient high hills and narrow slits of land, or coulees, in this corner of Wisconsin. I told Ted I enjoyed the outdoor life, although I could do without so much winter. Ted actually seemed to be interested. Feeling my confidence rising, I continued: "I'm glad to be away from New York's random violence, but I miss New York's choices and energy and variety. I miss the New York Public Library. I miss hearing West Indian women in the subway saying 'Just put a little of that powder in his coffee m'dear, and he won't give you any more trouble.' I miss seeing people or different colors, sizes and temperaments. Most of all, I miss my friends.

"But," I added, "my daughter has had a harder time adjusting to living here than I've had re-adjusting. A child who has just discovered the joys of strolling with her friends through Greenwich Village or browsing with them in Bloomingdale's can be devastated by being transplanted to a small midwestern community where kids can only go places if they are taken there by their parents. And while I am consoled for what I miss by the beauty and peace of this place, my daughter days, 'Beauty's boring. I miss the action.'"

"How old is she?"

"Twelve. Just twelve this month."

"Does she like sports?"

"Not too much."

"Has she made friends?"

"Janey's a very popular sixth grader."

I watched his face for a trace of the thought that my daughter must indeed be different from me if she was popular, but Ted just nodded in a reflective parent-to-parent way.

I was on the point of asking him about his children when Jack Ritter came back and told me that my car needed a new battery and the "damages" would be the figure he had named, one hundred dollars. I told him to repair the car and asked when it would be ready. Jack said by three o'clock. I started to say goodbye to Ted, but he asked if he could give me a lift, and I said I would appreciate a ride to the library. Ted said he would be glad to drop me off. He told his brother that if he did not drop in again to see him during the week, he would see him at their folks' on Sunday.

"Nice meeting you and doing business with you, Dr. Schaefer," Jack said to me. "So long, little brother," he called after Ted. The joke was that Ted was almost five inches taller than Jack. I felt a pang of envy for their good-natured brotherly banter. Janey had reason to complain about being an only child.

I walked with Ted to the curb where his car, a late model Buick, was parked. He opened the passenger door for me and I slid onto the front seat, conscious of the contrast between the new- chrome-and-leather smell of Ted's car and the old-car-mixed-with- cat odor of mine. Ted got into the car, adjusted a briefcase so that it would not crowd us on the seat and began driving toward the center of town. As he made a left turn into Main Street, Ted said, "My shop is down there," and nodded in the direction of the water tower by the riverside.

"Shop?"

"A screen printing firm I started five years ago."

I asked the obvious question: "What do you print?"

"Just about anything you'd want to put a message on: signs, banners, bumper stickers, magnetic signs, notebooks, pens, award plaques, photo cards, t-shirts, 3-d buttons."

"Those last two items are products my daughter collects. She may have samples of your work."

Ted quickly reached down with his right hand, flipped open the briefcase on the seat, and pulled out a catalog. Ted flipped through several pages, closed the catalog and moved it toward me across the top of the briefcase. "These are some of our products."

The catalog of Ted's company, Magnagraphics, showed photos of the items he had named; most of them were products for local retailers and manufacturers, but a conference notebook bore the name of General Mills and a promotional key chain had been made for Kentucky Fried Chicken.

"Your products look good. Is your company doing well?"

"Yes, we're making a go of it now, but it was tough at the beginning. It's hard to start a business in a small town; this small town, anyway." Ted spoke matter-of-factly, without complaint.

"Why? I would think that new business, small or large, would be welcome here."

"It isn't welcome if the established business community sees new business as encroaching on their turf. For example, two years ago, some people wanted to buy land out on the highway to open a restaurant. Well the Maleskis, who own the Hillside Fish and Seafood Restaurant, saw it as too much competition for their place and told the banks that they and members of their numerous family would take their money out if the banks financed the purchase, so the land remains unsold." Ted spoke as if we were continuing a conversation begun the previous day. My surprise at having my home town revealed to me overcame my self-consciousness. "Another example: last year two developers from LaCrosse wanted to build apartments on the riverfront. Well, for whatever reason, Keystone Milling Company opposed the deal, and since Keystone is one of the town's major employers, they used their influence to get the town council to stop the construction. Which is not to say that two years from now other developers with the right connections might not be approved."

"Did anyone else see you as a threat and try to stop you?"

"Yes and no. I'm too small to threaten anyone yet, but I pay my work force well and I provide benefits. Most of the companies in Star Lake pay hourly wages just a bit above minimum, and no benefits. If I ever expanded and became a larger company, they'd have to raise wages to compete with me. On the other hand, a number of companies in Star Lake maintain only factories here; the corporate headquarters – and the good management jobs – are in other cities. Winslow Industries, for example, which manufactures electric products, had its corporate headquarters in St. Louis. And Fibermight, which makes a variety of composite material for the aerospace and transportation industries, has its corporate headquarters in Orange County, California. In other words, if the workforce ever unionized and made demands, they might just close down and set up shop somewhere else with other non-unionized workers." I looked at Ted approvingly; the man had good politics. "Another aspect of doing business in Star Lake is giving other companies an incentive to help you. For example, Jim Hassenfuss owns the local AM radio station, KASE, but he also owns a construction company; he builds houses, so Halvorsen, who owns a rug company, buys advertising on KASE because Hassenfuss gives him the contract for carpeting in his houses. I didn't have much to trade when I got started."

"But you succeeded anyway."

"Mmmm. I'm in business, but I don't know that I would say I've succeeded yet. Let's just say I'm on my way, but struggling."

I was so absorbed in Ted's economics lesson, I did not hear what he said next.

"Excuse me?"

"Will you have dinner with me this Saturday evening?"

"Yes, I'd like to."

"Is six o'clock all right?"

"Yes, that's fine. Do you know where I live?"

"Yes."

"You do?"

"Yes, I do. I'll see you Saturday."

As I walked into the library, a Graeco-Roman structure that was a gift to Star Lake from a nineteenth-century lumber magnate, I felt disbelief that what I had once and for years yearned for and fantasized about had, in a matter of seconds, been offered to me: a date with Ted. But as excitement swept through me, I experienced a counter reaction, a determination not to become the helpless, infatuated female I had once been. I walked upstairs directly to the periodicals section and plucked the May issue of *Scientific American* from the rack. Settling into a comfortable chair, I turned to an article on youth unemployment by Ely Ginzberg. It told me that among nonwhites one third of youths and one half of young adults were unemployed; that college enrollment during the seventies among women of all ages had increased but among white males had declined. Ginzberg added parenthetically, "The figures confirm my impression as a member of a university faculty that during the 1960's many young men stayed in school in order to avoid military service during the Vietnam War." Oh, Professor Ginzberg, I thought, my husband did more than that to avoid the war. But he and all the young men who stayed in school were not wrong to oppose it.

Reading the article restored my sense of myself as a serious person concerned about national and world affairs. I felt I could, under the circumstances, let myself think about Ted Ritter. I had not seen him since the night we graduated from Star Lake High. He had won a football scholarship to UW, and during my first lonely weeks on the Madison campus, I continually fantasized about meeting him. I would sit in the Rathskeller, hoping Ted would come in, see me and ask to sit at my table. We would talk and I would be animated and charming. One meeting would lead to another. We would begin dating and he would break up officially with the cheerleader he had steady-dated in Star Lake. He would be on the football team, captaining the Wisconsin Badgers as he had captained the Star Lake Warriors, while I presided as his proud consort, and after college, his partner for life. But after Kennedy was assassinated

November of my freshman year, I felt my Ted fantasies were childish and I renounced them as a sacrifice to the memory of our martyred President. Later in my freshman year, the "Snicks," organizers from the Student Nonviolent Coordinating Committee, came to Madison recruiting volunteers for Freedom Summer. With my parents' reluctant consent—I was their only child and they did not want me to go, but my father, a Socialist, could not in good political conscience refuse permission—I went to Mississippi, secretly expecting to be killed. I was sent to Pilgrim's Crossing, a black community outside Hattiesburg, where I stayed at the home of a widow who was bringing up her dead daughter's two children. Each day, I went out with other volunteers to persuade people to register to vote. The hot, red dust of the unpaved roads bit my legs, but I enjoyed being greeted by the children who ran from their houses calling to me, enchanting me with their diphthonged version of my name, "Clay-uh, Clay-uh." Once, as I walked along on a road, I heard the slow, malevolent crunch of wheels on the road behind me. A car with two armed constables came alongside. "Are you fuckin' them niggers?" one asked. He held a rifle upright between himself and his partner; I was certain it was loaded, but I had no fear at all as I answered him, indignantly, primly, "No one in this community uses profanity. Why do you?" When they asked where I was staying, I gave them the address of the local office of COFO—the Council of Federated Organizations. "Where do you live?" they had asked, knowing I would not tell them the address of the family who was sheltering me. They arrested me for vagrancy and drove me to the jail. One constable got in the back seat with me. Referring to the cheap wraparound sunglasses I wore to protect my eyes from the strong Mississippi sun, he asked, "You with the Liberace sunglasses, are you fuckin' them niggers?" His voice was husky and his breathing was hard; I looked down from under the cover of the sunglasses and saw his hands jerking hard at himself through the chino pants of his uniform. When the constables arrived at the jail, they locked me in the dark smelly cell reserved for prostitutes and I stayed there until volunteers from the National Lawyers Guild came to bail me out. Later they got the charges against me dropped. On another evening, word came that members of the "council" – meaning the White Citizens Council – would ride. Then no one slept; we sat in a circle, the widow's grandson with a loaded rifle across his knees, while through the night cars with unlit headlights circled the house until dawn. I was sure I would die that night, but I was not at all frightened.

I went back to Madison with new pride and confidence. A story about me in the campus newspaper, *The Cardinal*, made me a minor celebrity. I dated young men with good politics and forgot about Ted until, near the end of my sophomore year, I realized he was no longer at UW. The anti-war movement started and I joined in campus demonstrations. One of the student leaders asked me out and at first, it seemed we were two equals joining forces. Like many of the people who dominated politics at Madison, David was a New Yorker. Except for his granny glasses, he reminded me of the pictures of Christ on the little pamphlets my Sunday School teachers gave me. He told me I was beautiful; he called me "the all American girl" and said he was so glad I was not a princess. When we were with his friends, he praised my hair, my skin, my "endlessly long legs." I saw that his friends looked skeptical and bored, but I was too flattered to recognize David's condescension. After we became lovers, I lost my heroic status and dwindled into "David's old lady." I did not mind my subordinate role at the time; only men, after all, were at risk from the draft, and, as Joan Baez told us, women say yes to men who say no. Besides, David dazzled me. With his sensual Jesus face, beard and long hair, David seemed a New Left messiah when he stood on the hill before Bascomb Hall, urging his fellow students on to acts of resistance against U.S. imperialism. I was proud to be his partner in struggle. The dearest wish of my heart was for us to stay together, dedicating our lives to the "Movement." But David never spoke of the future and I dared not question him. To steel myself against the separation I was sure would come, I made plans to join the Peace Corps. Then during Commencement Week, David suddenly asked me to marry him, and I, without a thought about his motivation for the abrupt proposal, gratefully said yes.

What had Ted been doing in the intervening years besides becoming an entrepreneur? He must have married. But if he was married now, he would never defy the mores of our community by asking me to have dinner with him. Then he must know that I am not married either. Who had told him about me? Why had he cared to know?

I put the *Scientific American* back in the rack and went to the current fiction section. Just shelves apart were two books I had been wanting to read: Marge Piercy's *Vida* and *Excellent Women* by Barbara Pym. Years before when I had taught the course "Women and Fiction" at Richmond Community college, and my students had liked Piercy's earlier novel, *Small Changes*, especially the beginning about a young woman from a working class family on her wedding day, Piercy's description of the bride's efforts to arrange her gown so that she could sit on the toilet without peeing on herself prompted the students to describe their own wedding and honeymoon mishaps. One woman brought in a photo of herself lifting her skirt as she entered the hired limousine, exposing the clearly marked price tag still pinned to the hem. Another woman confided, "Embarrassment kept me constipated all through the honeymoon." The descriptions led to a writing assignment; my students, women in their twenties through their sixties, turned their reminiscences into social history. War brides in the Forties had had "football" weddings: when servicemen grooms came home on leave, guests were hastily summoned to the ceremonies and at the receptions were served sandwiches thrown like footballs across the room. Brides in the post-war Eisenhower years had had formal, "godfather" weddings; "I held up my skirt," one woman wrote "and the guests threw in the amount of money they knew they were expected to give." Another student, the only divorcee besides me, described her Sixties wedding on a boat off the Florida Keys: the wedding guests had caught lobster for the wedding feast and she and her husband had written their vows. I reproduced their individual essays and photographs and gave each student a copy of the class's collective wedding album.

 Vida, I discovered as I began reading, was also rooted in the Sixties. The central character reminded me of Bernardine Dohrn, the former SDS leader, a fugitive since her arrest following the "days of rage" in Chicago. I had met Bernardine once, in July, 1967, during what David had called our "red honeymoon." After our civil marriage in the Madison City Hall, we spent a week in Star Lake. My parents were gracious and welcoming and I was ashamed because I knew they were deeply hurt by not having been invited to the wedding of their only child. Then David and I went to California and the Northwest, camping out or staying with people we knew through the "Movement." If our hosts were involved in community organizing activities related to housing, people's parks, or events connected with Vietnam Summer, we participated, too. But mostly we had just hung out, listened to music, made friends, and had, as I later realized but did not know then, the best time of our marriage. On our way east, we had stopped in Ann Arbor to attend "Radicals in the Professions," a conference SDS had sponsored to give people moving on to jobs or graduate school strategies for avoiding "the personal emptiness and social evil of traditional career patterns."

The packet of position papers we received when we registered for the conference included an issue of *New Left Notes* with a cover showing a blonde woman holding a rifle. The caption read, "The New American Woman." "She looks like you," David had said; "I'd better watch my step around you and the other revolutionary chicks."

David's joke reflected the drawing's empty symbolism, for the men at the conference were alert only to each other. While one paraded his rhetoric, the others listened in hostile respect, biting hangnails or stroking beards while they planned their own theory-filled comments. When a woman spoke, the men relaxed and became inattentive; when the woman finished, the men did not respond to her comments, until, of course, an idea she had expressed came out later from one of their mouths. Intimidated, the women failed to second one another or pursue points they wished to make. Except Bernardine Dohrn. Older than the students, a law school graduate, Bernardine had a command of Marxist dislectics, but she had her own eloquence as well, and the men respectfully listened to her ideas while lustfully watching her pretty face, shapely body, and the long, long legs revealed by her miniskirt. For Bernardine had regally eschewed the politically correct dowdiness adopted by other radical women, and appeared at every conference workshop in a different dress, sometimes wearing an extravagant wide-brimmed hat. When David spoke admiringly of "the queen of the left," I was not jealous; I also admired Bernardine and thought her one of the brightest people I had ever met. Most radicals were rude and remote, but Bernardine was accessible and polite. Like me, she was from a small Wisconsin town and had midwestern good manners that David had begun to tease me about. Bernardine was originally scheduled to stay for only the first two days of the conference before returning to New York where she lived with another radical lawyer, but she remained when one of the conference leaders asked her to stay. I never saw Bernardine again, but I often thought about her. I read her speeches and essays in *New Left Notes*, and when SDS sank into incomprehensible factionalism, I got into mental arguments with her, especially when the press reported her cheering Charles Manson after he and his groupies butchered Sharon Tate. In the summer of 1969, I joined a women's consciousness raising group. Feminism was being born, and the group followed it, like a divinely heralded infant, to lofts, basements, and churches. But from the moment of its birth, the women's movement had more than one mother trying to claim it as her own. The SDS women denounced feminism as white and bourgeois unless placed within the context of class struggle. Bernardine Dohrn had put other women down for being unconcerned with class struggle and the oppression of women of color; she warned against "flailing at our own middle class images." "To focus only on sexual exploitation and the tyranny of consumption," she warned, "does not develop a mass understanding of the causes of oppression, and it does not accurately point at the enemy." I remembered Bernardine as she had been two summers earlier in Ann Arbor and I recognized that, like the women she addressed, Bernardine was struggling with the tyranny of consumption and fear of losing connection to men.

During that summer of insurgent feminism, I toted Janey in her stroller, and went with my c-r group to almost every meeting announced on lampposts. One night in the parsonage living room of Washington Square Methodist Church, we found ourselves being invited to join a "women's militia" to fight "Pig Amerika" in Chicago. In the mandarin prose of Marxism, one Weatherwoman and then another gave us the rationale for the "Four Days of Rage." Bring the war back home was their theme, and Chicago was the focus of the action in revenge for the police riot at the 1968 Democratic Convention. "We're going to show Pig Daley that he doesn't own Chicago," one woman declared. Probably some women in that room had been in Chicago in 1968; those who had not been there remembered the television broadcasts, had heard the screams and seen the blood streaming from cracked heads. A second woman described the planned activities. While she was talking, the woman who had spoken before her sat down near me and spoke with another Weatherwoman. I overheard her complaining about her oppressive childhood in Scarsdale with a mother who was a "bourgeois housewife who played mahjongh all day." Then I heard another speaker say, "One of the actions we've planned for October is we're going to lead a mule train through the black community. Then we're going into all the high schools in the ghetto and yell 'jail break' and all the students will come out and join us." I found the words, "This is bizarre" escaping from my lips. The Scarsdale Weatherwoman turned to me and hissed, "I assure you, this is not bizarre. This is the first of one thousand struggles against U.S. imperialism." But my impulsive objection broke the spell; in a minute every one got up from chairs, couches, patches of floor and left the room.

Months later, the Weatherwomen were routed by the Chicago police, their rage reduced to a whimper. Studying the *New York Times* photo of the women being led away in tears to patrol wagons, I was angry with them for setting themselves up for a humiliating defeat and saddened that Bernardine Dohrn had been a leader of the foolish adventure. Bernardine went underground rather than stand trial. Still, over the years, I continued to feel a sisterly bond with her; if Bernardine had ever asked me for help, I would have given it.

I also felt a bond with Marge Piercy, another Movement alumna. However, I knew my students at

Fontbonne college would complain if I assigned them her novel about a fugitive revolutionary.

The young women in my current "Women and Literature" course were uncomfortable with most twentieth century authors. Woolf and Lessing perplexed them; American writers – Flannery O'Connor, Joan Didion, Joyce Carol Oates, Grace Paley, Alice Walker – confronted misfortune, injustice, violence, and complex relationships, aspects of life that were not part of my students' experience and, they were convinced, not intended to be. My Fontbonne students were at home with nineteenth century English writers like Austen and the Brontes, whose themes of marriage and money echoed their own aspirations, with the distinction that they wanted MBAs along with their Darcys and Rochesters.

I shall always prefer my students back at Richmond Community College who were not young, affluent and confident, like my Fontbonne students, but older, diffident, working class, familiar with hardship or even tragedy. They took my course with a raw eagerness that energized me; they read my assigned texts as primers in reclaiming their lives; they had needed me and acknowledged my leadership. The women at Fontbonne were condescending toward feminism. Yes, they acknowledged, women had been discriminated against in the past, but the struggle for equality had been won, and such remnants of blind prejudice that might still exist would surely not prevent their own unquestionable merit from being recognized and rewarded. The days of the crusades were over. During a discussion of Adrienne Rich's poem, "The Burning of Paper Instead of Children," I dropped my guard and referred to my activism in the Sixties. As if she had been waiting for the opportunity, one student, a long-haired blonde, looked up from her pretty painted fingernails and responded: "Professor Schaefer, you were part of a generation of idealists who made commitments to social justice. You worked to help other people, and to stop the war, and you made sacrifices to achieve those goals. For example, you probably don't have the career you might have achieved if you had been more ambitious for yourself."

"But I'm teaching you. How can one ask for a better career than that?"

"Well, okay, hah hah. But, look, Professor Schaefer, people my age look at what your generation accomplished and don't feel it was worth the sacrifice. At any rate, your generation is not a model we, that is, my generation, want to follow. We think we can accomplish more by pursuing our own ambition, achieving our personal goals rather than trying to change society."

I looked out the classrrom window at the green lawn and ivy-covered Gothic buildings across the quadrangle. Who would want to change a society like this one? "Do you deny that you have a threshold of expectation that was made possible by the efforts of my generation?"

"That may be true, but don't expect us to be grateful to you. You had a saying then, 'Power to the people.' Well, we don't believe everyone should have power. Poor people are not necessarily good, or entitled to be leaders. We see nothing wrong with moving up the corporate ladder or becoming rich."

Twenty carefully groomed heads nodded in agreement.

"If becoming a corporate officer is your goal, you will have to make yourself fit someone else's mold: think, behave, speak, even dress according to other people's expectations. I don't know if you consider that a sacrifice, but I do. And remember, there isn't room for all of you at the top. Your peers will be your competitors; my generation worked together for a common goal. I hope when you are all managers and one half of a two-career couple, you can look back at your twenties with as much satisfaction as I do. I and members of my generation did not follow patterns, we broke them. We did reshape society. We have made lasting changes. We did create opportunities. We did stop a war. We were part of something larger than ourselves. We spoke out. We were adventurous." I paused, then added. "Ah, and let us not forget romance. Those were extinct times. Can climbing the corporate ladder or acquiring wealth be as romantic and satisfying when one is young as moving with one's peers, one's sisters and brothers, comrades and lovers to change society. Dear students, I leave it to you to decide."

I had impressed the students, but I knew that the advantage was temporary. I could not for long penetrate their self- absorption. After that encounter, I did not make the mistake of revealing myself to them again. I have always despised the confessional, call-me-by-my-first-name professorial style, a Sixties teaching approach widely adopted at Richmond Community College. It seemed condescending and dishonest, although my "Women's Lit" students had been so like peers that I had encouraged them to use my first name and had shared information about myself. But I decided that scholarship was the way to establish credibility with my Fontbonne students. I gave fast-paced lectures, sending their hands racing to fill their notebooks with my words. I rejected plotty answers in class discussions, and demanded close textual analysis. I required clear thesis statements and detailed supporting evidence in essay examinations. I graded their term papers strictly. I was formal but fair, and I was not their friend. By the end of my first academic year, I sensed that I was grudgingly respected, more successful, in fact, than with my Richmond Community College students, whom I had loved, but whose need of me had been so great I inevitably disappointed them when I could not meet all their expectations. Then they had turned against me. That I should be more respected by students I cared less about troubled me, and I confided my sense of anomaly to Marge Fogarty, the English department chair, the patron who had rescued me when my career in New York came to a dead end.

"My dear, you're a professional. Teachers are not supposed to love their students any more than doctors are supposed to love their patients or lawyers their clients. I don't think you can perform as well as you should as a professional if you are emotionally involved with the people you are serving. One of the worst mistakes I ever made was to try to teach one of my children math. I was awful, both a rotten teacher and rotten mother; fortunately, I had enough sense to quit and hire a tutor before he turned off both math and me forever. Besides, I think a healthier classroom climate prevails when teacher and students are slightly, antagonistic. Just enough for each side to keep the other alert. I also see a wry justice at work when members of the Eighties generation challenge members of the Sixties generation as you once challenged your elders."

"At UW, dissent was the tradition; our elders cheered us on."

If Marge had brought me to Fontbonne as the point woman for dissent, the Pym novel would not be useful for that purpose. Barbara Pym had died in January, her reputation restored and her work once more in demand after years of neglect and undeserved oblivion. Her gentle novel about ordinary people making much of small chores and details would not provoke my students, but would please them by confirming their complacency. Still, there was no harm in giving them, once in a while, something they would like, and they would admire Pym's style, which had been compared to the admired Austen's. They would have warm, condescending feelings toward Pym's self-deprecating women, who would remind them of their mothers. I decided to include it in the course and put Piercy's book on the optional reading list to encourage the occasional rebels and doubters.

I checked out the books and left the library. I walked down Main Street to The Small Planet, a health food restaurant owned and run by two amiable, laid-back couples who had found a reasonable solution to the basic Sixties question of how to survive and stay decent. I ate a sandwich of muenster cheese, walnuts and bean sprouts grilled on pumpernickel bread and drank decaffeinated mint iced tea. Afterward I went to the post office for stamps, and then walked down to the river and sat on a bench on the levee reading the Pym novel until it was time to reclaim my car. I took a bus to the service station, paid Jack Ritter for restoring my Volvo, and drove home.

Janey was home from school when I arrived, and she and her friend Ellen were sprawled in front of the television watching *General Hospital*. If Janey had been alone, she would have been watching *Sesame Street*. After dragging my daughter, literally kicking and screaming from Greenwich Village last year, I enrolled her in my old grammar school, Longwood Elementary. Declaring "I've always been at the center of the in-group," Janey buried her resentment and, with a subtle ruthlessness that reminded me eerily of her father, she set about becoming leader of the pack, or "click" as these murderous children's clans are still called. She selected as her second in command Ellen Winters, a less aggressive and slightly less pretty girl whose only advantage over my daughter was that she had begun to menstruate and Janey had not. These two girls named themselves "itty-bitty-titty-committee" and, occasionally with other sixth graders, were often at our house. Sometimes I listened to their judgmental gossip about their peers. Once when they had worked themselves into hilarity, I heard Janey warn them, "Be careful, or my mom might tape record our conversation. That's what she used to do when I was a little kid living in New York and me and my friends used to act out fantasies." Janey told her friends about "the wedding." Dressing themselves in my old clothes, Janey and her friends had taken turns playing the roles of a marriage ceremony. The role each girl wanted, however, was not the bride, but the true power figure in the situation, the minister. "You should have heard us," Janey told her friends. "We said things like, 'Do you take this awful loving man to be your lawful heavenly husband.' Janey liked to listen to the tapes of scenes from her childhood, and I suspect she would be pleased if I did tape record her and her friends now.

As I watched Janey's and Ellen's neat butts rising over the v's of their neat jean legs like a pair of well-loaded bean shooters, I smelled a telltale flatulence hanging over them. When Janey was aware I was in the living room, she moved her arm, trying to hide a pile of cellophane wrappers.

"Hi, Mom," Janey said sheepishly.

"Hi, Janey. Never mind trying to conceal the evidence. Your Twinkie farts give you away."

"It was my fault, Mrs. Schaefer," Ellen righteously volunteered. I could imagine Janey making the same admission, in that same false, sweet, arching voice in Ellen's home. "I bought them on the way home from school."

"Mrs. Winters isn't fanatic like you are about junk food, Mom. She doesn't think you can die from an overdose of Cheese Doodles."

"Neither do I. But I don't think the chemicals in junk food are good for your body. The ones that don't leave in gaseous form, I mean. Besides, Twinkies are dangerous; a man in California claims he committed murder under their influence."

"I'm not going to become a Twinkie killer. But I like the taste of chemicals and it's fun to fart."

Ellen giggled self-consciously at Janey's frankness with me.

"Why is it," Janey asked Ellen, "that we enjoy our own body smells, but other people's are disgusting?"

Ellen shrugged and giggled, unwilling to be frank with Janey while I was present.

But Janey pursued the topic. "Do you like the smell of . . ." she began, but I interrupted her.

"Do you like the smell of another topic?"

Ellen supplied the new topic. "Mrs. Schaefer, could Janey sleep over at my house on Saturday? I've asked my mother and she said yes. You can even call her if you like."

"I recognize a set-up. Sure, why not?"

"Oh, snap. Thanks Mom."

"Not at all. And if the two of you are still hungry, slice yourselves carrot and celery sticks, okay? And if you're still not satisfied, make peanut butter sandwiches. Agreed? I'm going upstairs to my study. I'll be down in an hour and we can drop Ellen on our way to the supermarket."

Later, after driving Ellen home, Janey and I headed for IGA in the center of town. I turned on the car radio to a station that played "our" music, an area of shared taste between Janey's disco and my baroque that included the Beatles, Bruce Springsteen, and Stevie Wonder. The station was playing Bette Midler's *Stay With Me*.

"How was your day?" Janey asked, taking up the ritual of our daily reunion. "I thought you were going down to Madison. How come you came home so early?"

I made my narrative minimal and casual, but my alert daughter immediately understood the significance of the main event of the day.

"Oh, snap," Janey exclaimed and then began a volley of questions that continued after we entered the midtown IGA. I spoke of Ted in neutral terms, but Janey's imagination was stimulated. I felt resentful that all the effort I'd made for her was discounted, that when a man asked me out to dinner she was impressed.

"Is he married?"

"I don't know if he's been married, but he wouldn't have asked me out if he were married now. That just isn't done in Star Lake."

"Maybe he lives in another town," Janey suggested while she pulled out a box of Captain Crunch from the shelf. I took it from her hand and put it back on the shelf, then reached for a box of Cheerios.

"I don't like that cereal," Janey complained. "Can I at least have Corn Flakes? It's the only cereal in the 'good' category I like."

I put back the Cheerios and let Janey drop the Corn Flakes into the cart.

"Even if he does, I don't think he's married. He was decent in high school and seems decent now."

"You knew him in high school, but you didn't date him?"

"Not him. Not anyone. I only went to my senior prom because my mother and my aunt ganged up on my cousin Martin and made him take me." We turned into the household products aisle. Without comments or suggestions from Janey who trusted me in these matters, I selected a generic dishwashing product and cleanser.

"Oh, gross. How embarrassing. But if I had nobody to go to the prom with, I don't even have a cousin to take me against his will."

"You might not have that problem. I had so little self esteem, I never could imagine anyone wanting to take me, and that was the message I sent out. With your crusty charm, you'll either intrigue boys or intimidate them."

"It could go either way, huh?"

"Yes. Or you could ask a boy yourself. That wasn't done in my day."

"That's true, I could. It's hard to imagine that two years from now I might meet someone whom I'd be dating when I'm as old as you are. The boys in my class are so indescribably gross."

"They always are in sixth grade. But they're tadpoles. They'll change. They'll improve."

"Tadpoles become frogs, don't they? I want a prince. Wasn't Ted a prince?"

"I thought so at the time."

"Besides, that won't happen to me because I plan on leaving this town when I grow up, like you did, but I don't see myself coming back, except to see you, of course, if you're still here."

We were in the last aisle: pet food on one side and dairy products on the other.

"Yes, if I'm still alive. Oh, good, they're having a sale on Purina. Our cats won't have to eat El Cheapo cat food for a while."

"Oh, good. It's embarrassing to check out economy brands at the counter." Janie sucked in her teeth. "I wish you'd buy brand names all the time."

We finished shopping and checked out. I wheeled the cart out to the parking lot and we loaded the bags of groceries into the car. Janey returned the cart to the stack outside the market.

I drove home by way of River Road. A string of barges, pushed by a towboat, moved down the river. I glanced at the birds flying above the barge train, hoping to see a blue heron.

I thought of Janey's demand, "I want a prince." Janey was just two years shy of the age I had been when I first saw Ted. When Juliet first saw Romeo. Fourteen was passionate. Janey should not be gripped by such strong emotion. Not at fourteen.

Later? I don't regret my life, but I don't want my daughter to live it.

"What are you going to wear?" Janey asked when we were putting away the groceries.

"I don't know. Perhaps that dress that Grandma made for me. That linen dress. It's my favorite."

"Umm, maybe. You don't have much besides teaching clothes, running clothes, and relaxing clothes. The linen dress is okay, but it's not exciting. You need something to knock his socks off with."

"I do?"

"Yes. Why don't you buy something new?"

"Then Saturday becomes more than a date; it becomes an investment."

"Well, if Ted doesn't work out, you have something to knock someone else's socks off with."

"Why do you want me to knock someone's socks off?"

"You've been single for a long, long time. And you won't have Janey to kick around for much longer."

Despite my disciplined skepticism, Janey's mandate stirred memories and desires. The next morning, I did a hard workout of eight miles as an act of faith that I would be invited to compete in the New York City Marathon. I ate breakfast and saw Janey off to school. Then instead of driving down to the UW Library in Madison, I went to LaCrosse to shop. Until I went away to college, my mother had made all my clothes, sewing in the evening after dinner, bending over the Singer in the upstairs room that was now my study. The smoke from the cigarette that was always clamped between her lips curled like a grey ribbon in the light from the machine's lamp bulb; the swarming ashes were somehow always flicked off before they could fall on the fabric. But I did not appreciate my mother's effort, I resented it. I have more patience with my daughter's desire for brand-name products when I remember how I once yearned for the store-bought clothes other girls wore. Prowling through the attic after I first came back to Star Lake, I discovered the handmade clothes packed neatly in boxes. I studied the French seams of the dresses, the sturdy linings of the skirts, and then I wrote my mother. "I never realized," I obliquely apologized, "when I was in elementary school that I was wearing clothes that would cost a fortune if they were made today." Two weeks later, my mother sent me another sign of her silent, eloquent love: the dress of natural linen, elegant and superbly constructed. A note was folded in with the tissue: "Thanks for the kind words. I thought when I came to Florida, I'd never sew again, but I ran this up on a neighbor's machine just to see if I still had my touch. Hope you can use this. Dad and I send love to you and Janey."

In college, I'd acquired the casual, jean-based wardrobe all my peers wore. I took these clothes with me to New York when David and I moved to the Upper West Side apartment we had sub-leased from friends of friends. For my first meeting with her in-laws at their Oceanside, Long Island home, I wore an Indian cotton print dress, brass hoop earrings, and sandals. David's parents had been cold and cutting, especially his mother, who let me overhear her complain to David's father about the "shabby shiksa" their son had brought home. I was terribly hurt, especially when I contrasted his parents' meanness with my parents' generosity. My mother, who did not like to cook, had fussed over meals, baked cakes. David's mother set out an unappetizing spread of leftover "deli." I consoled myself with the thought of laughing afterward with David, who had for years mocked his parents' "boojie" values. What did his parents' unkindness matter so long as David, my partner and comrade, admired my blonde hair, blue eyes, and legs that "went on forever." His extravagant praise nourished my ego and bewitched me with a sense of my own beauty that I had never been allowed to have. He had taken the flax of me and spun it into gold. That night, as he drove us from his parents' home back to Manhattan in our secondhand car, David had asked, "Did you have to wear that schmatta?"

When I began teaching, I adopted the jeans-and-combat boots style of the early academic feminists. Later, as both the academy and the movement became more conservative, I softened – some would say regressed – to suits, silk blouses and tailored slacks, which were now the staples of my wardrobe and served all professional and social needs. For the first time in my life, I was searching for clothes that would make me sexually attractive. Seductive. Feverish and embarrassed, I searched impatiently through the shops, invoking, as I tried on garments and studied myself in dressing room mirrors, the critical view of my digital-eyed ex-mother-in-law. At last I found the correct dress: a brown and purple striped silk shirtwaist that transformed me into the woman I aspired to be – sophisticated, sexy and in control. I paid for the dress and left, promising myself as I drove home that the next day I would go down to the UW library in Madison to regain my sense of sober mission.

CHAPTER

1965 - 1970

My husband had been my first lover, and from our first time, a clumsy one. I was proud of being his partner in struggle, so I never expressed disappointment in our lovemaking. What did I know, after all? Each time he asked, "How was I?" I answered, "Fine, you were just fine." And, of course, he accepted my response without question. The only complaint I ever made – and that was because of the pain – was about his kissing. David liked to bite my lips; even when I told him he hurt me, he never stopped. He liked to kiss me that way. But he taught me to please him. I can still feel the pressure of David's fingers spreading over my head as he pushed my face down over his erect penis – as he might put a grapefruit half into a citrus press – and held it there until I gagged on his semen. (In the final days of our marriage, I found the courage to ask him, "Why did you make me go down on you when you never went down on me?" "Why did I never go down on you?" he echoed—he always repeated my questions—and then answered, "Why, Claire, dear, how was I to know you wanted me to; you never asked.") But during our honeymoon, he was ardent and tender, and his passion continued through our early days in New York. In the hot cavern of our top floor apartment, he exalted me with flattering words and pulled me down on the living room floor while on our borrowed stereo, Jim Morrison and The Doors commanded, "Come on, baby, light my fire."

In September, David began graduate work in sociology at Columbia and I became a temporary office worker, according to David's plan that he would develop theory while I developed political consciousness among the workers. The reality was that my job supported us. By October, I knew I was pregnant. David surprised me by being pleased. "How shall we live if I can't work?" I asked, and David had answered, "Don't worry, Babe, my parents will have to come through." I was ambivalent; having a baby would be more interesting than typing or filing, but I was afraid of being responsible for another life before I had lived my own. One year earlier, even months before, I had thought I would be at that very moment imparting literacy to the children of South American peasants. Instead, I rose each morning, and even after bouts of morning sickness, traveled on the West Side IRT to a midtown office where I performed a series of tedious assignments. My office mates, working wives from Queens and Brooklyn showed me where to put my pocketbook and were considerate when "my condition" showed, but it was laughable to think that I, the "temp," would ever rouse these placid family-loving women to struggle for control of corporate America. In the evenings I returned to shop for food, cook, and clean our sparsely furnished apartment. David's bridegroom ardor, which might have sustained me, had vanished. Our honeymoon passion had dwindled into perfunctory Sunday morning sex, coupled with a ritual David seemed to find more exciting than sex. He would roll over on his stomach and command me to straddle his back and squeeze out the pimples and blackheads his active glands had built and harbored under his oily skin. "Let me see it," he would say huskily after I had popped a big blackhead; I would present the pussworm to him on my fingertip, and he would study it as eagerly as if I had offered him a jewel on a velvet pillow. The memory of that Sunday morning ritual shames me, but I was too besotted with love to recoil from David's grossness or to recognize the contemptuousness of his demeaning request.

He was often away from the apartment, and when he was home, three or more undergraduates were usually with him, for he had quickly developed a following among the Columbia students, who were flattered to be asked to the apartment, and even more flattered to be interviewed. David transformed the raw data they spouted into his tape recorder into his dissertation, and still later, into a faddish, fast selling study of student radicals, *Portraits of a Generation*, which he parlayed, during the period when "soft" data were acceptable in academia, into a teaching position in, of course, California.

The last stages of my pregnancy coincided with the student strike at Columbia, a time of exhilaration for David and discomfort and depression for me. David exulted in his role as SDS alumnus and veteran organizer, and, while as a graduate student, he never attempted to project himself into the front ranks of building occupiers and strategists, he did enjoy a guru status among the novice radicals. They flocked to our apartment in the evenings; I had hoped, in my ballooning condition, to avoid them by staying in my bedroom, but I could not avoid their slim bodies during my many trips to the bathroom, which one of them seemed always to be occupying. One night, feeling my pee coming out all over me, I pounded on the door and screamed until the young male occupier, zipping his fly with one hand and clutching *New Left Notes* with the other, grudgingly exited, followed by the cloudy aroma of his recent bowel movement.

Janey was born on May 1, 1968, and my love for her was immediate and fierce. David and I spent the summer displaying her to members of his family – his parents were almost friendly to me then – and to my parents on a visit to the Midwest. We saw our college friends, but decided, for Janey's sake, not to participate in the demonstrations at the Democratic convention in Chicago. Although David and I were on friendly terms, I was aware of the absence of the intense lovemaking of the previous summer which I had allowed myself to hope would return after Janey was born.

In September, David resumed his graduate studies and I took one of the part-time secretarial jobs the university reserved for wives of graduate students. Our apartment was again crowded with student activists, including some women, as snobbish to me as their male counterparts, who were involved in opposing the strike by New York public school teachers against community boards demanding to control the schools. These young women talked tough about driving racist pig teachers out of the schools and making the schools accountable to third world parents and kids. One night I asked them if they were planning to teach, for that would seem to me to be the most effective way to change the schools. They said they were not planning to become teachers because they thought they could bring about more widespread and long lasting change by working in the legal, health care and academic professions. I saw that these future lawyers, doctors, and college professors regarded me as a failure, trapped with a baby and no profession. But I also saw that despite their harshness and self-absorption, they took their identities from men. As I watched them follow their lovers with their eyes and become distracted when a special voice came to them from another room, I recognized myself as I had been. Janey was my joy and comfort, but I was lonely. I missed my parents, my college friends, even the kind women I had met doing temporary office work. My job at Columbia, typing letters under the direction of a department secretary, answering the telephone and responding to students, was without interest or purpose, and if David could not take care of Janey, half of what I made went to a sitter.

The only consoling presence in my life at that time, my best friend, actually, was David's grandmother, Frieda. Back in Madison, David had boasted of "my grandmother, the Communist," and shortly after we came to New York, he took me up to the Bronx to meet her. Frieda had emigrated from Poland before the First World War because David's grandfather wanted to avoid conscription into the Czar's army. The young couple found work in the garment industry and started their family: a son, David's father, and a daughter, David's Aunt Sarah. Frieda soon became involved in the labor movement, but her husband became in Frieda's words, "a bourgeois turncoat, a capitalist exploiter, a sweatshop owner." Frieda and her husband divorced and divided their family; David's father went with his father and his Aunt Sarah stayed with her mother. Inspired by the Russian Revolution, Frieda joined the American Communist Party, met and married a fellow Party member who was also active in the labor movement. Frieda had another child, and she and her young husband, together with other young left-wing couples, turned their attention to finding a place in the country where they could escape with their children from stifling workplaces and apartments during the summer months. They bought land in the Catskills and set up Camp Nitgedaiget, which flourished as a recreation center for radicals during the Thirties. As their children grew, Frieda and her friends turned their attention to the need to provide decent, affordable living space in the city and, again, through collective effort, established the first cooperative apartment complex in New York City, known as "the Coops" on Allerton Avenue in the Bronx. They bought land and built according to a plan which included a line of single room apartments – "Section K" – for women who planned to remain single and devote their lives to the work of the Party. From the first, the Coops' founders intended that their housing would be integrated, and they recruited black families to join them as owner-tenants. They set up a day care center for workers' children. Taking up a skill she had developed at Nitgedaiget, Frieda became the cook, and was called "the lamb chop lady" because of her ability to provide meat for the children's meals even during the hard times of the Depression. Sarah, her younger sister, and their peers grew and thrived; they excelled in the city's public schools and colleges, and entered careers and professions while remaining faithful to the ideals their parents had taught them. Sarah, who became a successful magazine editor, was under pressure during the McCarthy era to deny her left-wing roots, but, Frieda said proudly, "She refused, even though she was in a difficult situation and thought at times she might lose her job. She always said, 'My mother is a Communist and I am proud of her.'"

David's grandfather, meanwhile, flourished as a clothing manufacturer. David's father joined him in the business, married, and moved to Long Island. He wanted his sons to become professional men. David's older brother, Aaron, had fulfilled one half of his father's plan by becoming a doctor, but David did not want to become a lawyer. During his radical period when, according to his mother, "nothing would have made him happier than to wake up one morning and find that his father and I were Negroes," he began visiting his grandmother. After David introduced me to her, I visited her, traveling up to the Bronx by subway on my own, even when David did not come with me. I saw her even more frequently after Janey was born. A deep affection grew between us. Frieda loved Janey and was delighted to have ties once again to the branch of the family that had informally disowned her. Through Frieda, I felt reconnected to my own forbearers, the *Acht-und-Vierzigers* who emigrated to America after their revolution in Germany failed. I told Frieda about my family, which includes on both sides

Socialists, Abolitionists, supporters of the LaFollettes and the Progressive movement that developed the reforms and programs which were the basis of the New Deal.

Frieda had countered, "The Wisconsin Idea gave us Social Security, but we have it in this country only because the Communists fought for it."

During our frequent long conversations over *chai* — tea — at the table in Frieda's small but pleasant kitchen, religion emerged as our principal area of disagreement. "I'm a Communist, an atheist, an American, and a Jew, in that order," Frieda declared. "Marx means more to me than Moses."

"And Methodism means more to me than Marxism," I replied. "My politics were shaped by my religion. The two often went together in my family. Some people in my family were conservative Lutherans, but others became Socialists because they believed Christ preached Socialism. Many of the early Socialists were ministers, and my family includes people who were both. My cousin, Martin, for example. His middle name is Luther, like Reverend King. Now, Frieda, you cannot deny the role the church played in the civil rights movement."

"No, of course not. But the church is an organization people created, and it was so powerful in the Black community because it was all they had. The civil rights movement achieved so much because people struggled together for a common goal. In struggle people's lives are enlarged and illuminated; they experience the truth of their own lives. That is the revelation, not laws inscribed on a stone tablet brought to them by a leader who descends in a cloud from a mountain top."

"But the revelation included more than the recognition of necessity. Blacks in the South were inspired and sustained by their faith. They have always seen their struggle in this country in Biblical terms, as a parallel to the exodus from Egypt. I went to Mississippi because of what I was taught as a child in Sunday school and church, and I found other women who were there for the same reason, especially white Southern women who could not bear the contradiction between what they had been taught churchgoing Christians were supposed to do and what churchgoing Christians were actually doing."

"I know what you experienced," Frieda said. "I experienced it too with the comrades, including those who came from bourgeois or even wealthy families. They could not bear the contradictions, either, but they recognized the contradictions were a result of class privilege, not faulty application of faith. And we struggled, just as you did, because we were guided by a vision of a better society than the one we knew."

"Frieda, I believe there must be mystery, yes, magic, to sustain the vision. I do believe in the spirit. Frieda, I cannot accept a totally materialistic explanation of the world."

"So who should get credit for what people achieve? God?"

"No, not God, an old white man with a beard who spied on me when I was a child. I hated God. But Jesus Christ was another matter. I used to daydream about him because of the picture of him that was on our Sunday School lessons. You know the picture of him with the light behind his long brown hair, the sensitive eyes looking off into the distance, away from the viewer, and that sensual bearded face. I fell in love with David because he reminded me of that picture of Jesus Christ."

"My grandson, the saviour. Very interesting. So I have Christ to thank that you're a member of my family. Do you believe the rest of the story about him—that his mother was a virgin and that he went right up to heaven when he died"

"No. I believe he was born and died as we all do, and that the myths that grew up around him were variations of other earlier religions. I think the real Jesus Christ was a political leader—a Jewish nationalist—but what attracted me to the legendary Christ was his womanliness. He loved children, he fed the hungry, he cured the sick. He was a nurturer."

"A Jewish mother."

"More likely a male version of the female deity in an ancient goddess-centered religion."

"This is all very interesting, Clarelleh, but I still prefer analysis to prophecy. I'll stick with Marx, who was also a very sexy fellow. Did Christ leave a bastard behind, too?"

"I never heard of one, although I'm surprised the claim has not been made. But Jesus did leave behind good organizers. Has Marx had disciples as effective as Peter and Paul? Will Communism last as long as Christianity?"

"I can tell you this: that there are more Communists in this world now than Christians. The age of faith is over, Claire. Around the world, people are unwilling to meekly, patiently bear oppression in this life for the sake of a reward in a mythical afterlife. They want to defeat their oppressors in this life."

"But class struggle demands faith, too. People have to be willing to work for changes they will not live to see."

"Yes, but we have enough examples of revolutionary change in the world already to be confident others will come. This place, for example, the Coops. I came here as a young woman; I brought up my children here, and I've lived here as a widow. Long ago we were forced to surrender collective ownership to private. But we established a model that other groups have followed. And the spirit of the place continues in the people who still live here and in our children who have gone elsewhere. I hope you won't make Janey embarrassed about her Communist great-grandmother. I don't believe in the afterlife, but I'll come back and haunt you if you do."

"That's unfair, Frieda. I'm proud of you. Both my grandmothers died young, driven to early graves by hard lives and mean husbands. You're the only grandmother I've got. Long before I met you, David bragged about his grandmother, the Communist."

"I'm useful to David as a weapon against his parents, who I'm sure are hoping I'm an enthusiasm that will pass, a part of his rebellion that he'll outgrow."

"That doesn't mean he will."

I showed more confidence in David than I actually felt, for he was beginning to seem embarrassed by my affection for Frieda and had asked me why I liked her so much.

"Why shouldn't I like her?" I replied. "She's everything you said she was and I admire her. Besides, she's the only member of your family who cares about Janey and me. Most of the time, your parents are rude to me, and they care much more about your brother's children than they do about Janey."

"My brother's children are boys and they're Jewish. You're not Jewish, so Janey's not Jewish."

"So they can't love her? Why is religion suddenly an issue? Why is the subject being raised now?"

"I'm merely pointing out that religion is an issue of importance to my parents, who, by the way, are helping to feed us and put a roof over our heads, so excuse them for not having your white bread Protestant good manners."

David's shifting loyalty and increasing distance frightened me. I dreaded abandonment and a return to my youthful loneliness, but I feared even more the loss of my tormenting dream that David and I would follow Frieda and her husband in the struggle for justice. Every day, like Scheherazade trying to invent the tale that would prolong her life another day, I tried to think of ways to restore his love. I never went to bed without showering first, scrubbing myself raw and douching, determined that no body odor should offend him. But David and I made love rarely, and he approached me reluctantly, as if he would rather be doing something else, like filing an income tax return. One night, reckless with despair, I refused to stay on the bottom. As I straddled David, the friction of his penis stimulated my clitoris, and I climaxed loudly with sobs and cries. David shushed me at once; "the neighbors will hear you," he scolded.

I took hope from his fondness for Janey. We were still a family, I told myself, as long as he cared for Janey. David enjoyed bragging about his May Day daughter. He bought a piece of red flannel in which to wrap his "red diaper baby" when he displayed her to his friends. One evening when we had guests, David went into Janey's room to put her in her costume. I followed him and stood against the doorway, cherishing the image of the devoted father holding his happy, gurgling baby over her crib, trying to use it as evidence against my inner certainty that our marriage was failing. "Shickie, little schickie," David crooned at Janey, "You saved your Daddy's ass, you kept him out of Vietnam." I gasped and David turned around to face me. He just smiled and shrugged; then holding Janey like a trophy, he walked past me into the living room.

After that evening, I moved in a holding pattern, numbly going through the routine of our life while my anger steeped. One Saturday, I went shopping for food while Janey napped and David worked at his desk. As I returned with my arms full of groceries, Janey's cries pierced the walls of the elevator cage as it crawled toward our floor. From the first floor to our floor, the sixth, my daughter's sobs echoed in the shaft. When the elevator finally stopped, I pushed open the door and ran to our apartment, dropped the bags, found my keys after long seconds of searching in my pocketbook, opened the door and raced down the hall to Janey's room. David followed me into the baby's room, trying to pretend she had just started crying. I picked her up, soothed her, laid her back down, and peeled away the fetid diaper. I cleaned her, changed her, comforted her, and laid her back in her crib. She was asleep immediately. Then I took the dirty diaper and strode through the hall into David's study. David was sitting at his desk, again absorbed in his work. I grabbed his attention rather quickly by holding the diaper over his head and asking, "How long did you let her sit in her shit, David? A half hour? An hour? If you ever leave her like that again," I began that clause intending to complete it with, "I'll wipe her shit all over you." But, following another impulse, I lowered the Pamper over David's desk and warned, I'll dip each and every one of your precious notes and drafts in it. Then you'll finally have to soil your hands on some family shit, David." The most satisfying memory I would take from my marriage was of myself at that rare moment of Amazonian anger, standing over David, who cringed with his arms stretched over his note cards and manuscript, and looked at me with fear, respect, and lust.

That was a turning point; I recognized that my marriage was, in effect, over, and began trying to take command of my life. I applied to and was accepted by the graduate English Department at New York University. I continued to work at Columbia, attending classes part time while David contributed more time to child care and also, at my insistence, reduced the flow of visitors to the apartment. I wanted to be involved in political life again, and joined an anti-war group, Resist. There I met other women also struggling in relationships with revolutionary men who were domestic tyrants. We formed a consciousness raising group and began meeting regularly.

At the same time the Columbia women were forming c-r groups; when their lovers became aware of the intimate discussions at the "chick-lib" meetings, they became uneasy. Their complaints alerted David, who told me, "I don't want you telling our private stuff to strangers, people I don't know and who may not be politically reliable."

"Why, David? Are you afraid there might be someone in the group who will see publishing opportunities and write a book about what goes on?"

"My manuscript is a sociological study, a seminal document of our epoch, not a collection of anecdotes from angry women spilling their guts about the men they live with. I don't expose people's intimate private lives."

I told him that we had no intimate life for me to expose. I saw him debating with himself about trying to reconcile with me, but even if he had once again become my ardent lover, I would not have renounced the group.

My closest friend in the group was the only other mother, Penny Wilson, a Texas farmer's daughter, a former airline stewardess who taught English in a New York City high school. Her husband, Dick, taught at Hofstra and worked intermittently on is doctorate.

"We met in graduate school," Penny told me. "We married while we were still students and found an apartment in the Village in a building filled with other graduate students. We went to classes and shared chores. We had meals dormitory style and drank beer in Chumley's in the evening. We had the most egalitarian, comradely marriage imaginable. And then I got pregnant. We moved to the East Village, but it might just as well have been the Midwest. He became Papa and went to work and I became Mama and stayed home and cooked, cleaned, and took care of the kid. When I had nothing but four walls and a screaming baby, I understood why women murder their children. If I hadn't had Tompkins Square Park and the company of other mothers, my daughter might not have survived her first year."

I felt close to Penny because she was the first woman near my own age I had met who was trying to combine motherhood with a political life. I respected her point of view. After the Weatherwoman meeting at Washington Square Methodist Church, Penny said, "I hate their kick-ass politics, their rhetoric and their rudeness. This damn war is driving me crazy, but I can't accept leadership from the likes of them. They're too young. Their 'smash monogamy, smash the state' line is out of the question for me. I'm trying to change my family life, not destroy it. That's the problem with the Left in this country. It doesn't accommodate family life. It doesn't leave a place for someone like me who is trying to make the world safe for democracy and get her laundry done."

In November, Penny, her seven-year-old Shirley and her five-year-old Bill, Janey and I went to the anti-war demonstration in Washington. Penny's friend, Barbara Meyers, came with us, but her two daughters, Christina, twelve, and Valerie, eight and ill with leukemia, stayed home with their father. The special train we were on was delayed for two hours because of a bomb scare, and we were among the last demonstrators to arrive in Washington. Nevertheless, we six women and children, with Janey in her foldup stroller, managed to ease through the crowds until we were at the Washington Monument. Chilled, blowing white breath, we heard the speakers who waited in and returned to a heated tent behind the platform. Dr. Spock, Dick Gregory, an anti-war G.I., an anti-war Wall Street businessman spoke to us; Peter, Paul, and Mary sang to us; David Dellenger, one of the "Chicago Seven," joked that because of the trial, Abby Hoffman and Jerry Rubin had nine-to-five jobs. On our way back to Union Station, we noticed that the government buildings were filled with young soldiers staring fearfully at us over their weapons. Shirley saw young women putting flowers on the bayonets that were sticking out from the gates of the buildings. One of the women gave Shirley a flower and brought her up to a building so she could drape her daisy over the bayonet of the rifle held in a startled soldier's hands. (Five years later, when I was teaching at Richmond, a young Black man in one of my remedial writing classes described that day, beginning with orders to travel from Fort Ord and ending with his still-amazed remembrance of "a girl putting a flower on my gun.") Then, the military acted on Attorney General Mitchell's orders to tear gas us. As our eyes and throats began to burn, we three women pulled out handkerchiefs and tissues, soaked them in water from the thermos I had providentially brought with me, and pretending we were playing a game, placed the handkerchiefs and tissues over the children's faces and led them back to the train. During the trip home, Penny, Barbara and I invented curses for each member of the Nixon administration. Barbara wished for a plague to carry off all their children.

In those days, David and I were living parallel lives. I was in the early stages of graduate study while David, nearing the completion of his doctorate was on a job search that resulted in an offer from a university in California.

"How much will you and Janey need to live on?"

"Twelve thousand a year," I replied promptly, expecting half.

David did not haggle too much because his parents were financing the separation, and I actually got more than I had expected. His parents sent me monthly payments of five hundred dollars until David's twenty-sixth birthday, when he was no longer at risk from the draft if I should charge him with abandonment. I was teaching by then, earning just enough to support Janey and me, but I remained patient, waiting for the other shoe to drop. And two years later, when David wanted a divorce in order to marry the daughter of a Los Angeles real estate developer, I asked for and got a cash settlement which I later used to buy my parents' house. I also got David's agreement to let me change Janey's last name to Schaefer.

May, 1980

"Are you going to wear makeup?"

I was in sweat pants and t-shirt, sitting on my bed with Vida propped on my bent knees and the cats spooled against my feet. Janey, in jean jacket, t-shirt and jeans, slouched in the doorway of my bedroom, the backpack stuffed with PJs and toilet articles dangling from her hand.

"I don't wear makeup ordinarily. Why should I now?"

Janey signed. "I thought just this once you'd break down, for your big date with Te-ed. You know, T-K-H-S-O."

"I'll just have to rely on the force of my personality to make an impression."

"But that's not sexy."

"I'm sorry about that. Janey, don't have high expectations of this evening. Reunions are often disappointing. We may not like each other. Do you want me to drive you to Ellen's?"

"No thanks, I'll walk."

"All right, then. Come here and kiss me good-bye. What time will you be home tomorrow?"

"Mr. Winters will probably drop me off on their way to church. If they ask me to go with them, should I say yes?"

"If you go to church with anyone, I'd rather you go with me."

"Good, that's what I'll tell them. I'll say, 'My mother is the custodian of my soul.' No, I won't. But do I have to go with you?"

"No, not if you don't want to. I'll expect you around 10:30 or 11:00. If I'm not here, I've gone to church."

"And I'll expect a full report from you."

After Janey left, I prepared myself for the evening with more care than I would have wanted Janey to witness. I felt uncomfortable as though I were passing through a ritual as I showered and shampooed my hair, wrapped myself in a towel afterward and applied an emory board to my toenails and a pumice stone to my heels. I stroked lotion over my body and into its crevices. I put on clean bikini underpants, new pantyhose, and a cotton slip, whirled a dryer through my hair, and then put on the new dress, after carefully removing price tags and flushing them away. I brushed and combed my hair, then put on pearl and gold earrings and a gold chain necklace. ("Why is jewelry okay and makeup not?" Janey had asked. "Jewelry has intrinsic beauty and value, especially if it's an heirloom, and makeup does not. Besides, I like jewelry and I don't like makeup.") I put on the only "dress" summer shoes I had, an elegant pair of cognac sling-back pumps, organized the matching shoulder strap pocketbook, and went down to the living room to wait for Ted, trying not to be aware that all my anointments and drapery were in anticipation of what I hoped would happen later in my bedroom that evening.

CHAPTER

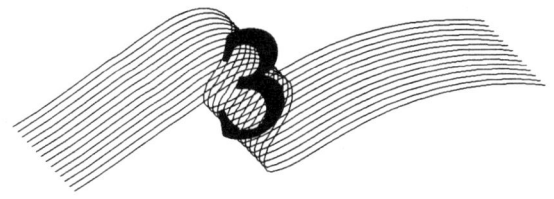

1970 - 1972

We moved down to the lower East Side. I rented a top floor apartment in a nicely renovated tenement on East Eleventh Street that had a small bedroom, a small kitchen, and a large living room with a skylight and a door opening onto a terrace-like fire escape. I joined the day care center in the basement of a neighborhood church that Penny, who lived only a few blocks away, had organized with other mothers. I delivered Janey one day when Penny was in charge and found her uncharacteristically depressed.

"What's wrong?" I asked as she listlessly distributed toys and games, organized play groups, and placated quarrelsome toddlers.

"Too many visits from the angel of death," she explained. "A woman who lives in my building, whom I've never liked too much or even known too well, is dying of cancer. She's divorced, has two preteenagers, and is not on good terms with her family. She did not want to die in a hospital, and so she asked her neighbors to see her through her final days. I've become part of a team of six women who take shifts around the clock, performing all the intimate, disgusting, and tasks necessary to keep a rapidly deteriorating body clean and comfortable. We also have arranged for her friends to care for her kids, supported her through difficult visits from relatives and negotiations with her ex-husband for the care of her children later."

As blonde as I but much shorter, Penny personified the Southern woman whose polite perkiness masks an iron will and a military mind.

"Well, I know you're extraordinary, Penny," I soothed. "But the true surprise is to find a half dozen women willing to submit themselves to such an ordeal."

Penny put on an oil cloth apron and joined a group of four-year-olds at a table set up for fingerpainting.

"The other women and I are just ordinary people rising to the demands of a difficult situation. And not one of us regrets it. Not one of us has missed a shift, no matter what else is going on in our lives. With the woman who is dying and the women who are caring for her, I've felt like a member of a religious community, more than I ever did in my years as an East Texas Baptist."

A toddler came over to the table and whispered loudly in Penny's ear. "I gotta go potty." Penny took her to the bathroom.

"You spoke of 'visits' from the angel of death," I said when Penny returned.

"Valerie is in the final stages of her illness. God, it will be a blessing when it's over. The chemotherapy made her hair fall out. She wore a wig to school and when it fell off, the kids made fun of her. And if watching your child die is not bad enough, her parents have too much money to receive any kind of public assistance, so Val's medical expenses have taken all their resources. Valerie's illness has drained their emotional resources as well." Penny put her face in her hands and shuddered. When she moved her hands away, her face had blue and yellow streaks on it. "Christine's been put on hold and of course feels both resentment and guilt toward her sister. My God, how do families bear such burdens? I'm beginning to believe Barbara's conspiracy theory. The government is filling the environment with enough poison to kill us off. When I was a child, except for an occasional accident or stillbirth, only old people – very old people – died."

I went to Bellevue to donate blood for Valerie, then in remission, but with little chance of surviving. She died the following week, and I went to the memorial service in the basement of Judson Memorial Church. The mourners sat on folding chairs while the minister spoke briefly about Valerie and then Christine read a poem she had written about how she had hated her sister for crowding her out of the family with her illness, but she had always loved her through the hatred and now would love and miss her always. There was no coffin, for Valerie had been cremated; just a table at the front of the room with Valerie's photograph and some of her drawings displayed. The sight of those drawings, so like Janey's drawings held by magnets on our refrigerator, connected me at once to the grief I would feel if

Janey died. I broke into heaving sobs; no one, not even Valerie's family, cried more loudly. Other mourners stared at me. Valerie's mother and father, for whom their daughter's long dying had been far more terrible than her death, sat motionless and dry-eyed. After the funeral, I began writing an essay. My thesis was that Barbara's charge that a poisoned environment took their daughter's life was not a paranoid fantasy. Valerie's death, the murders of students at Kent State and Jackson State, the drafting of young men to fight in Vietnam were part of the same condition: their government was willing to sacrifice the nation's young. That recognition gave me, as a mother, more motivation for political activism than I had had in the Sixties when I was single; the irony was that precisely because I was a mother, a single mother, I could not be the dedicated political activist I wished to be. I submitted the essay to the *Village Voice*. To my surprise, it was published. The day after the issue containing it appeared, a man identifying himself as Maurice Rothman called to tell me how moved he had been by my description of Valerie. He asked me to have dinner with him, but I refused.

"Oh, come on," he urged, "I'm not a freak or a pervert."

"What are you, then?"

"A shoe man."

"A what?"

"A shoe man. I'm an assistant shoe buyer at A & S."

"Men's shoes?"

"Women's."

"Why do men always sell women's shoes yet you never see women selling shoes to men?"

"I don't know. It's just the way things have always been. Have dinner with me and maybe you can persuade me to struggle in behalf of women shoe salespersons."

I agreed to have dinner with Maurice. When he came to the apartment, I was immediately attracted to him. He was taller than David, dark-haired, clean-shaven, and muscular. I knew I would never fall in love with him. Maurice was just what I needed then to restore my ego: an attractive partner for a meaningless relationship. We began an affair immediately. Maurice was earthy and uninhibited. His explicit enjoyment of sex, of sex with me, restored my confidence in my sexuality. But I soon found that sexual pleasure was all we could share, for Maurice was not a comrade, a fellow anti-war activist, but an ex-Marine who, though he had not served in Vietnam, spoke obsessively of bombing the "dinks" and "slopes" into extinction. When he first began spouting his crude red-neck propaganda, I thought he was joking. But I soon realized he was serious. He made fun of my "pinko" politics.

"My politics were up front in the article. If you don't like them, why did you call me?"

"Because you pinko women are good in bed."

Maurice was good in bed, too, even if he was a right wing nut.

But his angry racism disgusted me. He talked almost obsessively of how "spics" and "niggers" were ruining New York with their crime and welfare dependence. He made insulting remarks in the streets, loud enough to be heard by the people he was talking about. I was embarrassed, more than embarrassed, I felt I was betraying deeply held beliefs by maintaining a relationship with Maurice. Like the

Mississippi constable, he asked me if I had "slept with them" when I was in the South. But the flip side of his hostility was admiration. Maurice liked to talk "like a bro" and walk "like a dude." He was proud of his body and worked to maintain it. One room of his Yorkville tenement apartment was filled with body building equipment (I put Janey's tote bed on a pile of weight disks when I spent the night there); he ran five miles a day; he studied karate and earned a black belt. A command of martial arts is supposed to make people secure and unconfrontational in the street, but Maurice often carried chukka sticks with him, and spoke of wanting to get a gun. His racism and paranoia repelled me, and I tried to end the relationship. Then Maurice retreated, acknowledged his bad temper, and promised to try to change.

"Give me another chance," he asked, appealing to my reforming instincts, and I lingered in the relationship, until Janey provided the catalyst for ending it. At the beginning of our affair, Janey and I as a package had charmed Maurice. When we were in Central Park, he liked to pretend we were his family. But when Janey became her own self, bright, assertive, and nobody's fantasy baby, Maurice became disenchanted.

"She used to be a doll, now she's a dictator," he complained.

As soon as I realized Maurice was beginning to count Janey among his many antagonists, my attraction to him and his to me ended at once, as if we had turned off a switch. Yet Maurice refused to break off contact with me; he continued to call me, manipulating my maternal instincts until I found myself allowing him to assign me a new role as his confidante and counselor. Much of Maurice's anger was rooted in his shame at having dropped out of college and working at a job he hated. I urged him to get into a field he liked, sports and fitness, but he rejected my advice.

"I'd have to go back to college to get a degree in physical education; I left college to join the Marines. I don't want to go back."

Maurice went job hunting and got an offer from J.C. Penney to work as an assistant account executive.

"You'll still be in retailing," I warned. "It's a lateral move. You'll still be miserable."

Maurice took the job, hated it after two weeks, and was fired six months later.

This time Maurice took my advice. Using unemployment insurance, savings, and a loan from his father, a wealthy but stingy chiropractor who had previously been uncharacteristically negligent, I thought, for a Jewish man with an only son, Maurice enrolled in Hunter College, majoring in physical education. His student teaching assignment in a Bronx high school had the effect of softening his racism.

"I guess they're all right," he conceded after a semester of coaching Black and Hispanic boys. "They're just jocks like me."

Maurice graduated, but could not get a teaching job, so he went on to earn his master's degree in physical education, which, ironically, brought him right back to the corporate world when AT&T hired him to direct one of their fitness centers. Maurice was earning a good salary doing work he liked. His politics grew more liberal, although he continued to have occasional wide mood swings and to act out his ambivalence about his identity through vivid fantasies.

"Claire, I dreamt I saw Joe Hill last night, alive as you and me," was one of his frequent telephone greetings. Sometimes he spun out extended false reminiscences which sometimes involved his mother, a Viennese-born housewife completely dominated by her husband. "The miners loved my mother," he claimed. "She worked tirelessly organizing them against the bosses. They looked upon her as a mother; Mother Rothman, they called her and blessed her name."

But at heart, Maurice still identified with the aristocracy. When *Masterpiece Theatre* ran the "Upstairs, Downstairs" series, my telephone rang each Sunday evening at one minute past ten, and Maurice would greet me as the upper class family's wayward son, Captain "Maurice" Bellamy.

Despite lapses, I thought Maurice was turning out rather well, and I felt I had contributed to his transformation. He even went so far as to concede the Vietnam war was a mistake. I congratulated him for becoming a human being.

"Yeah," he agreed, "now all I need is a wife."

We both agreed Maurice should marry, but our project did not succeed. I cannot remember all the women who passed through Maurice's life: actresses, airline stewardesses, models, department store buyers, corporate women on the fast track; plain and pretty women, fat and thin women, women he met in the park, through introductions from friends, or advertisements in the *Village Voice*. His long affairs lasted for months; his brief ones for weeks or days. He spoke of some women with his former "spicks and niggers" contempt; these were "cunts and sluts."

(In these periods, his racism resurfaced). Of others he declared, "this is the one." But it never was. He introduced each promising candidate to me. I encouraged him in the early days of his bridesearch.

"When are you going to have that fixed?" Maurice had once asked me, referring to a flea-sized wart on my wrist.

"I don't know when or if I'll have it fixed, Maurice. Can't you accept me, warts and all?"

"I don't see why you should accept imperfections when you don't have to," he responded grimly.

After his breakup with a third almost-fiancee, I understood that Maurice's search for love was entwined with a search for warts. His involvement with a woman lasted until he found the reason it could not last. His pattern varied only when the woman was reluctant. Then Maurice's increased interest made him so persistent and intense, he drove her away. Often there were postscripts; Maurice would speak of having met a former lover who was now, to his regret, married to someone else.

"Of course, she's married to someone else," I said after one of these announcements. "You've had so many nice women in your life and you let them all get away. But tell me, Maurice why not one of them has ever been Jewish?"

"I prefer Christian women because they have *pom*, or what Gentiles might call class. Like when girls from good private schools ride on buses. When they sit down and their uniforms slide up, the space between knee sock and hem is divine, a shrine I could worship at."

"That's poetic, Maurice. Now tell me the real reason."

"Jewish women are always saying, 'Buy me, do me, get me, bring me, take me.' Christian women let me breathe."

"My ex-husband used to tell me he was so glad I wasn't a 'Jap.' It took me a while to realize 'shiksa' was another word for 'patsy.' I think the principal difference between you and my ex-husband, Maurice, is that your contempt surfaces before marriage."

"Nobody, nobody likes a smartass, Claire."

Ten years after we met, Maurice is still unmarried, and I doubt he will ever marry. But he is still my friend, warts and all. And the relationship has not been so one-sided, after all. Maurice encouraged me to run and coached me when I started. Running was very useful to me during another very bad period in my life. With Maurice's help, I would run in the New York City Marathon, for on June first, Maurice would line up with thousands of others at the main post office in New York and at midnight would drop two envelopes into the Road Runners Club chute, one for him and one for me, each containing a request for an application to run in the October race.

After Maurice, I grew cautious. In retrospect, I felt that as a single parent totally responsible for my child, I had been rash indeed to have rushed into intimacy with a stranger. I was appalled by reports of men who abused, or even killed, their lovers' children, as if driven by an enraged instinct to stamp out evidence of another man's potency, but I was even more appalled by the women who were so dependent for self esteem on identification with a male, that they allowed their lovers to hurt their children. Men were drawn to me; they approached me on the street or in the park when I was with

Janey. I dated a number of men I met casually, once, twice, usually no more than three times, for I resisted intimacy. I was cautious and they were ambivalent. Initially, they were charmed, as Maurice had been, by the Madonna-like composition of the blonde, blue-eyed mother with the blonde, blue-eyed child, but they quickly withdrew when they confronted the prospect of committing themselves to a family another man had created. I recognized myself as a member of a female sub-culture in New York: single parents of single children, brief early marriages behind us and long struggles ahead, vestals to children and work.

In the Fall of 1970, I had completed almost enough credits to earn a Master's degree and was aggressively applying for teaching jobs at the City University of New York. I was hired to teach writing at a two-year college in Brooklyn in a special program established for students entering City University under a new open admissions policy. I urged Penny, who had opposed the New York teachers' strike in 1968 and was unhappy teaching in a high school, to apply and she was hired as a reading teacher. Open Admissions had been rushed into life by university administrators in response to the city's increasingly restive minority population, but housewives and white working class adults also began flocking to the tuition-free colleges, whose faculties, if now obliged to accept them, were not about to take on the task of teaching them. For this purpose, separate programs were established at most of the CUNY branches, staffed by a disposable corps of remedial instructors like Penny and me. But even the knowledge that the Open Admissions students and their teachers were considered second class citizens did not curb my enthusiasm for the program. I discovered I liked teaching and had a gift for it; I liked my students, I was happy to be working with Penny, and I liked our program director, a gentle-mannered, Mississippi-born Black man named Jack Jackson, whose eyes had lit up during my interview for the position when I spoke of my civil rights work in his native state. I liked every one in the program, with one significant exception, a math teacher, Michael la Marca, who called the students "dummies and misfits" and ridiculed their lack of mastery of his subject.

"Why is he in this program?" I demanded of Jack Jackson. "How could you have hired someone who hates the students and makes racist remarks about them?"

"Perhaps you've noticed that I'm not totally in charge here. I don't make all the decisions. But I put the case to you, Claire, would you prefer to have me in charge of the program with Michael in it or someone else running the program — with Michael in it anyway?"

"Do I have some time to think it over? Seriously, who really is responsible for Michael being hired?"

"Keep your eyes open, Claire, and you'll unravel that and other mysteries."

Eventually I figured out that Michael's godfather was Augie Audino, a dean of the college. Then Penny and I began to speculate about other anomalies. Why, for example, had the president, a former mink rancher without a doctorate or any prior academic experience, been chosen when presumably many other candidates with appropriate credentials had applied for the position? Why were so many of the college administrators former priests or nuns? Why did one of the technical programs, architectural engineering, have a large paper enrollment of students from a mideastern country who were never visible in the classrooms? Penny came up with a partial explanation.

"Without inside information we won't know the answers to these and other mysteries, but it's clear that this place, and no doubt others, is like a huge tin box that the people in charge – I mean outside the college – use for making deals, paying off political debts, pacifying restless populations, giving the mob its cut, and, oh yes, giving their friends jobs."

"It's here some sleaze, there some sleaze, everywhere it's sleaze, sleaze on MacDonald's farm, in other words."

"No, not entirely. We're here and we're not sleazy, and I'm sure there are others here who are not cynical and care about what they're doing."

Jean Berns was one who cared. I met her when she came to observe me in the classroom. Since every one in the program was an untenured newcomer, the college personnel and budget committee had appointed a committee of tenured faculty to evaluate our teaching skills. On the day Jean visited my class, I had assigned a group of students to read their prepared essays and then respond to questions and comments from their classmates. One young woman was overcome by nervousness when she read her paper and began to stammer wildly. The other students looked down at their laps. I walked over to her, put my hand on her arms, and said, "I don't want to put you under pressure, but I know you can do this." At once the tension in the room eased. The student's back straightened and her speech cleared. Her classmates raised their heads, watching her as they listened attentively, nodding and smiling to encourage her through an occasional lapse. When she finished reading the essay, they asked intelligent questions and she gave sensible replies.

After the class, Jean said she was indebted to me for making it possible for her to "witness an epiphany." She wrote a positive evaluation. I was thrilled by external evidence that I was what I wanted to think I was, a good teacher. The required follow-up conference about the lesson was the beginning of a friendship. Jean had been teaching political science at the college since 1960 and had managed to keep her enthusiasm for teaching, her concern for the students, and her indignation at the college's shabby policies and practices, which included repeated denials of her requests for promotion.

"I'm one of three people in a department of twelve who have doctorates. I've published articles in scholarly journals and presented papers at conferences. Yet I'll probably be the oldest assistant professor in the western world. That seems to be fine with my colleagues. When the head of the English department learned I wanted a promotion, he asked me what my husband did. I told him my husband is an engineer. Then he said, "Assistant professor is as high as a married woman with a working husband has a right to go."

I introduced Jean to Penny, and Jean introduced me to Anne Schneider from the art department, "the only person at this college to be awarded a Guggenheim."

"Which at this college will not help me get tenure," Anne explained. "In fact, it will hurt my case because my colleagues are jealous."

We began meeting regularly. One day, Penny pointed out to us that our discussions were mainly about grievances.

"This is like c-r; bitch and moan, bitch and moan. If we're ever going to change things we don't like, we've got to get organized."

Penny's challenge motivated us to contact other women at the college. Jean drew up a questionnaire that we distributed, asking women at the college to evaluate their job satisfaction and to indicate if they were interested in forming an organization. The response was good; forty of the two hundred questionnaires we sent out were returned indicating a low rate of job satisfaction and a high rate of interest in forming an organization that would be, according to one respondent, "just a tad to the left of the Faculty Wives' Committee, which is all we have at present."

We scheduled a meeting, sent out an announcement and twenty-five women came. At our first meeting, we organized ourselves into The Faculty Women's Committee, a name we agreed sounded "assertive but not militant."

In the spring of 1971, when Jean was again denied a promotion by her department, she filed a charge of discrimination against the department and the college with the New York City Human Rights Commission. The case was not heard until almost a year later. By this time, the Coalition had grown in size and influence, having succeeded in heading off several non-reappointments and winning some promotions for its members. Twenty Coalition women attended the hearing in the Commission's headquarters in an office building on lower Broadway in Manhattan. Rows of folding chairs for spectators were on three sides of the hearing room; the commission members – women prominent in New York philanthropic circles – sat at a long table on the fourth side. Jean and her attorney, Madeline Robinson Steele, a well-known civil rights lawyer, sat on a chair in the center of a large, arena-like floor space, while the University's Associate Corporate Counselor, Pauline Blatt, paced around them, firing questions.

"Did you really write this?" Blatt screamed at Jean while shaking in her face a paper Jean had presented at a conference of political scientists.

"Yes," Jean replied calmly, "I was invited to give that paper as a result of another article I had written for one of the journals."

The women at the Commission table watched impassively as Blatt continued her attack on Jean.

"I don't believe this," Penny said. "It's like Jean's on trial for mass murder."

"I thought even in an adversary situation, there would be a measure of decorum," I said.

"Blatt's rudeness has a crude effectiveness," Anne acknowledged ruefully.

"I admire Jean's pluck," Penny observed, "but I could never keep my cool. If Blatt ever talked to me the way she did to Jean, I would have knocked her to the ground."

When Blatt finished, Jean's lawyer concluded the proceedings by questioning Jean and building her answers into a dignified response to Blatt's insults and charges of incompetency and inadequacy. We had naively expected a ruling from the Commission within a reasonable period, like six months at the most. We should have known better than to expect remedy from the Commission, whose members, after all, were political appointees, not an impartial, independent body. Two years after the hearing, the Commission still had not issued a ruling. In the interim, after several rounds of promotion decisions, Jean's department finally elevated her to the rank of associate professor. The case being moot, Jean withdrew her complaint.

"Once I challenged their perfect system, they set out to destroy me," Jean said of the experience. "They almost succeeded in making me believe I was as bad as they said I was. Filing the complaint cost me a great deal, but not filing it would have cost me even more."

One benefit from Jean's action was an outpouring of support from women at her own college and from other branches of CUNY as well. Lila Milini, a lecturer in the English Department at Brooklyn College, sensed in the mood of Jean's supporters a readiness to organize. She sent out a flier announcing a meeting at the CUNY Graduate Center on West 42nd Street in Manhattan. When Jean, Anne, Penny, I, and other women from Brooklyn Community college entered the auditorium on the evening of the meeting, it was full.

"Look at all of us," Penny said, "just beaming with we-are- not-alone euphoria."

Lila chaired the meeting, which moved efficiently toward an agreement to form the CUNY Women's Coalition, with the immediate goal of developing an affirmative action plan for the university. That, of course, was the high point. Subsequent Coalition meetings were often as boring as any academic meeting, but the incentive for attending was to meet women from other CUNY branches, hear gossip, learn about jobs. One evening, a woman from Richmond Community College told me there was an opening in the English Department and encouraged me to apply for it. I sent off my resume and a week later I got a call from the department secretary setting up an appointment for an interview. At the interview, I faced a circle of at least twenty members of the English department who questioned me about my philosophy of teaching, my experience in the civil rights movement, my progress toward my doctorate. Knowing the way had been prepared for me, I answered confidently, feeling, for the first time in my life, that I would be the winner in the contest. The next day, the chairperson, Esther Sternfeld, called to tell me I had been chosen for the appointment as assistant professor. I went back to the campus to get my teaching schedule, fill out tax and pension forms, and meet the officers of the college, but not the president, who, Esther explained, was out of the country "overseeing a program this college has set up jointly with a university in Nigeria."

"You'll meet him when he gets back," Esther promised. "Your experience in the civil rights and anti-war movements is just the kind of background he wants in new faculty. He has a law degree from the University of Chicago, was a dean at the New School before heading an anti-poverty program Bob Kennedy set up in Bedford-Stuyvesant. This college was a conservative technical college, the oldest in the CUNY system, set up after World War Two to give job skills to returning vets. Bob Wasserman came here determined to transform it into an innovative, liberal postsecondary institution, and he's pretty much succeeded, not, however, without making many enemies among the old line faculty."

CHAPTER

May, 1980

At six o'clock the doorbell rang. Ted was smiling, looking very pleased to see me. The sight of him certainly was pleasing me. His clothes were correct but casual: khaki twill trousers, a blue oxford cloth shirt, a tie with a modest pattern, and a navy wool blazer. A faint, clean scent came from him, and I pictured him in his shower preparing himself for me as I had minutes before prepared myself for him. I asked him if he wanted anything to drink and he asked for a glass of water. I went to the kitchen and filled two glasses of tap water and ice. When I returned to the living room, he was looking at the photographs on the mantel.

"Is this your daughter?"

"Yes, that's Janey. The photo was taken last year when we were still living in New York. That's her best friend, Julie, on the right."

"She looks like you. Will I meet her?"

"Not this evening. She's sleeping over at her friend's house."

"That's some fish," he said, nodding at another photo. "Your parents look happy. Where do they live now?"

"On the west coast of Florida, near Sarasota. I don't think two people ever enjoyed retirement as much as they do. Neither one of them ever really had a childhood, and now they're finally able to play. They fish, swim, play cards with their friends. Yes, they are happy."

"That sounds like the kind of life my father had in mind when he retired last year. He had worked hard and was looking forward to relaxing and traveling with my mother. But my mother said she's not ready to sit in the sun yet. All her life she did what he wanted her to do. She stopped working when he came back from the service. She got her teaching certificate and began teaching only when my brother and I were out of high school. Now she's become active in local Democratic politics. But she's not enthusiastic about Jimmy Carter."

"Who is? But I find the alternative unacceptable."

"Who is the woman in this picture? She looks like she is active in politics, too."

"That is Frieda, who was my former grandmother-in-law. That photo was taken at an anti-war demonstration in New York."

Ted pleased me by asking me to tell him about her. As I described Frieda, I was aware of how quickly he and I were at ease with each other and how much I was already enjoying myself.

"I loved Frieda," I concluded. "I remained close to her after my husband and I were divorced. She died two years ago, surrounded by her comrades, a committed Party member to the last."

"She sounds like my own grandmother, who was active in the Wisconsin suffrage movement. She was one of Belle LaFollette's ablest lieutenants."

"You had a suffragist grandmother?"

I looked at Ted, he looked back, widening his eyes in imiation of my surprised expression.

"I thought that would interest you. Now, who is the woman in this picture"

"That's Mrs. Johnson, the woman I stayed with when I went to Mississippi in 1964."

"There was an article in the *Star Lake Daily News* about you when you were down there."

I touched the photo.

"I still keep in touch with her. I call her every so often to find out how things are down there and how she is. She was old when I was down there; I don't know how old she is now, but she's still strong. All her adult life, she worked as a maid, 'but never in people's houses,' she told me. She worked in a local hospital and in a local television station. She bought her own home and that car she's standing so proudly in front of. She brought up her daughter's two children when her daughter died and she put her granddaughter through college. Now she's enjoying life. I took Janey down there two summers ago to see how things have changed. The civil rights movement really made a difference in that community. The roads are paved now and people get services. They have new homes and better jobs. Mrs. Johnson said, 'Used to be only the white man got the job. Now if you got the skills, you get the job.' The word went out when Janey and I stayed with her, and people came around to greet me. Janey was really impressed. She said, 'They act like you're a TV celebrity.'"

"You must feel good about what you did there."

The approval in Ted's voice felt nice too.

"Yes, I do. I was part of a movement that produced so much change for the better in people's lives. Oh, there have been problems. I've heard about young people committing crimes, getting involved with drugs, but the community as a whole is so much more prosperous, so much happier. And the change is permanent. Even if Reagan gets elected, things will never go back to what they were."

I saw Ted staring at his glass and asked if he would like some more water.

"No thanks. We should be going."

I took his glass and mine back to the kitchen and put them in the dishwasher. When I came back to the living room, he looked directly into my eyes. I knew he felt the electricity, too.

As we left the house, I looked up and down our street for neighbors who might be present to take note of my leaving home for the first time in the company of a man, but lawns and porches were vacant; people were probably in their houses eating dinner.

Ted opened the passenger door and I slid into the front seat. Before entering the car on the driver's side, Ted took off his blazer jacket and folded it over the back of the front seat. He started the car, drove to Highway 35 and headed south. He rolled down the window and rested his arm on the door. The wind flapped his sleeve and I thought of the arm

within it, seeing in my imagination the blondish brown hairs visible at the cuffs.
"Where are we going?"
"To Trempeleau?" His voice ended in a question, as if he were asking my approval.
"To Ed Sullivan's. Have you eaten there?"
"No. Sounds fine."
Ted drove to Highway 35, the Great River Road. I studied the Wisconsin bluffs, enjoying as I always do watching one peak fall into shadow before another, or a valley glow golden under the evening sun. Farms studded the bluffsides, their silos shining pink or purple in the twilight. "Pillars of debt," my mother had commented bitterly almost every time she had driven past them. "Don't marry a farmer," she had warned me. "It's a mean life and a woman is no more than a beast of burden." Her father had joined in milk strikes during the Depression. The farmers had dumped milk, blocked roads, and even planted bombs in cheese factories. They had clashed with National Guardsmen and been tear-gassed. But the strikes had failed, and the farmers did not get more money. "Hard times just made my father harder," my mother said. Her eyes had burned whenever she spoke of her "ruthlessly Germanic upbringing:" chores on bitter mornings, frequent beatings, waiting on her father and brothers at mealtimes. "'I need a fork, Anne Marie,' he'd say, and the sideboard with the silverware was inches from his hand, but I'd have to fetch it for him. My mother, my sister and I never sat down at the table; we ate their leftovers later, standing up in the kitchen. I wanted to be a teacher, but he didn't even want me to finish high school. 'What does a girl need school for?' he'd ask. I got a job with the phone company and moved

away as soon as I could, and not too long afterward I met another runaway who in the course of time became my husband and your father."

"Did your parents have a happy childhood?" I asked Ted.

"Yes, I think they did. They both grew up on farms. My father was the second of three kids; my mother was the next youngest of six."

"Who had the suffragette mother?"

"My mother. When I was a kid, my brother and I went to my mother's father's farm for the summer with all our cousins. it was like summer camp. God, we had a good time. I still go there for visits. Both those grandparents are still alive, but they've retired. Their second eldest son runs the farm for them. And if they can scale it down and make it profitable, one of his kids will probably take it over from him. My father's childhood was not as exuberant as my mother's. My mother's father, for example, would put a tree in each of his kid's rooms at Christmas. My father's father did not do things with so much style, but I think my father was happy. He was the younger son, so his older brother got the farm. My grandfather is dead; my grandmother lives in a Lutheran retirement home. My father visits her and his sister and brother from time to time, but there isn't as much warmth on that side of the family as on my mother's."

I was thinking enviously that I had no warm grandparents to remember at all.

"Family reunions with my mother's family are still a treat. My mother brought the fun of her childhood into ours, my brother and mine. When we were kids, she'd read us stories, but better yet, make them up. She played games with us and took us on trips. She liked being out of the house; she hated housework, but liked to cook. Then when we were older and wanted to be with our friends, she made our house the place where all the kids wanted to come. My mother liked having a lot of kids around; she wanted more kids, especially a daughter, but it didn't happen. My father was not so pleased to have his home turned into a playground. He'd come home from work and grumble, 'I had two kids when I left this morning, and that's the number I'd like to have now.' But my mother would say, 'I want our home to be a happy place,' and it was. I thought the good times would never end."

Ted stopped talking. I thought about his last statement. Then he said, "I take it that your parents did not have such a good time when they were young."

My parents' childhoods seemed Dickensian compared to the childhoods of Ted's parents. Briefly, I described my mother's life on the farm. I told him a little about my father's father, who had worked for Walter J. Kohler, the manufacturer of plumbing fixtures, in Kohler, Wisconsin. Kohler had set up a "workers' village" near Sheboygan; he built houses which the workers paid for out of deductions from their salaries, and set up groceries where they bought their food with what was left of their wages. During the Depression, workers found their maximum wages were below the NRA minimum and all hell broke loose in workers' paradise. The men went on strike and old Walter Kohler set his goons on the pickets. Both my grandfathers were tear-gassed in the Thirties. During the year-long strike, Kohler Village was occupied by armed National Guardsmen.

"My grandfather's class struggle against the bosses, however, did not prevent him from becoming a tyrant at home. Like my mother's father, he took out his frustration and rage on his family. My father enlisted in the army when the Second World War started and he never went home again. He has a brother and sister still living, but he rarely sees them. I have cousins I have never met. My mother loved her mother. When my grandmother became ill with diabetes, my mother's father was unwilling to pay for medical care, and she was too worn down from a life of servitude to demand it. She died when my mother was nineteen, two years after my mother had left home and took a job with the telephone company. My father went to work for the post office after the war and one of his buddies was dating my mother's friend. This couple introduced them. My mother is close to her sister, but we never had the kind of reunions you've described. Just an occasional visit with my cousin Martin, who reluctantly took me to the senior prom."

"I remember."

"Were you surprised to see me at the prom?"

"No. I don't remember exactly what I thought, but I was probably just pleased to see you had come to the dance because you didn't, as I remember, go out much."

"No, I didn't. My cousin Martin is now a Lutheran minister in Duluth."

Ted moved his right hand from the wheel to reach into the inner pocket of his blazer. He pulled out a billfold, spread it on the seat between us, and opened it to a plastic encased photo of a boy in a Brewers' cap holding a baseball bat to his right shoulder.

"While we're moving from past to present, let me show you a picture of my son, who's about a year older than your daughter."

"Well, we have certainly reproduced ourselves, physically, at least. Janey may look like me, but her personality is very different from mine. Your son seems to have your athletic ability as well as your looks."

"Yes, I think he has, although I can't take any credit for encouraging him. What skill he has, he's developed on his own."

"Where is he?"

"Right now he lives with his mother in Milwaukee. This summer, around the middle of August, he's coming to live with me. Here we are."

Ted drove the car into the crowded lot, and after a search for a space, parked it. He put on his blazer and locked the car. We entered the restaurant which was so full we had to wait in the bar area. A woman wearing an apron with shamrocks on it took our orders for drinks; I asked for mineral water and Ted ordered two bottles.

"You don't drink?"

"Yes, but not when I'm driving. Do you?"

"Wine with dinner sometimes, but nothing else."

We looked at each other and smiled, out of talk for the moment. When we had finished drinking our mineral water, the woman who served us told us our table was ready. We went into the restaurant where another woman led us through the tables filled by large families and parties of young people, seated us at a table, not next to the window, but close enough to it so that we could see the river, gave us menus, commanded us to enjoy our meal, and left. When a young man about Mike's age came to our table we were ready to order: red snapper for me and trout for Ted.

"Would you like a glass of wine?" Ted asked.

I did want one, but declined, not wanting to drink alone or risk watching Ted break his resolve by ordering a drink.

After the waiter had taken our order, we went over to the salad bar and filled plates, selecting items from icebound bowls containing crisp salad greens, fresh vegetables, assorted beans, chocolate pudding and lime jello with whipped cream. When we returned to the table, I felt comfortable enough to ask Ted to bring me up to date on his activities in the past seventeen years. But Ted intercepted me.

"I know you got married, moved to New York, had a child, got divorced after you left Madison. Tell me what else you were doing before you came back to Star Lake."

A little startled, but also pleased to have him switch the let's-talk-about-you roles, yet at the same time fearful of talking too much and boring him, I told Ted about teaching, about graduate school — even about Mackintosh. I told him about getting fired.

CHAPTER

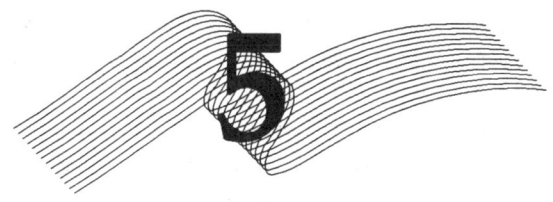

1972 - 1977

Other CUNY administrators saw Open Admissions as an odious, if necessary, concession to New York's increasingly restive minorities; Wasserman saw the policy as an opportunity to practice social engineering. He reached beyond Richmond's traditional student population of young public and parochial high school graduates to bring in housewives, veterans, working people, foreign students, high school students, and prisoners. A skillful fundraiser, Wasserman was able to get money from federal and foundation donors to establish New College, a form of counter-college to Richmond, in which he lodged an array of adventurously named programs – New Horizons (to provide "liberal arts enrichment to alienated youth"), Neighborhood Scholars (to bring high school students into the college), Multiversity (to set up branches of the college in Chinatown, and Bedford Styvesant), the Universal College (to encourage working class youth to become entrepreneurs) – along with an exchange program for Nigerians, a program for prisoners at the Great Kills Detention Center, and the university-wide alternative program, SEEK. New College was staffed by a faculty hired (and fired) by a Personnel and Budget which operated, over the objections of the faculty union, with actual independence from Richmond's regular P and B, and with nominal independence from Wasserman.

Wasserman's main support in the "traditional" college came from the English Department, although he was not without critics there, especially from "the senior men." One of these, Karl Spieler, a "tenured full," devoted a large part of a department meeting to a derisive description of a New College course, which he had observed "in a spirit of enlightened curiosity."

The teacher, he reported, "spent the entire period 'rapping' with the students with the stated goal of deciding collectively what the syllabus for the course would be. He accepted each of their inane remarks as a revelation, commenting with sacerdotal solemnity, 'I see what you're saying,' 'I hear where you're coming from,' and the inevitable 'Thank you for sharing that with us.' He concluded the class with an expression of gratitude for the 'learning experience' and a promise to continue the valuable discussion the next day. I could barely contain myself from calling the man an imposter, for he certainly is not a teacher. We're not paid to have students provide us with 'learning experiences.' It's our responsibility to use our experience and education to give them direction, to tell them what they need to learn and teach it to them, not to place the responsibility for their education in their own inadequate hands. And I mean education of substance, not trendy nonsense. Listen to this excuse for a social science course as it is described in a New College catalogue. It's called 'Urban Roots Revolution' and the course description states: 'At the completion of this course students will have acquired, through hands-on experience, skills in installing black boxes to prevent Ma Bell from further ripping them off, collecting survival rations from supermarkets, and securing shelter through a variety of means, including reprisals against greedy landlords.' This is not valid higher education; this is a course in crime."

Spieler was a vehement critic of Open Admissions and Affirmative Action, claiming that students admitted and faculty hired (like me) under those programs were unqualified for admission to or employment by the university. He was probably a racist and a sexist, but I felt his criticism had some merit. Before the end of my first semester at Richmond, I saw the college as a reflection of the best and worst of the Sixties legacy, its commitment to equity and justice marred by shoddy practices and unethical behavior.

During my first month at Richmond, new faculty members were invited to an orientation meeting sponsored by the administrators of New College programs. The meeting was held in the C building, one of the two-storied buildings facing on three sides of a quadrangle reserved for student-related matters from financial aid to counseling to organization offices. The A building was used for courses in the humanities; the B building was used for sciences; however, the alphabet structures did not end there, for because of the college's growth, lettered annexes had been added to each of the three main structures. Most of the New College courses and some of the regular college courses were taught in trailers lined up in a barracks formation on the campus.

When we new faculty entered the lounge where the meeting was held, the chairs, were arranged in the ubiquitous circle. One half of them were already occupied by Carlo Cremona, an ex-Jesuit who was dean of New College, the younger men who were directors of the New College programs, and some of their staff. The New College personnel almost outnumbered, in fact, the twelve or so new hires, but since some of us had "movement" credentials, I assumed Cremona thought we merited being courted as New College allies. My civil rights and anti-war activism, which I thought modest, nevertheless gave me status. Ariela Burstyn, the new hire in the History Department, whose Spanish mother had met her Polish father when they were both fighting on the Republican side during the Spanish Civil War, had worked with her ex-husband in a community organizing project in Cambridge for several years before coming to New York to begin graduate work at Columbia. Norma Reilly, a new hire in Neighborhood Scholars, had gone from SDS to organizing the New University Movement at the University of Nebraska while completing a doctorate in sociology. Another former SDSer, Shirley Benjamin, newly hired in the New Horizons program, had gone with the Venceremos Brigade to cut cane in Cuba. Ariela, Norma, and Shirley were renting a house together on Staten Island. The rest of the new hires had straight academic backgrounds, and the only one of these I knew was Trudy Markoff, new in the Social

Science department, who had a doctorate in philosophy and had published several articles. Cremona opened the meeting by briefly stating that New College programs were not always clearly understood and were sometimes controversial and that "this little meeting" was designed to explain the rationale and methodology of these programs to new faculty. Then Cremona turned the meeting over to his lieutenants. Henry Sharpley of SEEK spoke first, stating that the program's goal was to make students able to "manipulate the system instead of being manipulated by it," and "above all, to keep their eye on the main chance." He spoke at length in a roundabout way, but his major point seemed to be that his program, one of the largest in the CUNY system, owed its success to the large federal aid package it supplied to students. "We show them where the sugar tit is," Sharpley boasted. Seymour Abromowitz, director of Universal College, spoke next. Abromowitz, a large, chubby boyish-faced forty-year-old, was a genuine star, with a long and highly regarded background as a labor organizer and theorist, credentials he was transforming into a nontraditional doctorate at Union Graduate School. He spoke of the college's history, of its previous historic mission to feed the working class youth of Staten Island into civil service and corporate middle management, "which is admittedly a better break than working in Wendy's," but his program, Abromowitz explained, was designed to make students critical of these career patterns and to seek to find or create "optional and optimum workplaces." The next speaker was Phil Zweiback of New Horizons; he described his program's distinctive feature as "the expansion of a traditional academic experience into one which can turn on students who would ordinarily tune out. For example," Zweiback said, "we thought it would be nice if the students could experience theater in a socialist society, so I wrote a proposal that was funded and we were able to take thirty students to East Germany and the Soviet Union to see the Brecht and Moscow theaters."

"Without knowing German and Russian?" I asked.

The words had sprung from my lips like a genie from a bottle. At once I felt tension in the room. My question had signalled an "incorrect" attitude, arousing in my comrades the sudden, palpable suspicion, I had seen arise before at Left gatherings; it probably resembles the hostility that springs up in fundamentalist congregations when one among them questions the true faith.

"We had an orientation for the students before we went," the director replied coldly. "The differences in language did not prove a significant barrier, and the students had a meaningful learning experience."

People were cordial afterward; Cremona came over to me during the punch-and-cookies social aftermath, but I knew I had aroused suspicion. And the more I saw how Richmond functioned, the more my skepticism deepened. I learned, for example, that potentially disruptive student constituencies—Blacks and Hispanics—were co-opted through "perks" financed through the student activities fees or from felicitous grants like the one Zweiback had gotten. With minimally monitored funding allocated through the student government organization, students made long distance telephone calls, and entertained themselves and their friends; they went on "retreat" at upstate dude ranches, out-of-state resorts, hotels in Puerto Rico. The "regular" students at Richmond were aware and resentful of benefits they did not enjoy. What goaded them even more – and what threatened Wasserman's vaunted racial harmony at Richmond – was the sight of hundreds of minority students in a line that snaked from the bursar's office in C Building out to the quadrangle on the days financial aid checks were distributed. Many of these students were otherwise invisible on campus, but repeated academic failure for nonattendance or any other reason did not disqualify a student, for Sharpley refused to drop anyone from his program. Eventually, when student government organization excesses became too blatant, when, for example, one truly enterprising student was allowed to finance car payments, the administration was forced to modify its policy of permissiveness and install some modest reforms in disbursement of funds and oversight of expenditures. But nothing really changed, of course.

When I met Jean, Penny and Anne for a reunion dinner at the cafeteria on the eighteenth floor of the City University, "our club" on 42nd Street, and told them about the sleaze and shenanigans at Richmond, Anne said: "So what else is new?"

"That may be a disappointment but hardly a surprise," Jean added.

"But you do love the place?" asked Penny and the others exclaimed in unison: "Tell us about it!"

"The goal really is to do the best you can for everyone. Even the teachers who don't teach genuinely care about the students, almost all of whom have been written off, rejected by parents, teachers, children, spouses, the courts, their country. These students come to Richmond and encounter for the first time people who think they are worthwhile and capable of making a contribution. It's wonderful to hear a returning housewife talk about her newly discovered talent for science, or read a student's paper to a class and witness a sudden, brand new burst of self esteem appear on that student's face. Being part of that process of transformation and empowerment turns me on, keeps me high all the time."

"I'm glad to hear good things are happening somewhere in the university," Jean said.

"I'm envious," Anne said. "Find jobs for us there."

"What are the faculty like?" Penny asked. "Tell us about the men."

"They run the political spectrum, beginning with a group of right-wing troglodytes who came in when the college opened after the Second World War. Most of them were hired from industry to run the technical programs. They don't have academic credentials, but ironically, they now see themselves a defenders of intellectual standards against the brash Ph.Ds or near-Ph.Ds who've come in under Wasserman. The trogs hate Wasserman; they think the place has gone to hell under his administration. What they don't realize is that they flunked so many students out of the technical programs, or discouraged them from entering, the college's enrollment declined to a point that the college might have been closed. Wasserman was hired in a last ditch effort to keep the place alive."

"He's saved the trog's asses," Penny observed.

"That's right, but they still hate him. So does the faction that's slightly to the left, a strong centrist union group with some overlap with the trogs who oppose Wasserman because of his open contempt for faculty governance. The leader of this group is Craig Cameron from my department, who is vice-president of the faculty union university wide. Craig likes people to think he knows all the university gossip, and when he's about to share some of it with you, he says, 'If you repeat what I'm about to tell you, I'll deny saying it.' Craig also enjoys bragging about the Union's regularly scheduled meetings with Wasserman because Wasserman, who has a full bar in his office, brings out a bottle and allows Craig to think he can outdrink him."

"That's so macho," Anne said.

"Yes," I agreed, "in some ways the place is more like a frontier town than a college. But, drunk or sober, Wasserman is still the fastest gun, only he deflects most of the challenges and manipulates all the competing groups against each other: trogs who support the union until a grievance is filed against them for their terrible personnel practices, the union types who have to force the trogs to observe the contract and who are watchdogs to see the New College programs don't get more than their share of the college budget. The New College people, who have allies in the regular college, too, include a group of Black and Hispanic men with titles like 'Special Assistant to the President,' meaning they don't have a faculty line and serve at Wasserman's pleasure. These are men with good political connections, but few academic credentials. Wasserman has another group of men, Kennedy-era liberals with good academic credentials, who administer the special programs or develop projects Wasserman wants created and then loses interest in once they become successful. The new College people also include stars from the Sixties like Carleton Greene, the editor of a left-wing social policy journal who teaches in the New Horizons program, and Seymour Abromowitz, a former trade union activist."

"I know Seymour" Penny exclaimed. "That is, I really know his first ex-wife. She lives in my neighborhood."

"How many ex-wives does he have?" Anne asked.

We all perked up, eager for gossip with dessert.

"Two that I know of, plus assorted ex-live-in lovers and groupies."

"I had heard he was a womanizer," I said.

"That reputation is well-deserved. Less well-deserved is the reputation Seymour cultivates as a working class hero. His background is actually bourgeois. His mother was a concert pianist. He grew up in an atmosphere of European *kultur*. The working class connection comes from Mary Rose, his first wife. Her parents were factory workers. And not left-wing-Workmen's Circle-Jewish-intellectual factory workers; they were *goyische*, the real thing. Seymour and Mary Rose met when they were very young; no doubt each saw the other as a romantic figure. They married and had two kids who are grown up now. Then Seymour met his second wife, a college-educated journalist and Jewish, and left Mary Rose to bring up the kids by herself, mostly, with very little support from Seymour, who said alimony was medieval. He, of course, had his education by then, but Mary Rose had to get hers bit by bit while doing office temp work and bringing up her kids. She finally got a substitute teacher's license and works in my kids' school. Of course, maybe I'm being unfair to Seymour, but I do tend to see the wife's side of things."

After we stopped laughing, I said, "What Penny's been saying about Seymour Abromowitz reminds me of my ex-husband. I guess that's why the hairs on the back of my neck stand up when I'm around 'rad' men. I know for all their talk about sharing power and destroying authoritarian structures, they all want to be the tyrants they're trying to bring down. And in their hearts they are all male chauvinists. At a meeting Seymour and some others called at Richmond in order to bring the liberal and left factions together and prevent fratricidal conflict, Seymour was trying to make a point about the women's movement and referred to 'Fanny Howe,' obviously assuming all the women would recognize the name. I thought, 'Who's Fanny Howe?' and then I realized Seymour was talking about Florence Howe, and I took his Freudian slip as a comment on feminism and feminists: we're all 'Fannies' to him."

"It strikes me," Jean observed, "that each political group you've described – trogs, unionists, liberals and radicals – is extremely sexist. And I'm rather surprised, because the Richmond women I've met at the CUNY Coalition seem well organized and assertive. How are they responding to the situation?"

"We're a faction apart, but we don't control or even greatly influence the other and dominant political factions at Richmond. The women's group has had some success in advancing its agenda. For example, women in my department were determined the job I got was going to be filled by a woman. The group has developed women's studies courses in all humanities and social science departments. We've developed a proposal for a women's center on campus that we're asking Wasserman to get funded. And for the past two years, women students and faculty have been able to hold a conference on a woman-centered theme, with some money available to pay speakers."

"I'm happy for you but sad for us," Penny said. "Richmond is light years ahead of Brooklyn. We've yet to offer our first women's studies course."

"The Richmond women's group has done some solid work," I conceded, "and yet, the group seems to me less cohesive than the women at Brooklyn Community College. The Richmond women are fractionalized. The radical women have their own agenda and I feel them manipulating the group. The radical women never talk about feminism; they are uncomfortable being affiliated with 'bourgeois' women. In their eyes, only welfare mothers or third world women have valid concerns. In my opinion, they are afflicted with self hatred that renders them unable to declare themselves as acting in their own interest. And that self hatred feeds into the chauvinism of the radical men, who strongly influence them and through them, influence the women's group. Shirley Benjamin and Phil Cardinale, a radical man in my department are lovers. I imagine their pillow talk includes planning strategy for our meetings. I resent the radical women's lack of respect for the integrity of our group. I came out of a meeting one day and heard Norma Reilly reporting on what had been going on to Phil Cardinale; she mocked one of the speakers, Edith Goldberg, who had said, 'I'm not going to support any woman just because she's a woman. She's got to have credentials.' I was angry with Norma for exposing us and making fun of Edith. But I was not comfortable, either, with Edith's elitist feminism. Someone at the meeting, I've forgotten who, had a very good answer for Edith's insistence on credentials. She said, 'Edith, the standards are schlock, and we meet them.' Yes, we talk a lot about sisterhood at Richmond, but it's an abstraction. Richmond may be more advanced than Brooklyn in a lot of ways, but it lacks you folks. I miss you. I miss our friendship."

"Are you saying, Claire, that we're the best damn women you've ever known?"

"Why, sure, Anne, if you want me to."

But missing my friends was the only fly in my honeypot, for, despite my minor quarrels with the political factions at Richmond, I loved the place. From the first day I began teaching there, I felt, in the words of the Shaker hymn, I had come down where I ought to be. Everything about my life in those days – walking Janey to her Greenwich Village nursery school, traveling to Staten Island on the ferry, walking on campus, or facing my students – seemed wonderful. I fought the feeling that I did not deserve such happiness. Securing that happiness was connected to getting tenure, and while I was sure of a favorable decision under Wasserman, I felt my claim would be strengthened if I had my doctorate or was close to completing it when I came up for consideration in the Fall of 1976.

By January, 1973, after I had finished my course work and passed the comprehensive examination I set about developing a thesis topic and finding an advisor. I wanted to write about one of the women I had discovered after my Sixties activism had prompted me to search for American counterparts to Doris Lessing and Simone de Beauvoir. I read Walter Rideout's guide, *The Radical Novel in the United States*, and found that a tradition of political writing by women did indeed exist. Especially in the Thirties, women had transcended the limitation s of "women's fiction" to deal in novels, short stories, poems, and essays with the issues and struggles of the era: labor conflict, racism, communism, and fascism. Avidly I read women I had never heard of before: Mary Heaton Vorse, Josephine Herbst, Myra Page, Grace Lumpkin, Meridel Le Sueur, Josephine Johnson, Agnes Smedley, and Leane Zugsmith. I especially identified with Josephine Herbst, a midwesterner from a German-American family. The logical sponsor of a dissertation on Herbst was Walter Cole, the department's twentieth century fiction man. I had taken several courses with Cole, including his criticism seminar. Cole had directed all the seminar students to write papers on John Hawkes, a writer I was and am not interested in, but Cole was writing a book on him at the time. I went to talk to Cole during his office hours to speak to him about Herbst.

"Excellent choice," he assured me. "I knew her, you know. She died only a few years ago. Extraordinary woman. Refused as a matter of principle ever to take a taxi. She'd be out late, even when she was older and not in good health. Her friends would try to persuade her to take a cab home and she'd say, 'No, no,' and pop into the nearest subway."

"Would you be my thesis director?"

"Put something in writing and I'll get back to you."

Afterward, which is, of course, when you get the information you should have had originally, I learned of other graduate students' experiences with Cole. He was known to misplace meticulously prepared proposals, returning them a term later, sometimes with pages missing and almost always with a rejection. Reluctantly, I abandoned the Herbst project and turned to the only member of the department who had ever been friendly and responsive to my ideas, Mackintosh, one of the Romantics.

I did not like the English Romantics. The radical men of their day reminded me too much of the radical men of mine. Young Wordsworth went to France to witness the Revolution, fell in love with Annette Vallon, and had a child by her. Later, he returned to England, became conservative, and ignored Annette's letters to return to France to give their child his name. His adoring sister, Dorothy, kept house for him and also kept a journal of her encounters with homeless soldiers and poor widows which Wordsworth used as sources for his poetry. Later he married another adoring woman, and Dorothy, not too many years later, suffered what today we would probably call Alzheimer's disease. Shelley as a teenager had married another teenager, Harriet Westbrook, then grew disenchanted with her, fell in love with still another teenager, Mary Shelley, and eloped with her. Harriet drowned herself in the Serpentine. In time, Shelley grew disenchanted with Mary and would have probably left her, too, except he, a non-swimmer, drowned in a boating accident before he had the opportunity. Byron pursued women, was pursued by them; liked young men, as well, but probably loved no one so well as his sister. He declared one of his loves, Mary Shelley's half-sister, Claire Clairmont, an unfit mother, placed the daughter he had had by her in a convent where she died in a fire. Blake and Keats were probably the best poets and did not harm others, but I did not want to do a dissertation on any Romantic, not the least reason being that the dominant scholars in the field are as self-absorbed and chauvinistic as their subjects. My search for a feminist thesis resulted in a proposed study of the French Revolution from the point of view of four women writers: royalist Mary Berry, and republicans Ann Radcliffe, Helen Maria Williams, and Mary Wollstonecraft. Mackintosh seemed delighted to sponsor my dissertation; the proposal was sent round the department and approved, and I set energetically to work.

But before the first chapter was completed, I realized Mackintosh's interest in me was more personal than professional. At first I tried to make myself believe that this warmth was mentorly, but when our lunches together in Greenwich Village restaurants ended with Mackintosh's bony hand moving like a greedy crab across the tablecloth to snatch mine, when our conferences in his office ended with this thin, dry lips pressed against mine, I could not deceive myself about his real feeling. He never attempted to do more, or suggest an affair, but I was not attracted to him, a married man with a daughter my age. I was repelled by his caresses and resented them as inappropriate in our relationship. I considered looking for another advisor, but I was certain I would not find one among the cold men of the department or its lone woman, the medievalist and mysognyist, Marian Feldstein. My original high enthusiasm for the work dwindled into dislike, for it and for myself because I was compromised and powerless.

I escaped into the intense life at Richmond. My students brought me into contact with the city. In one composition class I had a student who dreamed of being an undertaker. He was studying for his license and serving an apprenticeship in a funeral parlor. His love of his work filled every writing assignment until I finally wrote across the top of a page, "I will not grade your next paper unless you write on another topic." I did permit him to use his vocation for fulfilling my course requirement that each student teach the class a five minute lesson.

In 1969, there had been a terrible industrial accident on Staten Island. While men were cleaning a tank at the liquified natural gas company, the gas had ignited and exploded, killing more than twenty men. My mortician student had assisted in preparing a number of bodies for burial. "It was one of the toughest jobs I ever expect to have in my life," he told the class. "I hope I never had to do that kind of job again. The staff at the funeral parlor worked day and night to restore the bodies which had been burned beyond recognition. We felt it was important to present the grieving families with loved ones they could put in open coffins, and in almost all cases, we were able to do that. Although the work was terrible, I am proud I had an opportunity to assist the staff. Being a good mortician is important to me because I can bring comfort to people at one of the most painful times of their lives." Afterwards, the supercilious humor which the students and, I confess, I had felt for Frank, the undertaker, was gone; even when he came to class in his embalming school uniform, he had our respect.

My most memorable class at Richmond was a composition class I taught in the evenings. All the students were adults who worked in the day, and all but one of them were married. The class worked in groups. Twenty-five students were divided into groups of five; I introduced a task, or topic of discussion for the groups, and after the group had worked together, one member from each group reported to the rest of the class about the group's findings. Then the students wrote an essay related to the discussion, and afterward, the students were invited to read their drafts. One night, a cop's wife read what she had written of her feelings about her husband's job. "We used to have other friends, but now we don't. Cops don't have any other friends but cops. And when they get together, they talk about their work. I think there are a lot of cops who are dangerous and who ought not to have weapons in their possession. I hate the violence of police work, and I hate the fear I have for my husband. Each time I iron his shirt, I wonder if it will be stained with his blood before his tour is over."

My favorite student in that class was a fireman who, in one essay, wrote of being on a search when a retarded child at Willowbrook had wandered away during an outing. "I never wanted anything more in my life than to find that child. We went from house to house in every neighborhood. We combed the parks, the woods, the beaches. For days we went in search groups all over Staten Island. Every time I saw a child by itself, I hoped it would be the missing child. It never was. Eventually the child's body was found in the lake near the picnic grounds. I have never been so depressed in my life as I was when I heard the news. Everyone was depressed, but I don't think any one was sorry they had made the effort to find the lost child." When it was the fireman's turn to give a lesson, he taught the class about fire safety, based on his own family's experience. They drilled regularly in his home, he told the class, and outlined the procedure his family followed, including the modification they had to make for one of his four children, a retarded daughter. My method of structuring the class for lots of student contact led to the formation of more than friendships, for as I drove off the campus one night, I realized a number of students were leaving their own cars on the lot and driving away in others.

In September, 1973, I met for the first time, my late afternoon class of ten male and five females, a reversal of the usual ratio. Six men in their twenties; two white men and two black men, all wearing dark glasses, were in their thirties. The four men gave off an aura that stopped me from introducing my usual first day getting acquainted gimmicks—having people go around giving their first names, then naming their favorite animals; students usually cannot recall each other's names, but they always remember each other's animal. Caught off balance, I set the students writing without warming them up; there was a tension in the classroom that I could not break. Suddenly, I thought, "they've done time," and realized that the quartet in dark glasses had come in to the college through the program at Arthur Kill Prison. Their menacing aura, a function of their defensiveness, intrigued three of the young women but intimidated the two others, who transferred out of the class. All the men in the class, including the ex-cons, were veterans. By the third class, we were comfortable with each other. I assigned the students to write in class and to hand in their work without putting their names on their papers; all would get credit for their work, I promised. ("How much credit?" "As much as you think it's worth.") The assignment gave the students the outlet I had intended. Confidings, confessions came to me about family problems, problems with lovers, about war experiences, about crime and punishments. "Can you imagine what it would be like to have the police come to your home one night and before your mother's eyes handcuff you and take you away to jail?" was in one of the papers, which I soon figured out had been written by Bill Schwartz, a large, square-bodied gravelly-voiced man of thirty-three whose reddish hair sprang out from his scalp like springs popping from a mattress. Bill wanted my attention, affection, and concern; I was what he called "a red carpet person," standing in for the mother he had betrayed, or who had betrayed him. Bill drew me into his life. I struggled with him over his drug habit, and the dealing he did not so much to support his habit but to enhance his self esteem. He had tremendous energy, charm and presence – magnetlike, drawing every one's attention when he walked into a room. But as he drew my attention, my affection and my concern, I found myself in a struggle: if I represented the good which attracted one side of him, his writing revealed the dark side against which I competed. In one paper, he boasted of teaming up with a buddy and, posing as cops, robbing a dealer of a load of hash. In another, he wrote of his dream of becoming a Mafia don, a dream that was enhanced during his honeymoon "when I got married many years ago." In Florida, his wife "bumped into" her aunt, who Bill learned to his pleased surprise, was married to Meyer Lansky. His wife's aunt invited them to visit their home, a place "like something from the Roman days." While his wife and her aunt talked, Bill went carefully from spotless room to spotless room; he picked up a statue in one of them, and a voice warned him not to drop it. The speaker was Meyer Lansky, who shocked Bill by being only five feet four and dressing "like he just got off the boat." If Bill's desire to redeem himself was nurtured at Richmond, so was his admiration for dark glamour. He confided once that Ariela, Norma, and Shirley were his clients. "They really do a lot of dope," he said admiringly. He shared a rented house in Port Richmond with other students, vets like him, but unlike him, lapsed Catholics, who gently mocked his affluent Long Island background. "How could a nice Jewish boy like you have gone into the army, Bill? Where did you go wrong You're the only Jew I ever knew who went to Nam." When the course was finished—too generously, I gave him a B—he remained my friend, invited me to the rock concerts he produced on campus, asked me to be the veterans' club faculty advisor. He did not let go, nor did I. He told me he was no longer doing drugs, no longer dealing. He was elected to the student government, became an officer. We had a long conversation the Friday before Christmas, 1974. He spoke of going on to a four year college upstate, living with his brother, becoming a professional rock concert producer. I went home exultant, thinking "I've won." That Sunday one of the Port Richmond communards telephoned to inform me that Bob had died of an overdose. Devastated, I wept all weekend. My grief made Janey anxious.

"Bill Schwartz died," I explained.

"Who?"

"You remember. I took you out to his house once. The house on Staten Island."

"With all the people in it? Was he the one who wore a hat all the time?"

"No. That was someone who came to the house. The people in the house called him The Hat. Bill had big red hair."

"I remember. He died?"

"Yes. And I feel very sad. That's why I'm crying, Janey. But I'm all right. There's nothing to worry about."

"Don't think about him if you're sad."

"I have to, Janey, because I cared about Bill. I thought he was going to be all right. That's why his death shocked me."

"Then how can you be sure you'll be all right?"

"I am. Bill didn't have kids. I have you. That's why I know I'll be all right."

"Oh. Okay."

I drove Bob's vet friends, Pete Shannon and Ralph Pena, and Pete's girl friend, Lois McIlvaine to the funeral in Oceanside.

"I won't be able to bear seeing Bill in his coffin," Lois sobbed.

"I don't think it's customary among Jews to have open coffins," I assured her.

"Bill finally did it" Ralph said. "He was determined to do himself in, despite everything his friends tried to do to stop him. He had us fooled, though. I thought after what happened last summer and all the promises he made to us afterward, he might..."

In the rear view mirror, I saw Pete nudge Ralph and nod toward me.

"What happened last summer?"

Pete told me that Bill had been hospitalized twice for drug overdoses; that he had almost died the second time and that he had promised his friends he would get help to kill his habit. I realized

Bill had wanted me to believe he had stopped using drugs because he was sure I would despise him if I knew the truth.

"I think Bill was trying to get help," Pete said. "I think his death may not have been an accident. Bill was on to something about the way student government money was being used. He made enemies. They may have had something to do with his death."

"I don't think Bill had any help at all in killing himself," I said.

The funeral parlor was jammed with Bill's friends, students and staff from the college. Milton Liebowitz, one of the vice-presidents. And Ariela Burstyn, who did a lot of dope and had been one of Bill's good customers. No point, though, in speaking angrily to her at Bill's funeral. Besides, I had never said a word to Ariela, never confronted her about encouraging Bill's dealing and using.

Bill's body, laid out in a blue wool suit, was on view in a satin lined coffin.

"A suit," Lois hissed. "What's Bill doing in a suit He never wore anything but jeans and overalls. That's how I want to remember him. Bill would die if he could see what they've done to him."

Lois began to giggle and cry. Pete Shannon brought Bill's mother over and introduced me as a professor from the college, one of Bill's teachers.

"Was my son straight?" she asked, seizing my arm. "Was my son clean of drugs when he died??"

"I don't know, Mrs. Schwartz, I..."

"Mrs. Steinholz. I'm remarried."

The words I had thought to tell her, parent to bereaved parent, went out of my head. "Mrs. Steinholz," I replied formally, "your son was one of the most popular students at the college. His friends and teachers will miss him greatly."

After the funeral service, we drove to the cemetery. Bill's mother, stepfather, grandmother, his two brothers and his sister stood near the grave as the rabbi said the prayer for the dead. The rest of us stood several feet away. Lois, Ariela, his sister, and I cried. Pete, Ralph, the dozen or so vets who had come remained stolidly dry-eyed, but that night, they went ritually to several bars and got falling-down drunk. Pete smashed his hand through a glass window, nearly severing a vein and was rushed to a hospital emergency room.

Besides the drama of love and death at Richmond, there was the drama of politics. How could there not be, with all of us Sixties people in residence, and Chairman Bob to stir things up if a lull should come? During my second year at Richmond, Wasserman, through his mysterious but always plentiful "discretionary funds" set up "The President's Series." The first distinguished visitor was Supreme Court Justice William O. Douglas, whose topic, the First Amendment, Chairman Bob claimed was his special passion. But Justice Douglas did not speak to us directly. Wasserman arranged that Douglas and he should sit in facing arm chairs on the stage of the auditorium, and he would question the Justice or comment on his responses. Chairman Bob called Justice Douglas "Bill;" Justice Douglas addressed Wasserman as "President Wasserman."

The Douglas evening went well and got Wasserman a lot of good press. Then Wasserman announced that in order to demonstrate his dedication to the First Amendment, he would invite William Shockley, Nobel Prize winner in physics and proponent of the racial inferiority of Blacks, to be his second Presidential speaker. Immediately, the campus was in turmoil, as Wasserman probably intended it to be. The administrators of the regular and New Colleges supported him, of course. Wasserman set them to work persuading faculty to wear buttons bearing the number "1," signifying support for the First Amendment. Most teachers in the New College and liberal teachers in the regular college opposed the invitation to Shockley on the grounds of his racism. This faction tried to make common cause with the Black faculty, but Wasserman called in his chips. At an emergency faculty meeting, Howard Fullham, one of Wasserman's special assistants, stood up — one hand extending from the arm of his leather-patched jacket sleeve held the bowl of his pipe so that the stem poked the air — and denounced Wasserman's opponents.

"I'm not threatened by William Shockley's theories, nor is any Black faculty member or student. Our achievements on this campus and elsewhere are ample refutation of his or any other racist's theories. No, William Shockley may come to this campus and depart, leaving nothing behind him. I repeat," Fullham said, poking the air with his pipe stem. "Shockley poses no threat to me. But I do feel a danger closer to home. I fear the ranting and manipulative demagoguery of leftists on this campus who are using Shockley's visit for their own ends. They will use Shockley's visit to lead Black students down the garden path to promote their own radical ideology."

Other Black faculty seemed embarrassed by Fullham's red-baiting, but did not speak in opposition either to him or to Wasserman. The Shockley opponents wisely did not respond in kind to Fullham's attack, but continued to hold meetings, issue statements, organize student opposition to Shockley's visit.

"The Women's Coalition Meeting has been changed from Thursday to tonight," Ariela Burstyn announced grimly as she passed me in the hallway one Monday.

"But I can't get a sitter on such short notice."

Ariela shrugged. "This is an emergency. We've got to respond to Shockley."

Ariela, Norma, and Shirley (with, I was sure, assistance from their male comrades and consorts) prepared a resolution condemning Shockley and Wasserman and persuaded the women at the meeting to endorse it. Wasserman, who had just allocated funds in the college budget for a women's center to be set up in one of the trailers, was understandably furious when the resolution was circulated. I would not have minded being on Wasserman's shit list, if I had supported the reason we were on it. I thought Wasserman should not have issued the invitation to Shockley in the first place and should have withdrawn it, but I believed our response was giving Shockley too much importance. I advocated calling for a boycott and using ridicule instead of rhetoric in our responses. Most of all, I disliked the way Ariela, Norma, and Stella had manipulated the Coalition. Other Coalition women had second thoughts about the way the resolution had been rammed through the Coalition and agreed at the next meeting that henceforth, no policy statement should be issued unless it had been introduced at one meeting and adopted at the next.

When Shockley did at last come to Richmond, students and teachers heckled him intensely and he refused to speak. The stop-Shockley campaign had embroiled the college for two months and, contrary to Fullham's prediction, his visit left much bad feeling behind.

I resumed work on my dissertation. I delivered chapters to Mackintosh. His dry kisses and caresses at the end of the meetings still made my toes curl; I still did not know how to get him to stop. He returned the chapters with directions for revision. I made them and resubmitted the chapters, which he returned again with further suggestions for revision. I tried to follow his directions without really understanding what I was doing, so far was I from the original design of my dissertation. In September, 1975 I delivered the completed manuscript to Mackintosh. Mackintosh then had to get a dissertation committee together because two of the three men appointed when the department approved my proposal had retired; the other was recovering from a heart attack. (During one of my many meetings with Mackintosh, I had asked, "Shouldn't my committee be looking at my chapters?" Mackintosh had not responded, perhaps confident that he could command the committee's approval, and I had made the mistake of not pressing him.) On Christmas Eve, I got a telegram from the department's graduate advisor informing me that the committee had found serious flaws in the dissertation and insisted it be thoroughly revised before it could be defended.

By an act of will I held myself together and kept the holiday rituals: putting small gifts in a red felt stocking by Janey's bed, and large gifts from my parents and me under the tree in the living room; playing albums of Christmas music, making pancakes for breakfast, recording a conversation with

Janey, letting her visit back and forth with her best friend, Julie, going for an afternoon walk, and eating a good dinner afterward. But the next day and all through the January intersession – the time I had planned to use for preparing for defending my thesis – depression settled over me like a skin of ice, a despair worse than what I had felt when my marriage failed. Self-betrayal is worse than betrayal by a loved one. And I had gained nothing by it. I could not go back to working with Mackintosh.

People I spoke to said, "Oh, committees always demand last minute changes. So you'll spend six more months on it and get the degree then." When I said I could not, they shrugged, their expressions letting me know they thought I was foolish. I could not explain to them, I could not even explain to Jean, Penny, or Anne why I could not go back to Mackintosh. Before the time when sexual harassment of graduate students by their advisors was acknowledged as not uncommon, I felt responsible for what had happened. I remained silent, feeling I was guilty for the sin that cannot speak its name. I did go to the department chairman and complained about the lack of proper supervision, but he insisted I must meet the committee's demands for revision. I realize now I should have gone directly to the president, told him exactly what had happened, threatened to sue Mackintosh and the university, and then sue indeed if they withheld my degree. I might not have succeeded, but at least I would have restored my self-respect by fighting back instead of retreating into passive, self-loathing shame over my complicity with Mackintosh. I was desperate enough to start a new doctorate at Union Graduate School.

Wasserman, however, was remarkably sympathetic, pointedly coming over to me at the next faculty meeting to tell me "things will work out." My department probably would not deny me tenure because I did not have my doctorate—only a handful did—but the P and B might. With Wasserman's support, their action would not matter, for Wasserman granted tenure to whom he pleased, no matter who opposed him. Years before, he had defied both the math department and the P and B to give tenure to Leonard Avner, a fine teacher who had offended his department less by his lack of a doctorate than by his deviance from their unwritten requirement that tenured faculty be not just Jews, but Orthodox Jews.

The financial crisis that gripped New York in the mid-seventies caught up with CUNY that spring. As part of a university-wide retrenchment, Busbee, CUNY's chancellor, and the trustees decided to merge Richmond Community College with the borough's senior college. In order to allay fears at the two colleges, the merger was called "federation," but every one understood that combining the two institutions did not mean that two sets of faculty would be retained. The contest for the presidency pitted Wasserman against Joseph Guelpi, so disliked by the faculty at Staten Island College that they, quietly, of course, let us know that they hoped our man would win. One of the coalition members at Staten Island, Randi Coopersmith of the History Department, came to a women's coalition meeting at Richmond and told us how Guelpi got his job at Richmond.

"When the former president retired, the CUNY trustees appointed a search committee at Staten Island, and I was one of the members. Now, Guelpi's predecessor had been president since the college opened. He was not a bad man, but he was not distinguished as a scholar or administrator, so the committee jumped at the opportunity to get someone really outstanding. We advertised in the Chronicle of Higher Education, we invited nominations and we assembled a truly impressive pool of candidates. We spent days and weeks interviewing these people, twelve finalists who traveled long distances at the university's expense to come to our campus. In the midst of this process, Busbee asked us, just as a favor to him, to interview his buddy, Guelpi, who was chairman of the English Department at City College. Well, we interviewed him and were distinctly unimpressed. We did not see him anywhere in the same league with the deans and vice-presidents of Ivy League and Big Ten colleges who were actually eager to come to Staten Island. Out of 200 candidates, we ranked Guelpi at about 190. After months of interviews and reinterviews, which we conducted while meeting our full loads of teaching and research responsibilities, we presented our list of three top choices to Busbee, two men and a woman who held high posts at major institutions. Well, you know by now what Busbee did. When we protested, he said we had, after all, interviewed Guelpi, and besides, he would be a more popular president among Staten Island's Italian-American community than any of our candidates.

'But Staten Island Italian-Americans are not that chauvinistic,' I told Busbee; 'they're sophisticated enough to prefer an outstanding president to someone mediocre from their own ethnic group.' But, of course, that argument went nowhere. The fix was in before we even started. You know, I wouldn't object to the old boy network so much if it worked. But

Guelpi's arrogant and tyrannical. He treats the faculty with contempt, and why not? We were powerless to stop him."

Wasserman used Guelpi's reputation for chopping people down to rally his faculty. Vowing that "they'll have to carry me out of here," he sent his supporters off to lobby on his behalf with the trustees. Meanwhile, as we would shortly learn, Wasserman was answering academic want ads in the *Chronicle of Higher Education*; also meanwhile, some of Wasserman's supporters were making surreptitious visits to Guelpi, "just in case." Wasserman's job search ended with an offer from Albion College, a multi-branched progressive midwestern college. Wasserman resigned to become president of Albion, and Guelpi was appointed head of the combined colleges, renamed the College of Richmond. However, word came back from the CUNY trustees that they would have appointed Wasserman if he had remained.

I made a practical decision to return to NYU and negotiate the terms for completing my dissertation with Thorgessen, the graduate advisor. Since Mackintosh had gone into full retirement, Thorgessen, a Coleridge scholar with aspirations to become the leading Romantic in the department, agreed to be my thesis director. Between us, we pared the original list of demands for revision down to a workable number, and I set to work.

Meanwhile, Guelpi was consolidating his power at Richmond. The mood of the campus changed profoundly. People no longer spoke of "experimental," "innovative," "cutting edge;" the new buzz words were "back to basics," "a return to standards," and "sound scholarship." The outs of the Wasserman era became triumphant, vindictive ins under Guelpi. Margaret Cavallo, elevated by Guelpi from head of the Chemistry Department to a deanship, appeared everywhere wearing a three-inch cross. Flamboyant, even promiscuous heterosexuality had been the norm under Wasserman; under Guelpi, the faculty became circumspect. Karl Spieler expelled his mistress from the Greenwich Village apartment he had for years declared to the IRS was his office, and brought his wife to faculty receptions. At the same time, however, homosexuality became voguish when Guelpi's gay vice-president signalled to people to come out of their Wasserman closets. In this climate I came up for tenure. Esther Sternfeld had promised me her support. Then Malcolm Doyle began meeting with her regularly. Joseph Berger, the deputy chairman, said one day, "Esther agrees with the person she's just had lunch with," and I heard his warning that I would be sacrificed.

"There was the smell of blood in the air," was Eliot Hoffman's description of the P and B meeting which ended in the denial of tenure to me and eight other candidates. Eliot, the theater department chair and a Guelpi refusenik, told me Guelpi had convinced the committee to turn me down by claiming evidence which indicated I would never get my doctorate. I was shaken, but rallied myself to prepare my appeal. Formerly, I would have appealed to the P and B, but now, because Guelpi claimed rejected candidates should get a "fresh hearing," I would appear before a new appellate body, consisting of three administrators appointed by Guelpi and four faculty members elected by their colleagues. Esther went with me when I appealed to the committee the first Wednesday in December, and embarrassed me by making the exaggerated claim that I had completed my dissertation. I suspect she was compensating for an inadequate defense of me before the P and B. But the appeal went well, and the next day Malcolm Doyle called to tell me the appeals committee had recommended that four other appellants and I be granted tenure. I was elated, for Guelpi had justified the change in the appeals procedure by persuading people that he would abide by the decision of the committee he had created. I had one happy weekend; then on Monday, one of my non-teaching days, I received a call from Henry Klein, a dean held over from the Wasserman administration whom Guelpi had designated to be his bad news bearer. Klein did not, of course, call me directly. His secretary asked me to "hold on for Dean Klein," and, as I held on for five minutes, I knew what the message was. I hung up; the telephone rang again, and Klein's secretary once more asked me to hold on for Klein. After another five minutes, I thought, "Why can't he dial his own damn phone," and hung up. On the third call, Klein delivered his by then redundant message. Guelpi had turned down his appeals committee's recommendation in my case and in my case only. The whole procedure had been a joke, I realized as I remembered my careful preparation, my lawyer-like assembly of material, and the committee's thoughtful reception of my argument. But Doyle, one of Guelpi's three appointees, knew when he congratulated me that Guelpi had decided to deny me tenure no matter how many hurdles I cleared or how many hoops I jumped through. And, since I was not Jewish, Italian, or a protected minority, he could fire me without political consequences. I made a formal request for his reasons; his reply was in a brief letter:

"The quality of your scholarship does not merit an appointment with tenure." I swiftly became a pariah. Some people were openly pleased by my firing. Others, including people I had thought were my friends, began not to see me. Criticisms came back to me; people who had never written more than memos were deriding my *Village Voice* articles as "unscholarly." My department wrote a letter of protest to Guelpi; the women's coalition protested, but people tired of the effort and support withered into resentment. I began to feel like an unburied corpse.

I fought despair by concentrating on my dissertation. I finished it in July and defended it in October. The committee awarded me my doctorate "with distinction." My other major concern was to keep my unhappiness from souring my relationship with Janey, and I like to think I succeeded. Striving toward these two goals left me with no resources for self-nurturing. My self-esteem withered.

If enough people turn against you, you turn against yourself. The leaders of the faculty union had not supported me; they, too, seemed to me to believe the college was well rid of me. I filed a grievance, but because I felt the union would not actively defend me, I did not pursue the grievance to the crucial third step, when it would be taken beyond the college and the university and submitted to an independent arbitrator. Too late I realized that I should have insisted on my rights and not let others' real or imagined opposition get in my way.

I did file a charge of discrimination against Guelpi with the New York State Commission on Human Rights, another mistake, I would discover. In its early days, the Commission had found for a complainant against a college; the college had appealed to the courts. Reluctant to intervene in academic decisions, the courts had overturned the ruling of the Commission, which thereafter retreated from aggressive advocacy and dwindled into a tame bureaucracy. A sympathetic attorney and a law student with the Women's Advocacy Center of NYU Law School assisted me through the grim and futile three day hearing. In the little room at the Commission's headquarters on Lower Broadway, the hearing officer presided while a law intern sat with me on one side facing two adversaries, Malcolm Doyle, representing the college, and for the university, associate counsel and scourge of womankind, Paula Blatt.

Doyle produced a months-old letter from David Harrington, the head of NYU's Graduate English Department, stating that an impasse had been reached in my dissertation and that I would probably never complete it. The letter, I realized, was the evidence Guelpi had used against me. The impact of the recognition stunned me. I had spent years earnestly meeting the requirements for a degree and paying hefty fees for the privilege, all the while teaching full time, rearing and supporting a child, and, having the burden of all these tasks increased by humiliating, unwanted sexual advances from my mentor. None of the facts of my life, known or unknown, had been of concern to Harrington, who rather than defend my interests, had used me to assist Doyle, a former colleague at NYU, in his new role as Guelpi's flunky. Harrington had not even bothered to check his information, for at the time he wrote the letter, I had almost completed my dissertation.

"Yes, she has her doctorate now," Doyle acknowledged at the hearing, "but at the time of her tenure decision, we had every reason to believe she would not complete it."

Paula Blatt, insulted me in the same banshee voice and with the same words she had used against Jean Berns seven years earlier.

"You didn't really write that article," she screamed. Then, pointing her finger at me and addressing the hearing officer, she yelled, "She wasn't fired because of discrimination, she was fired for cause. She didn't cut the mustard." Blatt was more persuasive than my collection of data showing that the majority of males in my department and in the college were not as well qualified as I; the Commission found that my firing had not been the result of discrimination.

CHAPTER

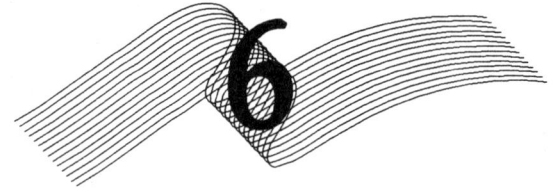

May, 1980

Ted had finished his dinner. I hurried to catch up.

"So you got your doctorate, but lost the job you loved." Ted's tone was neutral. Was he sympathetic or ironic?

"Yes. I actually would have preferred it the other way."

"That must have been rough. Working so hard and then losing the thing you worked for."

"It was. Especially when I was totally responsible for Janey's security and happiness."

"But you obviously landed on your feet."

"Excuse me a minute. I think I'd like some more salad."

When I returned, the words I had wanted to stop myself from saying came pouring out.

"Ted, when I got fired, people said, `Oh, Claire, I don't have to worry about you. You always land on your feet.' It was their way of avoiding feeling responsible for what had happened to me. I always wanted to say, `Worry about me.' So being told I always land on my feet is still upsetting."

"I didn't mean to upset you, Claire, but you have always seemed like someone who could take care of herself, no matter what."

"Even when I'm in despair inside."

"I can't believe you have ever despaired, no matter what happened to you. Besides, worse things could have happened to you. Worse things happen to people every day."

"Oh, Ted, you don't need to tell me that."

"No, I don't. Tell me what you did next."

I told Ted about the women of Project Change and my second job loss.

1977 - 1979

I answered countless want ads before being hired as director of a federally funded women's program at King's College, my third CUNY workplace. After accepting the position, I learned what my experience had led me to suspect but what my need for employment had kept me from confirming: that Project Change, sponsored jointly by the Kings College Women's Studies Program and its Women's Center, had a history of conflict. Betty Kaufman, director of the Women's Center, had wanted women recruited into the Project to participate in the Women's Center peer counseling program. But the original project director, Sibella Pinkham, had opposed her on the grounds that the minority women in the Project needed survival skills, not a counseling program that encouraged them to make excuses for themselves. Sibella might have survived if she had not also gone back to the community agencies that referred women to the Project and attacked the Women's Center as a "stronghold of militant lesbianism, which is counter to the lifestyle of minority culture." After weeks of daylong meetings which wrecked the Project's educational program and left the Project staff demoralized, Sibella had been forced to resign.

Enter Claire Schaeffer. I began rebuilding the Project by limiting the number and duration of the meetings between the Project and its sponsors/bosses and keeping the agenda focussed on programmatic rather than ideological issues. I was diplomatic with Betty and the women from the Women's Studies Department, but I shared Sibella's view that the Women's Center's counseling program would not help minority women; moreover, Italian-American women from Carroll Gardens and Irish-American women from Bay Ridge would absolutely refuse to discuss personal problems with strangers. Marylyn Ackerman and June Sabatino, the Project's counselors, and I developed a core curriculum of English Composition, Psychology or Sociology, and a basic college level Math course. Then I went to the head of each of these departments to make sure good teachers were assigned to the Project's sections of these courses.

Next, the counselors and I worked to stabilize the population of the Project. The original wide recruitment had simply encouraged women to use federal and state financial aid to enter the college; without preparation for the necessary adjustments to a full-time academic program, the women were set up for yet another failure. Overwhelmed, they left before completing a semester. Marylyn, June, and I devised a two-part evaluation procedure: a test to assess language and math skills and an interview.

"Who will look after your children while you are in school?" we asked women who came to the Project.

"A friend," they invariably replied.

"Will you pay her?"

"No."

"Then how can you be sure she will come every day? What will you do if she cannot take care of your children?"

Another friend, or their mothers would fill in, they assured us.

"What about your husband?" we probed. "How does he feel about your going back to school."

"Oh, he's all for it," they piously responded.

"Will he look after the children while you are doing homework?" Will he do housework? Shop for food? What if he thinks you might get a better job than he has?"

Our interview questionnaire made us seem like just another spy group, like welfare, and they met our questions artfully. Women who came into the Project continued to miss classes because of lack of child care; enraged husbands and lovers still tore up their textbooks or made them choose: that school or me. Some women were steadfast. "He has the same chance to advance himself as I do, but he doesn't want to," one woman told us; "but he can't stop me from trying to get ahead." But more often they chose their men. When one of our best students, the mother of two young children, realized her good grades would be more than her current lover's meager ego would bear, she became pregnant "so he'll have his own child to love," and dropped out of the program. "He'll only leave her eventually," June said sadly, "and then she'll have three kids to care for and no skills."

But where we could make ourselves seen as friends, where we could lead women to a realistic consideration of their problems, we could help them make plans and set goals. Some of them formed partnerships with others in the program and traded child care stints. They gave each other the support necessary, in some cases, to stand up to men, to say "I choose the school."

Our more difficult task was persuading women who could not write a coherent paragraph or do simple arithmetic that they should go to a program that could prepare them for their high school equivalency diploma. They wanted to come to college because of the financial aid package, and while many programs would accept them, the counselors and I agreed that we would not. These women hated us when we turned them away; they left the office sucking their teeth, rocking their heads, cursing us under their breath. We were another set of gatekeepers in their lives. They needed one of their own, Sibella, to give them straight talk and direction. I could not be of much help, either, to Black women in the Project who resented me and whom I discovered myself resenting. My experience in Mississippi had led me to expect every Black woman to be a hero; I did not know how to deal with the sleek, cynical women who strode into our office, casting their eyes slowly, contemptuously down my body and then up, taking in and reading back to me their measure of my dowdiness, for nothing in my wardrobe could match the smartness of their expensive, publicly-funded designer jeans, leather boots and handbags. I understood their connivance was a function of egos diminished by the burden of racism, yet I was shocked in my midwestern white Protestant soul by their manipulation and dishonesty.

A well-designed program might succeed if the measure of support supplied met precisely the amount of a client population's needs, but this population's needs exceeded our resources and would increase our failure rate. Although they spoke vaingloriously of becoming accountants, psychologists, and computer programmers, they knew as well as we did they lacked the skills and discipline necessary to achieve such goals. Sibella, or someone like her, could have said, "Get real, honey," and with humor, affection, and skepticism, might have turned the women toward realistic goals, demanded discipline, confronted backsliding, and praised successes. When I considered the loss to these women Sibella's firing represented, I resolved to try to find the humor to get past their sullen "get over" attitudes, and enough compassion and professional distance to encourage them to use available resources to move on to a better place.

The women refused to let me win them over. Their resistance to me was understandable, because I had replaced Sibella, but they would not even speak to the counselors who had been with the Project from its beginning. Anita was the only one they trusted.

Anita Wilson showed me the dark underbelly of the women's movement. Anita had grown up in misery, believing her mother did not love her. She married early a Black man whom she soon no longer loved. She had a daughter and a son and then worked at secretarial jobs she hated in order to help support them. Her children dropped out of school; her son was arrested several times for committing petty crimes. The women's movement inspired Anita to leave her husband, go back to school, and come out as a lesbian. She had enrolled in the Women's Center peer counseling program, and that connection led to her job with the Project, the high point of her career. When I was interviewed, Anita had looked at my resume and said "Those are impressive credentials." But I heard ambivalence in her voice. Later I learned that Anita had been offered the job after Sibella resigned and refused it. She was frightened of the responsibility, but would resent whoever accepted it. Anita created her own power base among the walking wounded. Women came to the door of our office, peered in; if Anita was not there, they would flee. "I'll come back later," they said when Mary, June or I asked if we could help them. When Anita was there, they sat at her desk, huddled with her in long whispered conferences that were not meant for the counselors or me to hear. During each conference, Anita took out a crystal on a string, dangled it over the hand of the woman sitting at her desk, and, I could only assume, interpret its motions to her. Anita gave women her card, encouraged them to call her at any time, and continued her counseling in late night telephone sessions. She was often out of the office on personal errands for the students, pleading with a professor to change a grade, or arranging for a woman to bypass our interview procedure and be admitted to the college. When we discovered what she was doing, we confronted her at a staff meeting.

"You're making the students suspicious of us and undermining the program," Mary said furiously. "You are not a trained counselor, and you should not be trying to counsel the students."

"I don't have a degree," Anita replied, "but I have had peer counseling training at the Women's Center and sometimes the women in our program are intimidated by professionals and prefer to talk to someone more like themselves."

"Anita," June said more calmly, "you are not helping the students by trying to solve their problems for them. That only continues their dependence. The correct function of counseling is to get people to confront their problems so they can solve them."

"If you disagree with our policies," Mary continued, "why don't you argue them out at the open staff meetings? If you think we're wrong, have enough confidence in your ideas and your ability to persuade us to challenge us openly. Don't go behind our backs."

"Besides," I added, "You may promise things you cannot deliver."

"I'll try to act more collectively," Anita conceded, but she looked away from us as she spoke. Later, we knew from the hard-eyed, resentful looks of her followers, that she had not stopped her subversive activities. But in all other areas, the Project was successful. Word-of-mouth brought more students in to the program and our retention rate climbed; our students were performing well; we were losing our reputation as a welfare mothers' program and were gaining respect within the college community. The

FAPSE program officers, who had feared they might have to write the Project off as an expensive, embarrassing failure, were pleased. But I knew that the Project's success would not save it. "Just when we've turned the Project into something good, Samuelson's going to kill it," June mourned.

Leila Samuelson was Dean of Continuing Education, the area where our program was housed in the college, and thus one of the people in control of our lives. Each time Samuelson, or rather her secretary, would summon me to her office, I would present myself precisely at the appointed time, and Samuelson would be on the telephone. Beckoning me in and assigning me a chair with a pointed pencil, she continued to scold or accuse her listener.

"Get me those registration figures by close of business Friday, or else," she would bark, then hang up and turn her attention to me, adjusting her previous abusiveness down to the level of commonplace rudeness which included, besides having kept me waiting, interrupting me, and sweeping me with bold, appraising looks. Her requests for progress reports were, I knew, linked to her fear that because of the Sibella debacle, FAPSE might cut its funding of the Project during the final year of the grant. Yet, she spoke of "the needs of our students," linked herself with the women's movement and me by referring to the struggle of academic women; she met with the FAPSE program officer and spoke of her plans for the Project, encouraging me and the FAPSE officer to think the Project had a future at Kings College. FAPSE actually increased its funding to the Project for its final "launchpad" year, and Samuelson was delighted. Then I asked to meet with Samuelson to discuss the Project's status when the college picked it up. "How can we pick up your program?" she asked, flicking me over with her calculator eyes. "It's not bringing in enough students to justify the expenditure. Besides, there's nothing your program is doing that other Continuing Education programs can't do as well or better."

"But FAPSE's funding increase in the final year of the grant was made with the understanding, which you encouraged, that the college would pick it up."

"Where is it written? I made a good-faith projection based on anticipated enrollments which have not materialized. I was too optimistic."

Enrollments were down in Continuing Education. Samuelson treated the directors of her continuing education programs so badly, only the toadies remained. Students wanted Saturday classes – the Project was the only continuing education program to schedule them – but Samuelson resisted that and other student requests, and was generally inaccessible. And then, of course, with CUNY's no-tuition policy at an end, enrollments were down throughout the university. But I was sure Samuelson had had accurate projections when she spoke with the FAPSE officer. Besides, our program threatened older programs and Samuelson had tenured staff to protect. As I left her office after one of our final meetings, I heard her tell her secretary, as Samuelson intended I should, "she must be crazy to think her college-for-bimbos program had a chance for survival."

I had performed well and been fired, twice; Samuelson, widely disliked, incompetent, whose performance evaluation, I had learned from one of her many enemies, "read like a twenty-page indictment," would remain and perhaps even rise at CUNY. The difference between our careers is explained by Samuelson's friendship from grammar school days with a woman, a former elementary school teacher whose leadership in Jewish women's organizations had brought an appointment as a CUNY trustee. Good people without political connections have succeeded at CUNY, but with them, no incompetent person has failed.

Knowing the Project would end did not keep Mary, June and me from enjoying our successes. In June, the Project would have its first graduate, Helen O'Rourke, brilliant, fat and forty. From the classmates who had become her first, her only friends, we learned that when Helen was a child, she was walking one day with her mother and older sister, when an out-of-control car mounted the curb and struck down her sister, killing the girl instantly. Helen's mother had said, "Why couldn't it have been you?" From that day on, Helen tried to atone for having lived. To the regret of the beloved nuns, and despite her honors in Latin, English and math, Helen dropped out of high school after her father died, and worked as a bookkeeper to support her family and send her two brothers, far less in love with learning than she, through college. She married, worked, had three sons, worked, kept house, went to church and PTA meetings. Still, she retained her fine mind and intellectual curiosity; she was thought of in her family and community as a freak. Sugar was her only consolation, her drug of choice. When Helen came to our office on the second floor of a building without elevators, we could hear her puffing in the hallway long before she dropped her swollen, self-abused body on our couch.

The Project delivered Helen from pariahdom; the best people in the world, so far as she was concerned, recognized and esteemed her talent. She took a double load of courses, maintained a double major in English and Accounting, earned an almost perfect grade point average, and still she went to church and PTA, kept house and cooked – preparing a hot meal for her husband and basketball-playing sons before she left for her evening classes; and still she tried to win her mother's love, shopping for her, doing her income tax returns, doing everything everyone to whom she felt responsible wanted her to do except give up her college work.

"I don't care what they say, I love this place," she would say with an unusual fierceness in her fat-lady's little girl voice.

Just after Christmas break in her last year, the elevators in one of the classroom buildings broke down. Helen had to walk from the first to the fourth floor for one class, over to another building for her next class, and back again to the third floor for her next class. When she went home that evening, she napped before preparing supper. One son, scheduled to play basketball, came in to waken her so she could get his meal ready. "Just fifteen minutes more," she asked. He came back exactly fifteen minutes later. Helen tried to get up, but fell back on the bed, dead before her head touched the pillow.

The students were stunned; I was saddened but not really shocked. I think Helen recognized that her life would never be as good again as it was at Kings College, that after she graduated, she would be, as far as prospective employers were concerned, a fat, overage housewife. The respect of faculty and students at Kings, coming after so many years of ridicule, would be followed by more rejection of an even worse kind than she had known. But I had lost another treasured student. How different Helen was from Bill, and yet how like him. Both had never received the love they needed from their mothers; both had used destructive substances as substitutes for love; both had understood they had reached the high point of their lives and subtly arranged to quit while they were ahead.

Several of Helen's grieving friends spoke to her parish priest about having her favorite teacher eulogize her at her funeral. The priest refused; "I don't want a Jew from Kings College speaking in my church," he told them.

"Helen was a sinner," he said, more than once over her coffin. "We can only enter Heaven as a little child," he warned. Helen had had a dispute with him, one of her friends told me, about Franklin D. Roosevelt. The priest, although a young man, had apparently been influenced by a parent or older relative who supported Father Coughlin, a bitter anti-Semite and Roosevelt critic. Helen had objected to a statement by the priest that Roosevelt had betrayed the United States to Stalin, refuting his charges with carefully assembled evidence in a well-reasoned argument. The unforgiving priest, whose Bay Ridge parish had eluded Vatican Two, was taking his revenge over her bier, and against, he no doubt hoped, her soul. I bit my lips to keep from disrupting the service, and muttered, "He's saying evil things about one of the best women I ever knew."

Just as at Bill Schwartz's funeral, college friends, in a sense the true family, sat on one side; the actual family sat on the other. "Look, the price tag on her dress is showing," Mary Francese, Helen's closest friend, said as Helen's mother entered the pew. "Helen bought that dress at Macy's as a Christmas present for her mother. "'Oh, I hope she likes it,' she'd kept saying. One of the first things Helen's mother said when she learned Helen died was 'Who's going to do my income tax now?'"

Enough students had cars so that we could all go to the cemetery. I spoke to Helen's husband, who seemed grief-stricken, but also flattered and puzzled by the sorrow of so many students and even more oddly, her teachers.

Mary, June, Anita and I organized a memorial service for Helen at the college. Helen's husband and three sons came and listened in embarrassment while the woman they had not respected was praised repeatedly by her teachers and many friends.

"Helen had more on the ball than I realized," Mr. O'Rourke said to me afterward while his three sons looked at their shoes. "She tried to tell me how much this place meant to her, but I confess I didn't take her seriously."

"She meant much to this college," I replied.

Later I had the cassette I had recorded during Helen's memorial dubbed at the college audio-video center and sent the copy to Mr. O'Rourke, hoping it would give him and his sons some painful moments.

In June, we sent a final report on the Project to FAPSE, and said our farewells. After vacationing in a lesbian commune in Vermont, Anita was going to work in a New Age health products store. Mary and June had applied to and had been accepted at separate out-of-state graduate schools. And I was about to jump on my next ice floe following Marge Fogarty's offer of a job at Fontbonne College.

CHAPTER

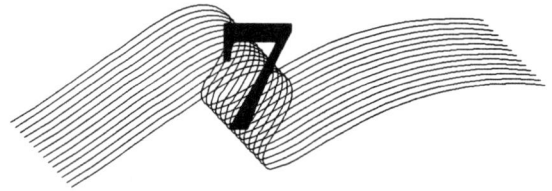

May, 1980

We were each drinking a second cup of coffee as I finished my narrative. I looked at Ted and said, "Now I'd like to know your history since you left Madison."

"As you know, I went to UW to play football, and like many a lad before and since, I discovered that players from other parts of Wisconsin, as well as out-of-staters, were better than I was. But even if I had been good, even if I had made the team, I probably wouldn't have stayed. I was lonely. I missed my high school buddies. We'd been together since we were little kids, had done everything together."

"And you were their leader."

"That's true. Not being leader of the pack was a blow to my ego. I might have made new friends, except I felt lost. Unlike you, I'm not a scholar. You felt right at home in Madison, didn't you?"

"Yes. For the first time."

"Well, I managed to get through a year and a half without flunking out, but I knew I couldn't go back. My parents were disappointed, but I felt I had to follow my buddies into the service."

"Did you go to Vietnam?"

"Yes. And you want to ask me what it was like."

"Yes."

"It was not what I expected it would be. I went over in the early days, when everyone thought we'd have a quick victory in months. I was just nineteen, feeling like a hero because I was carrying on the family tradition, and not my older brother, who'd been too young to fight in any war. Imagine, I actually felt he'd been cheated and I was the lucky one when I went in. My experience was probably like many others'. The war's an old, sad story now."

"Yes, but everyone's experience was not the same. When I was at Richmond, I was the advisor to the veterans on campus ..."

"Really? How did you get that assignment?"

"One of my students asked me to become the faculty advisor."

"He must have been persuasive."

"He was, although I was flattered to be asked."

"Really?"

"Yes."

"I'm surprised, because you were active in the anti-war movement at UW."

"I was anti-war, not anti-vet. I was always aware that boys I had grown up with were being sent to fight."

When I had protested the raising of Viet Cong flags at campus demonstrations, David had said it was important to show solidarity with their oppressed brothers and "besides chicks should leave those kind of tactical decisions to the guys."

"I thought none of you should have been sent to Vietnam, none of you should have risked your lives or been killed."

"And most people would agree with you now."

But they didn't then. People don't remember how unpopular opposition to the war was at the beginning. How do you feel?"

"Oh, there no question in my mind now that the war was a mistake. A close friend of mine who was in it says—and a lot of other people take the same position—that we could have won but the government lost its nerve and cheated us of victory. I think that argument is nonsense. We never could have sustained a military victory over time. Subduing a hostile population would have been a disastrous drain on resources. On the issues, your side was right. But I wasn't wrong to go there. I have people in my family and so do you to whom this country is precious because they could own a part of it. Never mind that they lost their shirts doing it."

"My mother used to say that in the old country the aristocracy owned the land; here the banks owned it."

"Nevertheless, many people feel proud and grateful to have even mortgaged land when they never could have owned land in the countries they came from. Most people here remember that, even if they're not farmers any more. That is why the men of the midwest have poured out their blood in this nation's wars. For honorable reasons, mostly, mixed in, of course with an ancient male desire to become a hero. I went because defending this nation is a family tradi tion, not because I wanted to burn huts and kill babies. When I came back, there were no parades. My father's name is on the plaque at the post office war memorial, but mine isn't and won't ever be. I can accept that. What I can't accept is being labeled a war criminal. And I was angry as hell when I came back at the anti-war movement for dumping a bum rap on us."

"Do you hold the anti-war movement responsible for that? Most of the people who were active where I was in New York understood that men who fought in the war were for the most part poor or working class, boys without options like the college students. The anti-war movement didn't turn against the vets; the vets were targeted as bad guys because people who had supported the war became ashamed of having backed a losing cause, and projected that shame onto the men who had fought a losing war."

"I went to the war early and came back when the anti-war movement was gaining momentum. I remember those posters of naked, burning children. The anti-war movement did change people's minds, and when people turned against the war, they turned against us, our guys became the bad guys." Ted looked away from me and studied the other diners.

"But there were atrocities. Lieutenant Calley and My Lai, the cigarette lighter igniting the thatch house."

"There have been atrocities in all wars. Men are sent to kill, not to Boy Scout camp. In most cases, they do what they have to do to stay alive."

I moved my hands from the table to my lap and studied my coffee cup. Then I raised my head and waited until Ted looked at me again.

"Was throwing prisoners out of helicopters doing only what had to be done? I remember the radio broadcasts of the Winter Soldier hearings; I listened to a combat veteran describing the way he and his comrades had raped Viet Cong women they had captured, then they put dynamite in the women's vaginas and blew them to pieces. He was remorseful, he cried when he told what he had done to the women. But I felt at the time that woman could have been me, that maybe those men were sorry afterward, but at the time they destroyed those women they had simply found an opportunity to act out their built-in rage. And violence against women has increased since the war. I don't know why men hate women, but they do, and I've felt that hatred. Two years ago, I was running in Central Park in New York. It was late on a weekday morning and there were few other runners in the park. When I got to the top of the park, where there are hilly woods on the side of the road, I heard a runner behind me, and I knew whoever it was wanted to hurt me. I ran as fast as I could but he was gaining on me. Fortunately, as I rounded the curve in the road, I saw two women running from the other direction. I ran across the road and changed direction. As I passed the man who had been following me, I saw his face, twisted with frustrated rage. He would have raped me if he had caught me, perhaps killed me. And I had done nothing to him, nothing. I'll never forget the shock of encountering such lethal anger. We reported him to the police, but of course, he was not there when they looked for him in their patrol car. And if he didn't get me that day, he probably hurt another woman, and I don't know how many others. Women are raped, beaten, mutilated, killed every day by men, men who are lovers, husbands, or strangers."

"What's all that got to do with the war?"

"The men who took their rage to Vietnam brought it back home, but even if they are not responsible for the increase in violence in our society, the atrocities committed there made violence more tolerable."

"You're slandering the men who fought in Vietnam."

"Am I?"

"Yes. I was a kid when I went to Vietnam. Innocent, like the other kids who went with me and those who went after me. We were proud to be defending our country; the pride was foolish, perhaps, but it sprang from decent instincts, not the depravity you're talking about. But Vietnam made men crazy. The people we were sent to help looked just like our enemies, or maybe they were our enemies. And when we did sort out our legitimate friends, the die-hard anti-communists, they were very often corrupt, certainly not worth sacrificing American lives for. That moral ambiguity was too much for nineteen-year-olds from nice small towns to handle. Then seeing guys we cared about being killed and hurt made us not care about choosing between friends and enemies. Treat them all like enemies if that was the way to survive. I never did anything monstrous in Vietnam, but I did what I felt was necessary, and I would have done more if I'd had to, without any remorse. Everything got turned upside down in Vietnam. The war was the most devastating, disorienting experiences this country's young men ever experienced, and lots of them did things they would not have done otherwise."

"I don't agree. I think in many cases that instinct for violence was there already, acquired early in life here and nurtured on playing fields, during hunting trips, in street games, in bars, on television and in films, and other forms of our popular culture." I was aware of my voice rising. Out of the corner of my eye, I saw our waiter coming toward us with a coffee pot and then he quicked moved in another direction.

I lowered my voice and continued. "But I concede that more Americans agree with you than with me. After all, how much hard time did any of the men convicted for the My Lai massacre actually do? Not day one, for most people in this country believe with you that the men did only what was necessary, and if a few hundred old men, women, and children were killed, so what? Why should any one feel remorse, let alone go to prison?"

"But the men who committed atrocities were a minority. And even at My Lai, men refused to carry out Calley's orders. And one man, Hugh Thompson, even turned against his own countrymen to protect civilians."

"I know. But at My Lai, the resisters were the minority. Most men followed orders. And Hugh Thompson took a lot of heat for reporting the massacre."

"Maybe if men like your husband had fought in Vietnam, it would have been a good clean war like the one our fathers fought." The anger in Ted's face and his sarcasm made me think I was getting to him.

I spoke more calmly. "My husband would not have elevated the moral climate of the war, but you may be right that if all classes of men had fought in Vietnam, the war might have been different. We think of our fathers' war as a good war because this country was not an aggressor and everyone supported the war. The men in our fathers' war were probably better behaved because they knew their country honored them. Perhaps acts of atrocity were committed, but by common agreement, they were covered up. The Vietnam war was a cynical venture. Johnson lied to the American public about the Tonkin Gulf incident; our government backed one corrupt leader after another, and if one of them became an embarrassment, like Diem, our beloved Kennedy allowed him to be assassinated; military leaders gave us 'body counts,' told stories about the brave South Vietnamese fighters. Maybe in early days when you fought, most men believed in the war and went willingly, but most of the veterans I knew at Staten Island went later; they were poor and working class men who felt they had no choice. The gap between lies and truth about the war de-stabilized them. One of the Staten Island vets used to go berserk periodically and cry about the one hundred twenty civilians he had gunned down."

"My point precisely."

"But these men were part of the underclass this country breeds to fight its wars. Of course, most of them were just trying to stay alive, but they had no reason not to commit atrocities, if the opportunity arose. They did not have a strong religious commitment, as Hugh Thompson had, or strong family and community ties, as Ted Ritter had, to keep them adhering to a moral code."

"Then how do you account for the Communist atrocities, like the Hue massacre after the Tet Offensive – which was a big failure by the way? The popular uprising the North Vietnamese expected did not happen. And if Americans brought their violence with them, because of flaws in the American male character, how do you account for the violence of the Vietnamese against their own people since we got out of Vietnam? How can you slander the fighting men of your own country when the enemy has been so much worse? Calley was an aberration." Ted took a sip of coffee. His cup rattled when he put it back on the saucer.

"Was he? I don't agree."

"He was an inexperienced officer whose bad judgement triggered a temporary madness. Hue, on the other hand, was a deliberate, ruthless, well-planned act of terrorism designed to intimidate and suppress a population. God, I resent your smooth, glib, shallow analysis of events you never witnessed and know nothing about. You think being an advisor to vets makes you an authority?"

Ted had raised his voice so I raised mine. "I never said it did, but how shallow can my analysis be if we reach the same conclusion that we never could have prevailed in Vietnam? I can't account for other countries' actions; I won't be made to explain or defend them. I know that by going to war against Vietnam, we lost the power to influence events there. If we had not waged that terrible war, with such a terrible, wasteful loss of life, just think of how much we might be able to shape the politics of Southeast Asia. Through diplomacy we might have gained political and economic advantages. Now we have no influence there at all. I can't explain Vietnamese terrorism, but I do know something about violence made-in-the-USA, and I feel responsible to try to stop it for our kids' sakes, yours and mine and everyone's.

And because of the anti-war movement, your son probably won't have to follow in your footsteps."

We were silent. I was aware of the clatter of other diners' plates being cleared. People were looking at us. I regretted having spent money for my new dress. I regretted all the time I had spent shopping for the dress, time I could have used for research. I could sense Ted wanting to get up and leave me as I wanted to get up and leave him. I was embarrassed to think I had wanted to seduce Ted. The evening was a disaster.

"Look," he said after a minute, "you did what you thought was right and so did I. Let's not attack each other for acting on our best instincts."

If Ted was trying to rescue the evening, I would match his effort.

"Agreed," I said.

"What does your ex-husband do now?"

"What does he do now? He lives in California with his second wife, the daughter of a real estate developer. They have two children, both boys. David is a social scientist, teaching at a university. He also heads his own management consulting firm. He specializes in assisting corporations who want to decertify unions or stop their organizing drives."

"What did his Communist grandmother think about the change in his politics?"

"Frieda recognized David as an opportunist before I did. David only visited his grandmother for the first time during his radical student days, and she was skeptical about him. But I'm more fortunate than most people whose marriages have failed. I got a grandmother—both of mine died when I was young—

and Janey has good memories of her great-grandmother."

"Does your ex-husband keep in contact with Janey"

"No, he's had no contact with Janey at all from the time we separated."

"That must have been hard on her."

"It has been at times. Janey's gone through periods of blaming herself or blaming me for his absence, mostly blaming me. And she missed the perks other kids of divorced parents got, like treats from indulgent part-time fathers. But kids adjust; eventually they accept whatever situation they're in as the normal one. Now she feels that if her father and his family don't want anything to do with her, she doesn't want anything to do with them."

"What does she think about not having her father's name?"

"Did your mother tell you that, too?"

"Yes."

"Janey was so young when David and I divorced, she never thought about it. In New York, who would care? When we moved back here and people asked her questions, teachers at school, for example, or kids whose parents remembered me, she was caught off guard at first, and blamed me: 'In New York, all my friends had divorced parents; here no one does.' But she recovered quickly and now presents herself as the great world's envoy to the provinces. 'People don't have to take their fathers' names any more,' she tells them. 'People have choices now,' she tells her friends; 'they can take their mother's name if they want to or hyphenate their parents' names. People aren't stuck,' she says. My clever daughter has turned a possible embarrassment into something chic, and I understand some of her friends are asking their parents if they have to be stuck with their fathers' names. I doubt if Schaefer is a popular name in Star Lake."

"You know, I was thinking as you were speaking of how I would feel if Michelle had asked me to let Teddy's name be changed. I would never have agreed to it."

"Well, of course not. Theodore Ritter, Junior. Besides, you've been involved in your son's life. David abandoned Janey. 'Michelle' is Michelle Duvalle, the captain of the cheerleaders in high school?"

"Yes."

"But you're not married now."

"No. No, I'm not. When I came back from Vietnam I was driven by one idea. I wanted to become like the most decent man I'd met in the war. He was a sergeant, only a few years older than the men he led, younger than my brother, but he was more than a brother to us. He cared about his men. He let them know he cared and wanted them to stay alive. His concern kept them alive, but it didn't work to save him. I still grieve for him. I thought if I could set up a place, start a business where I could be to other men what the sergeant had been to me, I could make up for his death, or in some way fill up the hole left by the deaths of some of my buddies. Meanwhile, I went through the motions of living the 'normal' life our parents had had. I married Michelle. A year later Teddy was born. I went back to school, got an engineering degree, got a job, learned what I needed to know to go out on my own, and started my business. I was working eighteen or more hours a day, and I wasn't available to Michelle even when I was home. I couldn't bring myself to tell Michelle about my anger or about why the business I was starting was so important to me. I left her with a lot of time to make the discovery that the script that worked for our parents wasn't working for her. She's a bright woman, and about the same time she began to think 'Hey, this isn't enough,' the women's movement was there to tell her, 'Damn right, this isn't enough.' She and some of her friends formed a group together . . ."

"A consciousness raising group?"

"Yes. Although sometimes I think of it as a 'pre-divorce group,' or 'find-out-who's-responsible-for-your-problems group. Anyway, Michelle and I worked our way toward separation. She went back to school for computer training and then got a job in a Milwaukee bank and moved there with Teddy. We were divorced in 1976 after ten years of marriage. She met a man in her company and remarried in 1978. Last year, she had a baby, a girl. Her husband's a decent guy, but he can't help loving his daughter more than Teddy. Teddy is feeling shut out. Michelle loves Teddy, but she wants what's best for him. She thinks Teddy would be happier if he lived with me full time. And I want him. I've missed my son, and now I think I'm ready to be a decent father."

Nothing turns me on toward a man like the sight of him being tender with his kids. I thought of Ted with his son and my warm feelings for him came back.

"I think that's one of the best things a man can be."

Our waiter came to the table then to clear the dishes and to ask if we wanted dessert. We each ordered ice cream and coffee.

"Do you think you'll get tenure at Fontbonne?"

"At this point I expect I shall, but the situation can change. If I don't get tenure, I'll find another way to make a living. I know I'm a survivor, now. I realize what I've told you must make you wonder why I or anyone would want to stay in a field where insecurity and low salaries are the norm. I like teaching. Teaching allows me time for family life and community life and for research and scholarship."

"What kind of research?"

"Like a lot of researchers, I'm going back to my roots. I'm doing a study of radical women of the midwest. I'm working on a book about women who wrote for *The Appeal to Reason*, *The Coming Nation*, and *Socialist Woman*.

"Oh, I'm sure I have some of those in my family, too.."

"Radical women? Really? Do you think your family would have any papers or letters?"

"I'll ask my mother. That's the kind of project she'd love. My mother has always been a fan of yours, by the way."

"Really?"

"Yes. She saw you studying in the Star Lake library back in high school days. She said she had never seen such concentration in her life. She said that you had substance. She's kept up with you over the years. She keeps up with all the people my brother and I went to school with. When my brother and I tease her, she says, 'I follow people's lives because I'm concerned about them, and they interest me more than characters in soap operas.'"

"I'm glad you told me about your mother. Knowing I have a fan in Star Lake gives me a lift. I'll feel like less of an oddball when I go to the Parents' Association meeting. This is still a community where most parents come in pairs."

Having covered the past and the present, we paused self consciously.

"Shall we leave?" Ted asked.

I said yes. Ted paid the bill. And since he had invited me to dinner, I had no qualms about letting him pay. We left the restaurant, returned to Ted's car and drove in deep silence back to my house. Ted turned the car into my driveway, and parked it in front of my garage. That should give the neighbors something to think about, I thought, as we walked up the porch stairs and entered the house. As soon as we were inside, I turned off the porch light. I faced him, we embraced and I felt myself falling, almost swooning, into Ted's kiss. Kissing Ted was wonderful. His mouth covered mine; his open lips made a light pressure against my lips and I could feel sensation in my own lips and tongue as well as his.

After a long kiss, we pulled gently apart, and I led Ted into the living room. I switched on a lamp. Ted took off his jacket. We sat down on the couch and embraced again. It's coming back to me, I thought: the hard breathing, the giddiness, the feeling of being swept away. How long had it been since I had done this?

"Shall we go upstairs?"

Ted nodded. We got up from the couch and went into the hallway; I switched on the hall light and led Ted up the carpeted stairs. The entire upper story was mine; my bedroom, study, and bath. When I had shown Janey to my old room, one of the two downstairs bedrooms, Janey had observed sharply, "Your parents kept you downstairs so they could have their privacy upstairs."

In my bedroom politeness halted passion. I went to my closet and got out a wooden hanger for Ted. He put his jacket on the hanger, placed it in the closet, and then moved toward me. Grinning like children about to skinnydip, we pulled off our clothes and flung them on the chair.

I folded down the spread and slid between the freshly changed cotton sheets, pulling Ted in beside me. "Oh, this is wonderful," he said when I kissed him. Elated and confident, I moved my tongue and lips over his face, his ears, his neck. I moved down his body, nibbling at the hair on his chest. I folded his hands over his chest. "I wanted to do this in the car," I confessed as I licked the hairs in the hollow of his wrists." Kneeling beside him, I darted my tongue into the hollows of his armpits, the crooks of his elbows. With a lack of inhibition I had never known before, I pushed my tongue into the sides of his groin; then let my mouth travel down his legs; I curled my tongue around the backs of his knees, pressed my lips against the arch of each foot. Then I moved up again, kissing the mound of his groin and taking his erect penis into my mouth.

When I again lay facing Ted, he turned me gently on my back, then kissed and stroked every part of my body. He spread my legs apart and moved his tongue into and between the lips of my vagina. I shrieked. Ted said, "Ah, yes, Claire, yes." When Ted brought his lips back to my mouth, the taste of my cunt on his tongue was sweet. He brought me to climax again as he came inside me. Afterward we held each other. I stared at the ceiling wondering what Ted was thinking, wondering if he had been as pleased as I had been, if I had stirred him as he had stirred me. I turned to face him. He was looking back at me, smiling. His arm was under me. He squeezed my shoulder affectionately and said, "That was so good."

"Yes, it was. I never would have dared to dream this would happen, seventeen years ago."

"Well, however much time it took, I'm glad it happened."

I wanted to say a great deal more, but prudence kept me silent. Better not to trust the intensity of my feelings just then. I might not feel this way for long, but just then I was very happy. At the same time fear, like an evil twin, was springing up beside my happiness. Oh, let it alone, I admonished myself. My life's been one long drought so far as pleasure is concerned. Take what comes and enjoy. Ted removed his arm from beneath my shoulder; we turned toward each other for an affectionate kiss before departing into companionable sleep.

A noise at the bedroom door awakened me. The clock on my night stand read 6:07. Chica and Jumbo, miffed at having been expelled from their usual place in my bed, were scratching, demanding to be fed. Let them wait; I wanted a few more minutes to enjoy my connubial position next to Ted. He was on his side, his smooth, unblemished back toward me. I carefully pulled back the sheet and blanket, got out of bed and quietly put on running clothes. I wrote a note for Ted: "It's 6:15. I'm out running. Be back in an hour." I left the note on the pillow, carefully opened the bedroom door, petted the cats and crooned away their jealousy, led them downstairs, fed them, and left the house. A quick warm-up, and I was off and running, through the center of town, and out to the lake.

The morning was glorious. I was exhilarated. This is the antidote to passion; I thought, testing my body, reasserting control over it by demanding efficiency from lungs and muscles, removing my body from the claim of a lover's caress on my skin and nerve endings. That was the problem with good sex: it could melt my willpower, turn my mind to mush. I completed a run around the lake and ran back toward home. I looked at my watch; six and one half miles in fifty-five minutes. A little more than eight minutes per mile. Good. Maybe I could break eight minutes by the time I ran in the New York marathon. I would have to run under eight minutes per mile if I wanted to come in by three hours and twenty minutes, the qualifying time for the Boston marathon. Why was I even thinking of running in another marathon? Unbidden, flashbacks came from the night before; I felt Ted's hands stroking me; I saw his face above and below me; I held a vision of myself in climax. I had never known such passion and tenderness, and I was sure I would never find it again. With whom could I share what I had shared with Ted? We were almost siblings, formed by a culture and traditions with origins in another country, transplanted to this country more than a century ago. Being of the same generation was an important bond; acting from common ideals, we had come down on opposite sides of our era's tidal event. Now we were old fogies at thirty-four, veterans of causes younger people thought of as quaint or quixotic.

When I returned to the bedroom, Ted was awake.
"How far did you run?"
"Eight miles."

Ted looked at the clock. It was seven thirty. Watching him divide time by distance, I felt the impulse to remind Ted I had fed the cats and warmed up first; even so, his eyebrows lifted and the center of his mouth moved upward, a small sign, but enough to warm my vanity.

"That's serious running. How long have you been at it?"

"Since 1974."

Ted smiled at me. "Ah, yes, I should have known you were an athlete. Did your daughter come home?"

"No, she's still asleep at her friend's house. Why?"

"I was between sleeping and waking when you left, and I heard you talking to someone. I assumed it was your daughter."

"I was talking to the cats. Janey never used up my supply of baby talk, but I certainly can't talk that way to her now. Children grow up, but a relationship with cats never changes. I had to do a lot of sweet talking to them this morning to make up for evicting them from their usual resting place last night."

I walked to the dresser to gather clean clothes before taking a shower. Ted was still lying with his arms under his head, languidly watching me. The sight of me pleased him. That excited me. I went over to the bed and kissed him lightly.

"Could I persuade you to come back to bed?"

"But I'm sweaty."

"That's nice, too."

I pulled off my clothes, returned to bed, and we made Sunday morning love. Not long afterward, I showered and dressed. While Ted used the bathroom, I went downstairs. In the living room I paused to select an album. With the thought that now that we were lovers it was all right to set the stage, create a mood, I put Glenn Gould's recording of Bach's *Fifth Brandenburg* on the stereo and went into the kitchen. When Ted came down, I fed us both breakfast: a grapefruit half, coffee, and toasted homemade bread. We sat facing each other across the kitchen table, holding hands, not saying much but smiling at the joke we were playing on our younger selves.

"If sex between my husband and me had been half as good as what we had last night, I would have tried to save my marriage."

"Sex between Michelle and me was okay, not great."

"Then how did you become so exquisite a lover This is wonderful. You're blushing. But I'm serious. How did someone I remember as the prince of jocks in high school transform himself..."

"Into a frog?"

"No. Into a wonderful bedfellow. Since I won't be able to concentrate for days, I'd like to know the reason."

"I was in bad shape after my divorce. I hadn't realized how much I would miss my son. And Michelle. They were the reason I had been working so hard, and when they weren't there, my motivation was gone. I didn't think I could talk to my family, since I was the first to get divorced, etc., although my mother, I'm sure, would have made an effort to understand. I did her a disservice, but that was the way I felt at the time. I needed to do something, so I went on a camping trip, which, believe it or not, I had never done before on my own. I borrowed a tent, a stove, and other camping gear from my folks and started out, and it wasn't until I was in the process of setting up the tent – with night falling fast around me – that I realized I knew zip about camping."

"None of your military experience helped?"

"No, it didn't. Finally, I became aware of my nearest neighbor in the park, an attractive young woman, camping alone, like me, but unlike me, she was totally competent. Her tent was up, and she was cooking a fine meal for herself, while I was struggling to get the tent erect on the poles, and it kept coming down, and I felt more foolish. I wanted darkness to come as quickly as possible. Even if I couldn't get the tent up and had to sleep under the stars, she wouldn't see me still struggling. I even heard her covering her laughter as she watched me. Finally, when I was too desperate to refuse an offer of help, she came over to me. She was nice enough to try not to smile, and she asked if she could help. I said yes, and then she began, with great patience, which I had often seen in women, and great skills and confidence, which I had not, to give me a course in camping. I followed her instructions just as if she were a scoutmaster, and within minutes, I had the tent up. Then, of course, I invited her inside for some beer. We spent the night together, and during that time, she gave me a course in sexuality. I had never talked about sex with a woman before. Michelle and I had made nice sounds, said sweet words to each other, but we never told each other what we liked and disliked. But this woman did. She even took my hand and guided me at times. And she touched me the same way. She made me tell her what I liked. She asked me what I had wanted to try and never tried and when she got that information, she used it. I had never spent a night like that in my life. We stayed together three days, having a wonderful time, exploring the park, climbing. I had never met a woman so skilled in so-called masculine ways. She was better than I at everything, but I didn't feel put down because of it. She had learned these skills as a kid, and loved doing them, and was eager to share them. She was a good teacher. That's probably what she's doing now; she was on her way to graduate school in Washington when I met her."

"Did you ever see her again?"

"No, we both realized we were going on to different places, and those three days were perfect as they were."

"What year was the camping trip?"

"1976. What has my sex life been like since, you're wondering? Mighty sparse. Things have loosened up, but people are still slightly uncomfortable around divorced men. By then all my friends had paired off or moved away."

"Why didn't you?"

"Because I like it here and don't want to leave. I'm close to my family and that fills a void somewhat. For social life, I meet young women from time to time when I'm traveling on business, bright, attractive women who are serious about their careers and are not interested in forming serious relationships with any men, single, married, or divorced."

"Haven't you ever wanted to remarry"

"Yes, have you?"

"Yes."

I listened to the big hand of the kitchen clock jumping from one second to the next. After seven leaps, Ted said, I'd better get my car out of your driveway before your neighbors notice it and begin

talking. Could we have dinner together next Saturday? And your daughter?"
"I'd like that. Why don't you come here?"
"I'd like that very much. I'll call you during the week."
I walked him to the front door. Suddenly shy, we shook hands, and Ted left. I watched him through the living room window as he got into his car and drove away. The street was still empty, but maybe neighbors were watching through curtained living room windows as I was. Let them watch. I went to the kitchen to straighten up before leaving for church. I would walk and get there early, in plenty of time for Joys and Sorrows.

CHAPTER

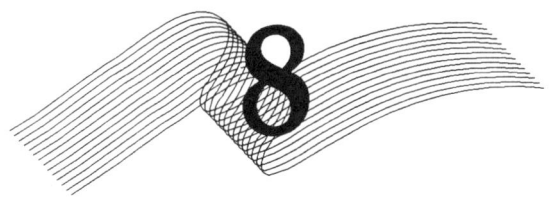

Gloria Hartman was playing *Sheep May Safely Graze* on the organ when I entered the church at twenty-five after nine. As flawed as Gloria's musicianship was, I preferred it to the recordings of timely rock music used when no volunteer was able to provide a musical prelude before the service. I sat in a middle pew and looked up, assuming an attitude of prayer. I was actually studying the ceiling, admiring once again the intricate lacing of the beautifully arched wooden staves, and thinking once again that if the church ever had a fire, the ceiling could not be replaced. In the less than a year since I had resumed membership in the church, I had become aware that a church with a moderate sized and far from affluent congregation like Broadway United Methodist was in constant financial need. Fuel was, of course, the greatest and an enormous expense; a winter that was over long or especially bitter could destroy a budget. The minister, Dan Baker, and the trustees, were kept on a constant round of fund raising, exhorting the membership to increase their pledges, and recruiting members. But the population was not growing; the newcomers, like the people on my block, did not quite replace the numbers of old-timers who had moved away or died.

Star Lake is a church-going community, with almost as many churches as bars to serve 25,000 people – but most people are already affiliated. Eight Catholic churches have served the town's blue collar population since Poles began coming here in the mid-nineteenth century to work in the lumber industry. The town's seven Lutheran churches serve middle class people and the town's business leaders. Of the three Methodist churches in town Star Lake United is the largest and most prosperous. It has beautiful stained glass windows (stained glass production is one of the town's industries), a full choir with a paid director, and two ministers. Immanuel United Methodist Church serves the remnants of a German congregation; it has a woman minister, but a conservative liturgy. Broadway United Methodist is the most progressive church; Dan Baker uses an inclusive liturgy, meaning God is not always referred to with male pronouns, and we sing from "the Yellow Book," a hymnal which includes feminine or collective nouns and pronouns, as in "God Rest Ye Merry, Gentle People," as well as hymns from Hispanic and Asian branches of the faith. The other mainstream religions – Baptist, Presbyterian, Congregational, Christian Scientist – each have one church; the remaining seventeen churches serve various fundamentalist and pentecostal sects, as well as Unitarians, Mormons, and the Bahai faith. Star Lake does not have a synagogue.

Broadway United Methodist Church attracts two kinds of congregants: people like me who can no longer have a spiritual relationship with a God who is a bearded white male and who want the church to be involved in social activism, and a smaller number of people who see more opportunity to achieve power in a smaller congregation than in one of the larger, more competitive congregations. The true believers deal with the opportunists and love the church in spite of its many shortcomings, which all too often impede our growth. One Sunday, I had heard a newcomer behind me whose voice was so lovely that I coveted it for our small choir, which unfortunately that Sunday, was unequal to inspection by a family looking for a church: Harry Sherman's reedy tenor, Helen Schmidt's harsh soprano, Edna Kent's wobbly contralto were clearly distinguishable in the choir's unaccompanied hymn. When the service ended, I turned to greet them; they were the perfect family: a young, attractive, affluent appearing couple with a son and daughter. While I was making my welcoming speech and encouraging the family to come again and be part of the church's warm and close community, Eugene Davis, the head trustee, was speeding toward them, eyes alight with the prospect of following my presentation with a closing. But the woman's pleasant, Southern-accented and noncommittal, "Well, now, we might just come again," let me know Eugene would be wasting his time. Either St. Martin's Lutheran or Star Lake United Methodist would win her.

Eugene's eyes had not lit up when I rejoined the church; a divorced woman without an independent income was not an especially valued addition to the church's well-coupled congregation. Besides, Banker Davis had correctly identified me as a potential social activist rather than a possible recruit to the fund-raising faction he headed. My politics were rooted in my early religious experience in this very church; now my politics had brought me back. Bella Abzug had been furious when people in the anti-war movement had carried Vietnamese flags. "Capture the American flag," she had commanded, and she had been right. Now I wanted progressive Christians to capture the cross from the fundamentalists. All of this I had explained to Janey, who remained skeptical; she said, "It still means praying to someone who doesn't exist, and that's creepy." Then, too, I found before I could work on my own political agenda, I first had to deal with the internal politics of the church, an aspect of religious life I had not seen as a devout, idealistic teenager.

Dan Baker had also been in Mississippi when I was there; then he was a newly ordained minister serving the National Council of Churches' Delta Ministry Project. I had not known Dan then, but I had heard of him when a local Klansman had attacked him. A picture of Dan, face bloodied, being led to a patrol car had been in the Hattiesburg newspaper and I had experienced a brief infatuation for him. Knowing that he had been appointed to Broadway United Methodist had been another incentive for rejoining, but I found Dan a different man from the one I had expected him to be. My friend Rebecca Swinton gave me the background on his transformation.

"Dan went through a Marxist stage, that was when he was in the civil rights movement. Then he experienced withdrawal; he next went through a Sufi period and is coming out of that into the New Age movement and an accommodation with the corporate culture. Mean Gene Davis is leading him in that direction because he wants the church to abandon what he considers its preposterous social action projects and pursue what really matters: an upwardly mobile congregation. But Eugene can't have it all his way. Dan's good angel is Sam Hartman, an ex-Alinsky organizer in Chicago who came here after burning out. He's back in action now and has gotten funds from the National Council of Churches to set up an ecumenical energy cooperative in the county. He's doing a good job at it, too. And as long as Sam remains one of the polar males in Dan's life, the church will sustain a social action commitment."

"Aren't there any influential women in the church?"

Kathy Hansen, my other church friend, answered.

"Sam's wife is influential, but she does the traditional things – organizes the Sunday School, plays the organ. Dan's wife, Evelyn, is a traditional minister's wife, and backs her husband one hundred percent. When we started a unit of United Methodist Women at the church and were defining its goals, Evelyn said the women of this church should do a better job of taking care of the church china and silver. We explained to her that UMW did not take on roles the church as a whole should assume, that UMW had an independent role to play, but that didn't stop her. She kept urging that we turn whatever funds we contributed or raised over to the church. Dan expects other women to look up at him worshipfully as his wife does. And a number do, literally. A minister can be a very attractive figure and some women in this church are infatuated with Dan. Rebecca and I started the social action committee, and kept it going, but if Sam Hartman didn't support it, we'd have a difficult time keeping it alive."

I then joined the social action committee and had helped plan the spring conference on alternate energy sources, which Kathy and Rebecca had strategically launched in order to cement Sam Hartman's support for projects less dear to his heart, such as battered women. I also joined the UMW chapter, and found myself linked, in the eyes of the other women, in an inevitable and somewhat isolated triumvirate with Kathy and Rebecca. "Triumvirate" is not the right word, as Rebecca had reminded me, "vir" meaning man; "trifeminae" is the accurate term, or "try-a-feminist." Kathy and Rebecca joked about their—our—pariah status. "Now that you're here, Claire," Kathy had said, "we could form a trio like the Supremes; if we could only sing, we could become a group and call ourselves, 'Every Woman's Nightmare.'"

"I prefer 'The Divorsays,' or how about 'The Triapariahs?" was Rebecca's suggestion.

Kathy was a librarian; she had graduated from UW-Milwaukee the year after I had graduated from UW-Madison, and had married her college sweetheart, keeping him from the war just as I had sheltered David. She had a son, Kenneth, just a year younger than Janey. Kathy had not spoken of the reasons for her divorce, or whether she or her husband had wanted it, and I did not feel I knew her well enough yet to probe. All she had told me on the subject was, "After my divorce became public knowledge, I was asked not to serve as den mother for my son's Boy Scout troop any more."

Rebecca was originally from South Carolina; she had lived in Chicago after graduating from the University of South Carolina in 1969. She had worked as a teacher before marrying a lawyer.

"He wasn't draft age, like the men y'all married; he was thirty, so I didn't rescue him; he rescued me from the Chicago public school system. Believe me I tried to show my gratitude. I even dressed the part."

Rebecca showed us a photo of herself as a young matron with teased hair, a strand of pearls, and a conservative, but frilly, dress, so different from the cas-

Legends of Good Women

ual, laid-back, clothing we all wore now that the three of us burst into laughter.

"I always carry this photo with me. When I'm in a funk and feeling down about myself, I take this out to remind myself of the me that was. It's a comfort to know I'll never sink that low again. The thought always cheers me."

Rebecca had refused to go back to teaching. She took computer courses at the UW extension services and was now a systems analyst for the State Division of Community Services. Unlike Kathy, she was not reluctant to discuss the breakup of her marriage.

"He thought I was a Southern belle, a child of the landed gentry instead of the daughter of two civil servants. I tried to live up to his expectations; I tried to be a devoted wife and gracious hostess in our suburban home, but I never felt real. I was playing a part and I just couldn't stand it after a while, especially when I found myself developing political opinions — I hadn't a blessed one before I married my husband, but he sure raised my consciousness. The problem was when I began arguing, for example, that bombing the Vietnamese to oblivion did not seem like a viable solution to resolving the conflict. He became furious; he wouldn't argue back, he'd just freeze me out, turn his back on me in bed, stop fucking, in other words, which was one of the few factors cementing the marriage, and that just made me angrier, and I'd find more issues to argue about, and he became more silent and more distant, so finally, I had to leave. My parents have never forgiven me, especially, my mother, who thinks if a man is a good provider and not abusive, there is no excuse for divorce. My ex has remarried and has a son, now. That's the only bad part. Now that he has a son and heir, he maintains very little contact with our daughter Sheila, and she, of course, holds me responsible for his negligence. I'm caught between reproaches from two generations; that does not seem fair."

My mother had never held my divorce against me; indeed, she had written me, "I guess it's all for the best," her way of telling me she thought I had recovered my sanity; but Janey blamed me for her father's abandonment of her as Sheila blamed Rebecca. I doted on Janey as mothers traditionally doted on sons, but she might still always hold me responsible for her father's negligence. I worried that Janey would define herself through male approval, that the feistiness that sometimes exasperated me but which I cherished in her would evaporate into subservience to some caddish male, or God forbid, a series of males, and my smartass would decline into a slut. If I remarried, would the presence of a male figure be what would preserve Janey from degradation?

I pondered these unholy matters through the opening words from the scripture and the first hymn. Just before the Sharing of Joys and Sorrows, Rebecca and Kathy joined me in the pew. If I remarried, I wondered, would I break up this gang of three? Then I tuned in to Joys and Sorrows because, as Rebecca, Kathy, and I agreed, that was our favorite part of the church service.

Helen Anderson asked for prayers for her mother who had been depressed since Helen's dad died. Dan asked Helen's mother's name and wrote it down; he would mention it later when he led us in prayer. Dan was conscientious about consoling his congregation. Tim Hamilton reported the joy that his sister, brother-in-law and niece were visiting his family for the weekend; Nancy Armstrong announced, "I have a joy that I have a new job, and so far I like it very much." The sharings were moderate joys and moderate sorrows;

Legends of Good Women

not a searing confiding: "I saw my brother last week; we have not seen each other in three years. He is a schizophrenic. I worry about him; I feel guilty about him, but I do not want him near my family," which Herb Armstrong, Nancy's husband, had shared with the congregation two months earlier. Or the other deep griefs that surged over illness, estrangement, death, loss of work and love, and all the forms of heartbreak that any randomly collected group of people will contain. I was happy for the joys, and saddened by the sorrows, but the sharings I relished were the gossipy revelations between joy and sorrow. The last segment of the Broadway United Methodist soap opera had been offered up by Molly Sherman, the wife of Harry Sherman, a lawyer, a church trustee, and choir member. Molly, an elementary school teacher, had formed a consciousness raising group with women at her school and now wanted some independence. During one of the UMW meetings, she had confided that she had never balanced a checkbook, and when she had asked to take control of her personal finances, Harry had resisted, but Molly had insisted and finally got her way. We were aware that Molly's efforts to "renegotiate my marriage" had produced tension, but one Sunday in April, Molly had stood up and began describing a "wonderful exchange" between herself and Harry that marked a turning point in their marriage. "In our years together, we've never known anything as wondrous as those moments we shared. It was like nothing we had known before." Molly continued speaking about the new marvel in her marriage, her high voice seeming to climb up into the staved roof. Rebecca nudged me and whispered, "I don't think she knows that what she's telling us is that she and Harry finally got it off. She finally had an orgasm." Molly was still glowing when she sat down, seeming to be unaware of the information she had shared about herself and Harry which, judging from the looks of embarrassment combined with amusement on several faces, others besides Rebecca had understood. I was without expectation then, that this Sunday would produce any titillation, and I was thinking that I was wrong to expect it in church, until Harriet Dunkel stood up. Harriet and her husband, Stanley, both of them social workers, had gone through a troubled period in their marriage. I had not liked Stanley ever since the Sunday, one of the first times I had come to church, when their nine-year-old son, Stanley Junior, had become restless during the service, and Stanley Senior, had taken him outside. We heard the whack of a blow on the side of the head, and a child's wail, and then Stanley Senior returned alone. I assumed that he had left his son outside to "cry it out" or had delivered him downstairs to the Sunday School. My suspicion that Stanley's Germanic sense of discipline also extended to his wife was subtly confirmed by Kathy and Rebecca, whom Harriet had made her confidantes during her estrangement from Stanley.

"We gave her a lot of support," Kathy explained one Sunday when she, Rebecca and I had lunch together after church. "Harriet was on the phone with one or both of us every evening, telling us about the stress she was under, working, and caring for her son, and being a wife, and trying to find her own identity. She felt Stanley belittled her, did not respect her, was "abusive;" she never came out and said it, but I sensed "abusive" included violence. We reassured her; we validated her feelings; we gave her lists of resources; we let her know that the end of marriage was not the end of the world, or one's sex life. This went on for weeks . . ."

Rebecca interrupted Kathy. "Months, actually, of almost nightly hours long telephone calls. Harriet told us she felt her confidence restored because of our support and encouragement, and she seemed on the verge of leaving her marriage. Then all of a sudden we weren't hearing from her."

"Until one Sunday we learned at church that Harriet was giving a dinner party. She and Stanley were giving a dinner party for other couples at the church."

We overheard a conversation about it; Harriet didn't have the guts to tell us herself. When we confronted her about it, she said we had been very helpful to her during a time of crisis, and she would never forget us . . ."

"Or 'cease to be grateful' . . ."

". . . but she didn't need 'all that' now; she realized her true destiny was to work through her marriage."

"I still like Harriet," Kathy had concluded; "she's basically a good person and very generous, but she burned us badly."

"Oh, lordy, yes. To lean on us, to use our precious time; godammit, while she was bitching and moaning to us, she was still with Stanley, who was after all paying some of the bills. We do the mother-father roles all by ourselves. And then to snub us. No, Kathy, I don't feel the spirit of forgiveness nudging me just yet," Rebecca had argued, "especially after she refused to go on the women's retreat because, she said, 'all women talk about on those things are clothes and hair styles.'"

Even though I was privy to Harriet's misuse of my friends, and though her anti- feminism foolish, I could not help but enjoy her occasional sharings, for Harriet was witty; she made us laugh. Reverend Baker was upset enough by levity in the church to move Joys and Sorrows to just before Pass the Peace, until he realized more people were coming in late during the service. Then he moved it back to the beginning, but put a note in the Sunday bulletin that "people who tend to remain silent should exert their will to speak, and people who talk often should constrain themselves to listen."

Then Harriet stood up. "I have my husband's permission to share our news with you," she began, and Kathy, Rebecca, and I glanced at each other quickly as she continued. "The Dunkels are about to take a new direction in their lives. After working at a job he does not like for more years than he cares to remember, Stanley, with my complete support, has resigned his position in order to complete a long unfulfilled commitment to scholarship. He is returning to graduate school full time in order to complete his course work and write his dissertation on George Eliot. And then, we both anticipate, he will embark on an academic career. It will be tough for us all to live on my salary, but I know we can count on your support. There are not many men who are secure enough to let their wives support them, but I'm proud to say that Stanley is not one of them."

There was subdued, scattered laughter when Harriet sat down, then a beat while people took in what she had revealed to them. I dared not look at Kathy or Rebecca, and they also kept their eyes on Reverend Baker, who, in his prayers, asked God to "bless new ventures," a phrase that covered Nancy Armstrong's getting a new job and Stanley Dunkel's quitting his. Oh, I could not wait to chew that over with Kathy and Rebecca. We sang a hymn, heard announcements about church and community meetings, heard an offertory anthem by the choir while the collection was taken, sang the non-sexist doxology, which strictly speaking was no longer a doxology, since the references to Father, Son, and Holy Ghost, and been changed to God the Creator of all. We passed peace; moving around to each other shaking hands an saying, "Peace be with you." This was the part of the service Janey disliked because, she claimed, her hands were sweaty and she was embarrassed to have other people touch them.

Then Reverend Baker spoke on "A Calm and Peaceful Mind." Jesus, he said, and called the Holy Spirit the Comforter, but most of us are closed to the action of the Spirit because we are not relaxed enough to let it in. We are made stressful by world events. But relaxation is a necessity, not a luxury; Jesus relaxed through meditation, and so should we, for a tense body makes a tense soul. Reverend Baker told us to close our eyes and count from ten backwards, trying to drive everything else from our minds. Then he led us in deep breathing, and after the deep breathing, he told us to think of a calm place, real or imaginary, where we could feel all our stress leaving our bodies and our souls. Then he asked us to describe what we had seen. Reverend Baker likes the parishioners to participate in the sermon part of the worship service, because participation makes people feel more involved in worship. I think because, also, it lessens the time he has to spend in preparation. Rebecca, originally a Southern Baptist, has a more traditional approach to religion and is driven frantic by what she calls his "New Agey excesses." And at times, I agree with her; for example, when Ayatollah Khomeni's fanaticism surfaced while the Iranian revolution was still young, Reverend Baker was referring to him as a "holy deliverer." But I find his sermons consistently interesting, even if they do not follow the prescribed pattern of scripture lessons, a practice that sets Rebecca fuming. "He does not follow the lectionary," she will declare occasionally, and if she will forgive him for forgetting communion one first Sunday, I do not think she will ever forget the omission.

When Reverend Baker asked people to speak of calm places, a few parishioners mentioned beautiful places around the state; someone spoke of being in the Upper Room with Jesus, and Harriet Dunkel said, "my back yard." Most agreed they felt tension falling away from their bodies, and their souls being soothed. Reverend Baker summarized the sharings and, gave us parting words; we sang the closing hymn, and went downstairs for coffee hour, another of my favorite parts of the Sunday ritual, because I like being part of this church community, even if the people in it are ambivalent about me. Encountering that feeling in others, in fact, is what makes me feel at home.

By tacit agreement, Rebecca, Kathy, and I separated to circulate among the other congregants. I went first to talk with Meg Patton, an elementary school teacher married to a former minister who now works for a union. They have one daughter, Diana, three years younger than Janey. I like Meg because she is down to earth and practical. She is the church treasurer, one of the few women in the congregation whose skills are recognized. She seems to be content in her marriage, allowing for normal connubial irritations, pleased with her child, and enthusiastic about her work, especially since she began teaching in the public school system after teaching in a Catholic elementary school. The nuns, Meg said, "are the most truly oppressed women I have ever encountered. Priests actually live very well; nuns live like paupers. They are very angry about it, but there is not much they can do. And the situation is worse since women stopped

Legends of Good Women

becoming nuns because now there is no base of support for the old nuns when they retire. I liked the sisters, but unless I wanted to share their poverty, I had to leave."

Today Meg asks me if I am still teaching. I tell her no, the term is over.

"Just a few more weeks, and I'll be finished for the summer, too, but when Diana goes to camp, that's when my freedom really begins."

Janey will be going to camp, too, I tell her, and we discuss the ritual of labels, sew- ins are better than iron-ons, we agree, but take too much time, and besides, your kid always comes home missing some of her clothes, but carrying someone else's. We tell each other to have a good week, and move on to greet others.

I smile and say hello to Gloria Hartman, who smiles tightly back at me, says, "Hello, Janey," and moves past me to talk to Betty Green, Eugene Davis's young second wife. Gloria, the director of a Montessori school, and, according to Rebecca and Kathy, widely respected for her work, dresses like a sixties woman in blouses, beads, long skirts, and sandals; she is stout and her graying hair is long and straggly. Gloria's earth mother image seems to result from an effort to deny, or at least efface, her professionalism. Although we have never had a disagreement, or even the mildest unpleasant encounter, I know she dislikes me; she typically calls me by my daughter's name, although Janey seldom comes to church. When I first became aware of Gloria's hostility, I had asked Rebecca why Gloria should be hostile to me. Rebecca had said that Gloria saw me as a threat because Sam might be attracted to me.

"But Sam doesn't like me either," I had protested.

"Not liking doesn't mean not touching. Just watch. If Sam starts talking to you, or any woman, Gloria, wherever else she might be, will suddenly be at Sam's side. And she has reason to be watchful. Sam has left home periodically on long, unexplained absences."

"But they seem so happily married. I remember once that Sam, while making some political point, said, 'I enjoy this,' – whatever it was – 'almost as much as making love to my wife.'"

"And the gratuitousness of that remark didn't immediately alert you to tension underneath?"

"How can a small-town Southern girl be such a cynic? Gloria and Sam sit together every Sunday in the same pew; fifth from the front on the right aisle."

"Yes, they work very hard at looking devoted. Oh, maybe you're right; I'm being uncharitable," Rebecca had acknowledged. "But what reason can you think of for Gloria's hostility?"

"I can't think of one, except for that defensiveness women who are lying to themselves about their husbands may feel when they encounter straight-up feminists."

I recalled Rebecca's words as I watched Gloria talk to Betty Green who was, if not defensive, evasive in her contacts with Rebecca, Kathy, and me.

"She used to be a feminist," Rebecca had said before filling me in on Betty's background. Before her marriage, Betty, now advanced in pregnancy, had been an officer in the bank which employed her husband; she was seen as a woman on the rise. Eugene had been married to someone else at the time and had two sons, now in college. When Betty and Eugene fell in love, her career and his marriage had ended. They had joined this church in the early days of their marriage, when Betty, according to Rebecca, had become active in UMW, and seemed more liberal politically than her husband. But by degrees, Betty had dwindled into a wife; the reason, Rebecca thought, was that Betty felt defensive about having a baby while her husband was putting two sons through college.

"Although I don't know why," Rebecca had said. "They obviously have more money than any other family in the church, not that that's saying much. They're affluent, for goodness sake; Betty could have a passel of kids Mean Gene could easily support. Well, whatever reason, she's become a pain in the posterior, like her husband. Just an echo; she, too now wonders aloud whether a social action committee really is consistent with the church's spiritual mission."

I watched Gloria Hartman, long-skirted and sandaled, hugging her shawl around her as she spoke to Betty Davis, who, in a dressed-for- success maternity suit, still looked like an executive on the fast track. If motherhood was a pod from outer space, it still had not taken over Betty's corporate world personality. I could not hear their conversation, but Gloria was probably subtly lobbying for her husband, not promoting one of his causes, but in her non-threatening, maternal way, keeping lines of communication open between the factions their husbands represented. Thinking that whatever differences they had with each other, they probably did not feel warmly toward me, I exchanged greetings with them and went on to speak to Marge Harrison, who, I was sure, did have warm feelings for me; for everyone, in fact. Not that Marge is indiscriminate, she is a joyful woman of good will, large, heavier than Gloria, and even more maternal looking. She is like many women in the church, a teacher; her husband, Pete, works at a number of trades. Currently he is a baker, one of the few men in the church who is not a professional. Marge and Pete have two children, a boy of seven, a girl of five. I had liked Marge from the first Sunday I had come to this church, but I really grew fond of her during the women's retreat.

We had gone to a Methodist camp, which is not as primitive as it sounds because the camp consists of a large residential building with dining and meeting rooms, plus several comfortable outlying cabins. A group of us had decided to walk into town; we mothers wanted to ease our guilt over being so happy away from our children by buying them something. We had not realized how far "town" was; we had been walking for over an hour and still had not reached it. Then, like a group of errant children, we were rescued; a station wagon pulled alongside with Marge at the wheel; she scooped us up, drove us into town and back to the camp when we had finished shopping.

Marge is always cheerful, but today she was radiant.

"You look very happy," I said.

"I am," she replied, "Pete and I finally are buying a house; it's going to be wonderful after living in a cramped apartment."

"I can appreciate how you feel," I told her. "When I first moved back here after living in a small New York apartment, I went from room to room, and went up and down stairs, thinking, 'All this space is mine.' The irony in my case is that the house I was marveling over was the one I had grown up in and never thought it was all that special. I wish you and your family much joy in your new home."

Marge promised to invite me to the housewarming. I moved on to greet other members of the church.

The older ones, my parents' age, I know only to say hello to, but those I know I like. Our common situation makes me feel close to Kathy and Rebecca, but I nevertheless like and admire the other women of this church. I am stirred by the burdens they bear. Jeanette Harris-Smith, a lawyer for a state agency who is married to a high school teacher and is the mother of two young children has had two bouts with breast cancer and a double mastectomy as a result. She worries, of course, about a recurrence of her own cancer, but also about other cancer victims she has come to know through the course of her treatment. Two Sundays ago she asked prayers for another young mother whose cancer had spread to her brain, and who was in her final hours. Jeanette also asked prayers for the sister who would care for her friend's two young children, and who has the burden of grief at losing a sister as well as the sudden responsibility of bringing up two children. Another young mother, Nan Woods-Hall, had a difficult second pregnancy and a long labor. She probably did not have the medical care she should have had, for her oxygen-starved baby was born with severe brain damage. The boy is growing like a slowly inflating doll who will never have more than an infantile mentality and motor skills. When she brings him to church, I look at the still, uncomprehending form, and hope, however wicked the impulse may be, for a quick end to its life.

The women's confidences, shared during the February retreat or during our UMW meetings, have made their concerns mine, and their flashes of biography are now etched into my awareness of them. One of the meetings was devoted to our ancestors; Gloria

Hartman, who led it, asked us to imagine our grandparents' lives and describe those lives to the others. Gloria's own contribution was one I clearly remember. She told us of her grandfather, a Norwegian immigrant who had settled in Minneapolis where he worked as a roofer until the glare of the sun reflecting on the tin he for years hammered onto housetops blinded him.

At that meeting, Gloria also asked us to imagine our parents' lives; Helen Schmidt supplied the memory I remember. Her widowed grandmother had lived with her family her grandmother and mother sang when they did the dishes together, and Helen sang their favorite song: "Nita, Juanita, let me linger by thy side. Nita, Juanita, my own true bride."

Not all the women in this church leave me dewy-eyed and lump-throated. Two I positively dislike. Martha Rosenquist, the very young and pregnant wife of rising young member of the history faculty at UW-LaCrosse, has told of how she andd her husband met twice in my hearing. When he was a brand-new Ph.D., he had taught at the Southern women's college she had attended. "Our history class was in the basement, and the windows were on the ground level. I used to love watching Jimmy be distracted by the sight of all the pretty legs walking by. I mean, every now and then, I knew that his lecture was blown clear out of his head by all those legs passing by just above his head. And the girls in the class were all in love with him. They'd come to class in low-cleavage dresses and short skirts and sit with their legs crossed and raise their hands and lean forward and say, 'Professor Rosenquist' in husky voices. When Jimmy and I started dating, we had to be circumspect, or thought we did. But after a while, we realized everybody knew and nobody cared. And then when Jimmy got this appointment up here, we got married. My parents love Jimmy, but they wish I'd gotten my degree first. Now, so do I."

Martha makes the other women feel protective, but the second time I heard her tell the story of her courtship, I could not help blurting out churlishly, "Do you think nobody would have cared about a professor dating a student if the genders were reversed, if the professor were female and the student male?"

"No," Martha replied, "I don't think that would have mattered. We had women professors at my college."

"But there were no male students, so we can't test your theory," I said with an edge in my voice. I sensed the other women thinking I was picking on Martha, but I could not help myself. I know part of my resentment is due to Martha's smugness, but most of it is due to jealousy of her husband, who can be serenely certain that he will have a distinguished academic career.

Shirley Mitchell is the other woman I do not like, and, as with Martha, my hostility has its origins in an encounter during the woman's retreat. Over the weekend, one of the dinner conversations was on theology; Shirley was silent as we discussed the misogyny in Genesis, most of the women agreeing that the emphasis on Eve's sinfulness in their early religious training had profoundly shaped their sense of inferiority.

"One thing I've never understood," I said, approaching the topic from another angle, "is if Eve was "the mother of all," did her sons "know" her as Adam did? Were Cain and Abel the original motherfuckers?"

I felt comfortable enough among the women to be so flippant, but I was assuming too much about Shirley as it turned out, or more likely, I sensed her probable reaction and was baiting her. Either way, her reaction was immediate and vehement.

"You are being blasphemous," she accused.

"Oh, Shirley, I was being facetious because I don't accept the creation story as the truth. The Bible has had many interpreters, and I believe Genesis is part of an ancient conspiracy of males to keep women in their place. You don't take the Bible literally do you? How can you be in this congregation if you do?"

"Reverend Baker comes close to the edge of what is doctrinally acceptable at times, that is true, but he has never, so far, crossed over the line. You, Claire, have indeed trespassed on Scripture. Yes, I believe in the Bible as the revealed word of God, and I also believe, as I believe in the Lord, that Satan is alive in this world and here in Wisconsin, spreading his snares for the unwatchful. You, Claire, are a heretic."

I admit I was alarmed. Shirley is a woman in her twenties, slim and fashionable, so like a pleasant, modern suburban housewife, that I was not prepared for the hard look of condemnation in her blue eyes as she made her accusation. If we were living centuries earlier, I would have been in real peril, a candidate for burning, in whatever community Shirley had influence.

"Yes, Shirley, by your standard I certainly am," I replied mildly, and by tacit agreement we all left the subject of theology. But even though we talked pleasantly afterward, I knew Shirley would unforgivingly remember my words each time she looked at me. The label "heretic" was firmly fixed in her mind next to my name and face, and "executioner" was fixed in my mind next to hers.

Shirley's husband Steve, was a seminary student when they met. "I went to a college that traditionally supplied ministers with their wives," she explained. However, Steve became a lawyer instead of a minister. Shirley sold textbooks to schools and colleges until she had her children. She has two young daughters, the second born after a difficult pregnancy involving months of confinement to bed, but Shirley's goal is to have three children, and with her steely will and contempt for pain, she will have them. And yet she surprised me during one of our more companionable times together during the retreat by talking in my presence of her husband.

"He has the most phenomenal metabolism," she boasted. "He has at least three bowel movements a day, while I'm lucky to have one."

Shirley gave more information about her husband, a pleasant, straight-arrow type, who at least to my not very well-trained eye, seems less fanatic than Shirley. But that one fact is riveted in my awareness of him, and each time I look at him, I think of his three evacuations per day. I do not think I should be in possession of that information. I think Shirley was more than indiscreet; her revelation was a betrayal of intimacy, perhaps unconscious, perhaps a subtle settling of scores.

As I left coffee hour, I heard an argument in progress at curbside between Kathy and Rebecca, on one side, and Harriet Dunkel on the other.

Harriet was saying, "Look, I think what you two are doing is well-intentioned, but misdirected. I think you would do yourselves and everyone else more good by finding rich husbands."

"I've already had a rich husband," Rebecca countered.

"Well maybe he wasn't Mr. Right. Go find Mr. Right Rich Husband. I'm not unsympathetic to battered women, and establishing a shelter may be a good idea. I just think it's all part of a losing battle. I think – " Harriet interrupted herself as the Armstrongs walked by.

"Nan, I'll call you this week about the four of us getting together for dinner, okay? Fine. Have a good week." She turned back to us. "Look, I think this is a man's world and the woman's movement is not going to change that fact. All that the women's movement has done has made life easier for men."

Harriet paused as the Davises left the church and as they crossed the path on their way to their Cadillac parked at the curb, she resumed in a hearty, for-public-consumption voice, "For example, no-fault divorce seemed a victory. Now men dump their wives and families and marry women their daughters' age. You see them on the Donahue show – men in their fifties with wives in their thirties bouncing babies on their laps and talking about discovering the joys of fatherhood. Well, what was that first family, an experiment? Did it not count? Will the wife the man has dumped find another husband when every man her own age is looking for someone half his?"

We all paused for a second to watch Eugene Davis open the passenger door for his wife and, after she had slowly settled her bulky body into the seat, slam it shut.

"But Harriet," Kathy remonstrated, "We're not really in disagreement about the basic unfairness women experience. Why are you so opposed to helping other women when you have such insight into and sympathy with them? We admire your organizing skills, your energy, and good-heartedness. That's why we came to you to be part of the sponsoring committee for the women's shelter."

Her husband was standing on the church stairs talking to Reverend Baker. As soon as he left the minister, Harriet walked toward him, calling back to us over her shoulder, "I'm sorry, I can't help you. Your project is not one of my priorities at the moment."

"But you never can tell," Kathy said softly, "It may be important to you one day."

CHAPTER

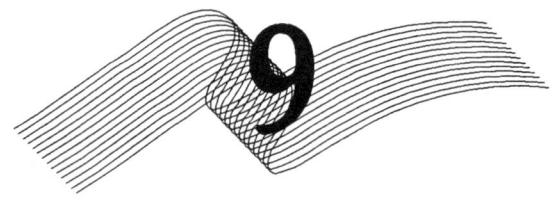

When he came to dinner, Ted brought us both flowers: a mixed bouquet for me and a single red rose, wrapped in its own florist paper, for Janey. At first she was confused by the gift of a rose, then she was pleased, and she fussed with my small supply of vases before settling, with a sign of dissatisfaction, on an ordinary white single-stem container. During dinner, Ted never excluded her from the conversation. He talked about school in a comradely, not in a condescending way.

"Where do you sit?"

"In the middle of the front."

"That's good, because if you sit in the back, the teacher knows you're trying to avoid doing work, and so she'll make a point of calling on you, but if you sit right in the front, your friends will think you're trying to be the pet. Middle of the front is respectable, but at the same time not a position of envy. That's a wise choice, Janey."

"I must be doing something right, because I get good grades," Janey boasted.

"That's true," I loyally seconded.

Legends of Good Women

Having lived in another part of Star Lake, Ted had not gone to Longwood Elementary, but he talked about his own school experiences, and Janey, who usually rolls her eyes when I reminisce about Longwood, listened with real interest do his discussion of teachers and their quirks, and of childhood pranks. Ted told a tale of cutting school with his buddies: "One day me and my friends," he began with a deliberate lack of grammar, and then corrected himself with a nod at me, "I mean, one day my friends and I . . ." The story ended with the pack of them being rounded up by the truant officer and being driven back to school to face the principal.

"Did you ever get into mischief?" Ted asked me. Janey snorted, and then became restrained when Ted looked at her.

"No, I never did, but only because no one ever asked me to cut school or break the rules. And I wasn't a leader the way you were, Ted, or the way Janey is now. I couldn't've led my friends astray."

"Do you mean you wish you had gotten into trouble when you were a kid?"

"Janey, I wish I hadn't been such a straight arrow. Yes, I wish I had some experiences of shared foolishness – nothing really wicked, of course – to look back on. I wish I had had more friends. Janey, I say that knowing you won't take it as permission to get yourself or your friends into trouble."

Janey said confidingly to Ted, "That's my mom manipulating me through positive re-enforcement."

I sensed Ted stiffen slightly. I think he found my daughter, the Greenwich Village smartass, a bit too brash. I felt myself become slightly defensive and resentful. Then he won my admiration again by asking Janey, "What does your school smell like? That's one of the things I remember about grammar school, the smells."

"Hmm, my room smells like, let me see, first there's paper from the books and the old lined yellow paper the teacher gives us for tests and sometimes there's her perfume, or the fluid from the thermofaxed sheets. There's different kinds of gum smells. Sometimes there's smelly socks and sneakers."

Ted sniffed with his eyes closed. "I remember library paste."

"Yes, but that smell is from kindergarten and the lower grades," Janey corrected. "Back then there was sometimes a pee smell, too."

"Wet wool and steam on rainy winter days," Ted continued.

"What did the high school you and my mom went to smell like?"

"High school doesn't have a distinctive odor because it's so much bigger and you move from room to room. Only certain rooms have odors—chem labs, locker rooms."

"And always the faint smell of cigarettes around the bathrooms," I added.

"You never smoked, did you?"

"Never did and don't now. Do you"

"We-ell," Janey began, and my eyes widened.

"Back in New York, me and my friend Julie tried it one day. We sneaked into St. Mark's churchyard and smoked a cigarette behind some bushes so we wouldn't leave a smell in our apartment and no spying adults could see us and report back to our mothers. Sorry, Mom, but I'm not the saintly child you were and besides, you said you wished you had had more mischief in your life."

"That does not mean that I want you to sow my share of wild oats."

"Don't worry, about smoking anyway. Both me and Julie, Julie and I, hated it."

After we had finished dinner, the three of us cleared the table. Ted and Janey toted in dishes, which I scraped, rinsed and stacked in the dishwasher. I wrapped plastic around the carcass of the chicken I would use for soup I would make the next day; then I put it and containers of leftover vegetables in the refrigerator, and set the cake in its clear domed pedestal on top of the refrigerator. I deliberately did not listen, the better not to be tempted to join in the conversation Ted and Janey continued, but I did note that it advanced beyond the topic of schooldays. It may have been about sports. I may have heard the word "Brewers" come out of my daughter's mouth.

We went into the living room after our chores were done and I put some of my Sixties records on the stereo. I began with the Beatles' "Sergeant Pepper's Lonely Hearts Club Band" album because it fits in the musical area Janey and I share. I played Credence Clearwater's "Bayou Country," "Cheap Thrills" with Big Brother and the Holding Company and Janis Joplin, and the Mamas and the Papas' "California Dreamin'." I played Sam Cooke's "Live at the Harlem Square Club, 1963" album, and at the "Twisting' the Night Away" cut, Ted and I spontaneously got up to dance. Janey was astonished.

"Did you actually dance the twist back then?"

"Yup. Want to give it a try?"

Ted turned from me and held out his hands to Janey, who reluctantly got up from the couch and began to dance, tentatively at first, but very soon with confidence and pleasure.

"What a corny dance," she said giggling while she began embellishing on the basic steps.

"But it's fun."

"Twistin'" ended the A side of the Cooke album; we listened to the B side, and then I played Otis Redding's "Pain in My Heart" album. We listened to the first four cuts, and then at the fifth cut, "You Send Me," Ted held out his hand and we danced. A slow dance, where a man traditionally leans with his groin, but with Ted, I did not feel myself being "led." We blended together like true partners, yet were restrained for Janey's sake. We danced through "I Need Your Loving'" and then listened to the B side; at "Louie, Louie," the three of us sang along. When the album was finished, Ted said he must leave. Janey and I walked him to the door. He shook hands with her, and said he had enjoyed meeting her. He kissed me on the cheek and said he would call me. After he left, Janey looked thoughtfully at the door and said, "He's neat."

"I think so, too."

"Do you think he liked me"

"I think your brashness startles, him, but yes, I think, on the whole, he likes you."

"That's good."

Janey was smiling widely, knowingly, and I knew she was enjoying a vision of displaying Ted to her friends.

"I had a good time."

"So did I. This was a good evening, but let's take one thing at a time, Janey."

Janey kissed me and, refusing to be warned, went smirking into her bedroom.

But Ted's behavior in the next weeks seemed to confirm Janey's expectations, for he often came over in the evenings just to talk with us or even watch television. Indeed, he was among us so often that Janey began to take him for granted. One Saturday night, Ted and I had dinner, a most mediocre one at a local restaurant and then went to his apartment. The knowledge that, in my role as responsible parent, I would go home at a fairly early hour, gave a furtive aura to our lovemaking. We were not tender with each other, but frantic, rough, delirious with roughness.

The next morning I went to church and Janey went with me. In the car, Janey asked "Do you have any special reason for wanting to go to church this morning, anything to ask God to forgive you for, for instance"

"Not a thing."

"You mean," Janey persisted, "you didn't do anything last night, for example, that was wicked or sinful?"

I parked the car before answering her.

"Janey, what you want to ask me is, did I make love with Ted last night. Well, I am not going to respond to that question, except to say that what I did was appropriate, not sinful, and that whatever I do, in or out of bed, is always governed by my sense of responsibility to you. Meeting your physical and emotional needs comes first in my life, but after that, whatever I do to meet my own needs is my business. At long last I seem to have a private life, and I do not intend to discuss it with you, so please, don't ask, me questions and don't speak of 'sin' or 'wickedness' to me."

Janey seemed to shrink and I was immediately remorseful. I need her spunk to reassure me she is all right.

"I was just happy for you, is all," she said defensively. "Why do you think I agreed to go to church without even an argument?"

I hugged her, and said I was pleased and proud of her for being happy for me. She squirmed out of my hug and stifling a laugh, we walked into church.

Days later Janey's school term ended; I packed her duffel and set off with her in our rejuvenated Volvo for her summer camp's pickup point. She had not wanted to go to camp, but chose it over the options of visiting her grandparents in Florida, or remaining at home with me and without her camp-bound, or vacation-homebound friends. She was silent in the car, remembering, I knew, the summer before when I had arranged for her to have one last four week session at Greenwich House Camp in New York. I had driven her back from Wisconsin, returned to complete renovations on the house, and then gone back to New York to drive her to the house I had worn myself out repairing in the hope Janey would be reconciled to moving to Wisconsin. Of course, Janey's reconciliation, when it came, would have no connection to my effort. A parent who expects gratitude from a child is a fool indeed.

Three other mothers were waiting with their children at the meeting place on the sidewalk in front of Kosciusko school when we arrived. Two of the kids, a girl and a boy, were younger than Janey and, judging from the anxiety in their mothers' eyes, first time campers. The other child was a girl close to Janey's age; she and Janey looked at each other with spontaneous dislike. Her mother and I grinned at each other.

"What is it?" I asked when I saw Janey grinning at me.

"I was remembering Greenwich House Camp—the way it was when the kids left. Not like this, a few kids and their mothers staring at each other and not talking, but a big crowd of kids from P.S. 41 and their parents, standing on Barrow Street, all talking to each other. Then the kids would go inside and the nurse would check each kid's hair for lice and poke between each kid's toes for athlete's foot. And then the bus would finally come, and the parents would go outside and then the kids would march out in a line between the parents. Always the boys went first. Why, in the five years I went there, couldn't the girls have gone first just one time?"

"I don't know. You should have raised the issue earlier."

"I wish I could go to Greenwich House Camp instead of Camp Birdbrain where you're sending me."

"It's a good camp. People at church knew of it and recommended it to me. Besides, even if we were still in New York, you couldn't go to Greenwich House Camp because you're over twelve years old."

"Isn't that age discrimination or something?"

"I remember those sendoffs, too. One year a woman waved at the bus with her plane ticket in her hand. As soon as the bus turned the corner, she went out to the airport and flew to London."

"That's cool."

"Do you know what the parents used to do when the kids left for camp?"

"What?"

"As soon as the bus turned the corner, we'd start cheering, 'Free at last, free at last.'"

"Hah, hah, so did the kids."

When Janey's camp bus arrived with kids already on it, a pleasant, serene young woman got out, introduced herself to the mothers as a camp administrator, introduced the mothers to each other, and gave us a capsule biography of each of our kids. The kids squirmed, but the mothers were reassured. The driver opened the bus's belly and threw in the duffels. The camp administrator told the two young kids they could sit up front with her and other "first timers."

"You two," she said, addressing Janey and the other girl, Allison, "can sit in the back since you're experienced campers, but if I need you to help with the younger ones, can I call on you?"

"Of course," they assured her. Janey and Allison smiled at each other, their enmity vanishing into the air from which it came, kissed their mothers, and boarded the bus. Seconds later, they were seated together in the rear of the bus, talking animatedly to one another while waving their experienced hands in the general direction of us, their mothers. I wished Allison's mother a pleasant summer and got back in the car, free at last, free at last.

In the days after Janey went to camp, Ted would come to my house when he finished work, but sometimes I went to his apartment. Ted was sometimes delayed by work obligations. I envied him because I was sure he did not have to shove me from his mind; the concentration I had been holding onto with such difficulty in the morning and afternoon vanished at four o'clock. I tried to keep faith with visionary Socialist women like the organizer, Kate Richard O'Hare, whose opposition to the First World War had led to a conviction under the 1917 Espionage Act and a term in Missouri's federal prison. Or the labor organizer, Lena Morrow Lewis, whose career had taken her from the lumber camps of the North to the alkaline roads of Mexico, from the Atlantic to the Pacific Oceans, and who, in seventeen years of lecturing, never spent more than fourteen consecutive nights in one place. Or Josephine Conger-Kaneko, publisher of *Progressive Woman*, a socialist-feminist magazine that hailed the achievements of other Socialist women and kept up the spirits of rural women, the isolated comrades. I felt unworthy to be the chronicler of such women, who, I was certain, would not have let themselves be distracted as I was allowing myself to be. Sex was my preoccupation. When I was not actually making love to Ted, I was reliving our times together in fantasy. I was in lust. I reminded myself of the middle-aged ex-nuns at Brooklyn Community College, who, newly released from celibacy, had behaved like infatuated teenagers. One of them, a dean, had sat on her date's lap at a college function, and I was as embarrassed for myself now as I had been for her then.

One night at Ted's apartment, we were eating a hasty post-coital supper and watching the evening news. When McNeill-Lehrer was over, Ted turned off the television and said, "My mother would like you to come for Sunday dinner."

"I'd like that," I tried not to sound ambivalent.

But except for a few tense minutes, the meeting with Ted's parents was actually very nice, and neither too much nor too little was made of me. Ted's father, Harry, in his sixties, described his status, "in active retirement." Harry is grey-haired, barrel-chested, well-muscled; Ted's brother resembles him. Ted's mother, Meta, in her early sixties, is still a beauty, like Ingrid Bergman, but blonder. She described herself as being "in active non-retirement. I do all the things I used to do, only for fewer people." Meta was involved in local Democratic politics.

"Raising her family wasn't enough for her," Harry complained at dinner. She no sooner got finished with them, than she decided she had political ambitions."

"What else could fill the void after we left home? I hope you have your eye on high public office, Mom, it's the only suitable substitute for the likes of us."

"Are you thinking of running for office?" I asked.

"Don't encourage her," Harry barked.

Meta answered that she might run for city council, and then changed the subject.

"Ted tells me you run."

"Yes."

"I'd like to try that. I used to be very athletic when I was in school. I played basketball, volleyball, softball; whatever sport they had, I played."

I spoke encouragingly, not sure how serious her intentions were. Harry held his head, groaning, and said, "Don't encourage her."

The meal was good: chicken, fresh vegetables, salad, and strawberries for dessert. Meta had a dishwasher, but we all – not just Meta and me – cleared the table and cleaned up afterward. In the kitchen, we talked of politics, reciting the litany of the failures of Carter's administration: unemployment, inflation, the Iranian hostages. Harry declared that he did not see much difference who is elected.

Oh yes, it does make a difference, Meta and I said together. We each wanted to continue, but I yielded to Meta.

"You'll see how much difference it makes when Reagan gets elected, and I'm certain he will be elected. I don't think people who will be affected are listening to Reagan, or are not believing him, but the man means what he says. He plans to take us back fifty years; he wants to revoke the New Deal, and as the daughter of Wisconsin Farmer-Labor people, I feel I've got something to defend."

Meta turned to her husband. "You must have a short memory if you don't remember how things used to be."

"But I do remember how things used to be. Look," Harry commanded, addressing me, "do you think I used to be a helpful husband, trotting after my wife like a trained puppy, carrying plates in my hand? No, once upon a time, when I came home, meals were waiting for me, and I didn't have anything to do with preparing them or cleaning up afterward."

Meta answered, "But you do less outside the home now, and I do more. Why shouldn't you do more of the household chores?"

"I'm not saying it's not fair, but I don't have to like it, do I? I'm saying I agree with Reagan on some things. I suppose you're for ERA."

I nodded.

We took positions on the four sides of the kitchen. Ted faced his father while I faced Meta. not really against ERA, Harry?"

"Perhaps, perhaps not. I just know I liked the way things used to be, especially around here. It's not fair. We spent most of our lives under one set of rules, and now everything's been turned upside down. Women's liberation. And you're involved with it, too, right?"

I nodded.

"Look at things this way, Dad. You had a good thing going for thirty years, so now you'll have to change for the next twenty or more years. I grew up expecting I'd have what you had, and the rules changed almost as soon as I became an adult. I'll never be able to look back on what you lived through, including being treated like a hero when you came home from the war. Cheer up, Dad. You're joining the rest of the male population in this country who are trying to cope with a social revolution."

"I don't think it's fair. To live your life one way, and then on the verge of your golden sunset years, be forced to become a 'now' person. I'm a 'then' person." Harry moved one of the chairs at the kitchen table and plopped down on it.

"Are you serious, Dad, or are you just trying out an idea? I can't believe you're serious, because you're too smart a man not to understand that life is not fair. You're a survivor of the Depression, after all."

"Don't worry, your father is too smart to vote against his own interests just because he's piqued with me."

"I sure hope so, Dad. I can understand not voting better than I can understand voting for Reagan."

"Why can you understand not voting, Ted?" I asked.

"Because I'm disgusted. I understand what Mother is saying, and I agree in principle, but neither side has anything to do with me, really. Right now, the people I most identify with are those eight guys who were lost in that messed-up, futile rescue mission to get out the hostages. I was also one of this country's expendable men, marginal to both sides. All sides, really."

Harry pointed his right index finger at his son.

"You'll see. One of these days, you'll find yourself in the same situation I'm in, at the beck and call of some woman just the way I am now. It's not the way a man should end his days."

He's whining, I thought unsypathetically.

"Dad, stop feeling sorry for yourself. Your days are far from ended. You went to a war and were welcomed back as a hero. You were able to start a business and build a home. You called the shots around here. Now it's time for a little payback. And you get to share your retirement years with an attractive and stimulating woman. Other men should be as lucky."

Meta smiled, obviously pleased by Ted's tribute.

"Thank you, Ted, but in all modesty, you're only paying me my due. Harry, you're damn lucky and you know it. I keep things lively for you."

Harry looked at the three of us and shook his head.

"No use arguing with any of you. I don't stand a chance around here."

Before we left Ted's parents' home, I asked Meta if she wanted to go running with me.

"Thank you, Claire, but I think what I'm going to do is persuade one of my friends, a woman nearer my age, to start running with me. I'll feel less eccentric if I have someone whose body is as old as mine to run with me."

"But you're in great shape, Meta."

"That's nice to hear, Claire, and I thank you, I really do, for your interest, but I think I need the support of someone who is at my stage of life. At your age, people accept and even expect you to do things differently from the rest of us. But at my age, every thing I do differently from the way other people do it is seen as strange, a sign of senility, perhaps."

She smiled and added, "Sometimes folks get angry if you take off in another direction when they expect you to go along with them."

In the car going home, I asked, "Why are you angry with your dad?"

"Do I seem angry?"

"Yes. Is it because he got a 'better deal' than you did?"

"Mmm. Maybe. That's part of it. Part of it is still wanting his approval. One time, years ago, I asked him about his war experience, man-to-man, letting on that I was ready to talk about mine, you know, swap war stories. He said, 'Just put it behind you, son, and get on with your life.' Of course, if I had wanted to talk to my mother, she would have listened."

"Maybe your father knows he got a better deal and feels guilty."

"Maybe, but I doubt it. He's cranky because he had everything his way and now he doesn't."

"What does being in 'active retirement' mean?"

"He manages some property he has acquired over the years. He fusses over his investments. What he likes to do mostly is go hunting and fishing with his cronies. How are your folks doing down in retirement land?"

"When you mentioned fishing, I thought perhaps you could send your father down to Florida to stay with my father for a while. My father always loved to fish, and now he does it every day. Of course, he brings home fish to eat and eases his conscience about having so much fun. My parents are happy, I think, for the first time in their lives. They do whatever they want to do every day of their lives. My mother gardens, my father fishes. They visit friends, go to parties. They still argue all the time, but now they also win trophies at dance contests. I'm happy for them, but I wish they didn't feel so guilty about having a good time."

"Your parents followed the same pattern; both worked and now they're both ready for retirement. My parents' lives are unsychronized, and my mother is feeling too frisky to retire."

"Did your father ever want to do something else than what he did?"

"If he had some youthful ambition that he buried, I don't know what it is. But I can encourage him to think about doing things he never got to do. You and my mother sure hit it off. Like the two of you are planning to take over the town."

"As you once said to me, this is a small town. Your mother and I would probably want something bigger than Star Lake."

"That's a bit alarming."

I wondered if Ted was thinking of his father's threat, but I did not ask.

My meeting with Ted's parents had gone well, but I avoided thinking about the next step – meeting Ted's friends.

One night at my house when we'd passed the news-watching stage of our domestic routine, Ted began reminiscing about high school. I ran upstairs, pulled the Star Lake High School, Class of 1963, yearbook from my bookshelf and returned to the living room. Sitting together on the couch, we began flicking through the pages. Touching each of the square photographs of our classmates' faces, Ted gave me capsule biographies of people whose names and faces I could not even recall: this one had gone into business with his dad, that one became a dentist in Chicago. Most of the men had gone into the service after high school, then on to business or careers. The women had gone almost directly into marriage, except for the predictable few who had become teachers or nurses. Now, some of the married women whose children verged on or had entered the teen years were, like Ted's ex-wife, returning to the work force. Most of our classmates had settled in the area, although a few had moved to Chicago, and one classmate lived in Los Angeles. Only two classmates, a male and a female, had not married.

Ted tapped one smiling face.

"I think this one's divorced."

"That makes three of us out of the Class of 63's what – 225 students?"

"That's about right. Three divorces and three deaths."

Ted tapped the faces of three boys. They had all gone into the service right after high school. They had all been on the football team.

"Three dead and five wounded. And we were in Vietnam during the early part of the conflict. Imagine what this country's high school yearbooks in the late Sixties must look like. All the holes."

Ted turned the pages of the yearbook to the section of candid photos. All the wounded men had also been athletes. But all the dead men had played on the football team with Ted.

He pointed to the faces of his dead buddies in the team photograph. Then his finger moved to the candid photos of the team in action during a game or clowning after practice. His finger caressed their faces. I moved my finger onto the page and touched the faces of these boys who looked more like sons to us now than peers, these children who had been sent to war.

"Good God, how young they were."

"Oh, yes, we were young."

For seconds, perhaps a minute, we fixed our eyes on the yearbook pages. Then Ted moved his finger back to the team photo and touched a face.

"That's my best friend, then and now, Bob McNeill."

"I remember him." Would I ever forget my hallway tormentor?

"Another vet?"

"Oh, yes, Bob's a vet. Now he's a policeman."

"And he's still your good buddy?"

"My closest friend."

We continued to stare at the photo, although I was not concentrating on it, and I do not think Ted was, either.

"Bob's married to another classmate, Sally Licari."

"I remember Sally." I flipped the pages back to the front of the book where the results of our senior poll were listed. "Yes, she was voted the most popular girl. I remember her as a nice girl . . ."

Legends of Good Women

"She still is."

". . . who threatened no one."

Ted gave me a sharp look.

"I'm not taking anything away from Sally," I explained, annoyed with myself for justifying the remark. "I was commenting on our primitive adolescent mentality. Sally was pretty, but not extraordinary; friendly, genuinely friendly, a nice, unchallenging, unexceptional person who conformed to the expectations of the era, which were much narrower, you will admit, for girls than for boys. Michelle, your ex-wife, was voted . . ."

"Please just say 'Michelle;' don't label her 'my ex-wife'."

"All right, Michelle was voted prettiest, but she would never have been voted 'most popular girl' because she made the other girls feel inferior. And, you'll notice, no girl won more than one title, while you were voted most popular boy, best athlete and most likely to succeed. You were a boy; you would have been allowed to be eccentric. Others of us were not. Me, for example, I don't come up in the poll at all."

Ted shrugged.

"A lot of people didn't come up. That doesn't mean they were not liked or even unpopular. You're too sore on the subject. We just weren't thinking about you. You seemed to be self-sufficient, content with your own company, somewhat stuckup – at least that's how you seemed to us, so we let you alone. All right, maybe we were a bit intimidated by your intelligence. But if you had met us halfway, or tried to be friendly, we would have responded."

"Perhaps. But if our classmates thought I was smart, why wasn't I voted the most intelligent? Who got that? Beverly Halversen, whose grades were not nearly as good as mine."

"Beverly was voted most intelligent because she lobbied for the title. If you had made an effort, you would have won."

"But why should I have tried to persuade people of something that was a fact. Other titles are subjective, but intelligence is demonstrated in grades. You, for example, were voted the best athlete on the undisputed evidence of your ability. I should have been able to claim 'most intelligent' for the same reason."

"You're still angry about what happened so long ago?"

"I guess I am. Not angry, hurt. I'm still hurt."

"Aah, poor neglected genius." Ted reached over and hugged me to him. Just before I became forgetful of everything, I remembered a fact from our past lives.

"Didn't you used to go with Sally before you went with Michelle?"

"Yes."

"Why did you break up with Sally?"

"Oh, Sally and I liked each other very much. We still do. But Bob wanted Sally so much, that I guess Sally and I recognized it as a force of nature. I stepped aside."

"Why?"

"I don't know. Anyway, that was then and this is now, and I have something else in mind."

Later I asked Ted if he saw Bob and Sally often. He said he saw them more than any of his other friends. He asked if I wanted to have dinner with Bob and Sally soon and I said of course I would.

CHAPTER

In the car driving out to the McNeill's house, the Sunday after the dinner with Ted's parents, Ted asked me to open the glove compartment. When I did, a pile of papers fell out.

"The first time I got into this car, I thought you were the neatest — I mean tidiest — man I'd ever met. Now this mess makes me feel more at home with you. You have a touch, just a touch of slob, just as I do."

"Well, the first time, I was trying to make a good impression. Weren't you? Anyway, it's time for you to see the warts, although," Ted took his eyes briefly away from the road and made a mock frown at me, "this is about as bad as it gets."

"All right, I'll try to respond in kind; that is, if I can think of any warts. Oh, I have one here." I tapped my wrist."

Ted smiled; after a pause, he said, "What I want you to find in that pile is a recent photograph of Bob. He's changed a lot since high school, and he'd notice if you seemed surprised.

The photo I pulled from the stack was of Bob and Sally standing in front of their house. Bob had aged.

The hairline of our yearbook picture had retreated from its widow's peak, exposing scoops of scalp. Facial lines extending from his nostrils etched his grinning mouth in parentheses. I was jolted, not so much by the aging I saw in Bob's face, but by what I could not put a name to until I studied the eyes, mentally cutting them from the smile, and felt the impact of the bitterness in them. Although I had known Bob, as I had known all my classmates, only from a distance, in high school I though he was sneaky – now I would add manipulative – and I still thought so, just as I still wondered why Ted had him as a friend. Sally still looked much as she had in high school: unexceptionally pretty, with a face more heart-shaped than oval, a wide mouth smiling as eagerly in the snapshot as it had in our yearbook, and dark brown eyes. I separated the eyes from the rest of the face and sensed anxiety in them. I remembered Sally as confident and enthusiastic, but perhaps I was reading too much into faces and expressions.

"Bob has changed a lot physically. Sally looks almost the same. How have they changed in personality?"

"Mmmm – superficially, Bob seems the same, like a big kid at times, but I should warn you, he's bitter about the war."

"Still?"

"Yes, still."

"Is this a set-up? Am I being brought out for a hate Jane Fonda session?"

"No. Do you really think I'd do something like that? But this is the big controversy of our generation and we'll probably argue about it for the rest of our lives, for years to come, anyhow. And Bob is still sensitive on the subject, so I wanted to prepare you."

"For what? What are you suggesting I do if Bob's sensitivity surfaces?"

"I'm not suggesting that you handle it in any particular way. I just didn't want you to be hurt or offended if he comments on your anti-war activism."

"How has Sally changed?"

"She also seems superficially the same. But she's less lighthearted than she was. She is a conscientious mother, a dedicated nurse, and, of course, Bob can be a handful."

We were about ten miles from the center of town when Ted turned off the highway onto a road with mail boxes stuck on posts. Two miles farther, he pulled into a driveway leading up to and past a modest white Victorian frame house. Fruit trees studded the lawn, along with an overturned tricycle; scattered toys, among which I recognized a Barbie's white styrene hair; and a child's wagon, in which a ginger cat sat looking as if it expected us to report to it first.

"Hello, Oscar," Ted called.

I asked and was told yes, there was indeed another cat, probably at the moment hiding fussily in the house, named Felix.

As we got out of the car and walked around to the front of the house, the door opened and Bob came out. He leaned against the door frame, pushing the screen door open with his left foot. He held a twelve ounce can of beer in his right hand, from which he took a long sip while watching us over the can's rim as we came on to the porch. His cheeks were puffed with beer after he had sipped; he gulped, moved one finger away from the can to point at us. We waited self consciously as he swallowed.

"Did you two plan your wardrobe together?"

Ted and I looked at each other. Until that moment neither of us had realized that we were both wearing white oxford cloth shirts with the sleeves rolled up and tan chino pants. Bob was dressed more casually in jeans and a striped, short-sleeved tee shirt. Bob transferred the beer can to his left hand, we shook hands and greeted one another, then he let us walk past him into the entry hall. I was expecting, hoping, to see Sally and their children, but no one else came. I followed Ted into the living room. Bob offered us drinks from an array on a dry sink that included an ice-lined bowl of beer cans, bottles of liquor, mixers, glasses, and more ice. Ted accepted beer, and seeing no wine, I asked for a glass of club soda. Ted sat down on the couch, Bob sat near him, and I took a chair facing them across a glass-topped wooden chest that served as a coffee table.

"I remember you; we had biology together sophomore year, didn't we?"

"Yes, we did."

"Yes, you were a good student, always had your lab reports in on time, got good grades."

There was an opening, but I could not think of what to say to fill it.

"But, Claire," Bob resumed, then paused to sip and cross his left ankle over his right knee before continuing, "my clearest memory of you is in the hallway during class change. You always seemed to be at your locker. Do you remember, Ted? Every time we went into the hall, there she was, at her locker."

Ted did not respond. I kept my eyes on Bob's face and said nothing.

"And then you went off to college while some of the rest of us went to war. I was away in Vietnam in those years, but folks back home were good enough to keep me up to date on my classmates. According to my sources, you went to Mississippi to help the Negroes. Then you went back to college and became active in the anti-war movement at Madison, married one of the leaders after graduation, and went off to New York City. Is that correct?"

"Yes." I looked at Ted. So far, apart from his hint at racist feelings, Bob seemed bland.

"So tell me, Claire, what have you been doing since?"

I summarized my life, giving the bare facts about my divorce, my daughter, avoiding words like "denied tenure" or "fired," listing jobs with the phrase "And then I worked . . ." and concluding with "I was offered and accepted a job at Fontbonne."

"You're not Catholic, are you?"

"No."

"I'm not much of a practicing Catholic myself, but I find it interesting that a non-Catholic would take a job at a Catholic college."

"I'm not the only Protestant and there are even several Jews at Fontbonne. It's now considered important at Catholic institutions of higher education to expose students to representatives of other faiths and ideologies."

"Oh, yeah. Vatican Two. So how do you like being back in Star Lake? I can't imagine living anywhere else or doing anything else but what I do – I guess Ted has told you that since my warrior days I've been a police officer – but how must the old town seem to someone who's been used to the big city?"

"It seems fine, just fine."

Where was Sally, I wondered. I hoped she and the children would appear before Bob and Ted drank more beer.

"Well, that's good. Hey, Ted, looks like you're ready for another brew."

Bob rose, took Ted's empty beer can to the dry sink, pulled a full can from the bowl, and poured it into Ted's glass. He took a can of beer for himself, popped the tab, and gulped from the can. Then, his cheeks puffed with beer, he pointed to my glass and widened his eyes. I shook my head, no, I did not want a refill. Then Bob sat down again and began discussing the Star Lake Park and Recreation softball league with Ted.

"Enjoy this season while it lasts, old man; next year we have to join the over-the-hill guys. Are you ready for that?"

"Bob and I play for a team that my company sponsors," Ted explained, "but next year we're ineligible to play in the regular division; we have to join the men's over-thirty-five division."

"Will you still play, Ted?" Bob asked.

"I don't know. I might continue to manage the team I sponsor, and see if I can't move it up to Division One. What about you?"

"Probably not, if you're not playing."

I was able to follow that conversation, but then they moved on to a litany of Wisconsin athletics. I heard references to the Bucks, the Brewers, the Badgers; I heard references to particular players, games, down to details of the plays. I tried to focus on what was being said, but found myself unable to follow or retain the substance of the dialogue. I was baffled and excluded, as I realized Bob intended me to be. But Ted was helping him to put me in my place. To distract myself from the resentment slowly overtaking me, I studied the room. The house's exterior showed neglect – it needed paint and the eaves drooped – but the inside, what I now saw of it, was the product of meticulous, devoted care. the floors, the frames of the two side windows, and the frames of the bowed front window were all of oak, brought up, with dedicated polishing, to a liquid, golden sheen. The oak banquette in the front window was lined on top with bright yellow corduroy cushions, a color which was picked up again in the pillows on the couch that was covered in grey flannel, as were the two chairs facing the couch. A large oval rag rug covered the floor, and shutters lined all the windows. A large globe lamp descended from a pole in a ceiling fixture that had once held a chandelier. The room was painted a dull white, but the details of the molding on the walls and ceiling were outlined in soft grey. A plant arrangement filled the dry sink which stood on one side of the entry into the hall, and a cabinet containing stereo equipment stood on the other. The walls were bare, except for a tapestry depicting women in nineteenth century dress seated around a table making a quilt. As I studied the room, concluding that hands other than Bob's were responsible for its welcoming attractiveness, I succeeded in blanking out the substance, but not the bantering tone of the conversation. Men have to talk to each other that way, I thought. Even close friends like Bob and Ted have to speak to each other above the lines.

"Where are Sally and the kids?" I asked.

"Yes," Ted echoed. "Where are they?"

Bob answered Ted: "Sally's out in the kitchen and the kids are with her. She's making dinner for our honored guest."

Then he turned to me. "Perhaps you'd like to go out and give her a hand," he said, smiling at me over the top of his beer can.

"Why don't we all go out and give her a hand?" I replied, smiling back.

Footsteps came toward us from the back of the house, and soon Sally, looking like a teenager in blue jeans and a yellow camp shirt, entered the room shepherding one girl about six who was holding a platter of skillfully carved vegetables and another girl who was probably ten who held a bowl of dip.

"Claire, oh it's so good to see you," Sally exclaimed. "You look wonderful. And, Ted, it's good you could come and bring Claire."

The girls placed the food on the table. Sally put down a pile of paper napkins and then introduced her daughters, who came forward solemnly as she presented them. "This is Daphne," Sally said, touching the shoulder of her older daughter, "and this is Enid."

Each girl held out her right hand, as I knew their mother had instructed them to do; I wanted to hug them, but, maintaining the formality they were striving for, shook their hands and said "How do you do" to each. Both girls wore jeans. Daphne looked at me directly, her hands on her hips, while Enid was coy, rolling her tongue around her mouth, and crossing one foot over the other. They were both pretty, but Enid, as she well knew, was cute.

"Where's your girl?" Daphne asked. She had no doubt been told about Janey and was disappointed I had not brought her as a playmate.

"She's away at camp."

"Do you miss her?"

"Yes, but I know she's having a good experience at camp, so I don't mind that she is away."

"Do you cry for her?" Enid wanted to know.

"No, because I know she is busy with sports and meeting new friends."

"Girls, why don't you pass the vegetables and dip around."

When they had done that chore, Sally assigned them to choose an album "and give it to your father to put on the stereo."

The girls went to the album rack next to the stereo, and without hesitation picked out an album – it seemed to have been preselected – and solemnly handed it to Bob, who, with that delicacy most males have for technology and seldom have for humans, placed it, thumb and index finger barely touching its surface, on the stereo. It was the Beatles' "Sergeant Pepper," and I was surprised at the choice. Bob nodded at me, as if to say, "this one's for you, kid."

"I'm sorry I wasn't here to greet you when you arrived," Sally apologized, "but I got a late start. One of the other nurses at the hospital was sick, and I had to work an extra shift."

"Sally, you should have called me," Ted said, "and we could have come for dinner another time."

"No, I wanted you to come. I was so pleased when Ted told me he was bringing you, Claire. I'm so happy to see you again."

I was flattered by Sally's genuine eagerness to see me, but puzzled, too, as we had barely known each other in high school. Also, I was embarrassed, because I could not honestly respond to her warmth.

Bob, who had been standing at the stereo, walked to the dry sink and took another can of beer. Whoosh went the tab. Was it his third or fourth since Ted and I had come to the house? And how many before? Sally was facing me and away from Bob, but I was sure I saw a flicker of anxiety on her face.

"Bob," Sally said, turning to face him, "I forgot to bring out pop for the girls. Would you please go and get it?"

There was a pause. I could hear a question being silently asked: "Why didn't you bring the pop?" Sally's eyes remained on Bob's face. Shrugging, he yielded and went to the kitchen. Sally asked questions and I gave answers about when I had actually returned to

Star Lake, how Janey liked her school, how my parents were, and how I liked teaching at Fontbonne.

"Gosh," Sally said wonderingly, after I told her I liked teaching at Fontbonne, "being a student at a woman's college seems to me one of the best things in the world. Imagine teaching at one. I want my girls to go to college, maybe Fontbonne, maybe a school away from here. But back when we were in high school, going to college seemed something only superior students like you were meant to do. You were always so focused, Claire; you knew what you were going to do. The rest of us were twits. At least I was."

"You were a twit, Mom?" Daphne asked, with a hint of incipient smart aleckiness that was in full bloom in my child.

"Yes, I was, but I outgrew it long before I had you, and now I'm a very smart person and don't you forget it."

Bob returned with two smallish glasses of coke which the girls accepted in disappointed silence. Ted had been listening to Sally and me while Bob and been out of the room, but now Bob claimed his attention when he sat down again in one of the chairs facing the couch.

I rose from my chair and went to examine the tapestry, which was four feet by six feet. "S. Licari McNeill" was woven into the bottom right hand corner.

"Sally, this is lovely," I exclaimed.

Sally leaped up and came to my side, the girls popping after her like jumping beans.

"Oh, do you really think so?"

Indeed I did. Sally had created a nineteenth century room, a room such as the one we were in might have been one hundred years before. A woman of about fifty sat at one end of a large table in the room's center, and two younger women, probably her grown daughters, sat at the other end. In the center were two other women, older than the daughters and younger than the mother, who probably were relatives or neighbors. All the women were working on a quilt spread across the table, while two children sat with their backs to the viewer, working at another task, which seemed to be matching pieces of cloth. All the women were concentrating on their work, but conversation had preceded the moment Sally had captured, and would follow afterward. I marveled at the way a silent, harmonious relationship and such vivid human expression had been evoked by the simple manipulation of colored fibres. The process seemed even more miraculous to me than paint, which was more pliable and cohesive than separate threads being woven in and out of other strands. To my eyes, the tapestry had the technical skill of hangings I had seem in museums, but the quality of the portraits reminded me of the genre paintings of the sixteenth and seventeenth century Dutch and Flemish schools. Sally's tapestry was clearly American in subject, but the scene was not flat or primitive. This was more than craft, this was art.

"Oh, do you really like it?" Sally was asking, testing me, sure I was only being nice.

"This is fine," I said authoritatively. There was silence behind us; then Bob suggested to Ted that they go outside and pitch horseshoes. Ted agreed and extended the invitation to Sally and me. We both declined. Daphne and Enid began tugging at their mother and asking when they would eat dinner.

"Go eat some more vegetables and let me enjoy my visit with Claire. We'll eat soon."

I asked Sally when she had learned to weave, and she told me she had more or less taught herself when she was a child, making use of an old loom that had been in her family. I asked when had she made this weaving. She told me one winter when Daphne was a baby, she had begun to think of her own mother and grandmother, and had started to remember stories that had come down to her.

"I was feeling blue one day, and started rummaging through the house for some work, not a household chore, but something that would cheer me up. I found this loom in the attic and decided to use it. Later the idea of making pictures of the stories I had heard as a child came to me. I made designs and wove them on the loom."

"Are there more?"

"Oh, yes, lots, upstairs in the room I've divided into a workroom for me and a playroom for the kids. Come on, I'd like to show you the house."

Sally's home, doll-sized as my own was, revealed a talent I had always envied: a skill with found objects. Common household items – rug beaters, old spatulas, and wooden spoons took on uncommon significance displayed on walls or placed among plants, bowls of dried ferns and flowers, or herb bouquets. The curtains and bedspreads were obviously homemade, not because they were clumsy, as mine would have been, but because they were unmistakably original. The layout of the house was simple: a dining room and a living room on either side of the entrance hall, a kitchen and pantry at the rear of the house. A flight of stairs in the central hallway led to two bedrooms and a bath in the front and sides of the house, and in the rear, a door leading to the work and play room. When Sally opened the door, I saw that almost the entire rear wall had been turned into a window; the front part of the room had been sectioned off by partitions into the children's play area, and shelves with their toys marked off still smaller spaces that were clearly Daphne's space, Enid's space, and sisterly space. Beyond, where the afternoon sun was bright, was the workspace to which Sally led me. Bins and chests for her materials were on one side and burlap sacks on the other; her loom was set up in the center, facing through the window to the back yard and neighboring fields and houses. It was certainly a space to dream and create in, and I knew beyond question that Bob had made no contribution to the construction of this room, that Sally had paid for it from her salary.

"May I see them?" I indicated the rolled up sacks and rugs on the side of the room. Sally nodded and began unfurling a tapestry, as large as the wall hanging in the living room, of a scene of women picketing in front of a building with a sign that read 'Oliver Mining Company.'

"Oh, Sally," I almost moaned, "this is so good."

Embarrassed, but very pleased, Sally explained, "Most people don't think of people from southern Italy as early settlers, but my folks were on the frontier. My father's people came earlier and became dairy farmers; that's why my father started the family's cheese business. My mother's folks came later and were laborers. One of my great-grandfathers was a miner on the Minnesota iron range and knew Carlo Tresca when he came to organize the miners for the I.W.W. I like to imagine the life the people in my family led, but I also like scenes closer to our own time because my mother and grandmothers spoke of events they had actually lived through and I remember the feeling that came into their voices as they spoke of their childhood."

Sally showed me some of these scenes; almost all of them showed women, men appeared only occasion ally. Noticing that Sally had left one of the sacks unopened, and thinking to spare her the labor of fetching it, I went to the sack and began to open it. Sally had been studying one of her weavings, and when she noticed what I was doing, she ran to my side.

"No, not that one;" she exclaimed, "that was one of my early failures and I'd rather not show it."

I relaxed my hold on the sack and Sally took it from me, but as she did, the sack fell open, and I saw blackened threads on the weaving inside; I smelt the sourness of scorched fibres.

"You didn't burn it?"

Sally shrugged and bent over the sack, avoiding an answer.

"Me want to go downstairs. Me hungry," Enid whined.

"Yeah, Mom," Daphne chorused. "When are we going to eat?"

"Soon, my dears, soon."

I helped Sally to repack the tapestries and the four of us descended to the living room, where Ted and Bob, having finished their horseshoe game, were laughing together. Bob was laughing very hard, in fact guffawing and slapping his leg like a teenager. Even Ted, who in my short experience of the two men together, was clearly the more mature and restrained of the pair, was now behaving in a way I could only describe as adolescent. Sally and I asked what was so funny and said we would like to laugh too, but the men just shook their heads and, when they were more in control of themselves, said they were sharing a joke we would not appreciate.

"It's stupid," Ted said.

"Professor Schaefer," Bob added, smiling meanly, "you wouldn't appreciate our humor, believe me."

Legends of Good Women

I stared into Bob's eyes and he stared into mine. We understood each other, or rather, I understood that he was isolating me from Ted, staking off experiences like humor, which only they, the men, could share. Bob darted his eyes at Ted, who was leaning back on the couch and staring at the ceiling with an innocent, silly grin on his face, and then back at me. Bob obviously felt some kind of triumph in having made Ted behave foolishly.

"Sit down, Claire, I'm just going to get dinner ready."

"Let me keep you company."

I did not want Bob to think he had succeeded in sending me off to do chores, but neither did I want to spend another minute in his company, or in Ted's either. Fuming, I followed Sally and the girls to the kitchen, where my anger melted, for Sally's kitchen was so well organized, I would have enjoyed working in it. The original cabinets—wooden doors and drawers below, workspace in the center, and glass doors on the cupboards above—were still in place. The stove, refrigerator, and sinks were modern but not too recent, and everything was clean and cheerful looking because of the white paint on the walls and stencilled trim around the windows.

Sally had obviously labored for hours in preparation. Crisply fried chicken was draining on the stove, a beautifully composed salad sat in a glass bowl, awaiting only dressing and tossing, ears of corn were piled near a large pot of water being brought to a boil, and a loaf of homemade bread was cooling on the kitchen window sill. Although everything looked ready, I was about to ask if I could help when I heard Ted and Bob coming toward the kitchen

"Could you use some help, Sally?" Ted asked in a bloated voice.

"Dear, could you use some help." Bob echoed.

"Not as much now as I could have used earlier, but please stay on good behavior."

Sally gave us assignments, and soon we were in the dining room, eating a meal that was even better tasting than it looked. Bob and Ted were concentrating on making themselves sober again; they lifted their forks carefully, and said "please pass me" often and with elaborate enunciation. Daphne and Enid put aside their skill as attention-getters in order to watch the grownups, or rather, the men, whose disguises they had easily penetrated. Remembering certain social occasions Janey and I had shared when she was closer to the McNeill girls' ages, I realized that an otherwise capable adult male is irresistible to little girls when he is temporarily not in control of himself. Sally and I maintained the conversation. I learned that Sally had become a licensed practical nurse before she had married, and hoped to continue her education when the girls were older.

"I'd like to be an R.N. and set up practice as a nurse-midwife.

"Sally, you remind me of a student I had years ago at Richmond Community College."

"Really?"

"Yes, she was a nurse and an artist, too, as you are."

The word "artist" had an impact on everyone; suddenly Bob, Ted, Daphne and Enid were looking with amazement at Sally.

"In fact, she decided to give up nursing when she was accepted at Yale University. In one of her essays, she wrote that she had found the courage to give up a secure career to begin a risky one because she had nearly died of a strange and never really diagnosed illness, and when she recovered, vowed never to fear taking chances again. But the principal way she resembled you, as I remember her, was that quality of alertness you have, that way of listening to what is said and done around you and putting separate pieces of information together into new patterns. I never saw my student's art work, but her own quality was so memorable, so strong, I'm sure I would have admired it. I certainly admire your tapestries, Sally. I think your work is really fine."

There was a short silence during which everyone else watched Sally, who darted nervous glances at each of us and then looked down at her plate.

"Pass me the chicken, Sal."

Sally passed the platter. Enid tugged at her arm and said, "Me want meat cut, Mommy." Daphne toppled her milk glass. Sally wiped up the spill with her napkin. Recognizing the diversions as a collective McNeill assault on Sally's emerging individuality, I continued to stroke it.

"Have you ever tried to sell your work, Sally?"

"No, no, I mean the weaving is something I do because it gives me so much pleasure. I never thought anyone would pay money for my work."

"You used the word 'work,' Sally. Why shouldn't someone pay you for your work if it is good?"

"I don't know why not; I just never thought of what I do as art work people would pay money for, hang up in their houses."

"Well, it is, believe me. I like your work so much, I'd pay money for it. I'm serious. I'd like to commission a weaving from you. You've weaved scenes from your own family life; how about weaving a scene from mine? If I told you a story about my mother's life, could you weave a tapestry of it?"

"Yes, I could. Are you serious, Claire? Do you really want me to weave something for you?"

"Yes, I do. I think it would be a lovely gift for my mother. Let's talk about your fee."

While I had begun negotiating with Sally, Bob had been chewing noisily on his chicken, and throwing the bones down on his plate. I had heard him begin another sporting conversation with Ted, but Ted answered Bob shortly and distractedly, restoring my good feeling toward him by paying primary attention to Sally and me. Bob appeared to be concentrating on his food, but as soon as I said the work "fee," he pushed his chair back, rose, and marched to the kitchen.

"More brew, Ted? Anyone?"

"No thanks."

Sally's face went from pleasure to alarm.

"Claire, I'll talk to you about it another time, okay? I've never thought about selling my work, so I don't even know what my fee should be."

"Sure, Sally, but remember, I'm serious. I'll call you during the week and we'll discuss it."

"All right. Come on, everyone, help me stack the dishes so we can have dessert."

"If I don't stack the dishes, does that mean I can't have dessert?" Bob haggled.

Sally did not answer him, but Ted nudged him and commanded, "Just stack, man." We all went out to the kitchen bearing plates and cutlery which Sally stacked in her dishwasher. After Sally had made coffee, dished homemade strawberry ice cream, and filled a plate with homemade chocolate chip cookies, we went back to the dining room to eat our dessert. Bob was silent, almost glum, the beginning of a mean drunk, I thought. Ted spoke to him about the softball league, about work, but Bob responded only in monosyllables. Sally's anxiety was palpable. She told the girls they might watch television for an hour before bedtime, and then, in the evident expectation that conversation would ensure good behavior, directed a question at me.

"Your students at Fontbonne must be very different from the students you had in New York."

"Yes, they are . . ."

As if realizing she had not given me enough fuel for discourse, Sally rushed to add:

"Were all your students in New York as interesting as the nurse who became an artist"

"Some were. I remember the special ones. The nurse was special. She worked in a hospital on the lower east side of Manhattan, near Chinatown, and wrote about her patients in one of her essays. I learned from her that Chinese women have a very difficult time giving birth because their pelvises are so narrow. When Chinese women give birth to baby girls, no one comes to see them or the babies. The women cry and say, "My husband will insist on having another baby because he wants a son, and the pain is so terrible, I don't want to have another child."

Suddenly I found Enid at my elbow, asking, "Don't Chinese men like liddew girls?"

"They prefer boys. Chinese men, and probably other kinds of men don't cherish their daughters as I am sure your father cherishes you."

"What's 'chewish'?"

"To love very much."

Enid looked quickly at her father and then down at the floor. Sally reached out her hand and Enid came to her, nestling against her side.

"Yes, Enid is a cherished child. So is Daphne."

"Just because a man wants to have sons, doesn't mean he doesn't love his daughters."

"Of course not," we three other grownups reassured Bob.

"I mean, it's reasonable, isn't it, for a Chinese man, or any other man, for that matter, to want a son? I mean, you've got a son, Ted. Aren't you glad you've got a son?"

"Yes, but I'd be glad if I had a daughter, too. Your girls are great, Bob."

"I know that. Don't think I don't know my kids are great. Right, Enid? Right, Daphne?"

Daphne came into the dining room. Both girls looked silently at their father, then Daphne took Enid's hand and they returned to their posts in front of the tv set.

"I'd like to hear more about your students, Claire," Sally prompted.

I felt no guilt at all about monopolizing the conversation. I did riffs on my memorable students, beginning with the apprentice undertaker. Seeing no yawns or glassy eyes when I had finished the mortician's tale, I went on to tell Sally, Bob, and Ted the fireman's tale.

"They don't seem at all like typical undergraduates; they seem more like peers," Ted observed.

"Yes," Sally agreed, "they seem like such interesting people. Staten Island must have been a wonderful experience for you."

"It was, Sally. Of course, the class the fireman was in was special, my all-time favorite. It was an evening class of twenty-five adults, all of them working, all but one married, who, in the aggregate, had produced over eighty children. I always have my writing classes work in groups of five or six, so they get to know each other by the end of the term. There is so little opportunity for social life in commuter colleges that students have told me my class was the only place where they were able to make friends. That methodology seemed to have been especially effective in that class, with one outcome I had not foreseen. I brought these people together; I introduced them to some good books; they became enthusiastic about ideas; they became decent writers; they became more confident; and they became turned on to each other. Everyone drove to class from work, but a number of cars remained on the parking lot afterward. I have often wondered how many extra-marital affairs had started in that class, and if any marriages broke up as a result. I had a fantasy once of being pursued by irate spouses."

I paused, reflecting on my former students, and then continued.

"Apart from releasing libidos, my class helped the students to produce some memorable writing, not only their essays, but the journals I asked them to keep. I had the class write a journal entry at the beginning of each class meeting and share what they had written with the other members of the group, and if they wanted to, with the rest of the class. One evening one woman read aloud what she had written about disliking being married to a cop. She wrote, 'We used to have other friends, but now we don't. Cops don't have any other friends but cops. And when they get together, they talk about their work. I think there are a lot of cops who are dangerous and ought not to have weapons in their possession. I hate the violence of police work, and I hate the fear I have for my husband. Each time I iron his shirt, I wonder if it will be stained with his blood before his tour is over.'"

When I had told the tale of the cop's wife, I sensed tension rather than appreciation, and then was aware, as I had probably known subconsciously, that Sally was a cop's wife and my tale may have had relevance to her situation. I was certain that there were connections when I saw Sally keep her eyes steadfastly on her plate. Bob was giving me a keen stare.

"Now my wife could never write an essay like that, could you, Sal?"

"What do you think I would write about being a cop's wife?"

"Well, that is has its difficult moments; any woman married to a man in uniformed service has some tense times, but it's a secure life—health benefits, pension, disability protection. Some women are never satisfied. Jeese, what does that woman who wrote that composition want? I don't think she had any business writing about her husband like that and letting all those people know their private stuff because she doesn't like his friends. God, Sally, I hope you don't ever let me down like that."

Husband and wife stared eloquently at each other. Then Sally told her daughters to go to bed. When they responded with the familiar, "Oh, ma, not yet," plea, she looked at them with a stern expression I had not expected, and they stopped their protesting and obeyed. They paused before going up to their room and Sally said, "Go on up, girls, I'll come up in a few minutes to say goodnight." She followed them with her eyes as they went upstairs, and then returned her attention to me.

"Claire, Staten Island must have been a really interesting place to teach."

"Yeah," Bob chorused, "why would you leave all those in-ter-es-ting students to come here and teach the virgins of Fontbonne? There's a naughty nickname we have locally for the school. Have you heard it?"

"No," I lied, having learned from my students early in my teaching days that the school was referred to by crude locals as "Cuntbun."

"Well, I won't tell it to you until I know you better. But how come you came back to teach here when you had a good or better job in New York?"

"I was fired, Bob; it's as simple as that."

Bob smiled, pleased at my response.

"Okay, but why did you decide to come here?? Couldn't you get a job anywhere else?"

"Yes, but Fontbonne seemed like the best job available."

"Really?"

"Yes."

Sally began clearing dessert dishes and coffee cups. Bob and Ted got up from the table and sauntered into the living room. I helped Sally clear and followed her into the kitchen. Sally set the dishes down on the sink and I helped her load them into the dishwasher.

"I'm going upstairs to say goodnight to the girls, Claire. Why don't you go back inside?"

"And interrupt the men at their port and cigars? No, I think I'll go outside for a while."

"All right. I'll be down in a few minutes."

I opened the kitchen door and went out into the back yard. It was too dark to see Sally's garden in detail, but I could discern in the outlines and patterns of her flowerbeds the evidence of her artistry. I had not even tried to start a garden in my yard because I had never even been able to keep house plants alive in my New York apartment. In minutes Sally joined me and the two of us watched the night sky, the trees in her back yard, and the trees, yards, and lighted houses of Sally's neighbors.

"I don't know if you're glad you've come back to live here, Claire; but I am. I never knew you in high school, you were kind of a mystery to everyone, but I hope we'll see each other often now."

I told Sally I also hoped that we would see each other often, withholding the comment that we would have little choice in the matter, since our menfolk seemed joined at the hip. The usual way out of these love-her-hate-him situations for my liberated friends was to see the wife without the husband. I wondered to myself if Sally could maintain a social life apart from Bob, whose company I wanted to avoid as much as possible.

Sally and I stood giggling at each other in the moonlight, as if we had just decided to go steady. Our friendship plighted, we turned and walked back to the house, our arms around each other's waists—I had to reach down to put my arm around Sally and walk leaning at an angle. At the door we dropped arms and giggled at each other again. Our good mood lasted until we went into the living room. Bob had resumed drinking beer and had persuaded Ted to join him. As Bob was a practiced drunk, he was seemingly more clear-headed than Ted, who had had much less beer than Bob, but was obviously inebriated. So much for that nice statement about not drinking when he drove. I did not trust myself to speak and thought I would simply leave and walk the fifteen or more miles home. Ted mollified me somewhat by standing up, taking the car keys out of his pocket and handing them to me.

"Shall we go?"

"Hey, man, you're still able to drive. Why are you giving her the keys?"

"Because I've had too much to drink to drive."

"Aw, man, you've got to be kidding. Handing over the keys like some kid. A good man drunk is better than a woman driver sober. Women drivers, no survivors."

"Claire's a good driver. I'd trust her with my life. I have to. I can't trust my life to me."

Summoning his habitual gentility, Ted thanked Sally for the wonderful meal and we left. Once outside the house, Ted was completely confused by the darkness and actually leaned on me for support as we went to the car. I opened the passenger door and helped him inside. As I pulled the car out of the driveway, I paused to smile and wave at Bob and Sally, who were watching us from the porch. As we reached the highway, I looked down at Ted, as he lay, barely conscious, against the front seat. His mouth was open and the sweat on his face gleamed in the glow from lights of oncoming cars. I decided that, instead of taking Ted home with me, I would bring him to his house, leave the car, and call a taxi to take me home. I heard Ted mumbling.

"What did you say?"

"I said, I guess I've shown you another wart."

I grinned, in spite of myself, almost loving him again. He mumbled something else.

"Excuse me?"

"I said, wasn't that a great evening?"

Every man I have ever known, my beloved included, suffers from what I call "field blindness," that is, the inability to see what is reality going on among people with whom they are in daily, even intimate, contact.

"Isn't it pretty to think so?" I answered.

CHAPTER

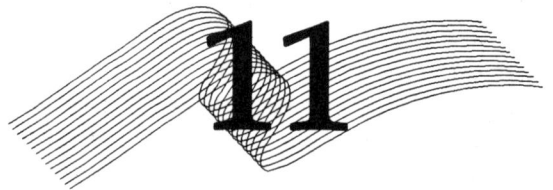

The next day, Sunday, I went to church. Before pausing for the sharing of joys and sorrows, Reverend suggested that that part of the service be renamed "the sharing of joys, sorrows, and concerns." The congregation stared back at him in resistance.

"No?" he retreated. "All right, forget the name change. Just a thought."

Despite a perceived rebuff, Reverend Dan went on to preach a rather good sermon on the evils of lying, which began, he told us, with lying to ourselves. After service, I listened to Kathy and Rebecca discuss the lobbying and fund raising they had been doing on behalf of the Star Lake Women's Resource Center's campaign to set up a battered women's shelter, which would serve not only Star Lake, but six surrounding communities as well.

"Is spouse abuse that serious a problem here?"

Kathy and Rebecca looked at me in astonishment, so I quickly answered my own naive question.

"Oh, of course it is. I've heard the cry in the night from a neighbor's house; I've seen tell-tale marks on women's faces in the supermarkets; I've heard the curt, abusive words men make to women as they leave the bars together. But I was still innocent when I left here for New York, and while I could accept the big city's wickedness, I always cherished the ideal of my hometown's innocence, and it's still hard for me to part with that myth, even after all you two have told me to disabuse me of it."

Kathy and Rebecca had filled me in on spicy items of local gossip; one county judge was widely believed to be a cocaine user and dealer. This same judge would routinely dismiss or lower charges against defendants in drug cases, but would ask women who charged their husbands with assault, "What did you do to provoke him?" Kathy and Rebecca had tried unsuccessfully to persuade the town's two women lawyers to run against Judge Somsen. Their only hope for getting rid of him lay with the ability of his principal antagonist, Star Lake's police chief, to catch the judge in the act of buying or selling, but that hope was extremely faint for the wily judge lived outside the county seat in a community whose tiny police force he had bribed.

Rebecca and Kathy had also told me of Star Lake's own crime of passion, which had occurred four years earlier. The long-married manager of the local Ace Hardware Store had fallen in love with his pretty assistant, the Homecoming Queen of Star Lake High in 1974.

"So to get rid of his wife," Kathy told me, "he hired a hit man from Chicago by placing an ad in Soldier of Fortune magazine and arranged for the man to kill his wife while he was out with their two sons shopping for a birthday present for her – he arranged for her to be killed on her birthday, a nice touch."

"Then when he came home with the kids," Rebecca continued, "he let them go into the house first with the present to surprise their mother, and of course, they discovered her body – she had been shot in the head – on the kitchen floor."

"He was a vicious bastard," Kathy added, "but fortunately he was a dumb vicious bastard. He paid off the hit man by sending cash and his wife's jewelry through the mail, which, of course, the police had been monitoring. They extradited the hit man who confessed the whole plot and went to prison; then they arrested the man who had hired him."

"Was his lover an accomplice?" I asked.

"The police never found enough evidence to charge her with being an accomplice to murder, but while her lover was on his way back to the county jail after a court appearance, she helped him escape . . ."

"The newspaper stories were always accompanied by a picture of her wearing her crown," Kathy interrupted.

"What happened to her?"

"She was arrested, tried, went to prison for two years."

"But she was rehabilitated. She moved to Milwaukee, went to UW, got a degree and is now, I understand a social worker. Is that right, Rebecca?"

"Yes."

"And what happened to the man?"

"Well, as I said, he was shorted in the brains department. He fled to Florida, used another name and applied for a job as manager at an Ace Hardware Store, but he gave his own name as a reference. When the Ace people checked back here, it was clear what he was up to; he was extradited, convicted, and is now in prison. A life sentence, I think."

Legends of Good Women

Now I had had my own glimpse into domestic stress. I told Rebecca and Kathy about meeting Sally after all these years and said I hoped to bring them together, but I did not tell them I suspected that Sally might be a candidate for their shelter. Kathy and Rebecca were especially interested in meeting Sally when I told them about her weavings.

"Would it be possible," I asked, "to arrange an exhibit of her work at the Women's Resource Center?"

"Yes, I think so," Kathy said.

"I think the Women's Resource Center could sponsor an exhibition," Rebecca amended, "but I don't think we have enough space at our office. We could arrange for an exhibition at the library or at the Arts Council; it would be a nice change for all the crisis stuff we do, but we don't have the womanpower to set it up or promote it, or get other organizations to co-sponsor it."

"I'll work on that," I volunteered impulsively. "I'd like to do something for the Women's Resource Center, but I haven't the skill, or frankly, the inclination to get involved in counseling or advocacy work."

"Good, Claire," Rebecca assented. "We have to get approval from the Board of Directors, but I'm sure they'll support it."

"And do you think our church's UMW would co-sponsor it?"

Kathy and Rebecca smiled mischievously at my question.

"I don't know," Kathy answered, "just mentioning the Resource Center makes the ladies of our church uncomfortable, but it would be worth having them turn us down for the pleasure of watching them squirm out of what they know in their hearts is their Christian duty."

"Enough of all this heavy talk," Rebecca declared. It's a beautiful day, our kids are away, why are we still in our Sunday best?"

We quickly organized an impromptu picnic out at the lake, passing the afternoon swimming, eating, gossiping about other church members, and talking politics – all of us were gloomily convinced by this time that Reagan's election was certain and discussed tactics for survival under the new regime. That evening, pleased that I had been able to forget Ted completely for several hours, I called him.

"Sorry about last night. Was I really stupid?"

"Is that a question? I was surprised."

"Disappointed?"

"Yes. A little."

"Sorry. Believe me when I say that I hardly ever drink too much. You know me well enough by now to know that I don't drink much at all."

"Why did you drink too much last night?"

"I've been thinking about that. I guess because I was tense about how well you and Bob would get along. I can't think of another reason. You know, Claire . . ."

"Yes? Know what?"

"You're almost too good to be true."

"I'm what?"

"You're an accomplished woman. You have high standards. Not many people can measure up. That creates a lot of pressure. I guess I was reacting to it."

"What you're really saying is I'm a pain in the ass."

"A tad. At times."

"Hmm."

"But I admire you. I want to measure up."

The revelation that Ted, my hero, was vulnerable to my judgement almost dissolved me. But I managed to stay cool.

"How are you feeling?"

"Better than I did. I still have a headache. I tried to call you."

"I went to church and then went on a picnic at the lake with my friends, Rebecca and Kathy. I've told you about them."

"The feminists."

"Yes, the feminists. Wanna make something of it?"

"No, I want to be friends. Thank you for getting me home in one piece."

"You're welcome."

"I'll talk to you during the week."

"Okay. Good night."

The next day, Meta surprised me with a telephone call and the announcement that she wanted to begin running. Could I take the time to run with her? I told her of course and then calculated when I could arrange to run with her. Maurice had proved a good friend; he had submitted my request for an application run in the Marathon to the New York Road Runners Club; I had received an invitation to apply; had applied and been accepted. I was now in serious training for the Marathon: eight miles every weekday morning and one long run of twelve to fifteen miles on one of the weekend days. I was reluctant to alter my schedule of warming up, running, post-running stretching, showering, breakfast, newspapers and national pubic radio between six and nine; work from nine until twelve; lunch and reading from twelve to one; and more work until three, three-thirty, or as long as I could go on. The rest of the day was mine; the evenings with Ted were my reward. Swallowing my ambivalence, I agreed to rearrange my schedule and run with Meta between seven and eight.

I asked Meta if she was serious enough about running to invest some money in a running bra and shoes. She said she would buy those items, and agreed to meet the next morning at the high school.

On Tuesday, I did my regular road work, toweled myself off afterward and drove downtown to meet Meta. She arrived as I did; we parked our cars in front of the high school and then went down the path between the wide green lawns, around to the back, and onto the field. This was the first time I had been this close to the building since I had graduated. I glanced at windows remembering myself in the classrooms; I thought of the long hallways where long ago I had sneaked longing looks at Meta's son.

I studied Meta's running clothes. She was wearing Brooks Lady Vantage shoes, a pair of cut-off jeans, and a tee shirt with the name of Ted's company on it. Meta is my height, but her body is larger, almost square. Her legs are still firm, but her breasts are large and pendulous. She had probably not been able to get one of the more supportive athletic bras with straps crossing in the back.

"Meta," I said, pointing, "You're going to bounce."

"I don't mind if you don't."

"I was thinking of comfort. I have very small breasts, and I never wear a bra, but I can't run without one. My breasts hurt if they bounce."

"We'll run very slowly, okay?"

I did exercises with Meta, explaining the purpose of each one, and encouraged her to think about what she felt her body needed, and what kind of exercise helped her. Then we ran slowly around the track. I saw that she very quickly experienced discomfort in her legs and that her lungs were not working efficiently. I explained she was feeling the way everyone did at the beginning, and with each new effort to increase speed and distance. We circled the track once and stopped.

"That was a quarter mile. Let's rest five minutes and do another quarter mile if you feel up to it."

Meta's eyes flashed with defiance, and I wondered what grievance or history of grievances was propelling her, on the cusp of senior citizenship, to take up such a demanding activity. I remembered the last mini-marathon I had run in Central Park in June, 1979. After the race, I was eating yogurt the race sponsors had provided, and found myself standing next to Eleanor Deutsch from Richmond's psychology department; I had never known her well, but remembered her as a decent, pleasant person. We compared finishing times, more than double Grete Waitz's winning time, but comfortably close to each other's. Eleanor explained that she had taken up running when she had turned fifty, declaring, "If I'm going to have hot flashes, I'm going to have them for a good reason." Then she asked if I remembered Seymour Abromowitz, and when I said I did indeed remember him, Eleanor introduced the woman standing next to her as Seymour's first ex-wife, Mary Rose, who immediately related the tale Penny Wilson had told me years before: that Seymour Abromowitz, Marxist scholar, author of The Politics of Hunger, had repeatedly reneged on support payments for his wife and two now-grown children.

"Seymour said he thought alimony was medieval. He agreed to child support, but at the time I did not know how to negotiate for inflation, for the kids' schooling. And he made chasing after him for the puny amounts he did agree to so humiliating. I was never free from anxiety."

"How did you support your children?"

"By doing temporary office work, substitute teaching, whatever."

Where was his sense of working class solidarity, I asked. Seymour always sprinkled his speeches on and off campus with references to his experiences as a labor organizer, and in the jeans and work shirts he always wore, gave off a working class hero aura that had attracted a second wife, now also an ex, and legendary numbers of women and girls.

"What continues to infuriate me is that Seymour's kids never had the benefits that Seymour himself had. You know, Seymour is from a prosperous family. Seymour had music lessons, everything an upper middle class kid could want. Seymour got his working class credentials from me."

I asked what Seymour and Mary Rose's kids were doing now, and was told that the son was trying to make his living as a rock musician and composer and that the daughter was trying to be an actress, but was working as a waitress. Both were living precariously. And what was Mary Rose doing now that her children were grown?

"I'm getting a doctorate through Union College's external program, and I'm training for the New York Marathon this fall."

What does it say about women's lives that in order to redeem ourselves in our own eyes, we feel compelled to drive ourselves to these Spartan extremes? Only with doctorates, only by running – and finishing in good time – do we seem to be able to like ourselves and believe ourselves worthy of respect. What was Meta, who had appeared so serene to me, making up to herself for? When we had finished our second lap around the track, and I had stretched and walked with Meta, I asked her why she had decided to begin running.

"Oh," she began after hunting for an answer, "I needed a challenge."

I sensed that Meta had more to say, and that she was weighing and selecting what she would tell me. I led us over to the wooden bleachers, the very bleachers where I had sat, watching with yearning as her son had scored touchdowns, and waited.

"All through the years when the children were growing up, Harry directed our lives; he built the business, then expanded it; he was active in community life then. When he retired, he seemed to want to keep to his old ways, see his old friends, do what he had done in the past, and I had this new energy. I was free of responsibility and I wanted to go in a new direction. I realized that Harry wasn't going to lead me to one anymore, so I had to figure one out for myself. Otherwise, well, otherwise, I knew I'd just wither up like a prune and die. And I'm not ready for that. I'm healthy. I feel good. Well, when I decided to become even more active in politics, that made Harry mope. We get on each other's nerves a lot."

Meta placed a hand on one of her knees and looked down.

"These sixty-two-year-old legs look very good for their age, but Claire, I once had a beautiful body."

"Meta, you're still a fine looking woman."

"Still. That's not the same as knowing you're beautiful. As feeling your husband become aroused when he sees other men admiring you. You remember how I looked."

Indeed I did. I remembered Meta on the night of graduation, her hair as blonde as mine is now.

"Well, I guess I'm running because I want to do something for my body. I don't want it to just decay."

I thought of Meta and Harry when they were the age Ted and I are now. When Ted was the age our kids are now, had he known his parents were sexual beings? My parents had been so reticent, that I had never been aware of their intimacy, even in our little house. I thought of Meta and Henry naked in their bedroom, embracing, diving into each other as Ted and I did. Then I thought of Ted and me at his parents' age; I envisioned Ted cold and unresponsive while I yearned for him. That would be hell.

"Meta, does politics provide a challenge for you?"

"Yes, but it's a source of frustration, too. Of course, I should have been a delegate to the Democratic convention. But the men of the organization see me as a threat, so they announce this plan to encourage younger members of the party by sending them as delegates, and I had to pretend I thought it was a good idea, too, or else get into a power struggle with those s.o.b.s I was sure to lose."

A group of boys, one of them holding a whiffle ball, came onto the field and began organizing themselves into a game. They paused and stared as two women in running clothes, one more elderly than the other, walked across the field with their arms across each other's shoulders. Being polite midwestern boys, however, they withheld comment and waited deferentially until the women passed them.

I thought of how much I would have liked to have had, how much I would like to have now, the kind of talk with my mother that I had had with Meta. I tried to picture my mother running with Meta and me, but the detail that came clearest to me was of a cigarette bobbing in her mouth as she ran. I weighed an offer of support to Meta, rejected it, and then heard the words coming from my mouth.

"Would it help, Meta, if I joined the organization and became your supporter? Have you thought of running for office?"

"It would help, Claire. And, no, I haven't thought of running for office, but I'm beginning to."

That night I called my mother.

"What was your happiest childhood memory?"

I expected a defensive response – "Why do you want to know?" – but my usually tight-lipped mother became expansive, perhaps because we were speaking long distance and I was paying for the call.

"I only have a few. Like the time my father and brothers went fishing when one of our cows was due to calf. The cow went into a difficult labor. My mother managed to tie a rope around the calf's legs, but the three of us – my mother, my sister, and I, couldn't pull the calf out, and cow and calf died. When my father got home – and he and my brothers had had plenty of beer to drink while they were fishing – he flew into a range, began pulling off his belt ready to beat the three of us. My mother just wailed with despair, but I was fourteen and tall, and I found the strength to stand up to him. 'Don't you dare touch us,' I said. 'You knew the cow was going to calf and you went off and left the mess to us. What happened is your fault, not ours.' And my father just shut his mouth and put his belt back in his pants."

"That was happy?"

"In a childhood as rotten as mine was, that was happy."

"Do you have another good memory."

"Well, the next and best time – and I wasn't a child any more – was the day I left. I had put up with my father until I had graduated from high school. I was so eager to get away that I was an A student all through my school years and skipped a whole year of grammar school. The day after I got my high school diploma, I packed a bag and went to the highway to wait for the bus to take me out of town. I hadn't told my mother, but she knew what I was planning, and when I came downstairs with the little suitcase I had borrowed from a friend, she pulled money that she'd hoarded and hidden somehow, and right in front of my father she handed it to me. 'Here,' she said, 'you'll need this.' I wish I could have done more for her, but living with my father cut her life short, and I never had the chance. What's your happiest memory, Claire?"

"Unlike you, I have a bunch of them. Nothing special. You trying to cook good meals for Christmas and sometimes succeeding, or making me cakes for my birthday when I knew you hated to cook. You bent over the sewing machine making me clothes while I watched in fascination as the ash grew longer on your cigarette. You haven't quit smoking, have you?"

"Is the Pope still Catholic? What else do you remember?"

"The time I was very sick with some childhood disease and woke up at last free of fever. Dad was sitting by my bed with a tray on his lap that held a glass of milk and a plate of buttered rye bread. I guzzled the milk and gobbled the bread. It was the best food I'd ever tasted in my life. But what I remember most was the look of concern on Dad's face when I opened my eyes. 'He loves me a lot,' I thought."

"That's a nice one. I'll tell him."

"Do. You and Dad gave me a lot of good memories. I'm trying to do the same for Janey."

"Yes. Well, give her our love," commanded my again taciturn mother as she concluded our conversation.

I called Sally, told her my mother's memories, and asked if she could transform one of them into a tapestry.

"Tapestry isn't as flexible as painting. The first scene you described has several emotions in it – fear, despair, anger, defiance – that creates too much vertical movement for the warp and weft to express. The leaving-home scene has mostly horizontal movement. Yes, I could make a tapestry of that."

"Fine. I want to give it to my mother for Christmas. Could you do it by then?"

"Sure."

"What's your price?"

"How much do you think it would be worth?"

"No, Sally. Name a price and I'll either accept it or we'll negotiate."

"Let's see. The materials will be . . ."

"Include the value of your time and art."

"Five hundred dollars?"

"Say it as a statement, Sally."

She did and I agreed to pay her one hundred dollars in advance and the balance when the tapestry was completed in December.

CHAPTER

For some time, longer than I had realized, I had survived or functioned well by keeping others out of my own awareness. While I was teaching, members of my department, significant college administrators, and students took up temporary residence in my consciousness, of which the principal tenant was Janey. I thought dutifully, if not daily, about my parents; more recently, Ted had become a major occupant. Neighbors, townspeople, people I saw in church got little attention, but my conscience always nudged me to pay more heed to them at a later date. I had not really committed myself to homecoming, I was still finding my way. I attended parents' meetings at Janey's school, and paid attention to all matters concerning her, but beyond a diligent performance at work, I had not seriously attempted to integrate, or reintegrate, myself into the community.

Now a number of people were on my mind, crowding the space that formerly had been occupied solely by Janey, Ted, and my work. I thought about Meta and Harry, both in sympathy and concern for their friction. My own parents had bumped along together, were no doubt still rubbing their rough temperaments against each other, but despite the example of my own family, I realized when I thought of Meta and Harry that I had always believed couples who stayed together that long had worked everything out between them, like a road worn smooth by continuous traffic. But Meta and Harry were suddenly confronting problems of adjustment, like a newly married couple. I was both comforted and mildly dismayed by their inharmony; it served as a reminder that maturity is not static, that even in old age, one must grow and solve problems, making mistakes in the process.

I continued to run with Meta, pleased that she did not want to drop our schedule, but remained faithful to it, and began soon to be concerned about increasing her distance and speed. In less than two weeks, Meta was going a mile at the high school track in fourteen minutes.

I thought often and with concern about Sally, who, I believed, was in a state of crisis and had been for some time. I wanted to talk about the McNeills with Ted, but I hesitated, out of an instinct that Ted would resent my asking him to look at problems in the marriage which he preferred not to see. The flip side of my silence was that I was beginning to feel parity with him. When we met now as an established couple, every night or every other night for dinner, I knew that we came to each other with a whole life. We each had work and we each had a series of other relationships demanding our attention. Through my connection to other women, to Ted's mother, I was, I dared confess to myself, developing roots. Whatever Ted and I might eventually be to one another, I did not want to establish myself in the community only through my connection to him; I wanted what I had never had when I was younger, my own identity in the town.

Yet passion grew. At five p.m. on each day I would be seeing Ted, I stopped the work I had made myself continue until that moment; then showered and anointed my body with one of the sweet-tasting, sweet smelling lotions I sought out and bought with the concentration of the passionate collector. Always in searches, I imagined Ted's hum of pleasure, his exquisite sigh. I was certain the clerks in the stores understood my motives when I made my purchases; I even anticipated bawdy winks and congratulatory nods. As I prepared myself, I imagined Ted preparing himself; each of us in our separate dwellings carefully cleansing and then readorning ourselves in fresh clothing that would be discarded minutes after we were together.

And when he was at last with me, or, less frequently, when I went to his apartment, I would fall, like Alice, into Wonderland as Ted kissed me into another kind of consciousness, not aware of anything but my deep, deep pleasure; more than pleasure, happiness. Sometimes, however, I would make myself aware of him, alert myself to his experience of me. That sensation was almost as marvelous as the joy he gave me, for Ted seemed not to know anything but me. Oh, he kissed me with such delight, audible in his sighs, moans, grunts, comic sounds, really, but in the context of his profoundly happy face, so wonderful to me. No one had ever before granted me such power; I had never had the joy of knowing I was responsible for another's joy, that I was capable of giving pleasure beyond bounds. In my limited experience, no one had ever allowed himself to reveal, if he felt it, such naked need to me. What Ted felt, he spoke of to me, instantly. Nothing original, nothing but words that are exchanged between couples who are happy together, but for me to hear, all through our lovemaking, phrases

Legends of Good Women

like, "Claire, this is so good," "Being inside you is so wonderful," brought an elation I had never known. And always, behind this pleasure, a part of my consciousness was critically comparing the joy of the present with Ted against the sadness I had known as a bride, when so full of ardor, of simple, wholesome love, I had been denied words and silly love noises. Oh, David had spoken to me in bed during the days when we were lovers, and even in the early days of our marriage. He had questioned me: "Was it good for you, Babe?" He had commanded: "Tell me how good you feel." But words of unbridled pleasure had never tumbled from his lips; I had never been praised, and later, when David had made up his mind to end our marriage, he remained silent during our brief, sporadic, loveless couplings, in order, I believe, to bring me more around to adopting his goal of ending our marriage because there was no love or even companionship in it.

Companionship followed lovemaking with Ted, always. Our companionship followed a cycle which, in sex, carried us through wild shifts of roles. I enjoyed the power I felt in bed with Ted; I loved the sense of command I felt when, astride Ted, I made the muscles of my vagina contract around his penis. I gloried in moving him, or causing him to move in ways that let me please him. With an intense concentration, I focused on him, on using my hands, my lips, my tongue to touch him in every open and closed or enfolded place in his body. But I held my breath when the power shifted, and I felt as if I were falling from a high place and knew I would be caught when Ted would open his eyes, and with a smile and an eye gleam, take command from me, toppling me or lifting me up, moving my body in a way I could not move his, except by direction or subtle pressure. Through every stroke, every move, though, he kissed me; no human contact had ever given me as much pleasure as Ted's lips on mine did. Out of bed, conscious, away from him, and in daylight, I thought of the Weavers' song, "Kisses sweeter than wine," and understood how the narrator of the song could commit himself for life to a woman whose kisses pleased him so much. In bed, kissing Ted, I was transported, almost in a Victorian swoon because of the sweet, firm, but never hard – or biting, like David – pressure of his warm, moist but never sloppy wet mouth. The cycle of lovemaking was wonderful, whether Ted or I initiated it. Each time we made love, though, we completed the cycle of roles; each of us was dominant and each of us was subordinate to the other, but subtly, never grotesquely. And I loved both poles. I reveled in mastery over Ted and bringing him to climax, seeing him achieve pleasure almost against his will, but I enjoyed just as much his dominance of me, of feeling in his power and subject to his will and direction, and knowing the range of sensation his lovemaking gave to me, all of it, from tenderness to silly or rough playfulness. And then, finally, however the cycle had begun, it always ended in partnership, in lying side by side and hand in hand, confiding to each other like siblings or comrades, staring up beyond the ceiling of my bedroom to the sky.

Ted spoke of the second stage of his struggle. When he returned from Vietnam, he worked at his father's auto body shop, with the understanding that his work would continue only until he could develop his own career, since Harry was on the verge of retirement, and Ted's brother was the designated heir, and the business could not expand enough to support more than one owner. Ted completed his degree, first at a UW extension and later at Madison, and then, with a small loan from his father, began his business.

"I can't believe how hard I worked in those early days – this was back in 1970. I was out all day, going to companies, trying to get orders, then working all night when I came back to get the orders ready. It was tough on Michelle; she was home all day with Ted, Junior, and I was away most of the time and too exhausted to be really with her when I did come home. I just wanted to sleep. And she had all this energy, frustrated energy, and nowhere to go with it. No wonder our marriage failed. Although it's sad. I was working so hard because I wanted to have a family and in the process, I lost my family. I can't blame Michelle, though. I'm not being noble. I really mean that, although I was bitter when she left me and took our son with her. I couldn't argue with her, though, when she said she didn't have a husband and Ted, Junior didn't have a father. Michelle was hit with too much too soon, just as I was, and I can see now she couldn't bear being in a place where she couldn't have any control over her life – just to wait for me to come home, and then when I did, all I did was sleep. And there wasn't much money, either. I just took out of the business what I could afford in the early days. Then, when orders began to increase, I hired workers, and, of course, paid them before myself. And there weren't any vacations, either. In fact, the first vacation I ever took in my adult life was the camping trip after my marriage ended I told you about. Hah. How's that for getting everything when I need it? Everything at the right time. Anyway, the business did grow, and some of the tension I had been feeling for years, tension I hadn't even realized I'd been feeling, began to melt away. Only after I started to relax could I understand why I had been working so hard, and then it was too late. If I had had any insight into why I was working so hard during my marriage, I might have made Michelle understand. If she could have shared, if I could have shared with her what I was feeling, perhaps we wouldn't have drifted apart. Perhaps. Only perhaps. She didn't know my side, and I didn't know hers. I can only guess that Michelle, like a lot of women, began to understand what she had been missing. I don't have to explain to you, I'm sure."

"But tell me what you understood about why you had driven yourself."

Ted began with the pronoun, "I," stopped, seemed short of breath, began again, repeated the pronoun, and again was short of breath. Then he was silent, fathering his thoughts as if preparing a statement; no, more than a statement, and I sensed that we were at a new stage in the relationship. I felt all at once deeply honored because I realized Ted was moving, or preparing to move, from confidence to confession, for what he had to say was not to be spoken without breaking some long-kept silence. I waited with grateful expectancy, as if a prize were to be bestowed upon me.

"I realize now," Ted said after minutes, "that the reason I drove myself so hard was to wipe out the Vietnam years. I had such a mix of feelings about the war, those times. Anger because of the waste; you and everyone who was against the war were right about it. It was a wrong war, and every decent and indecent man who was killed or wounded or hurt inside because of it was sacrificed for nothing, for worse than nothing, for a lie, a lie by our government about another government that was as bad as our so-called enemies said it was. But I was angry because we had gone for the right reasons, all of us dumb, innocent, decent kids went because our country called, and I'm not the only man in this country from a family with a tradition of patriotism, where love of country is real because in each family the memory is still strong of what it was not to have rights. But that love of country was exploited, and I'm angry that we were not honored for our loyalty; honored is off the scale of what we encountered. We're all ashamed of having been there, and we shouldn't be. And I and many others did things we wish we had not done, that we still all these years later feel guilty about. But we shouldn't bear that guilt alone."

Ted stopped speaking for a few seconds. And I knew the rush of confessional words had been interrupted by another consideration he did not want to share with me: that he was suddenly aware of me as being on the other side, as one who should share his guilt — for what deeds — as one who had made him feel ashamed of his participation in that war.

"Building a small company may not seem like a monumental achievement," he resumed, speaking more slowly and in a lower pitch, "but it was one way — the one way — I found that I could make up to men I knew, friends who died, make up to them for the loss of their lives. That sounds ridiculous. How could I presume to live the lives that were wasted. Oh my god, when they were not even out of their teens, some of them. But I threw myself into my work because I thought if I could make a go of it, the business would be some kind of memorial to them. And that was the way I worked. When things were tough, I just thought of one friend who had been killed when he had only four days of his tour left in Nam, or another buddy, ohmygod, what a fine athlete's body he had, blown up by a mine, and I pushed on. And it was the business, a small business, because it seemed like a logical place for me to go, and it was more than I had ever dreamed I could do. My father was the powerful figure in my life. He had started a business, and I always assumed my brother would take it over, and I always assumed some place would be found for me, but the war made me want to take responsibility for my own life, and maybe for others. And that's what happened. The first years were tough, but then it grew. I had employees on a payroll. Not that everything was progress in an upward line on the charts. During the recession of 1977, things began to slide. I was really scared. I had to lay off a couple of workers, and I felt bad about that. I never want to lose another man again. The business became a kind of — "

Atonement was the word I said to myself, but I waited for Ted to complete his sentence.

" — the business became a kind of double payoff. I felt I was paying the government back — getting even — because I wasn't even supposed to be alive, and my modest success was a kind of payoff to the men who never had a chance to build their own lives."

"I don't think that's so modest. I think establishing a business and keeping it going is a major accomplishment in these times. I've never done that — created something where nothing existed before, borrowed money at these high rates, dealt with banks . . ."

"Do you want to?"

"Do you think I could? I mean get money from a bank?"

"Do you mean would you be denied a loan because you're a woman. I don't think so. At least not that by itself. A shrewd banker would look at the soundness of your venture, your marketing plan; he'd measure your margin of profit against your overhead. Why, are you going to start a business? Just because

Legends of Good Women

I own one. Aren't you going to let us fellas have anything, macho woman?

"I was just curious. And no, I'm not going to start a business. At least, I don't have anything in mind right now. But I don't rule it out. I have a daughter, after all, and maybe I'd like to hand something down to her the way your father did to your brother. And you should be flattered that I want to emulate you. I admire your achievement. I admire the risk you took. I've always had the feeling that if I'm going to be truly liberated, I have to take the same risks men take."

"Would you go to war?"

"No, but I'd take the risks men who refused to go to war took."

I could hear Ted thinking, "Like the risks your husband took."

"I mean I would have been a conscientious objector. I wouldn't have gone to Canada.

"Oh, no. I know you wouldn't have. You would have made damn sure you collided with authority. Just like my mom. What's so funny?"

"I was thinking of that song, *I Want a Girl, Just Like the Girl That Married Dear Old Dad*. I don't think the songwriters had women like your mom and me in mind; old-fashioned was supposed to mean yielding and submissive, not tough and strong-minded like your mom and me."

"Doesn't the song go, 'A real old-fashioned girl, with heart so true?'"

"'One who'd love nobody else but you.' That's right. That's what the song says."

Ted took my hand and we lay there; comrades, lovers, everything it was possible to be, I was sure we each felt we could be to each other. But we did not say a word then. We held our breath and looked at the ceiling of my bedroom, and seemed to float above it.

CHAPTER

In early July, Ted asked me if I wanted to attend one of the softball league games. "Yes, all right," I agreed, trying to mask my ambivalence about attending a game. Once, in New York, I had walked with Janey past a school yard where boys were playing basketball while their girl friends waited outside on the curb, leaning against cars while they waited for the boys to pay attention to them.

"Don't ever, ever let me see you sitting on a car fender while some boy you like is playing a sport. I don't want you to be a cheerleader; I want you to be the one cheered."

Janey had looked at me with a tolerant puzzlement, nodded her head insincerely out of a sense that my temporary irrationality would pass. I really did not want to go to the softball game; I did not want to be a spectator, and I did not relish being introduced to Ted's buddies in that context. I would be Ted's lady, and not my own.

"Of course," I added for reassurance, "I think that would be fun." I was grateful Janey was away at camp and not present to witness my downfall.

"Sally will be there; at least she usually is. She and the kids."

"Oh, fine."

"Sally knows a lot of the other women who come. You might get to know some of them."

"Oh, I'd like that."

Another lie. While I probably would like to know the women who watched the softball games, I did not want to sit among them at the game in a loyal cluster of fans. Oh, the hell with it, I decided. I would swallow my resentment and go to the damn softball game. That's all it was.

At five o'clock the next evening, I drove to the park by the lake where the game would be played. I parked my car on the road and surveyed the field before I got out. It was early; players on opposing teams were practicing their swings or pitching to each other near the field, away from the backstop. Some of the early arriving players had brought their families and were picnicking at tables near the playing field by the lake. Why hadn't Ted suggested a pregame picnic? I might not have minded so much climbing into the narrow v-shaped bleachers afterward and sitting passively while a game was played. I could feel crankiness overtaking me, and struggled to put it down. I was hungry and decided to get some food to bring with me. I got out of the car and went to a drive-in across from the park. I bought pieces of fried chicken, french-fried potatoes, and cole slaw, and then walked to the park, trying to feel I belonged there, hoping grease would not leak through the bag holding my sodden food, avoiding the glances of players and wives who were having suppers out of well-packed picnic hampers. I heard my name called, and recognizing Sally's voice, walked to the table where she sat with Bob.

"Where are the kids?"

"At my mother's. I have the late shift tonight. When I go in at eleven, they stay with her, and I pick them up on my way home from work."

Sally offered me some of her chicken, beautifully deep fried, dry and crumbly; I yearned for it, but said no thanks.

"Are you sure? Have some ratatouille, then. Bob says it's awful. . ."

"Why do you make that stuff?" Bob asked in a grouchy voice.

"Because it's good. Because I get bored with potato salad or macaroni salad. Here, have some tabouleh."

"That's almost as bad. Just hand me another can of beer from the cooler."

"Is it a good idea to have more beer before a game?"

Bob just looked at Sally in stony anger; then he waved his hand impatiently, and Sally quickly pulled a can from the plastic cooler.

"Could I have some ratatouille, Sally? And some tabouleh? I asked.

"Sure, here, pass me your plate."

I tasted the food and told Sally most sincerely how good it was.

"What an elegant accompaniment to my humble fried chicken," I exclaimed, certain my language would infuriate Bob. "Where did you find time to make it? I once followed Julia Child's recipe for ratatouille and thought I would never finish."

"Do you really like it?"

"Of course I do. Sally, I haven't eaten at your home a lot, but enough to know you're a fine cook. Don't you know how good you are?"

Legends of Good Women

Sally smiled and shrugged. "Friends usually like what I cook. Sometimes the kids."

By this time, people were finishing their suppers, and the women, having repacked hampers, were seeking each other out and forming companionable clusters in the bleachers while the men joined the pre-game warmups, walking slowly and meditatively, their gait reflecting their bodies' adjustment from eating to preparation for exercise. My eyes flicked almost automatically to the road. Where was Ted? I knew Bob watched me. Then I saw Ted's car slowing down and being parked very near mine. Sally was packing up her food and I helped her. Bob walked out to meet Ted, who would have continued on his way to Sally and me, except Bob put one arm around his shoulder, talking to him, then turning him around and walking him to his teammates.

I told myself it was not reasonable to feel so much anger, but that message did not get through to my stomach, where my recently consumed meal was certainly dissolving in acidic juices. I walked with Sally to the bleachers, feeling so like a chump. What was I doing in this woman-as-watcher role when the man I had come to watch was ignoring me? At last two older men – the league umpires – arrived at the field and, as the game seemed about to begin, Ted broke away from his group and ran toward me, spilling out words: "higladyoucamesorryi'mlatehadalotofworksorrywe couldnteattogethergottorushnowgame'sabouttobegin-seeyoulatero.k.?"

"Okay, sure."

Sally and I joined the womenfolk in "our" side of the small v-shaped bleachers behind the backstop. I tried to imagine myself disembodied, looking down on the playing field as the game began. Ted's team were at bat first, and as one man took his place at home

- 253 -

plate, moving his body in that attractive way—hips twitching, bat held firmly above the shoulders—I looked at the other men on the bench, workers in his company, their buddies, and high school seniors he had recruited, all in yellow t-shirts with Ted's company's name in black letters on their backs. Their opponents wore blue t-shirts with their sponsor's name, Heller's Home Heating and Cooling. Sally greeted several of the women around us, who chatted with her briefly before we all dutifully turned our attention to the game. Bob was the first man at bat and made a base hit. We all responded with a modest, muted cheer, and other women turned, nodded their heads in a congratulatory manner toward Sally, who shrugged a message, "I had nothing to do with it." A second man went to bat, whom Sally identified to me as the husband of Ted's secretary-bookkeeper. Sally then identified the player's wife to me, a young woman sitting further down in the bleachers, who, as Sally described her to me, turned around and smiled at us. Her husband made a base hit, Bob reached second base, and we women again responded with ladylike enthusiasm. A third man, in his twenties like the bookkeeper's husband and, as Sally informed me, one of Ted's employees, came up at bat, but he struck out; the response of the women fans was a groan of unreproachful sympathy. The women on the other side of the aisle, wives and lovers of the men of the other team, made approving sounds just short of a cheer, meant to be heard as encouragement to their menfolk. The next man at bat, also in his twenties and one of Ted's employees, also made a base hit. There was applause from our side, but no congratulatory nods toward a woman. Doesn't he have a wife or lover, I wondered. Perhaps he does, but she doesn't like softball; perhaps she is at home studying molecular physics, or maybe he doesn't want her to come because he prefers to keep his private life his own. Perhaps he dates so many women, he doesn't want to be linked publicly with any of them.

The man following the unattached batter drew slight movement and low murmurs among the group of womenfolk to whom he was obviously connected. Could they not be mothers and sisters as well as wives? None of the women seemed old enough to be the mothers of any of the players. Indeed, I felt a pang as I realized Sally and I were probably the oldest women in the bleachers; the other women were in their twenties, and a couple even seemed to be teenagers.

Two balls and a strike were called against the batter, who then hit a pop fly to the pitcher. Ted came up to bat with two men on and two men out. Perfect. I wished perversely that he would strike out, but striking out would have been out of character. I heard the whonk clear across the field as Ted's bat sent the ball out to the edge of the park, and before it was recovered, Bob and the other man had come home and Ted had reached third base. Cheers from our side, and I became aware of a few heads turning slyly in my direction. Another man came up at bat, amid modest murmuring from the women. He struck out, and the murmuring became a "That's all right" sound as the teams changed sides.

As the other team arranged itself in its batting order, the women on our side relaxed while across the aisle, the women of "their" side became alert. The men of "our" side stationed themselves in the field and on the bases, and Ted went to the pitcher's mound. The first opposing batter took his position, and Ted altered his stance, leaning forward, curling his body, preparing his arms to hurl the ball, while reading signals from his team's catcher. I felt the old awe overtaking me.

The batter struck out without ever making contact with the ball; the second batter hit a pop fly to the infielder; the third man at bat managed to get a base hit. When the fourth batter took his place at bat, a slight stir accompanied him, and the words "a season with the Brewers" came my way. And this man did hit a long ball to the outfield, but swift recovery by the outfielder kept the batter at second base and the other man at third. When the fifth opposing batter came up, the situation was the one Ted had confronted, two men on and two men out. But Ted's pitching put three neat strikes in a row past the man, and the other side retired.

Scorelessness sharpened the opposing team's defensive play; their pitcher became a tougher adversary against the second inning lineup, and held Ted's team to only one base hit from one of the high school players who came up after a man had struck out. The two men who followed him made hits, one to right field and one to left, but good work by the outfielders got them tagged out at first base. However, when they went up to bat, Ted's pitching kept them scoreless.

In the third inning, I found my attention wandering. I began constructing my own field of inquiry, focusing on the women on "our" side. I was certain not one of them was a college graduate. Why? They reminded me of New York secretaries going out to lunch together, except they were more serious, but they had the collective lack of self-importance I had observed among women office workers who moved slowly, contentedly in a herd, not at all like the brisk-paced, briefcased, visionary and self-absorbed managerial women, confidently on the rise like my Fontbonne students.

The women in the bleachers talked to each other, but kept their eyes on the men in the field, like women who want to chat, but must also keep their attention on young children. They watched the game with more attention than I would have expected from people for whom game watching was a habit. What kind of men were these who needed so much looking after? At a distance, most of them seemed younger than Bob and Ted; all of them, except the high school students and Bob, had long hair and mustaches and or beards. Ted's hair, while long by midwestern standards, was not so long as the younger men's hair, and his mustache was smaller. I understood all at once that these men were vets, and then my attention wandered back to former students, the vets at Richmond Community College.

I remembered the young man in one of my remedial English classes who one day recalled the 1969 demonstration in Washington where Janey and I had first encountered tear gas. He had been stationed at Camp Pendleton, he said, when the order came for him and the men he served with to load themselves into convoys of drab green military trucks which then went to the capital. My student and his comrades were then issued weapons and stationed in and around the maze of federal buildings, from which positions they stared at the demonstrators over their bayoneted weapons.

"I didn't know what we were doing there;" my student had explained, "I didn't know what was going on. I just remember that when I was standing behind this big iron gate in front of one of those buildings, some girl came over and put a flower over my gun."

Lots of girls had placed flowers on guns that November day, but I liked to think the flower draping Janey and I had witnessed had been on the gun held by the young man I was teaching to construct sentences and paragraphs.

I had become advisor to the Richmond vets when Bill Schwartz, who had become my friend after he had been my student, brought them swarming around me, absorbing me into their colony like a quick bee. With the exception of Bill Schwartz, they were all Catholic, but like Bob McNeill, had long lapsed, the war having burned their Catholicism out of them. However, the need for that rigid structure they had shed persisted, and they huddled together, trying to adopt the mainstream trends of the era as a substitute for the dark gothic rituals they had known in childhood. But it was obvious to me, each time I visited Bill, his four mates and the live-in lady of one of them in the shabby frame building they shared together in the Port Richmond section of Staten Island, that body heat, rock and roll, and drugs could not replace dogma and sacraments. The "commune" did not survive more than five months after Bill's death, not that his survival would have altered the time of the collapse significantly. But while it sheltered them, energy abounded in that house, constantly athrob with vibrations from speakers in each of its rooms. The Port Richmond vets were a manic, good-natured group, except for Dave, who emerged from his room only to come to meals with the woman who shared his room but who was not, as Pete's Lois was, a functioning household member. She was not even known by name; indeed, we seldom even saw her face, because Dave was usually kissing her when he was not actually feeding himself at the table. The couple did not speak to the rest of the commune members, or even seem aware of them. They, or rather Dave, shuttled back and forth between bedroom and dining table – the woman fastened to Dave like an intravenous attachment, except for the occasions when Lois rebelled and insisted that she help with the food chores. I did not understand why Dave had been accepted as a member of the commune until after I had witnessed the first of his outbursts on campus, when at one of the purposeless but never-ending vet meetings in the Student Building, he had moved to the center of the group and shouted, "I can't stand it. I killed 300 people in Vietnam. I machine-gunned women and children. Do you know what it's like to carry that kind of guilt with you? Man, my head's exploding most of the time." Then I understood Dave's acceptance into the commune as a humanitarian act by the rest of the group. In its heyday, the commune spun off a satellite commune, another collection of Hispanic-, Italo-, and Irish-American vets and resident "old ladies" who settled in another run-down frame building near the mother house. The second group were less dependent on Bill Schwartz's radiant energy than were the group in the house on Park Avenue, but they were devoted to him nonetheless. These vets did not weep at Bill's funeral, but one member, Pat McNulty, later led the others to a local tavern, found an excuse to get drunk, smashed his hand through the bar window, and was dragged, arm upraised, to a hospital where emergency room doctors barely saved him from bleeding to death. The vets were at the center of the witches' cauldron the campus had become under open admissions, but they drew other, unmoldable elements to them. "The Hat," for example, was a brooding presence the vets did not encourage to come near them; they actively loathed, in fact, the strange young man who seemed never to speak, or bathe either, who always wore a black shirt, black trousers, and a large, broadbrimmed, high-crowned black hat, but they did not try to prevent him from circling near them. The personage of Frank Carpenter descended upon them from time to time. A grey-faced man in his forties, Frank had entered Richmond with Bill from the college's special program at Arthur Kill Reformatory. But unlike Bill, a three-time loser, Frank had only been caught once in his long criminal career, and he did not intend to be caught again. he swept down on Park Avenue, regaling the inmates with tales of his illicit adventures. And when they asked, "What's a rotten guy like you doing in college, Frank?" he answered, "I'm polishing up my act here. I figure with a humanities background for good conversation, and some computer courses for skills, I'll be able to set myself up in white collar crime, except with greater flair, more flamboyance. That's the difference between you and me, Bill. I learn from my mistakes, I don't repeat them. When I realized the most successful criminals in this country were the heads of corporations, I made those guys my models. In some ways, you're a smart guy, Bill; that's why I can't understand why you're still doing those dumb dope deals."

"I'm not, I'm not," Bill always protested when I was present, and perhaps he maintained what I later knew was a fiction when I was not present. Where are they now, those vets of yesteryear? How many have survived the shedding of their skins and have successfully entered new lives? And how many others have followed my darling Billy to his grave?

A player on Ted's team came up to bat, and after a call of a strike and a ball, made a hit to right field; the outfielder retrieved it, and as the runner reached second base, threw it to the third baseman, who also fumbled. The runner reached third base and was held there. Another batter came up, also made a base hit, and the man on third came home. His teammates surrounded him, ritualistically patting his ass in a moment of allowable male body contact and demonstrable affection.

I became distracted by the conversation of the four women in front of me. They were talking about their husbands, and I eavesdropped with a raw curiosity that surprised and embarrassed me.

"He lies all the time," the woman on the end to my right was saying. "He lies about the simplest things for no reason. Like telling our neighbor that his car can get forty-five miles to the gallon. Well, of course, it doesn't, and our neighbor knows it. He only makes himself look foolish when he lies like that. He went fishing with my father last weekend, after bragging about this place he knew where the fish were big and almost jumped out of the water at the bait. Well, when they came back, my father had this strange look on his face, and later I heard him tell my mother that he didn't know what Joe thought was so great about that fishing spot because the fish were puny and far between. He seems to need to make people believe that everything that's connected to him—his car, his fishing spot—is larger than life. And I feel embarrassed when my parents look at him when he's saying something they know is a lie. They look at him, they look at me, and the look at each other with this what-can-you-do-about-it expression on their faces."

The three women in front of me were silent for a minute. So was everyone else. The other women had been listening, too. Perhaps the woman speaking had addressed a common problem. I looked at Sally and saw that she also was thinking about what the woman had said.

I looked back at the game and saw that Ted's team was in the field. I asked Sally what inning it was and she told me bottom of the fourth.

"I know what you mean," the woman next to her said. "I mean not that John lies, but he does strange things that make me uncomfortable. When he comes home, for example, he never comes to where I am. He has to prowl through the house first. I hear him going from room to room picking things up, putting them down, opening drawers, closets. It drives me nuts listening to him. 'What are you looking for?' I ask, and he says, 'Nothing,' but he keeps prowling. And when he comes home after being out with his friends, and I've gone to bed, he'll come into the bedroom and walk around the bed when he thinks I'm asleep. He keeps walking around the bed, from one side to the other. Then he looks under the bed. I always hear him, even if I've been asleep. But I pretend I'm asleep, because I don't want to deal with it. It's creepy. Why do you think they do these damn things?"

"Oh, I'm sure, in some way, it goes back to that damn war."

"Yes, probably. And isn't it neat the way we have to deal with the problems the men brought home with them?"

The third woman, sitting next to the prowler's wife, spoke. "Look, not every man who went to Vietnam came home with problems, or, at any rate, problems he couldn't put behind them. I guess my husband saw as much action as anyone. I know he saw men who were his buddies get killed, and in pretty horrible ways, too. But he was able to put it all behind him. Not that he's forgotten what he went through. But he was able to move on, get on with his life. If he has problems, I don't know about them."

"Well, that's good for your husband," the first woman, the liar's wife, responded. "I'm glad he was able to come through it so well. But a lot of men didn't. Lots of men have problems because of the war."

"And the only people who are dealing with the problems are the women they're married to," the second woman, the prowler's wife countered.

"Or living with," the first woman added.

"Yeah. And it doesn't help either the men or the women to be told that a lot of men came through unscarred. I mean, I'm happy for your husband, I really am. But I don't want to have the additional burden of feeling – or have my husband feel – there's something wrong with him because he can't forget about Vietnam."

"And our husbands, by the way," the first woman added, "don't have very serious problems at all compared to what other men are living through."

"That's right," the fourth woman on the bench in front of Sally and me said. "I've been hearing about it. There's even a new term for it. Delayed Stress Syndrome, I think it's called."

"For example, take Marian," the first woman said, nodding at one of the young women I had associated with one of the high school players because she was so young, "who lives with Steve." She nodded at the first baseman, who seemed to me slightly younger than Ted. "She's been trying to deal with his drinking. The last time he went on a binge, she threatened to leave him, so he made a big show of pouring out all the liquor into the sink, but you know as soon as her back was turned, he went out and bought more."

"Steve's much older than she is, isn't he?"

"He's thirty-two; she's nineteen."

"That's young. Too young to be taking on all that."

"Sure is. What's more, he's been married before. Has a kid."

"Aah. Why does she stay with him? They're not married," the third woman asked..

"Maybe she feels she has to make everything right," the second woman responded. "Like us. We learned or have been made to believe that no matter what goes wrong with our husband or kids, it's up to us to fix it. And if we can't, there's something wrong with us."

"But Marian's nineteen," the third woman argued. "When I was nineteen, I was more of my own person than I am now. I was more selfish."

"And she's so pretty, too."

A stir on the field made us all start like schoolgirls when the teacher walks into the room. The other team had scored.

"It's three to three now," Sally said. "Tie score."

She was trying hard to keep her attention on the game, but I knew she was listening with as much interest as I was. The women sitting just before us were aware we were listening. They began to perform just a bit, choosing their words carefully, with concern for the effect.

"Perhaps you're right," the first woman said, responding to the second woman's point. Perhaps we do feel that if our kiss doesn't cure all the world's booboos, we're failures."

Her theory had merit. Certainly, I had labored for a long time under the burden of that sense of obligation. When I was first aware of problems in my marriage, I was sure I was doing something wrong. I had reviewed my discussions with David like textbooks, searching for some clue to where my error lay, to find what I had done or said to cause his coldness. Everything and nothing, I soon learned. My husband was too flagrant a rat to waste time on subtlety; he made his opportunism plain. When I was no longer useful to him, he left me. Later, with Maurice, who was not a major figure in my life, I still felt obliged to heal him if I could. And then with Billy, I appointed myself to the job of life-saver, and felt such defeat when he died. Again, I had the feeling of having omitted doing something or having done something wrong. And now with Ted – what? No. This time I wanted reciprocity. I wanted nurture and giving back for putting out. Was that growth? Was I becoming mature because I was now willing to have my needs taken care of? Or was the change in my feeling due to a long delayed burst of self-esteem. Was I finally ready to acknowledge that attention and care were my due?

I studied the first two women, who were both around thirty. One was slender, the other was overweight, very much overweight, but her flesh had a pink softness I could imagine would be very appealing to a man in search of maternal warmth and youthful innocence at the same time. Stout women could suggest both mother and child in one body. The slender first woman seemed healthy and athletic, but she, too, had an aura of vulnerability about her. The third woman, with the well-adjusted vet husband, was blonde, with her hair pulled back and clipped, and seemed more confident than the other women. The fourth woman, who had hardly spoken but who was as absorbed in the conversation as Sally was, was dark-haired, wore glasses, was thin, and seemed full of anxiety, perhaps because of a problem she could not bear to speak about. Three of the four women in front of me seemed lacking in self-esteem, perhaps the very quality which had drawn to them the men they had married, who no doubt had sensed the women would not run away from them because they would believe they had nowhere else to go.

And what of Sally? Certainly she was unaware of her worth, but surely Bob, whose ascetic Celtic nature had been drawn to Sally's Mediterranean warmth, was not. Sally's lack of self-esteem was expressed like a constant apology which was most evident in the pitch of her voice. When she told Enid and Daphne to do something, her voice rose almost to girlish shrillness, as if she doubted her right to command them, and with their children's killer instincts, they frequently disobeyed her.

I was beginning to be bored and resentful; I stared at the field without seeing what was happening.

"Do you come to every game?" I asked the women in front of me. They turned around, not yet making up their minds about me, but studying me, reserving their decision about me until they could confer afterward and come to consensus on Claire Schaefer.

"Almost every game," the first woman answered. She looked at the others, and they all smiled self-consciously.

"I notice none of you bring your kids to the game. Why don't you?"

"My kids are too young, the second woman answered. "Jean and I," she nodded toward the fourth woman, "bring our kids to one another's house and take turns hiring a babysitter."

"My children are older," the third woman said. "They have their own friends, so they do what they want. They'd be bored, and they're old enough to be by themselves."

"If the kids came, they'd be restless," Sally explained. "And then we'd have to look after them. We'd be distracted and the men would get nervous."

"Do you enjoy coming to the games?" I wondered if they would respond honestly.

The first woman pulled down the corners of her mouth and shrugged. After moments, the second woman answered, "I think we could all find things we'd rather do, but we don't mind coming. It's important to the guys for us to be here, and besides, we like seeing each other."

"Who says?" the first woman bantered. "Speak for yourself."

"Well, if you don't like me, I think you'd better try to like me since we see each other so much because our husbands stick together like glue. Our social contacts," the second woman added speaking in mock affectation, "are somewhat limited."

I remembered the Staten Island cop's wife. These women were also isolated by their husbands' refusal to associate with any but their own kind. Did Ted have any friends who were not vets? I knew I would never let myself be confined, to accept humbly this group of women, even if it included Sally whom I admired, as my complete circle of friends, but I was uneasy about the prospect of having to struggle to maintain a wider range of social contacts.

"You're not my only friends; I'm here by choice," the third woman said. "Look, Marty, I like you, warts and all. I like all of us VWs."

"VWs?" I asked, addressing these women directly.

"Vets' Wives, or Vets' Women," the third woman turned around and answered. "Hi, I'm Ellen Magnusson."

"Oh, Claire, I'm sorry," Sally apologized. "I should have introduced you. This is, of course, Ellen, and (nodding to the first woman) this is Martha Hoffman, Carol Shaw (second woman), and Jean Higgins (fourth woman).

A chorus of mutual hi's followed Sally's belated introduction. As soon as my presence had been acknowledged, the women became shy and the showing off stopped.

"Welcome," Martha said. "I've seen you at the library and once or twice out at the K-Mart. I knew you probably lived around here. How do you like it?"

"I like it. I grew up here."

"That's right," Carol said, as if she was just remembering what I was sure she and the other women already knew about me. "Sally said you, she, Bob, and Ted all went to high school together."

"Yes, we did. Before your time."

"Do you have kids?"

"I have a twelve-year old daughter."

"How does she like living here?" Jean asked.

"She's getting used to it. I think she's even beginning to like living here."

"Where did you live before?"

"New York."

"Wow. This must be a big change for her."

"It was, but as I said, she's getting used to it."

"My kids are too young for her," Carol said. "I've got a boy four and a girl three."

"My kids are boys," Ellen explained. "They're twelve and thirteen, but they're not interested in girls yet. They're a pair of oafs, both of them."

"You don't look old enough to have kids that age."

"They're from my first marriage. I got married right out of high school. I was crazy and my parents were right. But I've been lucky. My second husband is terrific, and better to my kids than their own father was."

"You think you'll have any more children?" Jean asked.

"I'd like to. I know he'd like to have a child, and I'd like to give him one. He's such a, well, such a good guy. But it all depends on the economy. If Rea-

Legends of Good Women

gan gets elected, and things get moving again, then we'll do it."

"You mean you'd let a decision like than depend on who gets elected?" Carol asked.

"When it's a question of a third child, yes. With this inflation and unemployment, yes. No one here has three kids, right? How many people do you know who have more than two these days? It's too hard. With one you have fun, with two, you make do, with three, you're up a tree."

"Do you think" I asked, "with the policies Reagan is talking about, things will really get better?"

"Well, can they get worse than they are now with Carter?"

"What's happening with the game?" Carol asked before I could respond to Ellen.

"We're at the top of the sixth," Jean answered. "We're leading four to three. Their team is at bat, and Ted has just struck one man out."

Carol and Martha turned to give me congratulatory smiles, meaning, I supposed, that "my man's" accomplishment was the same as my own. The in-and-out, hot-and-cold feeling I had been having ever since I had come to the game possessed me. My pleasure in watching Ted's fine body as he swiftly uncorked balls at opposing batters, my vanity in knowing others knew this still physically splendid man was my lover was countered by resentment at having my own identity limited by that connection. What mattered to me about myself would not matter to others; the esteem these women might feel for me would be due to my connection to Ted, to being – of all things – the boss's wife.

Jean turned her attention from the game to me. She was clearly on the point of asking me a question, but paused to light a cigarette; she was the only one of us who smoked.

"Sally says you teach at Fontbonne."

"That's right."

"Do you like it."

"Very much."

"What do you teach?"

"Freshman composition. Writing."

"I used to love to write in high school," Carol confided. "I wrote poems, and I kept a diary, you know, one of those books with a lock on it. I wore the key around my neck so my mother wouldn't be able to read it. I thought my secret writings were such hot stuff, I would die if anyone ever read them. I found some of my diaries while I was cleaning one day, and I laughed. They were so silly. All about my thoughts on boys. Thoughts, mind you. I hardly did anything until my senior year, when I finally began going steady."

"Going steady," Martha echoed. "Remember some of the boys we went steady with? I wonder how they turned out."

"Like the men we married," Carol declared.

"Oh, no," Ellen argued. "I married the guy I went steady with, and it was a big mistake. The man I'm married to now is much better."

"Well, sometimes the men we marry are better, and sometimes not," Jean said. "I still see some of the boys I went with in high school. I mean," she amended, "I see them around, shopping in the supermarket when they're with their kids and I'm with mine. And I sometimes think . . . oh, well, I guess married life is the same, no matter who you're married to."

"Are you kidding? You can't mean what you just said," Ellen objected hotly.

Legends of Good Women

"And sometimes," Carol continued smoothly, "we marry the boy we went steady with, and it turns out well. Sally went steady with Bob in high school, and they're married, and it's turned out fine."

Everyone turned to look at Sally, who smiled stiffly and kept her eyes on the field.

"Ted's retired the side," she announced. "He struck out three men in a row."

We all belatedly, guiltily became enthusiastic. Carol and Martha applauded, but I could not overcome my ambivalence to do more than smile, sit up straight, and become attentive as "our" team went up to bat. Bob went first, taking a call of two balls and two strikes before hitting a pop fly into the catcher's mitt. I did not turn consolingly to Sally as the others did, thinking defiantly that she had not struck out, Bob had. I knew Sally was watching what I saw: Bob turning from the base mound and throwing his bat in disgust as he walked toward the bench. Carol's husband, Joe, went up, made one strike, received one ball, made a hit to left field, ran to first, and was held there by good defensive play as the outfielder threw the ball to the first baseman, who, after Carol's husband was safe, threw the ball to the second baseman. Jean's husband, Hig, went up, connected with the first pitch and sent it out to left field, sufficient to land him on first, but not wide enough to assure safe passage for Joe to second base. After recovering the ball, the outfielder threw it to the second baseman, who tagged Joe out. My little group sat facing forward; was Carol miffed with Jean, I wondered, because Hig had caused Joe to be sacrificed? Ellen's husband, Tom, came up, struck once, received two balls, and hit a foul. Would he be walked, strike out, or hit a good one? The next pitch was high and inside; Tom went to first, Hig went to second, and Ted came up with two men on and two men out. Ted took a ball, swung and missed the second pitch, and then, with a resounding whock, sent the ball on a high wide arc out beyond the tree borders. Hig and Tom came in, and then, as Ted touched home base, the team was off the bench and running toward him. I was proud and at the same time at war with my pride. And ashamed of the split in my feelings. Why should I not be proud, as one athlete might feel proud of a teammate? Why did I fear too much identification with Ted? Because I did not want to have to struggle continually with the tendency of everyone around me to meld me into him, to see his accomplishments as mine, but never my accomplishments as mine, and certainly never his. The four women turned around, smiling widely.

"Don't look at me," I commanded. "I had nothing to do with it."

Martha's husband came up to bat, took a ball on the first pitch; then connected with the second pitch, hitting a ground ball which the infielder retrieved and sent to first base. He was out, but nobody cared; "our" side went to the field, and, to a woman, we cheered. "We" were leading now, and I tried to focus my attention on the game. All of us, the six women in my little group, kept our faces firmly forward, turning now and then to watch the responses of the women on "their" team. The first man up had taken a base hit from Ted; as Ted faced his second batter, he moved, or seemed to me to move, just like the pros. I was unreasonably pleased to see him move that way, to watch him read the catcher's—Tom's—signals, and glance quickly at the batter on first base.

Jean turned around, and I quickly bent down to tie my running shoe.

"It must be great to have all that education," she said to my bent head.

The four women turned around. By god, they were sure focussing on me this time.

"You have a Ph.D., don't you?" Carol asked.

I nodded, keeping my eyes on Ted, who had just taken a second strike from the man at bat.

"You're the first and only Ph.D. I ever met," Martha said, "and you seem normal. You're wearing plain, non-designer jeans just like we are."

"Still, that's a very impressive accomplishment," Carol said. "I was terrible in school. I think I'll be able to help my kids with their homework until the second grade. After that, I don't know what I'm going to do."

"How long did it take you to get your degree?" Ellen wanted to know, and I told her ten years from start to finish, explaining I had gone part-time while working and caring for Janey.

They all looked at me with open admiration, and I became uncomfortable. Martha said I must have had incredible determination, and I was tempted to make a flip remark about what a strong motivation a bad marriage can be, but decided not to open up that area of my life for discussion.

"If I had one part of the education you had, Claire, even a two-year degree, I'd feel so proud," Martha said.

"Yes," Ellen agreed, "I wish I'd followed my parents' advice. They wanted me to go to college. God, I can only appreciate now how I must have broken their hearts with my headstrong ways. If my sons try to follow my path, I'll tie them up until they come to their senses."

"Oh, I wish I had had parents like yours," Jean said, "but my parents were typical Germans, you know, *kinder, kichen, kuchen,* as far as women were concerned. They thought education was wasted on women, and besides, they never came out and said it, but they made me feel I wasn't bright enough for college. And my husband has never done much to make me feel they were wrong."

"Yeah," Martha agreed, "I wish I had more education. I'd like to be a nurse, like Sally, but Sally got her training before Bob came home from Vietnam. I think it's too hard to go to school when you're married and have kids. And can you imagine what our husbands would say if we told them we want to go to school? And how they'd feel about spending money for tuition?"

I could not resist jumping on my hobby horse then and said: "Every life is capable of change and growth."

"But part of my problem," Martha countered, "is that I don't even have ambitions for myself. Whenever I plan, I plan for him. I think of what he could do. I think how nice it would be if he went back to school and got his degree like Ted."

There was activity on the field, and we all turned, maybe reluctantly, to see what had happened. Ted had retired the other side scoreless and the team was comfortably ahead. The women turned their attention eagerly to themselves again. Everyone, including Sally, said that she spent more time planning for her husband than for herself. That her daydreams usually began "Wouldn't it be nice if . . .," but the subject of them was always her husband. I said why don't you make yourself the star of your fantasies. Why don't you all make a wish list. Martha began slowly, extravagantly with, "I wish my great-aunt would die and leave me her property, not that I wish her dead one minute sooner than she should be." Carol said she wished she had a million dollars, and everyone else said the same. Then they began to be serious, beginning with the easy things like a new bathroom, or furniture, or a car, and moved on to work-related desires. Jean wished for a job where she had at least one person under her instead of reporting to everyone in her office. Ellen said she'd like to work with animals, that she had always wanted to be a veterinarian. I suggested that she try to find a job in a veterinarian's office to test whether she really did want to be a vet. Perhaps her ambition was unrealistic, perhaps not, but she should at least make a step toward it. I was beginning to feel preachy, but the women seemed to want to hear what I had to say.

"I know from experience that when I was in the worst situation in my life, a group of women got me through it. I really think you ought to make that kind of commitment to each other, that is, spend time together, apart from baseball games, to talk more about what problems you have to deal with, and help each other toward solving them, or living through problems you can't solve. There's risk, of course. You have to trust each other and be reliable for each other."

"I'd like to be part of such a group," Sally said, and I realized she had hardly spoken at all before. "But I don't think I can manage to come to meetings because my work schedule changes frequently"

Martha, Ellen, Carol, and Jean said they could get together for a meeting, but I did not hear much conviction in their voices. They asked me if I would come. I did not want to be part of a "VW" group, and hated my snobbishness. Of course I'll join your group, I said.

A light roar came up to us from the field, and we all jumped guiltily. Jean's husband had hit a home run and was coming around to third base when we were finally aware of what he was doing.

"Oh, God," Jean spoke as if she were really praying, "that's the first home run he's hit this season; he's been wanting to hit one so badly, and I didn't even see it."

"Well, you saw him complete his run," Carol assured her.

"It won't be the same to him," Jean protested, almost tearfully. "He wants me to watch everything he does. I hope he didn't see me talking to you all."

We were silent, contemplating the unreasonableness of Jean's husband. I was appalled by Jean's sense of having sinned because she had not seen her husband at the moment of impact between his bat and the ball, but I was to be horrified minutes later when, after one of the high school players struck out, the game ended. Ted's team had won, but we did not know the exact score. As the teams knotted together to gather up their equipment, Jean's husband ran up into the bleachers, heading directly toward us. He was screaming, his face twisted with a rage beyond control.

"You dumb bitch," he roared at Jean, who bent her head humbly as if acknowledging his right to abuse her. "You were so busy yakking, you didn't see me get the home run I was aching for. How could you not be paying attention to me when I go up to bat I don't ask much from you, and God knows I get even less but, woman, why couldn't you have done this simple thing for me just once?"

His rage did not stop; it fed on itself, and he lapsed into a litany of old connubial grievances. I wanted to put my hands over my ears; I did not want to hear the insults he hurled at her, betraying intimacy, spraying with his spittle information we had no right to know about Jean's inadequacies as a homemaker and sexual partner, about flaws in her cooking and personal hygiene. The other women kept their faces lowered as the storm of his anger broke over our heads, but I kept my face toward him, looking at him, determined not to give him total victory over female abjection. His eyes flicked over the other women, especially me. My steady gaze was provoking him; he probably recognized me as a threat, the piper who might call these women away. He was tempted to extend his anger to us, to me most of all, but the awareness that he would have to deal with his teammates, whose somewhat favored possessions we were, braked his wrath.

The approach of our menfolk brought an end to his tirade. Ted came up behind Hig, put his hand on his shoulder, and said quietly and firmly, "That's enough now. Stop it."

Hig subsided. I involuntarily shook my head, and Ted gave me a quick warning glance that infuriated me. The women filed out of the bleachers, following the men like belled cows. It was a rout. What wimps we women are, I thought as I watched them meekly going down the stairs, their eyes on their feet. Our commitment to each other had evaporated; we had not even lingered long enough to make plans for meeting again. I looked back at Jean, whom we had abandoned. She was looking down at her folded hands, while Hig stood bending over her with his arms on his hips, and one leg up on the bench beside her, in a posture suggesting menacing exasperation. I stood and looked back, determined to wait until they left.

Ted went on until he realized I was not beside him, then turned back; he understood but did not much like what I was doing.

"Did you bring your car, Hig, or do you and Jean need a ride home?"

Slowly Hig turned to answer Ted's rhetorical question.

"It's all right, Ted. I've got the car. Thanks, anyway."

Hig resumed his brooding posture. I remained watching him and Jean, and Ted, beginning to resent me, waited and watched with me. In moments, Hig realized Ted was waiting, turned, understood the purpose of our vigil, and frowned.

"Go on, you two, we're coming."

Jean looked up, and, perhaps taking courage at seeing me there, or feeling embarrassed at having me watch her humiliation, stood up and walked down the benches while Hig came to the aisle and walked with Ted and me out of the bleachers, then ran to catch up with Jean who was crossing the field.

I moved abreast of Ted as we walked across the field. He looked at me but did not speak, and I was too angry to speak to him. As we approached our cars, though I made myself break silence. Our original plan had been that he would come back to my house after the game. But I was not in the mood to follow it any longer. I wanted to talk to Ted about what had happened, but I wanted to be calm first.

"Look, Ted, I'm too upset by what happened to drive right now. I want to walk first. If you're tired, you can go to my place and change if you'd like."

I saw his expression change just slightly, as if he was annoyed yet felt obliged to indulge me because I was dysfunctional due to some irrational but inexorable "female complaint."

"Why don't we walk together?"

His request and his tone were so reasonable, I would have been churlish to refuse him. I had wanted to be alone, but I felt myself thawing.

"Sure."

We walked toward and then beside the lake. The sun was setting, sending out some last glorious streaks across the sky. Birds were sending night calls to one another. The wind rose slightly, and I pulled on the sweat shirt I had tied around my waist. I was calmer, but when I spoke, I was aware of how inadequately my words expressed my feelings.

"That was awful."

Ted shrugged. I persisted. "Don't you think Hig's behavior was awful?"

"Tell me why you think it was so awful."

"Oh, my God, a man screams insults at his wife, says things about her that nobody has any business knowing, betrays her . . ."

As I remembered the scene, my anger renewed; I turned to face Ted and grab his elbows. "That kind of revelation is a betrayal. I don't see how any marriage could survive such a betrayal. You didn't hear what he said."

"Not this time."

"You mean this has happened before. Oh, my God. How can you be so complacent about it?"

"Maybe I don't think it's my business. In fact, maybe I think it would be entirely out of line for me to get between a man and his wife."

"A man and his wife," I mocked.

"Yes." Ted stared at me then, understanding my irony, amended his words.

"All right, A man and a woman. A husband and wife. I think I would be obnoxiously patronizing if I tried to give a man marital advice, which he might justifiably reject on the grounds that I was not qualified to give it. Besides, Hig's a good worker. That's all I think I have a right to expect from him. What would you have me do? What would you do? Isn't it up to Jean to change the situation? She seems to accept it."

I was not ready to tell Ted that every flawed marriage I saw — and that was the only kind of marriage I saw – drove me into a panic, made me feel the odds were against us if all our contemporaries were in bad marriages. I was afraid that Ted might one day play Hig's role while I played Jean's. No, that would never happen. Ted might be Hig, although I doubted such a transformation would occur, but I would for damn certain never be Jean.

"Jean accepts Hig's treatment of her because she has no self-esteem. And if she doesn't get support from anyone, she'll go on thinking the way Hig treats her is all she deserves. And what happens between them is our business. We have a stake in the happiness of our friends, of the people in the community, whether or not we've got a good marriage to hold up as an example. I have a right to tell someone that his actions toward his wife hurt me, and I have a right to tell a woman that her complacent acceptance of bad treatment from her husband gives me pain, makes my life more difficult because she's reenforcing the idea that men have a right to abuse women. And I don't think such a marriage can have a good effect on children."

Ted's face was serious. He was concentrating on what I was saying. I was beginning to know when my words were having an effect on him. I knew when he was on the verge of agreeing or thinking about agreeing with me when he looked down as he listened. When he looked into the distance, as he was now doing, I knew he was not in agreement with me.

"I can't believe you just think about a man's work performance, and let everything else alone."

"Well, believe it." Ted's voice was testy.

"Then you're contradicting everything you've told me about yourself. About following the example of the good lieutenant. Besides, I know you care about the well-being of others, apart from their work performance. Why are you being arbitrary in this case?"

"I'm not being arbitrary. I think there's a difference between being like the lieutenant, and acting like a mother hen, or getting involved with other men's quarrels with their wives."

"Maybe you think it's all right for Hig to abuse Jean."

"I don't think it's all right for Hig to abuse Jean, but I don't know that he was abusing her."

"You don't think what he said about her in public is abuse? I feel terrible knowing the things Hig said about her. I would think Jean would be humiliated knowing I've heard them. We just met. I think she admires me. In her place, I'd be ready to die if someone I had just met and liked heard such intimate, insulting information about me."

"Well, Jean will survive; she has before. I used to be upset by their quarrels, but I've learned to adjust to their pattern. It's their style of communicating."

"Style?" I was ready to explode at Ted's obtuseness and complacency.

"Yes, style. Whatever may seem wrong about the way they deal with one another, however awful it may seem to us, it seems to work for them. Hig blows off at Jean, and Jean accepts it. Maybe she even provokes it. Maybe what you identified as low self-esteem causes her to call forth from Hig the kind of treatment she thinks she deserves."

"That's my point exactly."

"Well, for whatever reasons, they stay together. And I guess, despite everything they do that might seem unloving and unlovely to the rest of us, they love each other."

"That's not love, that's bondage."

"It seems to keep them together," Ted said, pausing, perhaps waiting for me to pick up his attempt at humor. "Look, don't think you can come back here after all these years and begin changing everyone's life."

"I'm not."

"No? Well, those women usually follow the games pretty closely. But tonight they were all stirred up. Jean must have been pretty distracted not to pay attention to her husband when he was at bat. Don't stir things up until you know more about the people you're talking to. Don't move in like a one-minute miracle worker. Maybe life here isn't all it should be, but people are getting along in their own imperfect ways. Don't start telling everyone how to live."

"You remind me of those Southern racists who used to say, 'Our nigras were perfectly happy until those outside agitators started stirring them up.' If you think people are 'getting along,' you're blind to the evidence before you. And if I can 'stir things up' in any way at all, I'm damn well going to do it."

We had walked until the sun was almost down, and becoming aware of the near-darkness, the coolness rising from the lake, we turned toward our cars. And the question of whether we would spend the night together. Part of me wanted to drive off alone and stay alone, but the other part wanted reconciliation. As we each got into our own cars, I felt a moment of panic that Ted might go to his place and not mine, but he called to me as he pulled away from the curb, "See you back at your place?"

"Sure, why not?"

CHAPTER

In the week following the softball game, my idea of reintegrating myself into a community I had never really been part of seemed pathetic and unrealizable. I began even to doubt that I could rebuild my career; no one would be interested in my scholarship, and I would end my days as a hired scribe, impelling unwilling classes toward functional literacy. But if I could not establish myself in Star Lake, where could I go? I could not uproot Janey again. I quelled the slide toward despair by concentrating on routines. I increased my training from eight to nine miles each weekday morning, and made a plan to run twenty miles on Saturday. Ted and I were surfacy with each other. In bed, we drove each other like nails, banging and flailing at each other like passion machines, and all the while, anger lay just beneath the tip of tongue and under fingertips.

One morning, I called Meta and told her not to meet me at the high school, that I would come out to her place and we would run nearby, somewhere under trees because it was a humid day.

Harry was reading the newspaper when I arrived. He held it in his hand as he opened the door and greeted me with an ambivalent expression on his face.

"The athlete will be down in a few minutes," he grumped at me. "Do you want any coffee or anything?"

"How about a smile, Harry?"

He made a mock Cheshire cat grin at me, and sank behind his paper like a torpedoed ship. Meta came down; she flicked a look of exasperation at him, but did not say anything. I suggested to Meta that we get in my car and search for a good running place. We drove a short distance out of town into farming country and selected a sparsely traveled, unpaved, tree-lined road that led to state park land and a lake. I parked the car off the road, and we began to run. After trotting half a mile at Meta's pace, I was sweating heavily. So was Meta. I watched the sweat on her face turn gold and the skin under it turn pink.

"Maybe we should stop," I suggested.

"No, when the going gets tough, etc. What would Vince Lombardi say?"

"Who's Vince Lombardi? You know what I would like to do? I'd like to take off my shirt and bra. Why not? Men run without shirts."

"And we can always dive into the bushes if someone comes."

Meta and I stopped, pulled off our singlets and bras, wound them together and tied them around our waists. We began jogging again. I watched Meta's breasts and she watched mine. Hers were larger, but still firm. Her nipples were nice, too — not big, brown and hairy, but still pink and petite. Her skin was also nice. So would mine be when I was her age. We had our northern ancestors to thank for that. Was it the cold and the damp that got into our genes, giving us still moist skin when we were well into our sixties? Why was Harry so depressed? Meta was still a fine looking woman, bright and adventurous; she was what I aspired to be at her age, and I would think a man married to such a woman would be proud. I would not ask her about Harry because then I would feel obliged to share confidences about Ted, and I did not want to because Harry was not blood kin to me, but Ted was her baby.

"You've got nice tits, Meta."

"I know. So do you."

We ran silently for a while, just listening to wood sounds and the rhythmic pounding of our feet.

"Do you know what we're doing, Meta?"

"I think so, but tell me, Claire, what are we doing?"

"Jugging."

After running with Meta, I spent the rest of the day at home, working in my study. I was on the point of calling Ted when the phone rang; wanting us to move past hostility, I nearly cooed when I answered. "Hi there."

"Claire?"

"Yes."

"This is Helen. You know from the softball game last week?"

"Oh, hello, how are you?"

"Fine. Listen there's another game tomorrow evening."

"There is. So soon."

"Yeah. The team plays every week. Ted didn't tell you?"

"No. It must have slipped his mind, or he assumed I knew when they played." Or he never wanted me to darken his playing field to 'stir things up' again.

"Yeah. They play every week. Their turn comes up once a week in the division."

"Oh, I see."

"Well, the reason I was calling was I was talking to some of the girls, and they didn't know whether you would be coming again, and so I thought I would call to see if you were planning to come. Claire, I hope you'll come. I know we all kind of left with our tails between our legs. We didn't know what to do in the situation."

"Really? Ted told me that 'the situation' has occurred before."

"That doesn't mean we know how to handle it. That's why we wanted a chance to talk to you again."

"Sure, Helen, I'll be there."

"Good. I know we seem like a bunch of—well, wimps, to you, but we're just getting started, you know, just beginning to get our act together."

I assured her insincerely that I had not thought they were wimps. "You know, Claire, I'm glad, and I'm sure I speak for the others, I'm glad you're here. We needed someone to light a fire under us and get us moving."

All the words of my little feminist set speech flowed into my head—about how all they needed was recognition, having their consciousness raised, and that everything else they would do themselves, but, of course, I did not say them. I just thanked her for calling, assured her I would be in regular attendance at the games, and told her I was pleased to be of help. Then I said even more honestly that her call had made me happy, that I was really pleased that she and her friends wanted me to be there. I was grinning when I called Ted, feeling ready to say, "Someone wants me to come to the game even if you don't," but he was surprised and pleased.

"I thought that after what happened last week, you'd never want to come again."

"My sisters have asked me to come."

"Sisters, eh? I think some of us are in trouble."

"Well, some of you were in trouble long before I returned to town."

"Maybe. I'll see you tomorrow, then."

"Ted."

"Yes?"

"I know there's a women's softball league."

"Yes, but . . ."

"Don't worry, I'm not thinking of starting my own team. But couldn't there be a co-ed league, so men and women could play together?"

"That's not a bad idea. Will you manage a team?"

Oh, shit, I thought. That's the last thing I want to do.

"Of course I will."

"Good. Well, when you want to get started, I'll help you get the Park and Recreation Department to set up a league."

The next evening, I ate dinner at home and then drove to the field, arriving shortly before the game began. Helen grinned and waved at me as I walked to the bleachers, and, as I sat myself among them, the women greeted me as if I were their friend whose presence they now took for granted. Assuming Sally would be there, I had not called her, and so was disappointed not to find her there.

"She had a shift," Helen told me.

When the game began, I noticed the women talked among themselves as they had the first time I had come, but they kept their eyes fixed on the field and were attentive to the plays. Their conversation was subdued and casual, mostly about domestic concerns. They made no effort to "share" with me reports of progress toward the goals they had declared for themselves, and I avoided asking questions that would result in admissions, embarrassing to both them and me, that they had not taken any steps toward changing their lives. I decided that if unjudgmental, accepting friendship was what they wanted from me, that was what I would give them.

Ted's team took the lead over the team from Archway Electronics early in the game and maintained it steadily and unexcitingly. I let my mind wander, thinking most of Janey, whose letters from camp were terse and uncommunicative enough to let me know only that she was not unhappy, and was probably having a better time than she wanted to admit to having. I imagined Janey's scornful comments if she saw me in the role I had forbidden her ever to play: passive, supportive man-watching female.

When the game ended, I walked onto the field with Helen. We paired off with our menfolk and walked toward the line of our cars parked at the edge of the field. Ted and I were in the lead; I grinned at him and impulsively picked up his hand and swung it as we walked.

"Had a good day?"

"Yes, I did. I saw your mother yesterday. We had a good run together."

"She told me. She said you were interested in going into politics."

"I'm interested in supporting her. I promised I would get active so she would not feel so isolated."

"Are you interested in running for office yourself?"

"No, are you?"

I had asked the question flippantly, wanting to throw a challenge back at Ted, but the immediate denial I had expected did not come.

"You have thought about running for office." I stopped walking.

Ted turned back, a sheepish grin on his face. "Actually, I have. Do you think it's a wild idea?"

"No. No. I think it's a great idea. What office do you want to run for? Congress. When do you think you'll run?"

"Not any time soon. I want my business to be more firmly established than it is. And I'll have to become more active in civic affairs. But you really can see me as a candidate for office?"

"Sure. You're a natural. Attractive young entrepreneur. Home boy. Family man – sort of. Veteran. You're a natural. If I had your credentials, I'd run, too. Or maybe all I'd need would be your gender."

Nodding toward the teammates who were strolling over the field behind us, I said, "So this is part of your constituency."

"Yes, I suppose so. I suppose I thought of that when I started the league. But I also did it because I like the game. I wasn't just being opportunistic."

"I approve of healthy opportunism, or enlightened self interest. Actually, you intimidated me with your seeming lack of it. Actually, I like you even better now that I know you're harboring political ambitions. Actually, I think unalloyed altruism sucks. Actually, I'm getting quite horny."

"Well, that's one problem I can solve even before I run for office."

We turned and walked quickly toward the edge of the field.

"Meetcha back at your place," Ted said and ran to his car. As I walked to mine, I heard footfalls behind me, marching in cadence. And then I heard two or three men chanting sotto voce, "We're not fond-a, we're not fond-a Jane; we're not fond-a, we're not fond-a Jane." I recognized the voice of the man just behind me as Hig's. I turned and faced the men; Hig was in the lead; Jean was beside him. The vets and the VW's were grouped behind him. Not one woman would look me in the eye. In the rear, grinning with sardonic pleasure, was Bob. I was expecting a hostile challenge, but none came.

"Goodnight," they chorused as I walked to my car. They briefly resumed their march before separating into couples, each man leading his wife to the family car. They had made their point.

For the next three weeks, I continued out of stubbornness to watch Ted's team play. Although some of the teams, like Ted's, were sponsored by local merchants and entrepreneurs, most of the teams were sponsored by bar owners.

"Where do you think most of the players spend their time?" Ted replied when I asked the reason. "The bar owners couldn't very well refuse the sponsorship fee and the cost of t-shirts for the team if they wanted to stay in business."

"It's too bad that bars are such a big business here. No wonder the column under the police reports in the Star Lake Daily News is filled with DWIs."

"What do you expect from men who work at assembly line jobs for hourly wages with no benefits and frequent layoffs to do with their spare time? Organize book clubs?"

"Some of those men's wives do. And they work as supermarket checkers and K-Mart sales clerks."

"I suggest that it's still tougher for men. Men are brought up to expect more of themselves as far as jobs are concerned. A woman doesn't think of herself as a failure if she works as a sales clerk if she's bringing up kids. But a man thinks of himself as a failure if he can't support his kids better than his father supported him. When they realize they're never going to be better than their fathers, they become disappointed in themselves. And yes, men lack the skill, which women seem to have so abundantly, of verbalizing their feelings. So they drink. Look, I'm trying in my own small way to change the way a few men live. I'm trying to get them to want to have a stake in my business. If I can do that, maybe others can, too. So if you want to make a contribution, try to provide an alternative. Or at least try to understand why they do what they do."

And I did try. I made a point of talking to the men before and after the next game, to de-demonize myself in their eyes. I made an effort to be friendly to Bob. I even proposed that Sally, Bob, Ted, and I have a pre-game picnic.

It started off well. I prepared thick hamburger patties and grilled them on one of the park barbecue pits. Sally brought plates, plasticware, buns, potato chips, potato salad, and cole slaw. Bob and Ted brought the inevitable beer. I also supplied the hit of the meal, a chocolate layer cake, which was completely devoured.

For a while, the conversation went well. Bob began discussing the hostage situation.

"You know, Carter knew that if we let the Shah into this country, the Iranians would seize Americans. He even raised the issue with the Shah's buddies, Kissinger and David Rockefeller, when they asked him to let the Shah into this country. But Carter let himself be talked into it and the Iranians took over our embassy. Dammit, I wish Kissinger and Rockefeller were sitting blindfolded in some cell instead of our people."

"So do I," I said, able for the first time to agree with Bob on an issue.

"Really?"

"Yes, I do."

Bob got up from the table and strode around it as he spoke.

"Fortunately, Carter's days in office are numbered. Reagan's going to be elected and then things will be different. This country's going to get some respect again."

"I'm not voting for Reagan," Ted said.

"How can you say that? With the hostage crisis. With Carter handing over the Panama Canal? With inflation and unemployment up? With the rest of the world ready to spit at this country? You're going to vote for Carter? I don't believe you."

"Whatever Carter's faults and errors, I don't see it in my interest to vote for Reagan. Or yours, either. He's going to give tax benefits to the rich that you and I won't get. And with those tax advantages, rich people will be able to borrow more money, and that means money will be harder for people like me to borrow. No, I'm voting for Carter."

Bob stood behind Ted and Sally, glowering at me over their heads, convinced, of course, that I had influenced Ted's decision.

"Were the pictures I gave you helpful?" I asked Sally.

I had asked my mother to send me family pictures because I wanted to complete my family photo album. My question drew an enthusiastic response from Sally.

"Claire, I've never done this before. The photos you gave me of your mother as a girl, her mother, sister, brothers, and father, and the scene you described to me just took over my imagination. It was like I was standing in the room with them when it all happened. I've made sketches, of course. And I've started to set it up on the loom. I'm just thrilled with the way the work is going. I feel I should pay you for the experience."

"Sally, do you think you could banish the word 'should' from your vocabulary for a week?"

While we had been talking, Bob had been pacing. Now he stood behind Sally and Ted, facing me, his face filled with so much rage, I was shocked.

Then Ted said it was time to get ready to play. He and Bob left while Sally and I packed up and disposed of garbage before joining the other women in the bleachers to watch the team defeat Kelley's Corner Bar. If Ted's team won the following week, they would win the division championship and go to the Division playoffs.

If my efforts to ease Bob's hostility toward me had failed, they had pleased Ted, who hugged me after the game and put his arm around my waist as we walked to our cars, an unprecedented public gesture of affection.

Later, at my house, I reminded Ted that our kids would soon be with us.

"Do you think they'll like us?"

"My daughter likes me. I'm sure your son likes you."

"You know what I mean. Will your daughter like me? Will my son like you?"

"My daughter thinks you're 'neat,' which is the ultimate teenage superlative at this time. And I'm sure your son, if he has his father's good judgement, will like me."

"Will they like us as step-parents is what I'm asking."

"Is that what you're asking?"

"It is. What do you think?"

"I think you should start by asking me to be your wife. Let me amend that. I think we should start deciding if we want to be married. Then we can think of our kids."

"Shall we get married? What do you say?"

"I say, yup, let's."

"That's not a very romantic answer."

"It was as romantic as your proposal."

"Maybe. But you're the wordsmith."

"Oh, I see. We've amended the gender-based division of labor so that it's now the woman's job to make pretty speeches. O.K. I'll say this. What we've had in the past few weeks is the only passion I've every known. I've been married and I'm a mother, but I've never been a lover or a wife. You've been my wonderful, perfect lover, and I hope I've been that for you."

"Yes, you have."

"And you've made me see the possibilities of being a wife, of being a wife in a good marriage, anyway. I'm starting to get choked up."

"Me, too."

"All right, that's all the romance you're getting from me tonight. And about our kids. They'll just have to deal with our decision."

Ted went to Milwaukee on the 9th, and I ran twenty miles through hilly countryside, planning what Janey and I would do when she came home. I wanted to do a sports activity with her, but to my great disappointment, Janey had steadfastly refused to run. Perhaps Janey felt the only way she could define herself independently from me was not to attempt anything, not to risk failing, not to compete with me, or to compete with me by becoming a non-achiever. I also thought of Ted; I imagined him going to his former wife's home; I imagined Michelle and her husband solemnly but with good will, the husband secretly relieved, handing over Ted, Junior to the care of his father. Probably the person made most unhappy about the change in Ted, Junior's guardianship would be his three-year-old half-sister, who would lose a sibling and miss him. How did kids deal with such change? The society had moved in less than a century from extended family to nuclear family to modular family. What would be the eventual cost to Michelle's daughter and to other children who had brothers one morning they did not have the next, or who had to suddenly behave as siblings to strange children? Would they, as adults, be even more casual and noncommittal than adults were today? Perhaps I was exaggerating the effect. Perhaps Michelle's daughter would adapt quite well to losing her half-brother, whom she would see again, but whose departure from her parents' home would lessen tension and increase her space. Perhaps there would be a second, full sibling to replace him, and Michelle's daughter would then be the senior member. But then my train of thought brought me to the freezing recognition that if Ted, Junior was vacating one home, he would, in time, be part of another merged family – mine, and I thought of Janey, sassy and street-wise, suddenly a junior member in our reassembled family. Oh, Janey had reacted romantically to the idea of a Brady-bunch unit, but I knew the reality of living in a merged family would be quite different from her expectations; different and difficult. I pictured her, brimming with resentment at her loss of stature, and to a male child. She might regard that displacement as an unforgivable betrayal. Would I be able to forge us into a family?

Monday I went to pick up Janey at the point where I had left her six weeks before. The other mothers were there already or arrived shortly before I did, and we all gave each other a smile expressing resignation at ending our furlough from motherhood and pleasure at being reunited with our children. The mother of the girl Janey had instantly hated on the day of departure spoke to me.

"Allison wrote me that she and your daughter-is your daughter Janey? – well Allison and Janey have become fast friends."

"Really? I'm glad to learn that, because Janey writes only to give basic information, like "we arrived safely," and issue instructions, like "send comic books and chewing gum."

In seconds the bus arrived and delivered back to us the waiting children it had carried off in June. Allison was the first one off and Janey was right behind her. She gave me her birthday-candle smile and touched her eyebrows; the gesture was a joking reminder of her return from Greenwich House Camp two years before. On their last night, the campers in Janey's bunk – all fashion-minded P.S. 41'ers – had decided to give themselves the pencil-thin eyebrows then in fashion. They had paired off to shave each other's eyebrows, but Janey's partner had gone too far and removed one entire eyebrow, so Janey, to restore balance, had shaved off the other one. I had been pawing the sidewalk on Barrow Street, for whether going or returning, the Greenwich House bus was always late, but when the bus finally arrived and released my daughter, my smile of welcome turned to a gasp of shock as I beheld my eyebrowless child. This summer she had her eyebrows and, I hoped, every other part of her intact as well. Allison and Janey each said "Hi, Mom," and then turned to each other for a frantic final conversation while Allison's mother and I waited like patient chauffeurs. The smiling, competent camp representative came off the bus to oversee the unloading of luggage from the bins, and smiled at Allison's mother and me while nodding at our chatting

Legends of Good Women

daughters, silently citing the blooming friendship as evidence of the camp's good work.

"I think your daughters had a good summer," she reassured us.

"So did we," Allison's mother said under her breath to me as we collected our daughters' duffels. Then, with an exchange of promises to write, Allison and Janey allowed themselves to be parted and returned to the custody of their mothers. I put Janey's duffel in the back of the Volvo and got in front beside her. I studied her; she was taller, blonder, and something else. What internal changes had she experienced over the summer?

"Did you have a good time? Your only communications to me were a long series of demands, so I could not determine whether you were enjoying yourself."

"Actually, it was better than I expected. Actually, I had a good time."

"Praise indeed. What did you do? I would have liked to have had some idea of what your activities were."

"Water sports mostly. I learned to sail. That was neat. And I snorkeled. I also improved my swimming. The coach was very good and taught me how to strengthen my kick and helped me to breathe better. I got so good, in fact – "Janey pulled a small rectangular box from her shoulder bag and put it in my lap. Inside was a small medallion with a red, white and blue band that read "Camp Flambeau Sports Rally Day. First Prize in Swimming Event for Age Group."

" – I came in first in swimming for twelve-to-fourteen-years-old. I beat kids older than me. Than I. Do you think the medal is as nice as you get when you run in races?"

"It's better. Everyone who runs gets a medal for just finishing. Only swimmers who come in first get these."

"The people who come in first in other events get the same kind of medal. It's not unique."

"But it's still special. I'm proud of you, Janey."

"I had a great time, but I'm glad to see you again, Mom."

That was big stuff from Janey.

"Oh, my darling daughter, I'm so glad to see you, too."

I hugged Janey and she even hugged me back.

And I knew as soon as I turned the key in the ignition, Janey would change emotional directions.

"So, why are we spending all this time talking about me? Let's talk about what you have been doing."

"You know my routine. Work. Training for the marathon. Seeing friends."

"Have you been seeing a particular friend? Your letters to me were not full of information, either."

I had planned to stop at the Midtown IGA on the way home, but this conversation with Janey was becoming too important to interrupt.

"If you mean Ted, yes. I've been seeing him a great deal."

"And you mean he's still a friend. Not more than a friend?"

"What do you mean?"

"Well, I thought with me out of the way, you'd well. . .am I going to have a new father is what I want to know."

"I can't say yes or no to that yet, Janey, but I'd like you to think about the fact that before you have a new father, I will have a new husband. Think about that, Janey; think of me married."

Janey winced.

"No, I hadn't thought of that while I was at camp. I'd think about different situation and having Ted as my father. But I never saw you in it at all."

"Seems natural to me. That's what every kid wants. A father and a mother who relate totally to the child, and have very little to do with each other. Well, try to picture me married to Ted. How do you feel about your mother being a wife?"

"I don't know. I see pluses and minuses."

I decided not to explore positives and negatives with her. I had more information to give her.

"And Janey, you'd have to do even more sharing if Ted and I married. Ted has a son."

"But he lives in Milwaukee, I thought."

"Ted and his ex-wife have decided that Ted's son should live with him. If I married Ted, you'd have a brother. An older brother."

"Oh, snap."

I knew Janey better than to trust her first impulse to see the romantic aspects of the instant acquisition of what she assumed would be an attractive, popular older brother who would make her the envy of her friends and bring home his attractive male friends whom she, Circe-like, would transform into admirers. Janey, as alert — indeed, more alert than most teenagers — to her own self-interest would race on to grasp the less than attractive aspects of an expanded family unit. I knew Janey's first formed images of it would be public ones: four attractive people being admired by her friends and their parents. All her sense of inadequacy about her family situation would vanish, and I had to admit that her perception that our status would improve through my marriage to Ted was real. Reverend Baker would make his face to shine upon me if I became a domesticated woman; he might even welcome me into a leadership role. Yes, there would be public advantages, but while Janey might claim the attention of Ted, his son, and all of Ted's kinfolk, she would have to share mine with them, and with her adolescent greed, no amount of gain was acceptable if any loss of what she already had was necessary. And she would lose her status as only child, her seniority, and, if Ted and I had another child, her juniority as well.

"Would you have another child if you and Ted got married?"

"I don't know. I haven't gone that far in my thinking yet. But no, I don't think so."

Janey's question startled me. I watched her ponder the positives of that possibility—a cute baby sibling to cuddle, show off, and dominate and the negatives—sharing my and everyone's attention with an invincible competitor. Out of the corner of my eye, I watched Janey's face pass through shades of ambivalence, as she contemplated the variables, but I was beginning to be certain that Janey's awareness of an improvement in our status would be the most important factor in promoting her acceptance of the change in family life.

"Tell me more about becoming an athlete."

"What's there to tell? I thought you'd be pleased."

"I am. I'm delighted. I'd just like to know how it happened."

"Well, you always said you wanted me to be passionate about something. And at Camp Flambeau, you were really out of it if you weren't involved in at least one sport. You knew that, didn't you, when you sent me there?"

"Yes, but I also knew it wasn't one of those Spartan places where they threw you in the water to teach you to swim. The camp directors seemed humane to me, and you liked them at the interview when you agreed to go there."

"I did? I don't remember agreeing. I remember being told I would go."

"You agreed to be sent."

"Well, anyway, I liked the camp and the counselors were nice. They have a counselor-in-training program for former campers. Can I go there next summer so I can become a counselor when I'm old enough?"

"Sure, you can, if you still want to go there next summer. Tell me how you decided on swimming."

"Well, I've always liked it, even at Greenwich House Camp. I liked the other sports I tried, even archery, but I liked swimming best. I guess because I liked the counselor best."

"Ah."

"What does that mean?"

"It means I recognize a familiar trait. You've always done well or poorly in school according to how much or how little you liked your teacher."

"Well, I liked Cynthia. She was very patient with me. She made everything I did seem terrific. And so I became very good at swimming."

"Indeed. The best in your group."

"Can I continue training, Mom?"

"Certainly, if you still want to continue it on your own. Can you find the desire to keep swimming without Cynthia to encourage you?"

"I think so. Because I've become good at it. It's the first time in my life I've done anything better than anyone else. I'll bet I can swim better than you."

"I'm sure you can swim better than I can. And you could, with those long wonderful legs of yours, be a better runner than I am. I've always told you that, so don't try to make me feel that I've tried to make you feel inadequate. I've just tried to be a more useful model to you than my mother was to me."

"Wasn't your mother good to you?"

"Of course she was. But she was limited. She and my father did the best they could for me according to their understanding of what the best was. We just know more today. Especially about how to bring up girls."

"Well, I always knew you wanted me to have my own identity. I just had to find it in my own time in my own way. Now you won't have to worry about me sitting against some car waiting for some boy to finish playing basket ball with his buddies."

"I'm glad, because I think being disciplined about something you care about is the greatest protection I know against disappointment. No matter what happens, no matter who lets you down, if you can make demands on yourself and produce what you ask of yourself, you still have a measure of control over your life."

When we reached home, I became absorbed in sorting out Janey's clothes, determining what had been lost—a pair of shorts and a t-shirt—identifying what she had brought home that was not hers: a pair of shorts with a name tape in it which I returned to the camp to be sent on to the owners, with my futile hope that the other child had brought Janey's missing shorts home with her. For a treat, as part of a rebonding ritual, I took Janey out for pizza. The next day, I enrolled Janey at the YWCA so she could swim. She found some of her school friends had also returned from camp or their family's summer home, and visiting them entailed chauffeuring her or them. I gave up any claim to being a scholar, and decided to be a full-time mother until Janey went back to school. My only effort at self-definition was to stick to my training regimen.

CHAPTER

When Ted called I asked how he and his son were getting along.
"He's very uptight. We agree on sports, like the same teams, but he's, believe it or not, a bit of a right-winger. He thinks I should vote for Reagan."
"What did you say when he told you that?"
"That I would not vote in any event for Reagan."
"How did he react to that statement?"
Ted paused before admitting that he and his son were not experiencing the instant bonding they had expected and were a bit disappointed in each other. I felt guiltily fortunate, for although my Greenwich Village smartass daughter infuriated me at times, she never disappointed me. But how would a right-wing child deal with the prospect of having a left-wing stepmother and smartass stepsister?

Where had his politics come from, I asked Ted. Perhaps from his stepfather, perhaps on his own; his mother was not very political, but certainly was not a Reagan supporter. Ted was not sure what explained his son's conservative attitudes, but thought that possibly his longing for structure and permanence had made Reagan's call for a return to a mythically simple, authoritarian yesteryear attractive to his son.

We arranged for our kids to meet at dinner at the Happy Chef. Of course, they hated each other on sight. Janey, who can be formidably charming when she decides on that course, went through the teenage getting-acquainted litany with good humor: what year are you in? what's your best subject? what sports do you like? what music do you like? But young Ted resisted her surlily, and answered only in monosyllables, keeping his face down, begrudging us even the sight of his clear blue eyes. After a truly vigorous effort at thawing the boy, Janey looked across the table at me and widened her eyes expressively, signalling she had done all the making nice that could reasonably be expected of her. Ted saw the gesture and understood its meaning. I did not know whether he felt resentful of or sympathetic to our mother-daughter conspiracy, or whether he felt, as I did, that his son was behaving churlishly. We got through dinner, but since this first effort at Brady-bunching had been a failure, the Schaefer and Ritter families went their separate ways. As Janey and I set off for home, she let me have it about the behavior of Ted, Junior, whom we agreed to call Teddy to avoid confusion with his father. I had to agree with her that he had been a nerd, but I expressed pride at her forbearance in the face of his sullenness. I urged her to be patient, for I was certain he would come around. Janey replied that I was placing a lot of responsibility on a twelve-year-old. I said she could handle it, and she agreed to be patient a while longer.

The next day, I called Ted and suggested we all go for a swim at the lake because I wanted to show off Janey's skill. Ted said he thought a better plan was for him and Teddy to join us for dinner. Janey and I went to the lake by ourselves.

"Oh," Janey sighed after we had parked the car and were standing together at the lake shore, "I'm glad it's just the two of us out here."

I heard what Janey left unsaid: that the times for "just the two of us" might become rare and she would miss them if they did. I was uneasy because I shared Janey's apprehension.

Janey and I entered the lake together, but I remained standing near the shore while Janey swam out to the dock. I was filled with admiration as I watched her pull herself through the water with strong, even, strokes and propel herself with powerful flutter kicks; the Schaefer legs, I noted with pride, were serving another generation of female athletes. Her head moved so economically, less than a quarter turn, as she took breaths, and I realized as I watched her transform herself into a splendid, efficient swimmer that I was experiencing separation. For the first time, I was aware of Janey, not as my daughter, but as another being, different and apart from me. I was filled with a this-came-from-my-body? sense of wonder that made me both humble and proud.

When Janey climbed onto the dock, I began swimming out to join her. As I pulled myself up the ladder, I saw Janey smiling down at me, aware that she had already surpassed me as a swimmer, but content to be pleased with her own accomplishment, rather than to feel vindictively triumphant over me. We sat on the dock until the sun had dried our suits; then we dove into the water again. Janey swam around the lake while I moved in a smaller, slower circle around the dock. After twenty laps, I was ready to leave the lake, but I knew Janey would not stop swimming until after I did – for her generosity toward

Legends of Good Women

me did not mean she had abandoned competitiveness, now that she had at last found the area in which she could better me. I swam five more laps, decided I had made a respectable effort, and swam to shore. Janey joined me after she had circled the lake – for the twentieth time? – and we sat on towels until our suits were dry before returning home.

When Ted and his son rejoined us at seven, I noticed a slight change, a small lessening of surliness, in Teddy. He and Janey were silent during the meal, while his father and I reminisced about our school days, as if we were developing a routine. Janey was on the verge of boredom, having already heard most of what we were saying, but I could see that Teddy was trying to hide his interest.

"Your father was the most popular student in our class," I said to him. "He was an outstanding athlete; the local newspaper was always full of articles about him."

Turning to Ted, I asked, "Did you keep any of those articles?"

"No," Ted answered, wrinkling his nose. "Maybe my mother saved them, but I certainly didn't."

"Well, I hope she did, because I think your son would enjoy reading them."

Again addressing Teddy I said, "In addition to being a fine athlete, your father was a genuinely popular student. He was always at the center of a group, the obvious leader."

"Yeah? Well, I certainly won't follow in his footsteps. I'm known for being a negative personality."

Janey looked at him sharply, on the verge, I knew, of making a smart comment.

Before she had a chance to speak, Teddy asked me, "What were you doing while my father was playing football and being leader of the pack?"

A slightly nasty edge was in his voice, but I answered him evenly.

"I was a student, what used to be called a grind. Unlike your father, I was not popular. I was a loner."

"You were not disliked," Ted objected. "The rest of us thought you were self-sufficient, stand-offish. Actually, I think most of us thought you thought we were not bright enough for you."

"There must be some kind of lesson in this, for I wanted nothing more than to be part of a group. No, Ted, I remember certain looks, comments being passed while I walked through the halls. I wasn't benignly tolerated, I was rejected. You probably cannot imagine what high school was like for me because you were up there, one of the elite, everyone's hero—including mine—but I am not exaggerating when I say I was miserable in high school, and my misery was not my own making. Teenagers are cruel and judgmental, then and now. If you don't believe me, just listen to Janey and her friends discuss one of their peers who does not meet their arcane criteria for acceptability."

"Hey, just a minute, Mom, don't take it out on me and my friends just because you were unpopular in high school. And I don't think you should eavesdrop on confidential conversations I have with my friends." Janey looked indignant and sounded self-righteous. Where did she get such qualities?

Suddenly turning to Teddy, Janey asked, You know what my mom used to do when I was a little kid? She'd sneak up on me and my friends and tape record our cute little conversations."

"I don't eavesdrop, Janey. You and your friends openly criticize your classmates. And I'm not blaming you, I'm describing a rite of passage. Adolescents have to establish a pecking order to reassure themselves of their status in the tribe. Fortunately, as time goes on and as most young people become more secure and sure of themselves, they become more merciful. But right now you need to quell your own insecurity by seeing others as inferior."

"I'm not insecure; I'm confident," Janey countered. "I know I'm a super person."

"Does everyone share that opinion of you?" Teddy challenged.

"I'm not trying to cultivate mass appeal," Janey replied, archly, not too obviously reaching to match the competition. "Since I value quality over quantity, I have a small, but very select following. Wherever I've been, I've always been in the top click. What about you? What are your friends like?"

"I belong to an even smaller and even more select group than you do. Although most of the low-life types at the school I went to in Milwaukee did not have enough intelligence to recognize our superiority."

"What made you and your friends superior?" his father asked.

"If you had seen the rest of the student body in my school, you wouldn't have to ask. Of course, my friends and I were white and most of the students were black. That's for starters. But we were superior to the other white students, too."

After a heavy pause, Janey asked, "Are you a racist?"

"I think blacks are less intelligent that whites, yes. I think all the standard measurements of achievement make that fact clear."

"You're a racist," Janey declared.

"Okay, then, I'm a racist."

"Well, all my friends think racism's tacky."

"You're entitled to your opinion."

We were still sitting at the kitchen table, where we had eaten our evening meal; each of us was looking away from the others. I got up and began clearing the dishes. Janey got up from the table and helped me.

"What did you do after you graduated from Star Lake High, Claire?" Teddy smirked as if he already knew the answers and was trying to force an embarrassing admission from me.

Pushing down an impulse to snap;, "Call me Dr. Schaefer," I replied, "I went to UW-Madison, as your father did."

"Yeah, but he dropped out during his sophomore year to go to Vietnam. You stayed on and graduated, right?"

"Yes. And after I graduated I married Janey's father and went to live in New York. I got my graduate degrees there and taught until we came back here to Star Lake."

"When you were at UW, were you one of those Sixties campus radicals?"

Teddy was sitting with his chair tilted back, and his arms hanging down over its top. I looked past the challenging smartass expression on his face and sat down at the table.

"I sure was. I was active in the civil rights movement, so, of course, I don't agree with you that black people are inferior to whites. I can't stop you from being a racist if you choose to be one, but I must tell you I dislike racists."

"Were you against the Vietnam war?"

"Yes, I was. And I was active in the anti-war movement at Madison."

"So you and my father were on opposite sides."

"Yes."

"If you had it to do over, Ted, would you go to Vietnam?" Janey asked.

"Knowing no more than I did then, yes. Knowing what I know now, no."

"Then you and my mom aren't really on opposite sides."

"Not any more, if we ever were."

Turning to face Teddy with a "so there" look, Janey asked, "What do you and your friends like to do when you hang out together?"

"First of all, we don't 'hang out.' Hanging out is for people who don't know what to do with themselves, who need others to direct them. My friends and I meet for a purpose. We make plans and carry them out."

"Well, what do you do when you're together?"

"Any number of things. We pursue what interests us."

"Will you please tell me just what one of those interests are – is."

"All right. There's a game we like to play; it's more than a game, really. It's a challenge to the imagination and intelligence. It's called 'Dungeons and Dragons.' You probably haven't heard of it."

"Oh, that was popular a while back in New York City. It was popular among nerdy kids who were trying to be macho."

The telephone rang and I answered it at the wall extension. It was Meta, breathless and distressed."

"Oh, Claire, I'm so glad you're home. Is Ted there?"

"Yes, he is, Meta. What's wrong?"

"Something has happened that he should know about. Nothing concerning family, or his business, but he should know about it. I'd rather he tell you himself. Could I speak to him?"

"Sure. Just a minute."

Ted, reading my expression, grew alert and concerned. He reached for the phone, but I told him to go to the telephone in my bedroom. He bounded through the door and ran upstairs; when I heard him say, "Mom?" I hung up.

Janey and Teddy looked at me, mildly expecting a message, but when I did not offer one, they unconcernedly looked away from me and back at each other. Then Janey turned suddenly and announced, "Mom, I'm going to take Ted into my room and play some of my albums for him, okay?"

Janey knew my permission was not necessary; she was documenting how much effort she was putting into being nice to Teddy. She wanted me to know I owed her one and more.

"Sure," I said gratuitously.

They went into Janey's room and soon I heard and felt the vibrations of "her" music. I went into the back yard, closing only the screen door so Ted would know where I was when he returned to the kitchen, and stood gazing up at the sky, full of light and movement in the mid-August pattern of celestial activity. Despite the beauty of the night, I felt a wave of depression coming over me. I looked at the rectangle of light made by the window of Janey's bedroom. If I married Ted, I would have a racist step-son. I would be sharing my home with a child, I admitted to myself, I intensely disliked. In minutes, Ted joined me.

"What happened?"

Ted hesitated. I prodded.

"Your mother said it was not anything affecting your family or your business. What was it?"

"There's been an accident at Bob's house."

"What kind of accident? Is anyone hurt? Sally? The kids?"

"I'm not sure. I don't have the details. My mother did not know all that happened; she just told me that Sally's mother called her looking for me, wanting me to go over there if I could. I think I should go over there now."

"Why didn't Sally call here looking for you?"

"I don't know."

I knew Ted knew more than he was telling me, and I was rather certain I knew what kind of "accident" had happened at "Bob's house."

"What about Teddy?"

"I'll take him home. Or bring him to my mother's. Yes, that's what I'll do."

"He can stay here," I offered lamely.

In the twilight, I saw Ted smile, whether at my insincerity, or at the prospect of leaving his difficult son with me, I could not discern.

"No, thank you for the offer, but I'll take him with me."

As we walked together back to the house, Ted put his arm around my shoulder and I put mine around his waist; I felt him striving as I was to preserve camaraderie. When Ted summoned his son, both teenagers came from Janey's room. At the door, with our children watching, Ted kissed my cheek; the gesture was, for once, not masking passion, but represented all the affection either of us felt for the other at the moment.

"Call me; let me know what happened."

"I will," he promised without saying when.

CHAPTER

I spent much of the next week cementing the bond with Janey: shopping for school things, taking her to the local Y for swimming practice, even inquiring about coaching, and fixing good meals. I enjoyed serving Janey her favorite foods—pizza and pasta—but also surprising her with new recipes which she might resist at first and then enjoy in spite of herself. I loved seeing her eyes widen with pleasure at what was in her mouth, and then hearing her make smack-smack noises with her lips. But even more than good meals, Janey enjoyed shopping trips.

"That's what I enjoy doing best with you," she said.

"I know. I wish you would enjoy doing other things with me, too."

Not that Janey was a greedy kid. On the contrary, I would have to persuade her that she could have a desired item over her objection that it was too expensive. No, it was not the acquisition so much as the examination of things that pleased Janey and bored me.

"When you get to high school," I told her, "I'm going to give you a clothing allowance. Then you can shop with your friends."

Her face clouded, but she did not object. I felt a pang of guilt, even though I was sure her disappointment was not because she would not share an experience with me, but because she knew she would have less money at her disposal if it was a fixed amount. However, our week together was sweet indeed. I learned by signs – like finding the living room had been straightened or the kitchen sink cleaned – how much she too was enjoying the time with me. She was still in the aftermath of her camp experience, which while enjoyable, was not like being with people who loved one. The week after a child returns from camp is usually the best time of the year for a parent.

Sharing good times with Janey was one of the week's blessings; another was my training schedule – the marathon was a bit more than two months away, and I had completed an eight mile run in under one hour. I was chopping my time down past the eight minutes a mile mark; if I could work my time down to seven minutes a mile and sustain that speed on a long run, I might be able to complete the marathon in under three hours and twenty minutes. I would qualify for the Boston Marathon then, and that was my goal.

I continued my runs with Meta, and we chummily talked of other things, for Meta did not tell me what had drawn Ted away the past Saturday night, and I did not ask. Meta was up to two mile runs at fifteen minutes a mile. I told her I was pleased with her progress, but even prouder of her commitment. I suggested that she persuade some of her friends to run with her. My own training was becoming so intense that I found running with Meta a distraction, almost a hindrance

I would continue to run with her, but I did not want to begin resenting our time together. She said she had asked her friends, but they had all said they would not think of appearing in public in running shorts and exposing their bumpy, veiny, flabby flesh. It was all right, they said, for Meta, who was, "listen to this, Claire, 'well preserved.' Don't you love that phrase? As if I had been sitting in a barrel of brine like a pickle. I said, 'Look, sillies, the way to make yourself happier with your bodies is to use them.' I said a lot of things, but they regarded the idea with horror."

"Why don't you try again in the fall when the weather will be too cold for shorts. If they can cover themselves in sweatpants and shirts, they might be willing to run with you. Tell them if they run and do other exercise, by the time next summer comes, they'll be more pleased with their bodies and more willing to expose them."

"I'll try; I'll tell them that, but I don't know if I can persuade them to get off their butts. It's hard to believe that my friends who were once so young, full of dreams and mischief, are now such biddies. We shared so much; we were girls together, young women, wives and mothers, and now, in the blinking of an eye, they're timid. I still need playmates, friends to giggle and gossip with, tell dirty jokes with."

"Meta, you're one of my inspirations. I need to see someone else nagging the world into behaving decently. Please keep after those friends, Meta, until you've got them off and running, too. Why are you laughing?"

"I'm picturing all my white and grey-haired friends as runners, and I'm picturing the faces of all those teenaged boys who can't get to their track because all these sixty-plus women are using it."

Legends of Good Women

When we parted, Meta said, "I really like having you around, Claire. You add something to this town. Stick around, this time, heh?"

That was a big tribute from Meta; she gave me an opening, but I could not bring myself to ask Meta about what had taken Ted from my home Saturday evening.

When he called me at last that evening, and I asked how he was, how everything was, he paused just a moment before answering, "Everything's under control."

We were both silent then as I thought but did not say, "What's happened? Why can't you tell me? Why don't you trust me?" and Ted heard my silent questions but did not answer them.

"How is business?"

"Fine. The shop is humming. I may even put my son to work."

"What has he been doing while you're at work?"

"A great thing has happened. He and my father have become great buddies. They go everywhere together. My father shows him off to his cronies, and Teddy is a wonderful new audience for their stories about growing up during the Depression, going off to war in the Forties, coming back and 'starting up from scratch.' My father has even been telling my son about pranks I pulled when I was a kid."

"Such as?"

"Oh, I'll tell you another time, or let him tell you. He feels so triumphant about discovering my flaws. There are still moments of tension between us, moments when we don't know what to say to each other, but he and his grandfather took to each other immediately, as if they had been searching for each other, as, in a way, they had."

"I'm not enjoying celibacy."

"Neither am I. But it's only temporary. We'll work something out."

"How soon do you think that will be?"

"I'm pressed right now. I have a lot to take care of, but I promise we'll work something out soon. Listen, can you and Janey be at the game this Thursday?"

"Yes."

"O.K. My son and I will see you and Janey then. Could you bring some food?"

"Sure," I said, feeling deeply resentful and vowing not to fuss but bring only jock and teenager food: deli sandwiches, potato chips, and cokes.

I was too edgy to concentrate on work, which I had more or less put on the back burner of my intellectual kitchen until after Janey had returned to school and I had resumed teaching. Janey had already become bored with me and, in the heartless way of children, was on the telephone in order to reintegrate herself with her "click" of friends, most of whom had returned from camp or their families' summer homes. I wanted to spend time with someone who would appreciate me. I called Sally several times, but there was no answer. Perhaps she, Bob, and the kids were away. I tried to make myself tranquil, to ease my impatience for Thursday. I resolved to keep my resentment of Ted's secretiveness out of my voice when he called, and of course, broke the resolution immediately after "Hello."

"Look, something's wrong somewhere in your life, and I think we've grown close enough to each other for you to tell me what it is. What is it that has you so busy that you can't see me. I think I deserve an explanation."

I heard my impotent, nagging-wife words and hated them.

"Yes, you do deserve an explanation, but I'm asking you to wait for one because what is concerning me right now concerns others even more. I don't feel free to confide in you yet. Can you be patient a while longer?"

I said — what else? — of course I could.

Thursday I had the picnic meal ready long before Janey emerged from her bedroom bearing endorsements of her body parts like USDA stamps: an alligator on her yellow tee shirt above her budding breast and a designer's signature on her derriere.

Ted and his son were waiting for us when we arrived at the field. I handed the two packed shopping bags of food to Janey and Teddy, and walked with Ted behind them to the picnic table where I distributed the heavy, glutinous, but ultimately satisfying deli-bought sandwiches. After we had eaten, Ted went to greet his teammates. Teddy rose with him, for although he was too young to play, his father had told him he could sit on the bench with the team. Then I realized I had not seen Bob and Sally.

"Bob's not playing?"

"No."

"Why not? What's wrong?"

"He's not feeling well. He's been sick."

Ted's tone was casual, but his eyes were so serious when they met mine, I knew I had identified the center of crisis. I also knew I would have to wait for more specific information. Ted and his son left; Janey and I bagged and disposed of the picnic remains before climbing the bleachers to join "the girls." They made approving adult sounds about Janey, who did not seem at all embarrassed by them; in fact, she seemed to enjoy being fussed over.

"Has anyone seen Sally this week?" I asked.

"No," Carol responded. "I tried to reach her, but there was no answer. And Bob's not playing. Are they away?"

"Maybe one of the kids is sick," Jean suggested.

"That would account for Sally's absence, but it wouldn't keep Bob from playing," Carol answered.

No one seemed alarmed, and no one seemed to know more than I did; they seemed to know less, in fact. Meanwhile, I wanted to do my duty by "the girls;" I inquired encouragingly about goals in weight loss, job search, pursuit of education. I hoped Janey would not notice and tease me about my spectator role, a vain hope.

"Have you come to watch Ted in every game."

"No, not every game."

"My mother, the fan. My, how the mighty have fallen."

Ted's team defeated the Limelight Tavern team; the game the following week would determine whether Ted's team would be division champions and go on to play in the division play-offs.

"Our place or yours," Janey asked Ted impudently after the game.

"I need to shower, Janey. Maybe you and your mother would stop to pick up some ice cream while we go ahead and then you two can join us at the apartment."

"Mom?"

"Sure. What flavor would you two like."

"Coffee for me. Son?"

"Strawberry."

I'm committed to chocolate and Janey wants vanilla," I said. "We'll see you in half an hour."

One of the advantages of living in a dairy state is the choice of ice cream. All the ice cream stores in town make their own ice cream; Janey and I went to the one which, after a pleasant survey, I decided made the superior product; then we drove to Ted's apartment. Ted and his son were sitting on the living room couch watching the ten o'clock news. The coverage of the election campaign provoked a "Yuck, Reagan" from Janey.

"What's so great about Carter?" Teddy challenged.

"Nothing," Janey replied, "but Reagan is terrible. The election represents the choice between two evils, and Carter is the lesser of them."

"Oh, yeah; what about the economy? Carter's done a rotten job. Look at unemployment. Look at inflation."

"Maybe it's not so good now, but it will get worse under Reagan."

"How can that be when so much of our budget is committed to wasteful social programs. Reagan is going to cut down on government expenditures."

"No, he isn't; he's only going to put the money in different places, like the military, where few people will benefit. Look, your pop is not rich and neither is my mom; working people don't do well under Republican administrations; only rich people do well. A lot of people think that Reagan's cutbacks will affect other people, not themselves, but what he says he's going to do will affect everyone even if they don't think it will. Only Reagan's rich friends will be better off."

"What's wrong with being rich?"

Janey paused before answering, long enough to be aware of my attention to her argument, so I walked quickly to the kitchen and quietly took bowls from kitchen cabinets so I could hear Janey's answer.

"Nothing's wrong with being rich; I think it would be neat, in fact, if I could be sure that no one would suffer because I was rich. But what Reagan is going to do will benefit the few at the expense of the many."

"That's your mom talking; those aren't your own ideas."

"Even if I got them from her, they're my ideas now. Where do you get your ideas from?"

Ted, Junior remained silent.

"Your mom?"

"No." His voice was almost scornful.

"Your dad?"

"My real dad or my stepdad?"

"Whichever."

"My son and I have not advanced yet to the stage of having a political discussion, so I can't be held accountable for his opinions." As Ted entered the argument with a touch of lightness, I entered the living room bearing bowls heaped with ice cream and handed them to Teddy and Janey. I signalled with my eyes to Ted that I wanted him to follow me. In the kitchen I handed him his bowl. We stood by the sink silently and efficiently feeding ourselves ice cream.

"Now tell me what's been going on," I demanded when we were finished.

Ted took my bowl and rinsed it and his own under the faucet, then placed the two bowls on the drainer.

"Last Saturday, when my mother called, she told me that Sally's mother had called her, asking her to find me and to tell me to come to their house as soon as I could."

Ted stopped speaking and I kept myself from asking questions.

"It seems," he continued, "that every Friday night for months, maybe a year, Sally goes to an Al-anon meeting. Did you know that? Do you know what Al-anon is?"

"Yes. It's a support group for family members of alcoholics. But no, I didn't know that Sally went to their meetings."

"Neither did I. Usually she gets a sitter for the kids."

"Even if Bob's there at home."

"Yes. Anyway, last Friday night, the sitter couldn't come, so Sally took the kids to her mother's house, as she also does sometimes, and then she went on to the meeting. She planned to let the kids stay overnight with her mother and pick them up on Saturday morning. While she was away, Bob came home in a black mood to an empty house. Even though Sally has taken the kids to her mother's many times before, Bob felt he had been abandoned. Sally hadn't told him she was going to Al-anon meetings, but he guessed that her regular absence from home on nights when she wasn't working was connected to his—drinking. He also apparently confronted the fact that his wife didn't trust him to leave the kids alone with him. So he decided to become as bad as everyone seemed to think he was. Worse. He began drinking and by the time Sally came home, he was in a rage. He attacked her."

"Oh, no. Oh, my God, no," I exclaimed; then added, "I can't say I'm surprised."

"He beat her badly. Blacked her eyes, left contusions on her arms. She's black and blue all over. Fortunately, he didn't break her nose or jaw."

"Oh yes, fortunately."

Ted looked at me and quickly looked away. I didn't care about his feelings at that moment. I was so angry, I felt he should accept some responsibility for Bob's actions.

"You've seen her?"

"Yes, that was why my mother called. Sally managed to get away from Bob and lock herself in their bedroom. Bob broke down the door. Sally tried to call for help, but Bob tore the phone off the wall. She was able to take refuge finally in that room she uses as a studio and playroom for the kids, but she couldn't call out, and she began to be afraid that Bob might burn the house down."

"Has he ever started fires before?"

"Yes, but I didn't know he did until, well, until this weekend."

"The first time I went to their house, when Sally was showing me around, she took me up to her studio to show me her weavings. I found a sack with a scorched tapestry in it. Sally didn't say anything about it; tried to cover it up, in fact, but I sensed that Bob was responsible. He is so threatened by anything he can't control. I saw that in our first meeting. I knew he hated me, without reason. He saw me threatening his relationship with you. He no doubt attacked Sally because he sensed she was getting away from him. Surely he had revealed signs of paranoia before."

"Perhaps he did." Ted threw up his arms in mock concession. "And perhaps Sally and I, lacking your clear vision, did not read and respond to his signals."

Wanting to avoid a quarrel, I said nothing.

"Anyway, Sally's mother became concerned when Sally didn't come in the morning to pick up the kids. She tried to call, but of course the phone was out, so she began calling around. She tried the hospital, but Sally was not on duty. She tried Bob's precinct station, but he wasn't scheduled to be on duty, either."

"Did she say anything to Bob's co-workers about her fears?"

"She let whoever she spoke to know that she was trying to find Sally, that Sally had not come to get her children, which was most unlike her. The person she spoke to suggested that maybe they had gone away together, or were on their way to her house, or had just overslept."

Of course Bob's buddies would cover for him, I thought. They probably beat their wives once in a while, too. An unfair judgment, perhaps, but I was probably right.

"Finally Sally's mother tried to get me and when I didn't answer, she called my mother and managed to convince her that something was wrong. My mother drove out to their house."

"Gutsy lady, your mother."

"Yes, indeed. She couldn't get in, but she knew people were in the house, and she suspected that something was wrong. She thought she'd have a go at locating me before she called the police."

Would the police have come if she had called, I wondered silently.

"Then she kept calling your house and mine until she got me."

"What did you do after you left my house?"

"After I brought Ted home, I drove to Sally and Bob's. There weren't any lights on, but I heard sounds. The house was locked, and I knew if I tried to break in, I'd only upset Bob more."

"Then you had some idea of what was going on?"

"I had some idea Bob was in crisis. So, yes, on some level, I was aware of Bob's problems. Of course, I've been aware of Bob's state of mind. I was where he was; I know how he got that way."

Oh, the goddam Vietnam war, I screamed in my head. I'm sick of hearing that war used as an excuse for men's violence.

"I stood beneath the windows of their bedroom because I was sure that was where Bob was. And I kept talking, calling up reassurances, pleading with him to let me in. I think everything had gone farther than he had intended it to go and he needed someone to talk him back. After half an hour, he came down and let me in. He was still in a state of rage."

"A drunken rage?"

"Yes. He said, 'She's trying to take my kids from me. She's turning them against me. She thinks she's too good for me.' He said a lot of things. He told me where Sally was and I made him go outside while I went up to get her. I got Sally out of the house and into my car. Sally didn't want to go to her mother's because she didn't want her kids to see her, so I called my mother who came and got Teddy and took him to her house and then she came back and stayed with Sally while I went back and got Bob and took him to the VA hospital. Sunday I went back to their house and cleaned the place up. I went to Fleet Farm and bought a new door for the bedroom and put it in. Sally called her sister in Eau Claire who came and got the kids and then I took Sally to her mother's. Sally hasn't been to work all week, but the bruises are beginning to lighten. I've been shuttling back and forth between them all week. God is it only Thursday? The counselors at the hospital got after Bob. They forced him to confront his drinking problem and insisted he get himself into an outpatient counseling program. Bob is full of contrition. He says he'll do anything to get his family back. He's agreed to enter the program.

"Will Sally go back to him?"

"What's the alternative?"

"What do you mean, what's the alternative? Not going back to him."

"You can't be serious. You're talking about breaking up a family. Do you want everybody to be in our club?"

"No, certainly not. But it's been obvious to me ever since I came back that something is terribly wrong in their marriage. How can it not have been obvious to you, who have known them through the years, who sees them frequently, that Sally and the kids walk on eggs when they're around Bob? I felt it. He hates me. He hated me on sight. He's irrational. You must have seen it. And heard it."

"I've seen problems, of course, but. . ."

"Yes?"

"It all goes back to the war. And don't, goddammit, roll your eyes or smirk. Bob . . ."

"I'll roll my eyes," I interrupted in a hoarse whisper, "I'll smirk, I'll make any response, voluntary or involuntary, to what I disagree with. I will not excuse Bob's behavior because of a bad war experience almost twenty years old. And I won't walk on eggs around you."

Ted was furious; maybe he wanted to strike me, and maybe he also knew that if he abused me, he would only prove my point. For whatever reason, he restrained himself and, after minutes of heavy breathing, answered me in a level tone.

"I'm not excusing Bob's behavior, but I do think his experience in Vietnam is a big factor. And the antiwar movement making him feel disgraced didn't help his state of mind."

"But Bob doesn't feel disgraced. He thinks the only thing wrong was that the war wasn't allowed to go on. His anger comes from being denied a victory."

"That's his public position."

"That's his private position, too."

"Maybe, but contempt expressed for men who fought for what they thought was a just cause, for doing their patriotic duty is still another burden he carries. Yes, it increases his anger and makes it even more difficult to admit he has a problem."

"So what do you see happening?"

"I see them getting back together and really working on their problems. Bob's agreed to go to the Vets' counseling program. And to go to a marriage counselor with Sally. Sally's agreed. Bob's fixing up the place as a peace offering before Sally comes home. Why are you shaking your head?"

"Because I think if Sally goes back, she's giving him permission to abuse her again, I don't care what promises Bob has made. He'll say anything to get what he wants. Control."

We were silent together for moments; then we walked into the living room just as Janey was saying angrily to Ted, Junior, "My father's Jewish."

CHAPTER

"What was that all about?" I asked Janey on the drive home after a terse parting from Ted and his son. Long silence, then: "Teddy had been asking me how I liked living in New York and what was it like, and I had been telling them about my friends, and what we did. I told him about going to St. Marks' on Saturday afternoons for double features, and going skating, and hanging out in Washington Square Park, and riding our bikes in Central Park. I told him about P.S. 41, and then he asked if any of my friends were colored, and I said black, no one uses the word colored any more, and yes, one of my friends was a black Puerto Rican and another had a black father and a white mother, and so what, and Teddy said maybe my friends were exceptions, but he hated going to school with black kids; that they stole and vandalized property, and didn't know how to behave in school. He said he hated going to school with them or being anywhere around them and he was glad Reagan was going to be president because then all their welfare would be cut off and they'd have to get jobs. Then I said my experience had been different from his; P.S. 41 was a middle class school, so everybody, no matter what they were, all acted the same, that is, we all were pretty well-behaved, or maybe the richest kids among us were the most obnoxious. And then Ted said he'd bet the richest, most obnoxious kids were Jewish, and I said some were, some weren't, that some of the rich kids at my school were black and Asian as well as Jewish, and some of them were obnoxious and some weren't, and then I said rich and obnoxious don't always go together. You're not rich, but you're certainly obnoxious, so how do you explain it, and before you start in on Jews, I want you to know that my father's Jewish."

I let some silence ride between us. Then Janey shared her thoughts with me.

"You know, Mom, I used to think some, not all, but some of the things Teddy was saying. Not about my friends, of course, or the kids at P.S. 41, or at Greenwich House Camp, but when I traveled around the city, I'd see groups of Black kids and they were awful. They were rowdy and they scared me; I didn't want them to notice me the way they would pick on some poor kids whose pants were too high above their socks. I hated the way they talked with loud, high, whiny voices and their awful language. Every other words was 'fuck' or 'shit.' But when I heard Teddy talking against them, my first instinct was to defend them. There wasn't a thing he said that at some time I hadn't thought myself, and yet when I heard those thoughts come out of his mouth, they sounded so awful, I had to argue against them. They sounded so ignorant."

I let some more silence ride between us.
"You know what's funny?"
"What?"

"Some of my friends here say the same things Teddy was saying about blacks, except they say them about Indians."

"Oh?"

"Yes, it's weird to hear the same stuff, you know, they live off welfare; they're too lazy to get jobs; all they do is get drunk. The only difference is they hate the Indians for having more fishing rights."

"Does your sweet-faced friend, Ellen Winters, say things like that about the Indians?"

A pause.

"Yes."

"But you have warned her not to say things like that in front of me."

"I didn't have to. She knows."

"That's the best, in fact, the only good piece of information I've had all day. But I thought you told Teddy your friends think racism's tacky."

"My friends in New York do."

A pause.

"Mom?"

"Yes?"

"I miss 11th Street."

So did I, but I kept silent.

"We couldn't move back, could we?"

"No. We're here for the duration."

"Duration of what?"

"Janey, I don't know how long, right now. For you, until you go away to college."

"Are you going to be stuck here for the rest of your life?

"I promise you, if I feel 'stuck,' I'll leave."

"You know what I miss about 11th Street? Everybody was different. Here everybody's the same."

"Janey, you're exaggerating. Wisconsin has a diverse population. There are just more people like us, that's all. A blonde woman and a blonde daughter stand out in a community where everybody else is dark. That's what you miss, isn't it? Standing out in the crowd."

"Yeah, sort of. I was the only blonde, blue-eyed kid in all of P.S. 41, practically. In my school now, every kid in my class almost is blonde."

"Sorry about that. But there are disadvantages to being exotic, as you might have found out if we had stayed in New York. Here, at least, we have our own group. We're not all alone."

"That's true. Still, I miss seeing other kinds of people. I miss Jews and Black Puerto Ricans and Chinese people. I'm surprised you'd want to live in a place that is as lily white as Star Lake."

I did not want to explain to Janey that I felt I had a choice between living in New York with all its ethnic diversity or moving to a less interesting community where I had a home and a chance at rebuilding my career.

"It was more interesting living on 11th Street," I acknowledged.

"What are we going to do about Ted? I mean Ted, Joon-yor."

Janey made a face when she said his name, but I understood that her question meant she recognized as our common problem becoming part of a larger family that included an obnoxious male who, in his present state, was not acceptable as a brother.

"I think we have to consider how much of what Teddy says he actually feels and how much is due to his feeling of powerlessness. His home situation was not happy, and his school situation wasn't happy, so he came to see the behavior he did not like in black teenagers as part of his situation, something he had to accept, even be victimized by. He never had a chance

Legends of Good Women

to put the behavior he hated into perspective. We'd be as angry as Teddy if we felt powerless; if we had to live only with the effect of the situation..."

"But you're not answering the question. What are we going to do?"

"I think we should be patient with him. And not take what he says too seriously. I think Teddy is doing what you do in new situations. He's testing us. 'This is my worst. Love it if you dare'."

"I do that?"

"Don't you?"

"Hmm, yeah, maybe."

"I think we should ignore as much of it as we can. Don't let him bait you. Or just tell him he sounds stupid."

"That will be easy."

Janey came over and put her arms around me. She doesn't do that often, and while I understand the reason, I do miss hugs and kisses, so I gratefully accept the affection she does permit herself to bestow. I never stop hugging her, of course.

"This has been a nice chat, Mother."

"I've enjoyed it, too. Goodnight."

For all my soothing, optimistic talk, I was concerned about Ted, Junior's bigotry. I had softened Maurice's racism, but that accomplishment did not mean I could win over Teddy. People change; they are capable of growth, but what if Teddy remained firm in his attitudes? I would not want to live with a potential klansman or neo-Nazi.

I was also anxious about Sally. Were the bruises on her face and body turning from blue and purple to yellow and green? If she had returned to work by now, with all her co-workers knowing what had happened to her, would she be pitied? And what of patients? Would she be allowed to care for them, or would hospital policy not permit a woman who bore the marks of a beating to minister to patients on the grounds that nurses need to be representatives of the health to which they promise to restore the sick and injured? I wanted to see her, or at least speak to her, but when I had called her mother's home the day after Ted had told me what had happened, Sally's mother left the telephone to talk with Sally and had returned with the message that Sally appreciated my concern, but she would be grateful if I would understand that she did not wish to talk with anyone just yet. Sally would, her mother promised, get in touch with me very soon.

School and college began. On the first day, Janey dressed and redressed herself for the occasion of entering eighth grade. Janey's little girlness had been so different from mine that what memories I had held of my own childhood had not served me well, if at all, in parenting her. But watching Janey select and then reject clothing, striving to create an image that would instill admiration in all beholders and silence all detractors, I felt I was watching a film of the adolescent me. Janey was becoming a co-woman in the household; next year she would be in high school, and ten minutes later she would go off to college, where, please Goddess, she would not make the mistakes I had made. I had that mother's ancient pang as I watched her: why it was only yesterday that I had held her in my arms, nursed her, changed her diaper.

"You look nice," I said when she at last came to breakfast.

"I do? Really?" There it was: a smile like birthday candles.

"Would I lie to you? But then, it's only a mother's opinion."

"I know, but I'll take all the help I can get."

I drove her to school and then went on to the college. Registration began at 10 a.m., so I spent the time between nine and ten with colleagues in the English Department. Standing in the reception area, clutching paper cups of coffee, plucking at Danish and rolls in white delicatessen paper, we made that humming sound together that academic folk make when they play the early fall game of how-we-spent-our-summers. Most of our efforts had been modest but academically respectable: a summer in London for one; a NEA seminar for another; another colleague had prepared a fellowship application for research support, urging the rest of us to "get some money while there's some still left; one more year under the Carter budget and then forget it; Reagan will want bombs, not books."

Except for the two Republicans, we nodded into our coffee cups. The future was looking brown.

Marge Fogarty was dashing around, or running into her office, obviously involved with administrative matters. I studied her as she went past, trying to read whether her movements indicated a budget crisis, or simply the usual beginning-of-term furor. No, Marge did not look agonized, as she would have if a momentary ax had to be lowered over one of us. I went off to my registration assignment without a qualm.

While I was registering students, welcoming the new ones, most of whom seemed younger than they should be. Was it starting to happen at age thirty-five that I felt my distance from them? When I first began teaching, I had worried that students not much younger than I might not accept my authority. Now I was seeing them as just slightly older than Janey. Had such maternal feelings been aroused in me before by their confused and anxious faces? They approached my table clutching their instruction sheets, cards, and bulletins, and I tried to reassure them in my kiss-booboo voice. As I handed them the cards for a section of freshman composition, I answered the invariable "I'm not very good at writing" with "Well, that's why we require you to take this course." Occasionally, there was a querulous "I don't see why I have to take a course I don't want." But such obdurance was unusual; most of the newcomers, like decades of their predecessors, were young Catholic women, bred to docility. And I had to admit to myself I liked the nervousness I found in the students; they were approaching higher education respectfully, aware that they were being challenged.

My registration stint over, I went in search of Marge and found her typing furiously on her office computer, a cloud of smoke ringing her head like a halo. I had long ago had to settle with myself the argument of whether I liked Marge because or in spite of her sharing with my mother the habit of chain smoking. I knew reminding her once again that cigarette smoke was bad for the computer was futile, so I waved my hand ostentatiously.

"I know you're in there somewhere, Marge."

"O.K., youngster, sit down and make yourself useful. What's the word for money that has been set aside to hire a particular person?"

"Encumbered."

"Thanks. I should know all that grantsman talk by now. I guess I think all this money from the government is sinful, so I blank out now and again."

"But you're so good at grantsmanship, Marge. I can only guess how accomplished a sinner you would be if you decided to be truly wicked."

"Only one who believes in eternal damnation can be really imaginative about sin."

"I can't believe you believe in Hell, Marge."

"No, but it's fun to imagine one's enemies there."

"Besides, Marge, if grantsmanship is sinful, and you and I know it isn't, you will not have to trouble your soul about it much if Reagan gets elected."

"Ach, don't remind me. The Irish are so good at producing politicians. Why does this one have to be such a wretched exception?"

"Good Irish politicians, eh? Like the late Senator from this state?"

Marge pretended she was about to throw her ash tray at me.

"No, wise guy. I was thinking of a late president of the modern era and a still living former Senator from a neighboring state who bears the same name as the fellow you refer to. That's for openers. Oh, what am I doing trying to revise my heritage? Irish politicians are rascally and successful because of their ruthlessness and instinct for the jugular, the Kennedys not excepted. I think Eugene MaCarthy's ambivalence about the rest of the breed—his obvious and intense desire to prove to himself and everyone else that he was superior to the rest of us rascals did him in, politically. It's Reagan I don't like, and I'm trying to tell myself he's exceptional."

"If it is any consolation to you, Marge, I don't think people think of him as Irish. He's been Wasped."

"Well, whatever. But you're right about what he'll do with the funding. The days when a Catholic women's college's efforts to turn liberal made them the darling of foundations and federal agencies are fast drawing to a close. But we'll have one more year under the Carter budget, so let's work as hard as we can this fall to develop fundable programs under new criteria, because when the gravy days are over, no one will remember how much overhead we brought into the college, or how much released time we bought for them."

I heard Marge's warning. One of the reasons she had persuaded the department to support her decision to hire me was her assumption that I would be able to bring in funding. I had in my first year written a small grant proposal for computer hardware and software; the proposal had been funded, but when I came up for tenure, my funding skills would no doubt be a factor. Would they be sufficient to get money from shrinking funding sources?

"Now," Marge said, with a final punch on the keyboard that set the printer whining and rolling out pages, "what can I do for you, Claire?"

"I have a friend," I said, launching a fairy tale narrative about Sally, a friend from high school who had married a classmate, taken nurse's training, seen her husband off to the war, borne two children, and through this normal, housewifely existence had developed a wondrous skill, and like Ariadne, could weave magic tableaus. Could Fontbonne be a sponsor of an exhibit of her tapestries?

"That could be a worthwhile project. Tell me more about Sally."

"She's Italian; her husband's Irish."

"A nice Catholic girl?"

"Is there any other kind of Catholic girl?"

"Does her husband support her interest in weaving? Does he like it and brag about it to his friends?"

Marge's voice became ironic. I shook my head. Marge grunted.

"Oh, sure. Just make sure supper's on time. Then you may go and paint the Sistine Chapel. That is, if you've got your mother to look after the kids. Where would the exhibit be held?"

"The Women's Resource Center of Star Lake would probably be interested in sponsoring it."

"Absolutely not." Marge's mouth pressed into a thin line and her face reddened.

"Why not?"

"It's a pro-abortion outfit. A Catholic women's college, no matter how progressive, cannot be in any way affiliated with it."

"The Women's Resource Center is involved in advocacy, principally of battered women. It doesn't do abortion counseling."

"It make referrals to abortion clinics."

"It makes referrals to counseling centers that present a woman with options. The Women's Resource Center is pro-choice, not pro-abortion."

"Same thing, as far as I'm concerned. How active are you in this Women's Resource Center?"

I wanted to say, "That's none of your business, Marge," but of course I did not.

"I'm not active," I acknowledged, "but friends of mine are."

"Well, it might be prudent, my dear, to keep your distance."

Sensing myself dismissed, I left her office far less sure of myself than I had entered.

I called Sally's mother when I returned home and spoke as convincingly as I could to persuade her to persuade Sally to talk to me. Sally's mother told me to hang up and wait five minutes.

Ten minutes later, Sally called me; her voice was so thick when she said hello, I could almost see her puffy lips and bruised jaw. I told her bluntly I wanted to see her, to comfort her, and above all I did not want her to feel like hiding from the world.

"Claire, I'm grateful for your concern, but I'm not ready to see anyone. It's even hard dealing with my mother. She doesn't like to look at me, although I'm not the first abused woman in our family."

"But you'll be the last."

"Yeah, maybe. At least I can see that my kids know better."

"Why won't you see me?"

"I'm ashamed."

"But, goddammit, you didn't do anything wrong."

"I know; of course I know. But I hate the way I look. It shouldn't have happened to me. Bob shouldn't have done this to me. No one should have done this to me. If I were the person I think I am, or liked to think I am, no one should have been able to do this to me. Bob would never have hurt the person I thought I was. My mother would never have not looked at the person I thought I was. And I don't want my kids to see me."

"See me, Sally. It's not fair to punish yourself. Or me."

"Okay," she said, and I got into my car and drove to her mother's house. Sally met me at the door and quickly led me to the living room. I sat down on a couch. Sally sat on a chair across from me. I looked past the sea colors of Sally's face and into her eyes while we continued our conversation.

"Bob never attacked you before? Or gave signs that he might hurt you?"

"He flared up a lot. He yelled at me when we had arguments or he didn't like something I did, but that had been part of our life for so long, I had no idea that this time would be so bad. It started when I came back from an Alanon meeting. Alanon is . . ."

"I know."

"When I started going on a regular basis, Bob asked me about it and I told him. He didn't like my going, but he accepted it. At least I thought he did. Until Friday night when he went on and on about it. And began going back into our marriage about all kinds of other things. Garbage. It was like he was going through garbage and throwing it at me, all the while getting angrier and angrier. Until I knew that he was going to hurt me, and there was no way I could get out of it. Oh, my God, that was such an awful feeling. That the man I had been married to for thirteen, almost fourteen years was going to beat me up, and I couldn't do anything to stop him. I felt so worthless, so useless. What was the point of my life if he could do this to me, just slap me around, move me in front of him with slapshots as if I were nothing more than a hockey puck? I ran upstairs into the bedroom, but he came after me. I couldn't even call the police because I knew they were all Bob's buddies and wouldn't do a thing."

"Was that the reason, Sally? You're entitled to protection even from Bob's buddies. Weren't you protecting him, even then, by not calling?"

"Maybe I was. Or maybe I was so ashamed, I didn't want them to know he could treat me that way. I tried to call Ted but he wasn't home. And then Bob broke the bedroom door down. He tore out the telephone, but I managed to get into the studio. That door was thicker and Bob couldn't break it down. I stayed there all the next day, but I knew when I didn't show up at my mother's on Saturday, she'd try to find out what happened to me."

I put my arms around Sally and held her. Mrs. Licari came into the room, a round woman in a black business suit: widow and entrepreneur. The intimacy Sally and I were sharing alarmed her, for she bobbed right back out of the room without pausing to ask if we wanted something to eat. As Mrs. Licari retreated,

I thought of my students in Staten Island, Italian-American women who spoke with bitterness of their own mothers, women that had suffered in their own marriages yet steadfastly refused to sympathize with their own daughters. "Why do our mothers seem to feel that, because they had a rotten time, we have to have one, too?" Was that Sally's mother's reaction? Or did her mother retreat because she felt helpless and could not bear the feeling?

I sat down on the couch. "What will you do now?"

I don't know. I'm just dealing with immediate things like when I can get the kids, when I can get back to work. I haven't thought about the larger things like whether I'm going to live with Bob again. I'm still so angry, I'm still in so much pain, I don't want to think about it. But I know I have to. I have to act immediately. Well, day after tomorrow, at the latest. Oh, my God, Claire, I don't know how I'll ever be able to live with him again, to look at him without remembering what happened. And yet, I don't know what else to do. I can't live with my mother. I know there are such places as battered women's shelters, but I can't see myself moving into one. I'm a healer; my ego is very much invested in my sense of myself as a person who makes other people well, not as a person in need of care herself. Although I know I am. I'm not ready to accept myself as a hurt person. Besides, shelters are temporary arrangements, aren't they?"

"Yes, they are. What about moving into an apartment?"

"An apartment. I don't know, Claire. I love my home. And if I left it, that would be punishing me. I don't want to leave my home. I don't see why I should leave it. And why should the kids leave it? I can't disrupt their lives."

"But won't living with the tension be just as disruptive to them?"

"Yes, they're frightened of him. And if we lived apart, I could get some medical help for the kids. Bob has absolutely refused to let them be tested to see if they have any genetic damage from the herbicides that might have infected him during the war. He consistently denies that anything might be wrong, but won't let me find out if there is. And I'm scared for the kids. Daphne has a very short attention span. And Enid might also have some learning disabilities."

"If they were boys, would he care more?"

"Possibly."

"The solution seems to be for Bob to leave."

"Certainly for the present, I think that would be best. I don't see how we can live together again unless he gets counseling. And that is something he has always refused to do. And I don't think he'll move out of the house, either. God what a mess. Who would have thought, Claire, when we were back in high school, that some day we'd be having this conversation? Of course, there were signs, even then. Bob was so jealous if he even imagined I was looking at someone else. You may not remember, but in sophomore year, I dated Ted for a while."

"I remember."

"Yes, well, Ted and I dated each other briefly; I think he was the first one I'd ever dated more than once. But Bob was so persistent, and Ted and I were so aware of his interest in me, that I think Ted was scared off, or decided to back out. Bob came to me one day and asked if I would go out with him. He said Ted knew he was asking me out and it was all right with him."

"Was it all right with you?"

"I felt I didn't have any choice in the matter. But even now Bob sometimes brings up Ted's name. His jealousy was a sign I should have paid attention to. But I was brought up to believe that if I did what other people wanted and expected of me, everything would be all right."

"Sally, when you were showing me your weavings, one of them was burnt. Did Bob do that?"

"Yes, that was another sign I ignored. How much more of a warning does one need when a man starts a fire? Bob began to hate my weaving, which I turned to more and more to overcome my feelings of helplessness about his drinking. And I succeeded in creating a life apart from him in my studio. The kids and I would go in there and be safe. When I would start to work on the loom, begin to create a tapestry, I knew that life would go on; I could overcome the terror I felt when Bob's drinking became so intense. The kids wouldn't be scared in there. And Bob felt left out. He knew we had claimed our own territory in the studio. He had no control over us there, and he began to hate my weaving. So one Sunday when I was working and the kids were with my mother, he went in there and dragged some of my pieces out on the lawn and set fire to them. He burned up two I especially loved. When I came home with the kids, I pulled into the driveway as he was coming out with some more pieces to burn. I took the kids into the house and upstairs and left them in the studio. Then I went downstairs and wrestled with Bob over the weavings. I managed to pull out the one that was scorched before it was totally destroyed. And I managed to save the others he had stacked up ready to throw on the fire. I'm grateful that he set the fire away from the house, or he might have burned it up, too. Looking back on what happened, it seems so clear that he was desperate and I should have demanded he do something, insist that he either get therapy or move out. But I guess even then I realized he wouldn't do either. He swore to me later that he'd never try to destroy my weavings again, and he hasn't. Now, he's trying to destroy me. But I guess I accepted his word because I wanted to believe him. And I guess I felt guilty about having created a life apart from him. The old if-I'd-been-the-right-kind-of-wife syndrome. Isn't that dumb?"

"Maybe. But it's a common failing. I've certainly refused to look at the truth in a relationship because I didn't want to believe it."

"Really? You always seem so much in command of yourself, Claire. I never would have believed that you had problems, made mistakes in a relationship like that. And yet I know you must have had problems. Marriages have ended with the two people remaining friends, but not if the wife insists not only on having her own name back, but that her child have it, too. You never talked about it, though, so I thought that if you were so good at handling problems, why should I talk about my problems? Bob and I go back so far together. I didn't have any brothers, and in Italian families, men are gods. So I never even thought about what I wanted. I thought about what the men in my life wanted. First my father and then Bob. We've known each other so long, shared so many of the same experiences. Even now, when I hear the music from that period, if I'm angry, the anger dissolves. One of the reason I find it hard to think about leaving Bob is that we do share so many experiences. Going back before Vietnam, of course. And I guess I also feel the war is responsible for the things I dislike in him."

"Such as? Beside, of course, the violence."

"It's all related, really. The drinking, of course. And his racism, which has become worse since Bob became a policeman. Of course, not all cops are racists, but Bob's friends are. I hate the way they talk about Blacks and Jews and especially the Indians. You know, police are very clannish; they don't socialize with other people outside the force. Cops and their wives. We tried that a few times years ago, but Bob, to give him credit, realized I hated being with them, so he confines his socializing to drinking with his buddies and going off with them on hunting-and-drinking trips up north. You know, you and Ted are the first couple-friends we've had in years. Ted's always been a friend, and thank God, because Bob's different when he's around Ted; he's always looked up to Ted. But I'm so glad to have another woman friend at last."

Sally was beginning to be teary, and I was becoming uncomfortable, so I told her about my plan of her to have an exhibit of weavings at the Women's Resource Center. Of course, I had to persuade Sally that her weavings were worth exhibiting, that not only would people want to see her work, they would want to buy it, too. But after I made her believe me, she became enthusiastic, and she became vital again, like a drooping plant springing back after watering. I went over the plan for the exhibit in broad outline, and then Sally began supplying details. I left Sally's house very pleased with myself.

CHAPTER

I went to the last game before the league playoffs to bring my meetings with the VW's to some kind of closure. I knew Sally would be mortified if the women knew that Bob had assaulted her, so I excused her absence through a form of the truth, that Sally and her children were visiting her family. I asked each of the women, trying very hard not to seem like a teacher marking term papers, what she had done to meet the goal she had set of herself. In almost all cases, not much. Don't worry, I assured them, trying to put conviction in my voice, if it doesn't happen now, you'll do it another time. Reevaluate your goals. If one thing isn't do-able, try another. If you don't lose two pounds in a week, try to lose one pound.

"You know, it's really weird," Jean reflected, "every time I try to lose weight, he brings more beer and ice cream into the house and seems to want pasta and steak and potatoes more than ever. It's as though he deliberately tries to keep me from losing weight, although he sure teases the hell out of me for being overweight."

I now understood Sally's silence during the first meeting I had had with these women. She had seen her own situation mirrored in theirs and had hated the reflection. She had understood the husbands of these women had a stake in keeping them overweight and unemployed, for in their insecurity, they were certain if their wives had any other options they would go out the door.

I told the women about the planned exhibit of Sally's weavings at the Art Center. They said how nice for Sally, how pleased they were that her talent would be recognized, but I heard in their voices a trace of the ambivalence Jean's husband felt when she said she wanted to lose weight. Someone might go on to a better life and they'd still be stuck. I urged them to go to the Women's Resource Center. They said they were sorry the games were ending because they had liked talking to me. I was embarrassed by their pleasure in knowing a woman with "brains." I wanted to destroy that lack of self-esteem in them, but I knew they had to find the will to destroy it themselves. And I also knew that if they found their own egos, they might have to make choices, including those their husbands feared.

The game ended; Ted's team had lost and I was secretly pleased, for I would not feel obliged to follow his team to whatever city won the bid to have the playoff games. I saw Ted and his son with Bob and felt my teeth setting on edge. Why was that man playing softball? Why was he living in his house? I ran to the car to avoid speaking to him, or to Ted, his faithful advocate, who at that moment I also hated.

In the following days, I put aside my concern for Sally and my anger at Bob as I prepared for the Marathon. As if in the grip of some religious compulsion, I rose each weekday morning at 5:30 for road work, alternating speed running with relaxed distance running. I listened to my body, trying to see it as I ran like a blue and red skeletal-muscular diagram. I studied the stress I felt, mostly in my calves when I did long runs. I studied the effect of the food I ate on the quality of my running the way a mechanic studies the impact of fuel on an engine. And, of course, I asked myself why I was putting myself under such stress. And after the New York Marathon, would I need to run in other races? The Boston Marathon? No. This was a one time thing, a need to kiss off a bad part of my life and release myself from a sense of failure. I had to be intense because I could let it go so easily unless I was compulsive. As I completed my training, I became furious with Jimmy Carter for prohibiting American athletes from participating in the Moscow Olympics. The Russians had not retreated one foot from Afghanistan, and meanwhile athletes who had trained for years toward a peak of fitness that for many of them would not come again had been robbed of an opportunity toward which they had committed sections of their lives. But I would nevertheless vote for him.

I tried to bury my depression about the imminent election of Ronald Reagan and what I was certain would be a major change in American political life; I avoided thinking about the unresolved conflict with Ted about Bob; instead I plucked at evidence that, in my personal world, at least, all would be well. Kathy and Rebecca had persuaded the United Methodist Women to co-sponsor Sally's exhibit of weavings with the Women's Resource Center. And the exhibition, I hoped, would lead to a new direction in Sally's life. Janey seemed to be enjoying junior high school, and, judging from the intense use of the telephone (I had bought an extension for Janey to honor her entry into junior high school and it had quickly become an extension of her arm), the reason was an as yet unidentified — to me — male eighth grader. My courses were going well, but of course, I always love my fall classes until Thanksgiving, when students are obviously behind in reading and writing assignments, and the classrooms resound hollowly with the silent panic of unprepared young people. My training regimen absorbed me; I was beginning to feel that I would complete the Marathon in a respectable time, that if I did not come in at 3:20, I would be close enough to it for the difference not to matter to me.

In the second week of September, Meta called to cancel our running appointments. I was pleased not to have to feel responsible for her, to be able to think only of my own training, but I was disappointed to lose her company.

"Why are you acting like George Steinbrenner and firing your coach?"

"Because I found someone my own age to run with. Now I won't have you to kick around any more."

"Who?"

"Harry."

"Really? How did you manage that?"

"I managed to convince him that since he couldn't lick me, he'd better join me. We ran together for the first time this weekend. Just a little trot but it was fun. I went fishing with him. And I decided I had been missing a lot of fun there, too."

"Sounds like you two crossed a couple of important bridges this weekend."

"Yes." Meta giggled. I could almost see her blushing. "It's nice to find out that senior citizenship is not without surprises and adventures."

Legends of Good Women

"I hope I have some of that ahead of me, too. I'll miss you, Meta; that is, I'll miss running with you, but I'm glad you've found a better partner for yourself."

I was feeling pleased with life in general and myself in particular; my anger at Ted had passed. We had had several stiff conversations, but had not seen each other in weeks. After Janey had pointedly asked for the third time, "What's happened to Ted?" —I called Ted and told him I would like to take him to dinner at Michael's in LaCrosse on Saturday evening. He agreed. When Ted got in the car, I tried to ease the way back to closeness by bubbling on, as I drove out of town and onto Highway 35 about my classes, my training, his parents running together, and the project I had launched on Sally's behalf.

No response from Ted. I ran out of happy energy and we drove in silence.

"Why am I getting on your nerves?" I demanded finally.

"You're on a roll, and I'm not. It's unfair of me to hold that against you, but I do. Okay? I have some business problems. they don't concern you, but . . ."

"Why do you say that? I have no qualms about complaining to you about everything that goes wrong in my life, from a bad department meeting to Janey's math problems. Why can't you feel you can tell me what's bothering you?"

"All right. An order I was counting on did not come through. I didn't get the business I went after, and I feel disappointed with myself. Not to mention the more serious matter of a cash flow problem. I have a bank payment coming due and, of course, workers must be paid regularly, whether the boss does or not."

"I'm sorry. If I can help you in your business-write letters, design advertising, plan market strategies, I'll be happy to do it."

"I know." His tone was softer, but I heard resistance.

"Do you think you could ask me to do something like that. I'll do it as a consultant. You could pay me a fee. Then you should feel all right about it."

Ted looked at me and smiled for the first time that evening. He reached around my back and rocked my right shoulder lightly, pal-like.

"Yes, I think I could ask you to help me. I've never thought about it."

"Well, think about it. What else is bothering you?"

"I didn't like hearing about my parents running together from you. I know my mother considers you part of the family, but I still think I have certain rights as a son, and they include hearing family matters first."

Resisting the impulse to say, "Stop being petty," I replied, "Your mother confided in me as a friend, a running partner, not as a family member."

"Maybe."

"Is that all that's bothering you? Or have I done something else you don't like?"

"What you're doing for Sally is terrific. I just wish you were trying to do something for Bob, too."

I felt all my conciliatory instincts vanish in a cloud of anger. With great effort, I kept my voice even.

"But Sally's been shattered. Her never-very-strong ego has been almost entirely destroyed. She can't face her kids. She's devastated. And Bob's the one who is responsible. I can't bring myself to think of helping him now."

"Claire, how we handle this problem between Sally and Bob..."

"Yes, this problem."

"Don't be sarcastic. We're choosing up sides and we should be working together to help them as a couple. I know Bob is the villain in this and he knows it, too. And I think it's crucial that he be helped to not be a villain. He's shattered, too, thinking he's destroyed the best part of his life. Please, please try to see that he needs help, too. That it's not one woman that needs help, but a family that must be put back together. And that it is important to us that we work together to help them. I don't want to become Bob's advocate and your adversary because you're lining up with Sally."

"I hear the logic of what you are saying. But it's very difficult for me to do what you ask. I do see Bob as a villain. I think Sally is one of the best people I know. And I see Bob as someone who tried to destroy her."

"I don't mean to excuse what he did, but he beat her. He didn't try to destroy her."

"People have been known to die from beatings. How can you minimize what he did? He could have killed her. He did not have anything on his mind when he attacked her except the instinct to hurt her, and the consequences of his actions might have been Sally's death."

"I don't think so. I think he never would have gone that far. He would have stopped."

"Is that why she hid? Ran from room to room like a trapped animal. Sally didn't seem to think he would stop in time. What's 'in time'? After he had blackened one eye and broken her nose? After two eyes and a broken nose? Would he have been satisfied to stop after breaking an arm? I don't understand how you can be so complacent, how you can minimize what Bob did."

"I'm not minimizing what Bob did. He isn't either. He feels like a beast."

And well he should, I thought.

"The awful thing he did only makes him certain he is as bad as he always thought he was. Understand something, please. In Vietnam—"

The war again, I thought. Was the war going to be cited as an exculpatory factor in every vet's wrongdoing, like the-devil-made-me-do-it?

"—men did things they never would have done under any other circumstance. We were all so young, we had no idea of what was going on. Overnight we had to throw out everything we had learned all our lives, do things we had always been taught were the worst things we could do, and then try to live with that knowledge afterward. But the things we had done at the time seemed like the only things we could do in order to survive."

"Ted, you and I come from the same tradition. We believe in free will, and neither Marxism nor modern warfare can drive out of our minds the belief that no matter how powerful the influences around us are, if we are human beings, we accept responsibility for our actions, or our humanity has no meaning. And I believe Bob is responsible for his actions. And I believe with all my heart that if a woman returns to a man who has hurt her, she is giving him permission to hurt her again. So I cannot join you in trying to bring that family back together again."

"But without his family, Bob feels he has nothing, is nothing."

"Forgive me for stating the obvious, but shouldn't he have thought of that before?"

"But he's feared it so long. He was afraid Sally would leave him because he thought she should. And so he reacted against what he saw as inevitable. Bob's not a complex man, not an introspective man, but even more complicated people than he have acted as he has, have acted to bring about the very thing they most fear. In Bob's case, he thinks he does not deserve his family."

"Bob and I are in rare agreement there."

"But he will die without them. I know he will."

"You lost your family. You've survived. Why do you think Bob is so much more fragile than you are?"

"I never needed Michelle the way Bob needs Sally."

"You mean that he is to survive at her expense. At the expense of his family. And I refuse to agree to assist in that kind of bargain. And, once again, I don't think Vietnam is the originator of all sin. The things you've described in Bob were there before he went to Vietnam. At least I'm convinced they are. I didn't know Bob in high school, but I think his rigidity, his macho attitude, his drinking had their origins back then. Maybe everything is worse now, but it started then. You know what his family was like. They must have contributed to making him what he is. But that is all in the past. And if you want to help Bob, you've got to get him to live in the present. I don't understand why you are willing to accept in him a standard of behavior so much lower than your own. Why have you never confronted him about his drinking?"

"Why haven't I confronted him about his drinking?"

"Oh, please don't do that—answer a question with a question. My ex-husband used to do that in order to evade me. He never answered my questions with statements."

"I'm' not trying to evade you. I'm saying the question out loud because I have asked myself that so many times. Like everyone else, I have my areas of willful blindness. I know Bob drinks more than he should, but he's usually careful never to drink too much when I'm around. He always seemed in control of himself. So I always told myself, if he could control himself with me, he could control himself at other times. He surely couldn't stay on the police force if he drank too much. And I don't know why I did not confront him about it; I probably did not want to assume – I don't know the real answer, Claire."

I had turned off Highway 35 on to Ward Avenue, entered the restaurant parking lot and parked the car. But neither Ted nor I moved. We sat facing straight ahead, as other diners entered or left their cars, occasionally with a curious glance at us.

"That first time we went to their house, I was ready to jump out of my skin by the time the evening ended. I could have made a chain of beer can tabs long enough to wind around the entire house. By the time we left, Bob was in the last stage before falling down drunk. And you had sense enough to give me the key to your car. Bob began to hate me from that moment. No, he began to hate me from the moment he saw me. The moment he heard about me."

"You're exaggerating. He doesn't hate you."

"No?" I turned to Ted and waited until he looked at me. "You're too honest to pretend he likes me. Is he glad I'm in your life. Will welcome me as the partner of his best friend."

"No. But hate is too strong a word."

"But drinking problem is not."

"No, but Bob comes by his problem almost naturally. Both his parents came from large, hardscrabble families. His father is a factory worker. He was 4F during World War Two, and it was a matter of some shame to the family. Bob's grandparents drank, his parents drank – still do – and his older brother drinks;

I don't know if his younger brother drinks or if his sisters drink. And then, for some reason – I guess this happens sometimes in large families – Bob's father did not love him as much as he loved his other children. Bob had one older brother who did not drink. He's dead."

"A boating accident, wasn't it? It happened when we were in high school."

"Yes. Do you remember the circumstances?"

"No."

"Bob's two older brothers were at a party at the home of a friend who lived in a house near the lake. When the drinking got out of hand, Bob's brother who didn't drink said he was going to borrow a rowboat and go out on the lake to fish. He asked his brother to come with him, but the brother said, no, he wanted to stay at the party. Time went by and the brother and his friends were quite drunk, but they were also bored. The friend who was giving the party had a motor boat, so they took it out on the lake. Bob's brother was steering, with as much control as if he were driving a car."

"And he killed his brother."

"Yes. The only other boat on the lake that night, and he managed to smash right into it. But when Bob's family heard the news, his father said, not to the son who had killed his brother, whom he loved, but to Bob . . ."

"I know what he said. He said, 'Why couldn't it have been you?'"

"Yes. Maybe that helps you to understand my commitment to Bob. By the way, Bob never told me what his father had said; one of his sisters did. I didn't go to Bob's house often, and Bob didn't like having me there. We both preferred being at my house. The family wasn't poor; they just didn't live well. His parents could have afforded to give Bob money for clothes, but they felt they would spoil him if he didn't work for everything he got. Bob always had to scrounge for money for everything in high school. That he was on the football team at all was a miracle, because he still had to work after practice. Being on the team was the only thing that made him feel good about himself, until he went to war. Can you imagine Vietnam being the best thing that ever happened to you? He was kind of getting even with his father, bettering his old man, who had been rejected for service, and who had been afraid his sons would get ahead of him so he tried to keep them down. College was never thought of; if Bob's mother had supported him, he might have gone. Bob's younger brother later got a football scholarship, but Bob had not been good enough. So his only option was the service. The only real blessing in his life was Sally; that's the reason I want so much for them to stay together. Bob's had so damn little in his life."

"All the more reason, I think, for him to treat what was precious in his life with care and respect."

Ted nodded. We were silent together for moments.

"You went with Sally before you went with Michelle. Why did you break up?"

"No particular reason. I knew Bob liked her, and I began to think she liked him, so I bowed out."

"Sally's so true-blue. I can't imagine she lost interest in you."

"I felt the relationship did not matter that much to her. And I wasn't in pain because of it. I was a happy guy. I had a good family. I was an athlete – "

"A star athlete."

"O.K. enough. I was well liked."

"The most popular boy in our class. Everyone admired you."

"All right. I knew I had all the good things in life. Things other people did not have and wanted so much they hurt. So if I help a friend to have some of what I had, I was happy to do it. That all sounds more noble than it should."

"How did you all come to this arrangement? Did the three of you have a meeting and agree that from thenceforth Sally would be Bob's girl?"

"No. We changed partners gradually. I think it started when Bob asked me one day if I was going to marry Sally. And I said I didn't know, that I wasn't going to think about marriage until after college. And I think he said that if he had someone like Sally in his life, he would never let her get away. I had known that Bob liked Sally, but that was the first time he had spoken of his feeling. He was intense. I was awed by his feeling."

"What was your feeling for Sally at the time? What was hers for you?"

"We didn't discuss our feelings at length or often. Every six weeks or so, I'd say, 'Gee, Sally you're neat,' or something as elegant, and Sally would say, 'I think you're neat, too,' and we'd kiss each other self-consciously and giggle."

"Let me understand how the switch was made. You and Sally agreed between you that she should become Bob's girlfriend?"

"There was no agreement. It just happened. I said to Sally, 'You know, Bob likes you very much.' And she said, 'Does he?' or 'He does?' and we were silent for a while and then talked of other things. I began to think that Sally might prefer to be with Bob, but what impressed me more, I think, was the intensity of feeling Bob had for her. I knew I didn't feel that way about Sally, so I started to slide out of the relationship."

"Ah, yes. Teenage males and sliding out of relationships."

"Understand, please, that I was careful about feelings because I respected them. I wasn't ready for that kind of intensity, but I knew people who were. I saw them at a stage of life I wasn't ready for. I knew I was a popular guy and that girls liked me. I didn't think I deserved that kind of admiration. What did playing football have to do with the kind of person I was? Intense feelings scared me then, but if other people were ready for them, fine. And if Bob felt intensely about Sally, I thought why shouldn't she have a chance to have someone feel about her the way I could not."

"But you never discussed your decision with Sally, so you don't know if she wanted to change boyfriends."

"No."

What arrogance, I thought; aloud, I asked Ted if he would have married Sally if they had stayed together.

"Perhaps. You've probably noticed I'm not a rover. It's a family trait. Once we Ritters find someone we like, we tend to stay with that person. Enough of this serious talk. Let's go eat. I'm famished."

The sky was navy blue and the air was chilly as we walked from the parking lot to the restaurant. Affection had returned, but I was caught in a mood of sadness. I thought of the poem I had learned in fourth grade about an aristocrat who rides by a field and recognizes a peasant woman as right for him, but he knows class boundaries make marriage between them impossible. "Of all the words of tongue and pen," the refrain goes, "the saddest are these: 'It might have been.'" Would Sally have willingly given up Ted if she had not thought he was just trying to dump her in a nice way? Not for all Janey's designer jeans.

CHAPTER

During the last week of September, three weeks before the Marathon, I felt my stomach rocking with nervousness every day. To compensate to Janey for my lopsided diet – pasta every other night, salad and bread on off nights – I financed a supply of fast food; my garbage embarrassed me with its overflow of Chinese food containers and folded pizza boxes, but Janey was delighted with her diet. If I were not so involved with training, I might have been annoyed for her clear preference for such food over my – in ordinary times – thoughtfully prepared, balanced meals.

On Saturday, I did my second twenty mile run. The weather was cool and crisp, but not windy, exactly the weather I hoped for New York. To prepare for the hill on the Verrazano Bridge, I plotted a course that took me through the hills of Trempeleau. As I leaned into the upgrade, I felt my calves straining. I tried to relax without slowing down, to let my back kick accelerate me and then use the momentum on the down grade. That was a successful tactic, for my five mile split was 38 minutes. At ten miles, I was running at just under eight minutes a mile, but at fifteen miles I was over eight minutes, and I was beginning to feel stress in my thighs. I was slowing down, but if I could keep from cramping, I would complete the run. At eighteen miles, the sugar was almost gone from my muscles, and threads of fire were in them instead. I completed the course in two hours, forty-three minutes, a time that did not indicate a Marathon finish of under three hours and twenty minutes, My goal was still to be eligible for the Boston Marathon even if I did not want to run in it.

Ted called midweek to ask Janey and me to come to a family dinner at his parents' home the following Sunday in honor of their forty-fifth wedding anniversary. His brother and sister-in-law were taking care of the main course, he said, and I asked if his brother was doing the cooking. Ted acknowledged that his sister-in-law was doing most of the cooking, but after all, his brother was older than he and had not had the opportunity to become as enlightened as he, Ted, had become. Ted said he was making bread and bringing salad, that a cake had been ordered, and Janey and I could bring wine if we liked. Ted sounded cheerful, so I asked him about his business. Things were in good shape, he assured me. And Bob? Ted said Bob seemed to recognize his problem and had agreed to enter a counseling program. But I thought he had already agreed to that. Yes, but he had not been going regularly. When he had finally realized he might lose his family, he had agreed to see his counselor twice a week. And what about Sally? Sally and the kids were moving back into the house this week. Did Ted mean that Sally and Bob were going back together as if nothing had happened. No, Bob would be staying downstairs until he and Sally could, well, until Sally was ready to be fully reconciled with Bob. But Ted was confident that Bob was really getting his act together, and that he and Sally would work everything out.

I was certain that Bob was being crafty, that he would remain in counseling only until he was accepted back in their bedroom. I was thinking, "Sally, don't be fooled, don't go back." Ted heard my unspoken thought and ended the conversation with a brusque "See you Sunday."

On Sunday, I ran eight miles in the morning and went to church with Janey. Because Janey was self-conscious about her sweaty hands, I went in first while she waited in the vestibule until Pass-the-Peace was over and she could join me in the pew for Sharing of Joys and Sorrows. The big news that day came from Eugene Davis, who popped up before anyone else to announce what his ear-to-ear grin told us: that Betty had given birth the previous Friday to a seven pound, eight ounce boy, Neal de Havilland Davis.

"Is that his first child?" Janey whispered wonderingly to me.

"No," I whispered back, "he has two grown children from a previous marriage."

"I guess he feels pleased with himself that he can still make babies at his age," Janey impishly whispered.

Eugene completed his announcement that he would provide cigars to the men and chocolates to the women, "or vice versa" during coffee hour.

Reverend Baker followed the lectuary and gave a sermon on the blessing of friendship; we most emulated Christ, he said, when we were unselfish in friendship. After the service, Gloria Hartman came over during coffee hour and told me the executive committee of UMW wanted to meet Sally, look at her art work, and discuss with her what was necessary to co-sponsor her exhibit. I promised to set up a meeting for one of the times Gloria suggested, A Saturday or Sunday afternoon.

Janey and I went home, read the papers, and then, in the middle of the afternoon, drove with the wine I had bought over to Harry and Meta's house. Cars were in the driveway when we arrived.

"I love to come to a house and see that lots of people have arrived before us," Janey said as we walked to the door.

"Then people will notice you when you come in. I thought you didn't like to have people paying attention to you."

"Only when I don't know the people."

"But you don't know all the people. You don't know Ted's brother and his sons."

"But I know Ted and his son. Besides, it's better to come in after other people and have a fuss made over you than to be first and feel weird."

I rang the bell, and as if he had been waiting on the other side, a very attractive boy just a bit over Janey's age and height opened the door and stared at Janey, obviously matching her reality to prior reports. He did not seem disappointed.

"Hi," he said, moving back with the door to let us enter the hallway, "I'm Bill."

We returned the greetings, Janey ever so smoothly telling Bill that she was pleased to meet him. I was aware of people watching the encounter in the living room to the right of the hallway; then Ted came forward and, taking the plastic sac of wine bottles from me, directed us to help ourselves from the selection of soft drinks and juices, cheeses, crackers and fruit that had been arranged on the hall buffet. I took Janey into the living room and presented her to Meta, who shook Janey's hand and told her she had been looking forward to meeting her and hoped to see her often.

"As you can see, I have a number of grandsons, but no young female friends. Your mother has been kind enough to be my pal during the summer. We have been running together, she may have told you, but she is more serious about running than I ever intend to be. Fortunately, my husband, Harry, runs with me now. But I'd still like to have a young female for company now and then, and to help keep my grandsons civil. You know Ted, Junior, and you just met Bill, and this is his older brother, Mike."

Janey's back was to me as she faced Meta's grandsons, but I envisioned quite clearly the glint in her eye as she realized what her status in this family would be if she and I joined it. Teddy must have drawn the same conclusion, for I saw him look resentfully at Janey.

Meta directed us all into the living room. I sat on a sofa and Ted brought over his sister-in-law, Marian. He introduced us and then, like a true midwestern male, went to join his father and brother. "If I join this family," I thought, "I'll have my work cut out for me." Meanwhile, Marian, a pleasant, attractive woman, who unselfconsciously told me her history.

"Unlike the rest of you, I'm not from this area. I grew up in industrial Ohio. My father was a steel worker who always wanted to be a farmer – living with the mills always in view, with smoke always in the air, will do that to you. But when I got out of high school, he decided to move. We'd come to Wisconsin on summer vacations and this place looked like heaven. So on one trip, he looked for a business with an owner who wanted to retire – he realized by then that he wasn't cut out to be a farmer – and he found one, a shoe store, so he bought the business. I worked in the store, of course."

"How did you meet your husband?"

"I met him when I got my first car. I drove into his station and asked for gas, and he was smart enough – he told me later – to realize I had just bought my first car and to understand just how I felt about it. You know that pride you have when you've done the first big thing in your life without help from anyone?"

I nodded to Marian but my attention was wandering to Janey, at the center of a cluster at the front window. Bill, whose back was to me, was doing most of the talking, and very animatedly. What about? Probably some aspect of pop culture. I realized suddenly that he was "on," performing for Janey's benefit, and I felt pangs of pride and loss. His older brother, who sat next to Janey in the window seat, was as susceptible to Janey on the grounds of her extreme youth, though he clearly approved of her. Janey's eyes met mine then, and the corners of her mouth tightened as she tried to repress a triumphant smile.

" . . . that feeling," Marian was saying, "and was sympathetic to it." 'A full tank, please,' I said for the first time in my life, hoping my voice would not give that fact away. He filled my tank and then he wiped my windows, without leaving streaks, and cleaned the front of the car, tapping the cloth once or twice against the hood, as if he didn't want to leave it. Then he said, 'This is a nice car.' Then I blurted out everything. Later he told me that when he saw me come into the station, 'driving that buggy like it was a baby carriage with my firstborn inside,' he had fallen in love at first sight. I guess I felt the same, because we've been together ever since and we've been very happy. I don't claim any credit for that, really, because many nice people have not been so lucky as us. Luck is what accounts for our good marriage; luck and the fact that we're both modest people. No demons drive us; we just take things as they come and enjoy them, especially our kids?"

I did not agree with Marian at all that luck was the key to a successful marriage, but I did not want to argue with her then. I took the safer course and agreed with her that children were a great joy. Marian was good enough to pick up that cue and tell me that Janey was attractive and intelligent looking and certainly seemed to be holding her own with the boys. Then, having paid respect to my child, she spoke of her own children.

"My older boy has athletic ability, like his uncle, certainly not his father. Does Ted's son have athletic talent, do you think?"

"I don't know. Possibly. My daughter is an athlete, though. She won a prize for swimming at her summer camp."

"Then she must get it from you. I understand you're running in the New York City marathon."

I began to like Marian. She asked me how many miles I ran a day, and I told her, and she said she couldn't run a city block, and I said, of course, she could; her mother-in-law was up to a mile.

"But Meta's a dynamo and I'm—let's face it, lazy. My younger son isn't an athlete, either. He has his father's sociable nature. You know, most boys are grouchy, well, maybe not all of them, but maybe you've noticed how boys lack social skills. Most of them are not even civilized until they're twenty-one when they remember to say 'God bless you' when you sneeze. But until that time, they might just as well be living in a remote Amazonian village. But as you can see, my younger son can entertain people. I think he gets that skill from his grandmother. Ted has probably told you about Meta's skill as a storyteller."

"Yes, but I'm sure your son owes his talent to his parents, as well. You laughed at his jokes, listened to his anecdotes; he would not have developed his skill without encouragement."

"It's good of you to say so."

"But I mean it. And your older son has social skills, too."

"Yes," she agreed, as we turned our attention to the group under discussion, "he does. But he has confidence because he's an athlete. His younger brother has to work harder at feeling he's accepted. He has to be the entertainer."

And indeed he did, for he was still pumping his arms and shaking his head, riveting the attention of the group to his words, and just when I was beginning to be impatient with Janey for allowing herself to be placed in the role of listener, she spoke, just a few words, but each boy listened to her. Mike and Bill kept their eyes on Janey, but Teddy's eyes moved from face to face and then he looked away.

"Mmmm," Marian said. Just then, Harry, who had probably also been observing the group, walked over to them. He addressed them all, but slipped his arm around Teddy's shoulders.

Marian looked at me and smiled. "We all need to be the apple of someone's eye," she said.

One of the two women Meta had hired to cook and serve the dinner, came into the living room and whispered to Meta. "This is Mrs. Hermann, everyone," Meta said. Then Meta went over to Harry, took his arm and drew him into the center of the room. "Mrs. Hermann has informed me that dinner is ready, so family and friends, let us eat."

We all filed into the dining room. Meta directed the two adult couples to one side of the table, the four "young persons" to the other; she and Harry took their places at either end. Mrs. Hermann brought out the wine bottles I had brought and placed them opened on the sideboard. With aplomb, Harry picked up one bottle, examined it with his eyes widening in approval, I noted with satisfaction, and then poured it into the adults' wine glasses. A second woman came out of the kitchen, whom Meta introduced to us as Mrs. Gunderson, and offered a selection of soda cans to the remaining "young persons." When each of us had a beverage, Jack rose with his wine glass in hand and offered a toast to his parents, saluting their success in two of life's most difficult tasks: marriage and parenting. He congratulated them for having made a "good and lasting" marriage and for having produced "two of the finest sons any parents could hope for." When he and Ted were kids, Jack reminisced, "you were the parents our friends most admired; this was the house where everyone wanted to hang out."

"What I want most to thank you for is for staying interesting and for not getting in a rut. I'm proud to have parents who can still teach me something. Family and friends, I give you my parents, Meta and Harry, two of the sexiest senior citizens I know."

"Meta and Harry," we all chorused, and then Mrs. Gunderson brought in a platter of carved turkey and set it before Meta; Mrs. Hermann followed her, setting a neatly sliced ham before Harry. While the anniversary couple served themselves and then passed the platters, Mrs. Hermann and Mrs. Gunderson brought in bowls, plates and platters of food: mashed potatoes, broccoli, carrots, gravy, freshly made and wonderfully tart cranberry sauce, still warm loaves of bread and sweet butter. We all helped ourselves and passed them on before settling down to silent consumption of the feast. For almost ten minutes, we ate

Legends of Good Women

in silence. Then, as plates and bowls once again were passed around the table, conversations bloomed. Seated between Jack and Ted, I listened to their fraternal banter and exchanged a few comments with Meta and Marian, while across from me, Janey, seated between Mike and Bill, was enjoying being at the center of sibling rivalry. Ted, Junior was in a dialogue with his grandfather. But the high point of the dinner for me was the pleased smiles Janey occasionally flashed at me across the table. For the first time since she was my smiling, cherubic infant, I had won her unqualified approval. A long time between strokes.

After we had devoured all they had set before us, Meta's two temporary employees returned to the dining room, stacked the dishes and removed them. Minutes later, they returned, first bringing cups, saucers, coffee, cream and sugar, and then, the two women brought in the cake: a long three-layered rectangle iced with vanilla butter frosting and topped by marzipan miniatures of the places that had been important in Harry's and Meta's lives. Recognizing a miniature school as a replica of the one she herself recently attended, Janey exclaimed, "You both went there?"

"Yes, indeed," Harry answered. "We met there. The first time I saw Meta, or took notice of her, was in third grade. We were playing in the school yard during recess, and she had fallen and torn her stocking."

"Girls weren't lucky enough to have jeans in those days, Janey," Meta explained, "We wore long skirts and long stockings, long thick woolen stockings in winter, cotton ones in summer."

"How did they stay up?"

As Meta was about to answer Janey, Harry took back the conversation.

"I'll let you stay mystified a while longer until I finish my story, if you don't mind. As I was saying, the first time I noticed this lady who was destined to be my wife, she had torn her stocking, but to keep the hole from showing, she had blackened her knee with a piece of coal. I saw what she had done; I looked at her; she knew I knew, and we smiled. I thought to myself 'She's a spunky type; I'd like to know her.' I still would."

"You've been more romantic in public than I remember you being. I hope I don't have to wait another forty-five years."

"A few words of praise from you might inspire me."

"Later, perhaps. The answer to your question, Janey, is garter belts. We held up our stockings with garter belts. Later, of course, we wore more complicated garments, contraptions of bone and rubber."

Meta looked at me and smiled, probably remembering the day we had been 'jugging.' "Oh, those days are gone forever."

Half the cake had been eaten; the kids were contemplating seconds. Some of the marzipan milestones had been doled out—the school to Harry, the replica of the gas station to Jack who had inherited it. A military cap, representing Harry's World War II service, remained on the cake, along with a fishing rod, signifying his retirement, and a running shoe and a donkey, signifying Meta's new interests. When we had finished dessert, Meta commanded us to stack our dishes and bring them into the kitchen—Mrs. Hermann and Mrs. Gunderson had departed—and we all obediently filed out and lined up inside the kitchen to give Meta dishes which she arranged on the kitchen sink counter while Harry removed the earlier dishes, still warm from the dishwasher, and handed them to his sons to put in the cupboards. All of us, adults and children, waited for Meta and Harry to tell us we were through with our chores.

"All right, everyone," Harry said in dismissing us, "I think we've done all that can be done here. Let's go into the living room."

We all did an about face and went from the kitchen back through the dining room and into the living room. The kids were self-conscious in arranging themselves on the couches. The two younger boys wanted to sit next to Janey, but did not want to seem to compete with each other. Mike settled the tacit competition by boldly sitting next to Janey, confident that his action would not be interpreted as anything but flattery to a girl obviously too young for him to be interested in seriously. I sensed that Janey understood his motivation but accepted the gesture as a means of maintaining her leverage with the other two. My smartass, alas, would become a coquette.

Meta went upstairs and returned to the living room with several photograph albums, and gathering Janey and me to her on either side, began turning the pages of her and Harry's family histories. Most of the pictures were taken when the subjects had established themselves in a new land with a measure of prosperity they wanted to commemorate, so, since they lived before every family had at least one camera, they had gone to a photographer's studio to mount themselves stiffly before his camera. The men, most of them with mustaches, stood in their bowler hats in back of the women who sat clustered in the center with children around them.

"Now those were indeed the days of binding undergarments," said Meta, pointing to one of the women in a photo of a group that included Harry's mother, his aunt, his sister and brother, father and uncle, and two cousins.

I said, "I can't believe the women wore those garments for more than an hour or two at a time. It must have ben torture to wear something that pinched them in the waist like that."

"The span of a man's hand. That was the ideal size for a woman's waist. And my mother tried to achieve it," said Harry.

"Not my mother," Meta countered. "Nor did she go around looking like a pouter pigeon. Look at the way their bosoms are pushed up. Oh, it makes me ache to look at them."

"And look at the clothes," Marian added, standing behind us, looking at the pictures over Meta's shoulder. "The women are wearing cotton dresses, so it must have been summer. Think of how long it took them to wash and iron their clothes, not to mention the undergarments. And look, even Harry is wearing a frilly shirt. Harry, did you wear shirts like that all the time?

"No, that was only because we were having our pictures taken. Most of the time I wore plain cotton shirts and knickers. I don't even remember that shirt. I probably hated it because I couldn't play in it. When I was a kid, we never saw our parents out of their clothes. But one day, I walked by my parents' bedroom door early in the morning. The door was opened and I looked in. My mother had her back to my father and was holding on to the bedstead, and my father had his leg up and his knee against my mother's back, and he had the laces of her corset in his hand and she was saying, 'Pull harder, Herman, pull harder.' That was more intimacy than I could stand. They didn't see me, but I ran back to my room, jumped in bed and pulled the covers over my head. I guess, thinking about it now, I didn't like being reminded that they had a life together. They were my mother and father, not husband and wife."

"Now my parents," Meta said, holding up a photo, "were openly affectionate with each other. Look, this is my mother. She wore long dresses – all the women did, but you can tell she didn't crush her insides; she's flat, straight up and down. My mother was athletic. She was a good swimmer. She still swims. I don't think she plays tennis any more."

"Where is she?" I asked.

"She lives in a small cottage she shares with a group of other widows in the northern part of the state. She's still active. They all are. They knew each other in childhood; most of their mothers were active in the campaign for female suffrage in 1913."

Harry broke off his conversation with Jack and Ted, who were sitting together on the opposite couch, and called out: "Which my grandfather was vehemently opposed to."

"All you beer-drinking Germans were," Meta answered him crisply.

"Damn right."

"Yes, I've read about that," I said. "The Germans were convinced the women would bring in prohibition if they got the vote."

"That was part of it, but I don't think the whole of it," Meta said. "I think the men were afraid they would lose control of the women if women were able to vote."

"They were right," Harry answered stubbornly.

"Isn't it ironic, Dad, that your grandfather opposed women's suffrage and you're married to a politician?"

"Yes, Ted, I'm aware of the irony."

"Yes, Ted, and I like to think that the ghost of my grandmother is smiling triumphantly at the ghost of Harry's grandfather."

Good natured banter—husband teasing wife about her relatives, wife teasing husband about his, brother recalling antics of brother filled the afternoon as Meta opened the albums, turned pages, and selected kinfolk to recall for us. Family anecdotes unraveled like a long skein of yarn patched from many sources. One story Meta told was about her paternal grandmother, blind in her later years, who had lived with Meta's family. Once when Meta's mother had been called away while in the midst of preparing cake batter, she had asked her blind mother-in-law to guard the cake batter from the family cat, who ate whatever food the family left unguarded. Meta's grandmother had sat at the table pounding it, but the cat, somehow sensing her infirmity, had leaped up, not on the table where the bounce of its paws would have given it away, but onto a chair, and then the cat had quietly pulled itself onto the table. When Meta's mother returned, she saw the cat lapping up the batter while her blind mother-in-law was still futilely slapping the table.

Once during the sharing of memories, I looked at the kids, who seemed as fascinated at what they were hearing as I was. Even Mike and Bill, who had heard each anecdote more than once before, seemed enthralled. Young people may be bored with, or resent, stories where a moral is being drawn—"When I was your age"—but these stories had no message; these stories were their history and heritage, and the subjects were people with more authenticity and individuality than the cookie cutter cute families on sitcoms.

In the evening, exclaiming almost in unison, "I can't believe I'm hungry after all I ate," we trooped out to the kitchen again to nibble on leftovers, drink more coffee or soda, and gossip about contemporaries. That exchange was even more fun for the kids because they were hearing inside information on people they knew as respected adults. The principal of Janey's elementary school, for example, had in childhood been the "bratty" younger sister of Meta's best friend.

And when it was clear that Harry and Meta, in spite of their health and vigor, were tiring, I signalled to Janey that it was time to go. She sighed as she does when I wake her before she has finished a good dream, but she came agreeably, after sincerely and heartily hugging Meta and Harry – winning their hearts, I was delighted to see – and shaking hands formally with Ted, his brother, Marian, and the three cousins. "God, Janey," I thought, "you do things well when you want to."

CHAPTER

After Meta and Harry's anniversary party, the stress and anxiety I had felt since I had begun preparing for the Marathon fell away. I was going to finish the Marathon in a decent but unspectacular time, and if I did not qualify for Boston, so what? I had new energy in the classroom, and my courses were off to a very good start; I felt the students' interest during classes and their hum of approving comments as they left the room. With euphoria-born efficiency, I arranged with Sally for the UMW women to come to her home on Saturday to view her tapestries. And looking with confidence toward the future, I decided I needed to know more about business, not only Ted's but about the economic situation of our community. I wanted to acquire skills so that if I chose, I could also become a risk-taking entrepreneur. Like so many women, I had a fear of acquiring money, investing it and making it grow to the point of wealth. Part of the fear was a residue of Sixties idealism, when all wealth seemed rooted in some form of oppression in the workplace and pollution of the environment. But much of the fear was rooted in my – and most women's – socialization. While we believed we would lose the purity of our souls if we became seekers of wealth; we needed to think of ourselves as privileged and others in need of help. We could become ambitious only on behalf of others. I wanted to abandon my modesty and become ambitious for myself.

When I returned home Monday afternoon, I found Janey still somewhat aloft from the previous day's male attention, which I concluded, from her glinting eye and smiling mouth, she had used to mint coins of admiration from her girl friends. Who were her girl friends now, I asked. Were she and Ellen still good friends?"

"Yes." The word traveled up and down over a hill of ambivalence.

"What is it? You don't like her as much this term as last?"

"Ye-es. But I've met some new friends I like better."

"But you two are still friends?"

"Yes. I eat with her every day, and I go to her house and she goes to mine, same routine as last year, but I'd like to enlarge my circle of friends. There are some kids in junior high from different elementary schools, and they're really neat. The problem is Ellen is kind of boring at times. She's afraid to try something new. And she said her mother wouldn't let her date until high school."

"She sounds like a most unreasonable woman. Is dating something you're ready for now?"

"I would be if there were anyone worth looking at or spending time with, but the boys in eighth grade are all jerks. So immature. They've started to notice girls now, and they've got this system of animal noises. In the morning before we go into school, they stand in the school yard and make noises according to how good looking a girl is or if she has a nice personality. Stephanie—that's one of the neat new kids I've met—and I have figured out that, according to their system, they make chicken noises if they think a girl is cute or has a nice personality; they gobble like a turkey or bark like a dog if they think she's ugly or awful, and they meow if she's so-so; no, they moo if a girl is fat; they meow if she's cute."

"That sounds mean."

"It is. And it can be so embarrassing. I told you they were gross."

"They sure sound gross. Oh, well, give them time. They'll grow up and get better."

"Do you really believe that?"

"I like to think I do. You know who I think is nice? I think Bill is nice."

"I knew you were going to say that. He's the kind of kid every girl's mother likes."

"Well, don't you think he's nice?"

"Yeah, he's o.k., but I don't think he's my type."

"Your type of what?"

"Oh, I could like him as a friend, but I don't think I would like him as a boy friend."

"Why? Why can't a friend be a boy friend?"

"Because a friend is like a brother, and a boy friend is definitely not like a brother. A boy friend is more interesting; he's sexier. A friend you can trust. A boy friend you can't."

"Oh, dear. Oh, well, I think Bill is sweet-natured and trustworthy. And I hope you don't have to live to be as old as I am before you realize how valuable and important those qualities are in a friend, boy friend,

lover, husband, whatever. And I hope you won't resist liking Bill because your mom likes him."
"Mom?"
"Yes?"
"Why can't we live in the good part of town?"
"What's wrong with this part of town?"
"When I told Stephanie where I lived, she said, 'Oh, you live in Polacktown.'"
Before I could respond, the telephone rang, and Janey answered it. I knew from her greeting it was Ted. Holding her hand over the receiver, she handed it to me, whispering, "Speaking of men of whom my mom approves."
I told Ted that I had just been having a woman-to-woman talk with Janey and asked him if he had had a man-to-man talk with Ted, Junior yet.
"You mean about women, girls?"
"Yes."
"It's a little early yet, both in my relationship with my son and in his own development. I think he likes some of the girls in his class, or one girl, anyway, but he prefers not to talk about anything but sports. I've avoided asking any pointed questions. But the reason I'm calling, in fact, is that his aunt and uncle have invited him for dinner. Do you think you could get away for a couple of hours and have dinner with me?"
And sex. His brother and sister-in-law were tactfully making time for us to be together while at the same time trying to thaw Teddy's hostility.
"Let me check with Janey."
"Yes," she said before I asked her, "you may have dinner with Ted."
"Janey gives me her permission to have dinner with you."

"I'll be by in ten minutes."
"I'd like to shower first."
"Shower here."
"Okay. Come and pick me up."
"I'm leaving right now."
"You sound like you're in a great mood."
"I am."

I tried to stop grinning as I put the receiver back on its cradle and returned to the living room. Janey looked up from the book she had open and resting on her belly to inspect me.

"You deserve some time alone with Ted, Mom. You two haven't had much time alone together. You must find that very frustrating."

"You are the source of my frustration at the moment, smartass. I'm disappointed that after all your splendid anti-racist talk, you should bring home a new form of ethnic bias from one of your 'really neat' new friends. I don't understand. In New York, on East Eleventh Street, we lived among Poles, Puerto Ricans, Blacks, Irish, Jews. Why does it matter now?"

"New York was different. There were so many people, no one was in the out group. This is a small town. One group is always on the bottom. And I like to be among the top group."

I felt that Janey was a stranger to me then. Realizing that further discussion was pointless, I went upstairs to put some toilet items and a clean pair of underpants into my bag. I went back downstairs just as the doorbell rang. I called goodnight to Janey and greeted Ted.

"This is wonderful weather for running. I hope it holds until after the Marathon, make that after the election."

"Do you think the weather will affect the outcome?"

"Not really. Reagan's going to win. But the defeat for Carter will be worse if the weather is bad."

When we reached Ted's apartment, he opened the door cautiously and brought me inside.

"I didn't have time to clean the place today, and I wasn't sure what kind of shape my son would leave it in. Why don't you sit down while I go check the bathroom."

"I won't love you any the less if your tub has a ring in it."

"Humor me. We're not occupying the same household yet. Besides, you prepare your place for me, don't you?"

"Yes, I do. All right, clean if you must. Just don't throw your standards of bachelor fastidiousness up to me one day as a form of reproach."

I waited in the livingroom while Ted did his chores.

"All right," he said when he rejoined me. "I think my bathroom is clean enough for you now. You can take a shower first."

"I won't be long."

"No, don't be," he said, the words coming out of him with a huskiness that was turning me to water. As I walked past him, he slid his hand down my back, and held me against him. We began kissing, pecking at each other like ravenous birds. In seconds we would not be able to stop, so I pulled myself away and went into the bathroom, closing the door. I showered and slipped into the spare freshly laundered terry bathrobe Ted had hung on the back of the bathroom door for me. I opened the door and went into the bedroom. Ted had brought in a bottle of cold chablis and two glasses on a tray he had set down on the short bookshelves beneath his bedroom window. He was sitting in an easy chair, watching the evening news. When I entered the room, he rose and poured the wine into two glasses, handed me one, and we stood together, arms around each other's waists, facing the newscaster, watching clips of the presidential campaign, local and world events, but more conscious of each other than of the information particles floating out to us from the 21-inch screen.

"I'll be back in minutes," Ted promised, setting his glass down on the tray, and, flinging his bathrobe over his shoulder, went out of the bedroom and into the bathroom.

I pulled back the bedspread and climbed between fresh sheets; alone, I was more attentive to the news program.

In minutes Ted did indeed return to me, and when my own gaze settled fully on his face, he turned the television set off and joined me in bed. We settled back against the pillows; heat would rise again; it was seven o'clock, and we had time to talk.

"Now tell me why you're in such a good mood."

"Three reasons. I feel everything coming together at once. Everything I've been working for or thinking about seems to be right within grasp or about to happen. First, I just signed a contract with a company of some size. It's exactly the kind of order that my own shop can handle by working to capacity, and if this order is followed by others, the shop should be humming steadily, with no slack, no hustle on my part from contract to contract with slack time in between. My profit situation should begin to change, and I might begin to be able to make a decent living from the business. For years, I was scrambling to make child support payments to Michelle now I'm off the hook there since Teddy lives with me. Then I scrambled to make payrolls, and in between pay my rent, feed myself, pay bills, and buy presents for my family once in a while. My financial situation is changing. This contract will, I'm sure, lead to others, not only from this company. I'm going to be a breadwinner again on a scale that pleases me, and that fits in with the second and more important reason for why I feel on top of the world. You felt it yesterday, didn't you, what a special day it was?"

"Oh, yes."

"I can't tell you how good I felt, balancing the table at my folks' house instead of being the odd man, the bachelor son that I've been for so many years. Not that my parents and brother and sister-in-law haven't been gracious, or ever made me feel uncomfortable, but I think you can understand why one wants to be part of a well-matched couple."

"Indeed."

"Well, yesterday, for the first time in years, I felt I was holding up my end in the family gathering department. And you were the reason. I was proud to have you there with me. I could see us years from now at other holiday gatherings. I felt like a citizen."

I turned and kissed his face and then the rest of him. I made love to Ted, who let me embrace him, arouse him, who rewarded me with love sounds. And then, when I had brought him to readiness, he came back from his private sphere of pleasure to bring me to mine.

Afterward, we lay side by side, holding hands, feeling jolly and giggly, like loving playmates, the best of friends.

"I'm thirty-five," I said.

"So am I. So?"

"Nothing. I'm not sure whether I'm feeling disappointment that I had to live so long without this kind of joy, or that I'm amazed and grateful that it has come at last."

"Well, whatever. We both deserve good things. We've waited a long time."

"Did you do things traditionally the first time you were married."

"Pretty much. Michelle took charge of that part of or lives. It wasn't bad. It was nice, in fact people fussing over us."

"Well, I got married in a municipal building. I didn't even have a friend at my wedding. Not even my parents. I'd like to do it more traditionally this time, if you don't mind."

"Not at all. What would you like? An engagement ring?"

"Oh, yes. I'd like that very much. Maybe not a diamond, but a nice ring. An heirloom, perhaps. Is there something in your family?"

"I don't know. Most of the stuff has been parceled out by now. My mother did give Michelle something—a pin or earrings—I don't remember, but I didn't ask for it back, whatever it was. I'll ask my mother if there's anything left. If not, I'll buy you something. An old-fashioned ring okay?"

"Fine. And I want a period of courtship. Not where you do all the courting, but where we court each other. Bring each other flowers, do nice things for each other, lots of surprises and treats. Would you like that?"

"Yes, I would."

"What are you thinking about?" I asked.

"I'm enjoying the image of you coming to my apartment holding a surprise bouquet of flowers behind your back, or holding out your fists and saying, 'Which hand do you want?'"

"I'll have a present in each one. I like to give presents."

"I know. So do I."

"When shall we tell our kids?"

"How about this weekend?"

"All right," I agreed.

I was in a state of calm elation, living through the moment and reliving moments that had just passed; if I could not extend this night in real time, I would make it last in memory. As Ted was driving me back home, one memory rose to the surface.

"Ted, earlier you said you had three reasons for feeling good. I know what the first two are. What was the third?"

"It's Bob. He's making the most amazing progress. I saw him last night, briefly after I left my folks', and I couldn't believe the change in him in so short a time. He is seeing his counselor. And separate from that, he and Sally have made an appointment with a marriage counselor. He has stopped drinking, and he is talking about going to college, or taking some courses that would advance his career. I wish you could have seen him, Claire. He has a new determination. He says he has finally realized what he could lose, and if he is going to keep his family together, he has to be the one to change. He was so positive, so mature. I went away from him feeling so great. I wanted to shout, 'We've won, we've won.'"

"That's wonderful," I said, and tried to mean what I said. I tried to resist the feeling of deja vu and alarm that rose within me. Back at my house, Ted left me on the porch, and, for the sake of watchful neighbors – or a daughter trying not to be seen from a darkened window – we cheek-kissed each other. I entered the house with a big grin on my face, but I could not make the twinge of fear and doubt leave the back of my neck.

CHAPTER

The next day Janey was expecting my report. Evading her was easy in the morning when she was preoccupied with preparing herself for an appearance at school, but at dinner I felt her scrutiny. I kept the conversation focussed on her, on school, for she was far enough into the term to have revised her opinions of her teachers. People she had liked the first day now seemed less magical, while those she had hated on sight were not as obnoxious as she had first believed. I inquired about each of her subjects: what were her assignments, how far along on them was she, what tests had she had, and how were her grades. As usual, Janey was off to her mediocre beginning, which could curve either way by the end of the term or stay depressingly the same. All of Janey's teachers—from Open Classroom advocates to Montessori specialists to back-to-basics traditionalists—had moved their heads in sad resignation when I visited them on Parents' Night conferences, and told me, "Janey doesn't work up to her potential." And while I agonized over the gap between Janey's potential and her performance, I had come to realize I could do little to change her. Not lectures, scolding, punishment, nor bribery could alter her motivation. I tried to comfort myself by relying on Janey's healthy self-interest which would keep her from real peril. She had always passed her subjects and probably always would, and when she did not feel she had to avoid competing with me to maintain her identity, she might even become passionate about her intellectual life.

"Are you going to marry Ted?" She sprang the question on me after I had completed my interrogation of her.

"How do you feel about my marrying him?"

"I think it would be really neat. I mean, I like Ted all right; you could do a lot worse, but I think his family's great."

Janey added shyly, "I'd like to be part of a family like that. So tell me, are you? will we?"

"I won't say yes and I won't say no right now. I'll tell you this weekend if Ted and I will get married."

"That means yes."

"I didn't say that."

"Of course it does. You must think I'm dumb. You wouldn't wait until this weekend to tell me you're not going to marry him."

The telephone rang, conveniently saving me from acknowledging the loss of another debate to my daughter. Knowing Ted was calling, I answered it in the kitchen. I talked to him and leaned against the swinging door into the dining room, in order to let Janey, who was pretending to do her homework at the table, hear our very dull adult discussion of our work, the election campaign, the weather, predictions for marathon weekend. Janey grew so bored she gave up pretending she was not listening and turned in her chair to suck her teeth in exasperation. I was pleased that, with all her sophistication, Janey did not know

Legends of Good Women

that Ted and I were consciously teasing ourselves and each other by talking platitudes while thinking sexy thoughts. Only once did a rise in my voice signal to Janey that Ted had said something interesting.

"Oh that would be super," said I, reduced to adolescent vocabulary. Janey's eyebrows shot up, but she would have to wait until I was off the telephone to find out the "really neat" plan of Ted's.

"I'm tied up with work," Ted said, "so I probably won't see you until the weekend. We'll talk before tomorrow."

"Yes, I'll speak to you then," I replied coolly, and said goodnight.

"Ted said he would try to come to New York the weekend of the Marathon," I informed Janey as I went into the living room to settle down with student papers.

"Oh? Will he bring his son?"

"Probably. Unless he leaves Teddy with Harry and Meta."

"I wish . . ."

I heard the rest of Janey's unfinished sentence: that one or both of Teddy's cousins would come instead.

"I know what you wish. I thought you were looking forward to spending that weekend with Julie."

"I am, but it would still be fun to have these healthy-looking boys from Wisconsin to show off to my friends in new York."

"True, but that is not even a possibility."

I sprawled out on the couch reading papers, searching for the graceful comment that would encourage each student to improve her writing while at the same time getting her to accept my judgement that it needed improvement and providing the direction for achieving the improvement I desired. I was aware of Janey in the next room, doing her homework in her looseleaf notebook. We were aware of each other, and Janey looked up.

"Well, it will be nice to have a family, but I'll miss this, too."

Suddenly, I too was aware of the "this" – the intimacy – we would be leaving behind. Until that moment I had not realized Janey would achieve her long-held goal of getting me to stop walking around nude. But that was a small gain when paired with the loss of the closeness that Janey, despite our frequent irritation with one another, had shared since her birth. We sat reflecting on the irony of our situation: as we were on the verge of putting aside what had seemed a flaw in our family structure, the just-the-two-of-us quality of our lives, we realized how much that structure had bonded us together.

"Janey," I said, "I can give up going around bare-assed, but I won't give up my special bond with you."

We silently continued our thoughts about the family life that was to come. I knew Janey was thinking as I was, that we had a lot of work before us to make ourselves feel motherly or sisterly to Ted's son.

"Don't worry," I said, answering her thoughts, "we'll lick him into shape. Come here and give your old Mom a hug."

And Janey, bless her, came running to me like the eager little darling she once had been.

In the next days, I functioned with a sense of being in transition, of wondering how my impending marriage would affect my professional relationships. I was certain that my colleagues and students would view me with new respect, and I was trying to fight a sense of guilt about achieving mobility through marriage. But I defended myself to my feminist consciousness: "I shall have a family, a support system. I shall not be vulnerable and alone. If things go wrong, I shall have people I can count on for help." Nevertheless, I could not shake off a sense that I was wimping out, that struggling alone in adversity had given me a sense of my courage and a self-respect I could not have as a married woman.

On Saturday, I drove out with Kathy and Rebecca—Gloria had begged off and delegated her proxy to her fellow officers—to Sally's home. I was pleased to find that Bob was not around. Sally—whose still-mottled face revealed her domestic history to my canny friends—explained that he had gone fishing. Sally introduced Daphne and Enid to Kathy and Rebecca, who spoke to the girls in a woman-to-woman way that charmed them. However, when we followed Sally up to her studio, and she unrolled her tapestries for us, it was the adults' turn to be charmed. More than charmed, really, for I could sense, by the silence that followed Sally's presentation of each weaving, that Kathy and Rebecca were experiencing the same recognition of being in the presence of fine works of art that I had felt when I had first seen them.

After Sally had shown us the weavings, we went back downstairs to the living room, where Sally served us coffee and cake and we made plans for the exhibit. We agreed that January would be a good time, for the holidays would be over and the exhibit would draw people from the surrounding communities. Rebecca and Kathy, efficiently making notes on yellow pads, were outlining the publicity campaign, listing organizations to be contacted. We did not hear Bob come in until he was standing in the living room, after, I was sure, having come in quietly so he could listen to us in the hallway before entering the room. Rebecca, Kathy, and I all saw him before Sally did. She had been talking, but when she saw her husband, she stopped. We witnessed resentment flicker in his eyes, and fear in hers. Daphne and Enid, who had been going in and out of the house, cheerfully interrupting us from time to time and demanding their mother's attention, became very still when they saw their father, quickly chorused, "May we be excused, Mom?" and went upstairs.

"I thought you were fishing."

"I was. I got bored. I see you've been busy." Bob's voice had an edge of disapproval in it.

"Yes. We've been planning the exhibit of my stuff at the Art Center. I told you about it."

"Yes, you did." The disapproval remained in Bob's voice.

"Oh, excuse me," Sally apologized, and then introduced everyone else to Bob.

"So you're all here to help my wife in her art career. That's really great. Well, I'll leave you all to it, then. Sally, I'm going to wash the car. Just call me when dinner's ready. Nice meeting you all."

Bob was smiling as he left, but his hostility toward us was palpable. So was Sally's tension, which quickly broke everyone's concentration. We excused ourselves as quickly as we could. Kathy and Rebecca promised to get the formal approval for the rest of the UMW leadership – "a given," they assured Sally, and get back to her about the promotion campaign.

"I would say that is one troubled marriage," Rebecca said in the car. "Is there anything you're not telling us, Claire? Anything about the McNeills we should know?"

"There is something I'm not telling you," I said after a pause. "But whether you should know it or not is not for me to decide. I'm sorry, but I don't feel I can break a confidence."

Legends of Good Women

"Never mind," Kathy said. "We can fill in the blanks."

"It's a classic situation," agreed Rebecca. "God, what a control freak. And we're doing something that will give her autonomy. He hated us on sight. And you started this project, Claire. He must really have it in for you."

"I'm glad you agree with me. Someone I've been seeing, who's Bob's best friend, thinks I'm paranoid about Bob."

"Oh, that's a piece of news, Claire," Kathy crowed. "Who is this person you've been seeing?"

"Someone I knew in high school. I told you, Sally, Bob and I were classmates in high school."

"And this person is Bob's best friend?"

"Yes, but he's very different. Really. He just won't abandon Bob as a friend because they were in the war together."

"All right if you say so, Claire," Rebecca conceded. "But that Bob gives me the creeps. Do you think he might try to destroy her weavings before the exhibit?"

Rebecca's question jolted me. I knew Ted had either been conned by Bob or had allowed himself to be deceived about Bob's true state of mind. Exactly how dangerous was Bob? When I dropped Kathy and Rebecca off at Kathy's house, Rebecca asked if and when they might meet the "person I'd been seeing," and I told them I might bring him to church one Sunday. I left them smiling at me ambivalently.

When I got home, Janey was waiting for me with a message to call Ted. The night before we had decided that the four of us should go to dinner. This was to be the weekend we announced our plans to marry to our children, although in our telephone conversations during the week, we had both become shy about when and how we would announce our decision to our children. Janey smiled in her brightest smartass way when she gave me the message, adding, "Ted told me the four of us were going out to dinner together. Is there any special reason Ted, Junior and I have been included on your date?"

"Any time the four of us are together is a special occasion," I said. Janey snorted at me.

When I reached Ted at home, he asked, most solicitously what I had been doing. I told him about the visit to Sally, how much the women liked both Sally and her weavings, and how enthusiastic we were about the exhibition. I refrained from telling him I thought his optimistic assessment of Bob's condition was inaccurate. "I look forward to seeing her work."

"You've never seen her tapestries?"

"No."

"How is that possible?"

"Sally did not talk about them often. I mean I knew she did weaving, but I thought it was a hobby, like needlepoint, not a major commitment. And Bob never spoke of it much either, so I had no idea she was serious."

"Well, you have a treat coming. Sally's work, in my opinion, is major."

Ted asked if I thought taking the kids to Shannon's in Fountain City for dinner would be a good idea, and I said I thought it would be fine. Then Ted got to the point.

"Look, Claire, I know we decided we would tell our kids this weekend about our plans, but, well, I tested the water earlier; that is, I tried to get my son's feelings about my remarrying some day, and he became upset. He knew exactly what I meant, and so he created a skit about his life, as if he were a tv newscaster, pretending to hold a microphone and talking into a camera about his life as a baby, 'oops, we preempt this family by a divorce, folks,' and then with his mother, 'We preempt this family with a marriage," and then with the birth of his sister, 'We preempt this child with a baby sister,' 'and now, ladies and gentlemen, we preempt this family with a father,' and finally, 'We preempt this transient adolescent once again, ladies and gentlemen with a remarriage – a stepmother and a stepsister.' I think, Claire, we should wait awhile before announcing our – what we plan to do."

"Are you talking about postponing the announcement or the event?"

"The announcement. We hadn't actually decided when the event itself would take place. But I thought the spring. I still think so."

"Fine. No problem."

"You're upset."

"A tad. It will pass. I understand. So, I'll see you and your son in an hour?"

"Fine."

Janey, with her vixen's ears and instincts, had deduced from my comments and tone the substance of our discussion.

"You and Ted are not going to make an announcement tonight because his son objects."

I nodded yes.

"Well, I don't think I want to be in the same family with such a creep, anyway."

I tried to coax Janey into a mood of civility, but only half-heartedly because I was having difficulty getting myself into a civil mood. When Ted came to call for us in his car, Janey complained, "Look, they're the men, the drivers, and we're the women, the passengers."

I asked Ted as we entered the car, if, for the sake of Janey's and my needs for equality, we could go in our car on our next outing. Ted said sure, he would like to be called for, chauffeured to a restaurant or movie and then brought home. Janey was mollified until Ted, Junior, jeered at Janey, "Are you one of those libbers, too, like your mom?"

It was a difficult dinner, and neither sports nor school, the usual conversation stimulators, could keep us engaged. Fortunately, the food—the other three had steak and I ate pasta—was good, and we could make several distracting trips to the salad bar. When Janey and I returned from one of those sorties, I heard Ted and his son talking about hunting.

"You're going on a hunting trip?" I asked.

"Yes, when the season opens." Ted replied.

"I didn't know you hunted."

"I've been working so hard for so long, I haven't had time to go hunting. But yes, like most men of the midwest, I'm a hunter. And I look forward to going hunting with my son."

"Do you eat the meat of the animals you kill?" Janey asked.

"Yes, but not all of it. I usually parcel it out among family and friends. Deer meat—venison—is very good."

I almost said, "Don't ever bring home a deer carcass for me to prepare."

"Yeah," his son added with a vicious smile, "deer meat's good; veggies are for wimps."

"My mom is no wimp and neither am I."

"Are you a vegetarian, too, Janey?" Ted, Junior asked.

"I am now."

"Then I hope you enjoyed that steak because I assume it was the last one you'll ever eat."

The kids had dessert while Ted and I had coffee, none of us saying much to one another. I had a vision of myself leaving the table, taking Janey, summoning a taxi home, packing our bags and going to the airport. Mexico? Tahiti? New York? I suddenly wanted very much to be living on East 11th Street again.

After dinner – Ted paid for himself and his son, I paid for Janey and me – we went outside and discussed what we should do next. I wanted to go home and so, I knew, did everyone else, but neither Ted nor I was willing to concede another failed outing. We decided to go to Valley View Mall to see a film.

Driving home afterward, I spoke again of the visit to Sally's and how enthusiastic we all were about the exhibit of her work in January.

"I don't think Bob was too pleased, however."

"Oh? Why?"

"I don't mean he said anything in opposition. He came in later, toward the end of our visit, and Sally, who had been so cheerful and enthusiastic became tense and distracted. Bob made the approving comments, but all of us sensed he did not really like the plan."

"Maybe he did mean what he said. Why not give him the benefit of the doubt?"

"Why not, indeed. You're right. We should take Bob at his word."

"I mean he's trying very hard to regain his position in the marriage. And if Sally exhibits her work and everyone is making a fuss over her, he has to make an even greater effort at adjustment. At a time when he needs all the support he can get, he'll have to deal with something that will make him feel even more insecure."

I was so frozen with anger, I did not trust myself to speak for minutes.

"I was thinking how wonderful it was that Sally had some recognition at last and a much-needed lift to her spirits. Are you suggesting that she once again put her life on hold because of Bob?"

"That's not what I'm suggesting and you know it," Ted snapped.

We rode on in silence; Janey and I almost jumped from the car when we reached our house. Teddy jumped out of the car and moved to the front seat. We all said a terse good night; Janey and I turned and walked quickly to our front door while Ted, who had not turned off the ignition, pulled away from the curb.

Sunday I went to church, reflecting with embarrassment as I stared at the ceiling on the fantasies I had allowed myself to have about being married here. The previous night's outing had certainly dented my smug pre-nuptial certainty. No, the marriage was not off, I assured myself, just not a top priority at the moment with either Ted or me. After the service, Kathy, Rebecca, and Gloria called a special meeting of the UMW leadership. Kathy and Rebecca reported enthusiastically on Sally's tapestries and outlined the plans we had made. UMW formally voted to co-sponsor the exhibit, and I left the meeting consoling myself with a sense of accomplishment.

Finding Janey up and dressed, but looking glum when I got home, I said her three favorite words, "Let's go shopping."

CHAPTER

During the week, Ted and I communicated by telephone almost daily, discussing my work, his work, his clients, my students, our children. By tacit agreement, we avoided intimacy, or the subject of marriage, and yet I felt no strong impulse to rupture our relationship, nor did I sense such an impulse in Ted. I did refer to my departure for New York in a week, but he did not repeat his intention to come to New York, nor did I press him, fearing both his resolve to come and his withdrawal from the commitment.

I did some easy running during the week, planning to run fifteen miles on Sunday, five miles on Monday, Tuesday, and Wednesday, and then rest until the Marathon in New York on Sunday the 19th of October. I was taking care of other details, like arranging with one of Janey's friends to come to the house while we were away to feed the cats in return for a fee of five dollars. For two reasons I also wanted to see Sally once before I left for New York; the better reason was that I wanted to maintain her enthusiasm and self confidence about the exhibit; the less good reason was a wish to prove myself right about my suspicions that Bob's recovery was simply not happening. I tried twice to reach her, but got no answer; on Friday afternoon, Bob answered.

"Bob? This is Claire. How are you?" Maybe I should not have asked that question; I should have pretended to assume he was all right.

"I'm fine, Claire; how are you?"

Politeness was making us both itchy.

"I'm fine, Bob, thank you. Is Sally there?"

"No, she isn't."

"Is she working? I've tried to reach her all week."

"She's not working now. She's been working overtime all week, and so have I. The kids have been at her mother's. She's with them now—probably shopping at K-Mart—but I'm sure she'd like to see you. If you drove out, I'm sure she'd be back by the time you got here. I just woke up, but I'm sure she won't be gone long, or she'd have left a note."

A half hour later, when I arrived at their house, the car was in the driveway. I pulled into the driveway and parked behind their car. As I approached the house, Bob opened the front door, and held it open as I went in. Standing a little behind the door, he made a gesture toward the upstairs, and I went up, calling Sally's name as I ascended. But when I was halfway up, the silence and its meaning became clear to me. I turned around, and nearly fell back when I saw Bob facing me, one step below me, but his head was level with mine and his bloodshot eyes were staring right into mine. Then I saw the beer can in the hand the door had hidden from me as I came in. He was drunk and he was mean, and the backs of my knees broke into a sweat.

"Where's Sally? I saw the car in the driveway. Isn't she here?"

Legends of Good Women

"Sorry, Claire. I woke up in a fog," Bob explained with a nasty chuckle. "I forgot that Sally and the kids went away with her sister last night. They're going to spend the weekend, I think. She'll be back Sunday, I'm sure. Sorry I made you come out all this way." His apology was mockingly insincere.

Bob swayed a bit and reached for the bannister. He got his hand on it the second try. He took up all the room on the staircase; I could not slip past him, nor even in his unbalanced state could I push him out of my way. He took a sip of beer, staring at me over the rim of the can as he had the very first time I had come to his house. He moved toward me, and in order to avoid him, I had to step backwards up the stairs. I hated him then. I turned and ran up the remaining steps to the second floor, and turned to face him with my hands on my hips.

"That's all right," I said in a civilized English professor voice. "I'll just leave Sally a note and be on my way."

"Don't run. Stay and talk to me. We've never had a chat, you and I. And maybe we should get to know each other better, since Ted tells me the two of you will be getting married."

As he spoke, Bob followed me up the stairs; then he paused, his left foot on the top step, his right foot on the step below it. Then he leaned forward, rested his left arm on his left leg, held his left wrist with his right hand and jiggled the beer can in his left hand. The sound of the swishing liquid seemed menacing.

"Yes, we are."

"Gee, that's nice. I hope you'll make Ted happy. He's a great guy. Do you appreciate what a great guy he is?"

"Yes, I do. And I think we'll make each other happy."

"Well, I hope so. He certainly deserves it. Ted's a prince, don't you think?"

"I think he's a fine and honorable man. The best I've ever known."

"'A fine and honorable man. The best I've every known.' That's nice. And that's a nice thing to say, to be say, to be a—"

"To have said about him?"

"Yes. That's what I meant. Gee, you're smart. But you should be. You're a pee aich dee, aren't you?"

"Yes."

"I must be a lucky man. I have a friend who's a fine and honorable man. And he's going to marry a college professor, a pee aich dee. An I have a fine wife an' two great kids. I'm a lucky man."

"Yes, you are."

Bob put out his right arm against the wall and, still holding the beer can, grasped the bannister with his left hand. Having blocked off passage, he studied me as if I were prey he would dispose of when he thought of the way which most pleased him.

"Yes, I'm a lucky man. I have a great friend; Ted's been my friend since we were kids. I've been Ted's friend longer than you have, Claire. We went to the war together."

"Yes, I know."

"You haven't known Ted very long at all. Oh, yes, I know," he continued in a mocking falsetto, 'we were all in high school together.' "But you weren't our friend then, Claire. You were a brain. You were above the rest of us."

"No, I wasn't. I didn't have friends."

"Really? No kidding. You were just a wallflower when all along I thought you were a snob? How about that? Well, you sure have made up for past performance, Claire. Just think, you came back to your home

Legends of Good Women

town, and in no time at all, you caught the best man in it. You worked fast, Claire."

"Ted worked as fast as I did, Bob."

"Oh, yeah. Ted could have had anybody he wanted. What else was there for you? If you didn't get Ted, who else was there in this town for you?"

"You're right, Bob. Ted could have had anyone he wanted and he chose me. Ted and I chose each other. I should think you would want your friend to be happy."

At my response, Bob's face reflected confusion, but as he decoded my words, his face showed hatred for me, such as I had not seen on a man's face since that day summers ago when I ran in Central Park. Then he masked his anger with a grim smile.

"Who says I don't? But I still want him to be my best friend. And I don't think he will be after you and he are married. Because you don't like me, Claire, do you? You think I'm a bum, a wife-beater and a drunk."

"Bob, I didn't start out disliking you. I knew very quickly you didn't like me. And yes, I think you drink too much, but so do a lot of men. I never have called anyone a bum, even people everyone thinks of and labels as bums. Yes, I grieve when people behave badly because I have an idea of how people ought to behave, and I think every one is in danger when humans behave in inhuman ways."

Bob waved the hand holding the beer can and some of the beer slopped out and fell over the bannister onto the floor below. His breath was awful.

"Oh, you're so good, I can't stand it. Cut the bullshit, will you? 'Every one is in danger when humans behave in inhuman ways.' You're so full of shit, I can't believe it. You tight-assed bitch, you don't know what the world is like. I'll tell you. I've been in danger. I've been where the guy you're fighting to defend will shave you in the morning and poison your water at night. And that's not just true in Vietnam. I've been in danger on my job. I see human nature every day, and it's dog-eat-dog."

"Is Ted like that? Is Ted dog-eat-dog?"

"No, he's the best there is, but he's the exception. He's rare."

"He told me you were improving, that you were dealing with your problem. He was so happy when you began going to the counseling program and told him you would continue in it. He was so happy when he believed you were trying to stop your drinking."

"Yes, I know. If I could do all that for anyone, I'd do it for Ted. For old St. Ted. But I can't stand going to the V.A. Hospital twice a week and sitting down to spill my guts to some fag-Jew-shrink. What does he know? While I was out risking my life, he dodged the draft to get the education that makes him an expert so he can interpret my life for me. He doesn't know fuck-all about my life. And as for my drinking, I can manage it, except once in a while. I'll just have to be more careful. I don't mind letting you see me drink, Claire, because you don't count with me. The people who count aren't here right now to see me."

Bob was building his anger toward me as Sally had said he had built anger toward her before beating her. I thought I could lower his anger by continuing to speak calmly.

"Bob, if you don't like the psychiatrist you're working with, why don't you ask for someone whose background is closer to your own? There must be psychiatrists who are also vets in the program, and surely you can be assigned to one of them."

As soon as I made the suggestion, I realized I had undermined his rationale for quitting the program, leaving him with only his rage, which he turned on me. As he began backing me down the hallway, I realized I should have said, "You're absolutely right, Bob. How could you continue in a program with a gay Jewish draft-dodging shrink?"

"What's the point of counseling anyway? I'm going to lose everything. And you're responsible. It isn't enough that you're going to take my best friend from me."

"You're wrong, Bob. I don't see us making a foursome, but I'd never try to keep Ted from seeing you. You mean a great deal to him. I have married friends, women who are married whose husbands I don't care for, or who don't care for me. . ."

"I bet they don't."

". . .and I see the wives without the husbands. People understand that couples don't always have to have the same friends."

"Yeah, yeah, more of that women's lib bullshit. I don't believe it. Ted wouldn't want to see me, I know. And my wife won't want to stay married to me, and you don't want her to stay married to me, admit that you don't."

Bob advanced until he was inches from me, his face above mine. He grabbed my arm. I tried to look dignified, not frightened.

"Let go of my arm, Bob."

He hesitated just seconds before releasing my arm, but I watched the pupils of his eyes, reduced to pins by alcohol, waver in their irises. I was far from safe. This man was determined to hurt me. How was I going to get out? I tried to think of what I could say to calm him, but he was using his own words to fuel the impulse that was driving him, and would soon find the combination that would permit him to do what he wanted to do.

"What did you come here for? To help plan that exhibit? To give Sally more ideas that will change her, make her dissatisfied with her life? Who the hell do you think you are, coming back to your home town and one, two, three, you're playing games with people's lives. But what if what you're planning for her flops? What then? You'll drop her and go on to something else. Maybe you're playing with Ted's life, too. I just hope Ted is man enough to keep you in line. But I'm afraid you've turned him into a wimp. I don't think he understands women like you the way I do. I know what you need; I've known it from the minute I laid eyes on you. I'm going to show you what a real man is like. I'll bet you've never had someone like me inside you."

He dropped the beer can and grabbed my shoulders. I put out both hands and gently pushed against his chest, and then slowly, carefully took a step toward him, just as if I was not at all ready to pee all over myself in terror.

Bob's eyes widened in surprise at my resistance. He pushed me again, forcing me down the hallway toward the bedroom. I managed to turn my body so my back was to the wall.

"No," I shouted. With all the strength I could summon I struck my arms against the insides of his arms as they reached out to grab me. I had the satisfaction of hearing him grunt. Then he stood before me, one arm holding the other, confusion on his face as he considered his next move. I was surprised that he had not struck me, and then I realized that beating me would leave evidence. Ted would know what he had done. But rape he could deny. Again, I tried to distract him.

"What would you gain..." I paused before saying "raping me" and finished the question: "...assaulting

Legends of Good Women

me? You have no reason to hate me, really, or to be angry with Sally."

He waited, his eyes reflecting indecision. Would he stop or try again to rape me?

"Bob," I said, in a miraculously calm voice, "you know your wife has a great gift. Her weavings are wonderful If I didn't help her promote it, in time, someone else would. Talent like hers can't be hidden forever."

"What's so great about those rags she puts together? They're just pictures."

"If they're just pictures, why did you try to burn them?"

"Because they made her forget herself, and her place. She got so wrapped up in her weaving, she didn't have time for me or the kids."

"That's not fair. Sally's a devoted wife and mother."

"Well, my devoted wife has locked up her weavings so I can't even see them. That's how devoted she is."

I had succeeded in giving him another target. He moved away from me and down the hall to Sally's workroom, where the gold circle of a newly installed lock gleamed in the door just above the knob.

"She's shut me out, the bitch, she's shut me out. I can't even be allowed near her precious tapestries."

He kicked the door once and then repeatedly. I ran down the stairs and opened the front door of the house. I could get to my car before Bob could reach me, but he was no longer interested in hurting me. I could hear the wood of the door begin to splinter. Soon Bob would have Sally's tapestries in his hands and would be unable to stop himself from destroying them. It can't be helped, I thought, and then thought again, I can't let Sally's work be sacrificed. I went back into the house and walked upstairs, watching Bob throw himself against the door and crying, "It's not fair, it's not fair. Everything I have is being taken from me." I saw him as I had never seen him, a pathetic, hopeless wretch. I pitied him, but I knew him to be incurable.

At the top of the stairs, I spoke to him, as softly and gently as I could make the words come.

"Bob, please stop. Please stop. If you destroy Sally's work, she'll never forgive you. You'll lose her forever, and the kids. And you'll never forgive yourself."

And he stopped, leaned against the door, and just sobbed.

"You're right. You're right. Oh, God help me, how did it get to be this way? All my life, I've been shit. You can't know what it is, to know that you're rotten inside, absolutely rotten, and to have such good people around you who trust you, love you. And to know you're not worthy to kiss the ground they walk on."

"You're not shit, Bob. No one is."

"Yes, I am. You don't know. I told you, you don't know anything. Please, go away. I won't hurt Sally's stuff. I promise."

I had to believe him, because I had done everything I could. I went outside and got in my car and drove home, where I lay down and slept until Janey came home from school. I awoke and made dinner for us, and tried to make myself believe another crisis had passed.

CHAPTER

After dinner, Ted called, in high spirits suggesting that Janey and I join him and his son in a "real old-fashioned evening – movie and ice cream afterwards."

"That sounds wonderful, Ted," I said, hating not being able to match his spontaneity and good mood, "but I have an awful headache. I'm sorry, but I don't think I'm up to it, this evening."

"I'm sorry, too, but it can't be helped if you're not feeling well. I'm flexible. Would you like me to come over and rub your temples, or something else?"

"Thanks, but I'm not fit company tonight. I just want to go to bed and sleep it off. I'll be all right tomorrow. Why don't you and Ted, Junior come over for a late breakfast or an early lunch. We can go for a drive with the kids and then go out for dinner together, the four of us."

"All right. That sounds fine with me. Are you sure you'll be all right tomorrow?

"Yes, I promise. I know my head by now. A long sleep will cure it."

Ted said goodnight with disappointment in his voice. As I returned to the living room, Janey looked at me with puzzlement and resentment.

"You never said you had a headache. You seemed all right at dinner."

"I don't tell you everything that's wrong with me. Sometimes I suffer in silence."

"Maybe you don't tell me in words, but you always let me know when something's wrong with you."

"Well, this time I surprised you," I said, trying to make my voice sound as if the matter were closed. "Now I'm going up to my room. I really do feel awful. What are you going to do?"

"Watch television. Do my homework. What else is there to do?" Janey asked sulkily.

I went to my room and lay down, not at all sleepy, but allowing the full awfulness of the day's events to overtake me. I edited out my final feelings when I had left Bob, that the guy was sadly beyond help, and allowed the anger I had repressed during the time he had menaced me to take over. I kept seeing Bob's face against mine and then over me; the scene kept playing itself out on a loop that would not stop. I relived the humiliation of having been in the power of someone who wanted to hurt me; I had had to be very careful; I had not dared to say what I wanted to say. I had been forced to use the weapons of the weak and craven: guile and deceit. No, no, I had only done what sane people do in the presence of berserk men. But women had to walk carefully all the time. Sally did, or how could she have lived with Bob so many years? Well, I hoped she did not live with him one more year, one more day. And yet, for reasons I could not clearly understand, I would not tell Ted what had happened.

Legends of Good Women

After hours, I heard Janey click off the television set, snap her textbook shut, and go into her room, slamming the door lightly, probably with the peevish wish that the sound would waken me if I slept. Had there been a problem? Had a newly forming relationship gone sour? Had one of the "really neat" new friends lost her glamour or been unkind? Had Janey wanted to confide some problem to me? Or had she just wanted company that evening, since no other friend was available? Refusing to let Janey's mood make me feel guilty, oozing myself out of the delayed spasms of anger, I finally drifted off to sleep.

I slept well and late; Janey was up when I awoke. In fact, her voice on the telephone wakened me. I could not hear what Janey was saying, but the earnestness in the voice drifted up to me through the bedroom door. I concluded that Janey had encountered a problem in a relationship and was trying to resolve it. I dressed for running and went downstairs. Hearing me, Janey interrupted her conversation on the kitchen telephone and peered around the kitchen door, cradling the receiver against her sweet young chest.

"Are you going running?"

"Yes. I'll be gone for about three hours. And then Ted and his son should be coming over. If they call, tell them I'm expecting them about twelve for lunch or brunch. You eat what you want, meanwhile."

I went to the sink and drank two glasses of water. I took two bananas from the bowl on the counter. Not wanting to keep her friend dangling and not wanting to continue the interrupted conversation in my hearing, Janey began giving her friend a play-by-play account of my activities.

"My mother's here with me. She's going running. I told you she's running in the New York City Marathon . . . Of course, I'm going with her; I'm still a kid, after all . . . Yeah, there are people I could stay with, but I want to go and see my mother run in the Marathon. Wouldn't you? Does your mother run? No, not many moms do out here. Bye, Mom."

I kissed Janey as I went past her and gently brought the kitchen door to a halt before it could bang against her. As I went through the dining and living rooms, I could hear Janey still in diversionary chatter.

"My mom's going to run fifteen miles now. She's taking bananas with her so she won't. . ."

Outside I exercised on the front lawn. I put my cotton gloves on and set off, holding a banana in each hand. I had planned my running course with two alternate turn-around points, one at seven and one half miles and the other at nine miles. I decided to take the longer course, and finished the eighteen miles in two hours, twenty minutes and some change, or less than eight minutes a mile. I should have been exhilarated, but the Marathon was beginning to be less important to me than having the event behind me. I returned to the house, stretched languidly to return my well-worked muscles to normalcy, and ate the bananas which I had fortunately not needed to ease cramps during the run. Janey was glumly watching television.

"What's the matter?"

"Oh, I wanted to make plans to go somewhere with Stephanie, but you've made plans for Ted and his grouchy son, and I'm just sitting here waiting for you to get back. When are they coming over?"

"Very soon. Around noon. I'll call them now."

Teddy answered. I had spoken to him so seldom on the telephone that I was shocked by the young sound of his voice. His slightly wavery "Hello" reminded me that he was a kid, and vulnerable before he was anything else, grouchy or whatever.

"Hello, Teddy; this is Claire. How are you?"

I did not want to ask for his father immediately, but I couldn't think of much to say to him. He spared me a search for words.

"I'm fine, Claire. My father's not here. Claire, I don't know where he is. He got a call early this morning, and woke me up and told me he had to take care of a sudden emergency. He said he'd be back when he could and not to worry."

"Well, I'm sure that's what it was, Ted, an emergency. Perhaps something at work came up."

"Not at eight on a Saturday morning. Besides, I haven't lived with my father long, but I know he'd never be as upset as he was by something at work."

The boy's voice rose then, reaching a part of me he had never touched before.

"I think you're right, Teddy; I don't think your father would be that upset over a business matter. Something must have happened to someone your father cares about, but whatever it is, I know he can handle it. Did you call your grandparents?"

"No, but if anything had happened to them, Dad would have told me."

Yes, he would have. His son did not have a range of possibilities to work with. He probably did not know immediately, as I did, what the source of his father's distress was. What had he imagined then?

"Teddy, shall I come and get you and bring you here? We can leave a note for your father."

"Okay."

"I'll pick you up in twenty minutes."

When I went back to the living room, Janey had turned off the television set, and had overheard enough of the conversation to figure out the rest. She asked if she could go with me, and I said she could. I ran upstairs to shower and change, and then we drove to Ted's apartment. The boy was standing on the lawn in front of the apartment complex waiting for us. As I drove the car alongside the curb, Janey got out and let Teddy get in next to me. I dared to kiss and hug him, and he not only let me, he hugged me back. I looked up at Janey in time to see the little smile she was trying to suppress. When the three of us were back at the house, Janey whispered, "I knew you could handle that situation, Mom."

"You mean you think I'm a good mother?"

"Of course."

"Well, tell me that once in a while. Who's going to reward me if you don't?"

But Janey was not listening to me; she was too impressed by Teddy's vulnerability. In his fear that he had once again been abandoned, Teddy had revealed himself as a child in need of comfort, and once Janey had the opportunity to feel superior, she immediately became generous. While I prepared lunch of peanut butter and jam sandwiches, apple juice, potato chips, carrot and celery sticks, Janey took Teddy into her room, and soon the rarely heard pinging of her electronic games sent darts of sound out to the kitchen. I called the kids in to help me set up the food on the kitchen table. We ate every bit of food I had set on the table, and then Janey got out a tin of cookies from the refrigerator.

"Homemade?" Teddy asked on the third cookie.

"My mom makes everything from scratch," Janey replied.

She went to the living room and put one of her albums on the record player; we continued our running argument about "her" music versus "mine." Teddy asked why I liked Sixties music and which artists were my favorites. I explained that the Beatles, Bob Dylan, Judy Collins, Joan Baez, Jimmy Hendrix, and Phil Ochs had been troubadours to my generation. People who were young in the Sixties saw themselves as having a mission, and the singers and musicians we admired had endorsed our sense of mission and inspired us to do what we thought was important.

"You all thought you were going to make the world a better place, huh?"

"Yes, we did. Maybe we didn't do everything we set out to do, and maybe mistakes were made. But I think the country is a better place because of the civil rights and anti-war movements."

"And the women's movement," Janey added.

"My father said you risked your life when you went down south in the civil rights movement."

"That's right. My mom was arrested. She could have been killed."

"Janey, most of the time I worked in the heat trying to get people to register to vote. Most of the time there was no danger."

"But you did risk your life to help Black people get their rights."

"Yes."

"I don't understand how or why you could have done that."

"I'd like to tell you why I did, but I think I'll save my explanation for another time."

"Well, anyway, I think it's neat that my father likes a woman who's got guts, even if I don't agree with you."

I thanked Teddy for his kind words and suggested we three play a game of scrabble. We cleared the dishes, Janey ran to her room for the game and we played it on the kitchen table, scrapping with each other amiably. Janey made the word "booze" early in the game; Teddy challenged it as slang, demanded a dictionary, was given one, and found the word in it. When Teddy took longer than Janey thought he should have for his turn, she got our egg timer from the kitchen closet. I turned up mostly low-point vowels at the beginning of the game, and high point consonants at the end, when I could do very little with them. The match was a genuine one between Janey and Teddy, and Janey won narrowly, thanks to a strategically reserved "s" which she used when all her other tiles had been placed, making a plural of Teddy's word, "bet."

The kids went into Janey's room then, while I sat in the living room, grading papers while trying to keep the cats from leaving paw prints on my students' essays and also trying to keep from thinking about the reason for Ted's unexplained absence.. In the middle of this peace, Teddy came out of Janey's room and said, "It really is strange that my father hasn't called."

"Yes, it is. But he counts on us, I think to know he knows he can rely on us."

Teddy accepted that statement and turned to go back to Janey's room. Then he turned back to me and said, "But something awful must have happened to keep him away all day without telephoning us. What do you think could have happened?"

"I don't know," I replied, trying to make myself believe what I said. I was guiltily certain that Ted had been called to intervene in another crisis, and perhaps Bob had harmed Sally even more seriously than before.

Soon another meal would have to be prepared, so I went into the kitchen to plan it. I really did need to go to a supermarket, but I did not want to leave the house. A shopping trip would be a pleasant diversion for the kids, but I was afraid Ted might call while we were out. I began mixing batter for a cake; somehow those ingredients were always present in my pantry. And I would make vegetable stew for our main course.

The sweet kitchen odors drifted into Janey's room at the precise moment when the kids' stomachs were reminding them they were empty again. Janey and Ted came to ask if they could help, meaning could they make the time when they could eat again come sooner. When they connected the smell of vanilla with the cake I was making for dessert, Teddy and Janey spontaneously and simultaneously made little smacking noises with their lips. Janey and I laughed and Teddy looked puzzled. Janey explained that Teddy had made the sound she always makes when she realizes her mom is making something good to eat. Teddy's unselfconscious gesture, coupled with the tenderness he had shown me earlier were softening me into thinking I might be able to accept him as my son.

I fed us and kept us cheerful, and then, at eight o'clock after we had eaten, cleaned up, and were sitting in the living room watching tv and passing around a bowl of freshly popped corn, the telephone rang. Ted was calling to ask if Teddy was at our house.

"Yes, he is. He's been worried about you. He said you had been called on an emergency."

"Yes."

"And?"

"Bob's dead."

"Bob?" I was stunned for the moment, but not really surprised. "How did that happen?"

"Gunshot. An accident. I'll tell you more when I see you."

"Shall I tell Teddy?"

"Yes. Please. Can he stay with you overnight? Or until I get there?"

"Of course."

When I told Teddy and Janey that Bob was dead, their responses were quite different. Janey did not really know Bob, but had deduced that I disliked him, and knowing that I was not feeling grief for him, responded without much sincerity, "Oh, that's too bad." Teddy, however, was truly shocked. He had liked Bob, having seen only Bob's remnant personality: cheerful, supportive older male and willing surrogate father.

Janey asked where Sally had been when Bob had been killed. I said I did not know; perhaps with her sister.

"What about his children?" Janey asked. "How will they feel?"

"They will be very unhappy, I'm sure; the loss of a parent is a terrible thing. But they are young and healthy, and have other people to love them. They shall recover."

I let our spell of somber questioning continue for a while, and then, sensing both grief and an impatience with grief in the children, I turned on the television set again, hoping for the silliest program possible. Where was Gilligan's Island when I needed it? Then I made another bowl of popcorn.

I made up the bed in the guest room; when I returned to the living room, Janey said Teddy did not have a toothbrush or pajamas; I said I always have a supply of fresh toothbrushes, and Teddy could have as a pajama top one of my father's old shirts that I keep in my closet for painting chores.

We were all ready for bed at eleven. I kissed Janey, then Teddy. Janey held out her hand as if unsure where to place it, and finished by patting his shoulder. He smiled at her, said "Good night," and we all went to bed.

But I remained awake for hours, reviewing the events, not only of the past days, but going back to my first encounter with Bob. One is usually able, after the fact, to read the signs pointing to the event they signal, but in Bob's case, the phrase "dangerous to himself and others" would have seemed to point more to others, to a final scenario involving the taking of hostages, the random gunning down of citizens by a gunner on a tower, one final act of destruction in which the author was only the final victim. Only in my last awful solo encounter with him could the man's despair be seen, and then the harm he had meant to do to me had kept me from feeling concern for him. I was not glad he was dead, but I was enormously relieved.

My experience of death was still limited. I had not known my own grandparents well enough to love them or mourn their deaths; I had loved Frieda but, while I missed her, I could not mourn such a well-lived life. The only other deaths I had known – Bill Schwartz's, Helen O'Rourke's, and now Bob McNeill's were all – indirectly self-inflicted and all three were related to a sense of lack of parental love. Helen's early life had so ironically paralleled Bob's: the death of a preferred sibling coupled with the same awful rejecting words from a parent: "Why couldn't it have been you?" And yet Helen had never become bitter; her life had been dedicated to earning other people's love, to serving others, not hurting them as Bob's had been. To equate the difference in gender with the difference in behavior might satisfy my feminist soul but seemed simplistic. Bill's death had come when he appeared to have licked his problems, when he was a student leader and people were eager to present him with opportunities. He had told me just days before his death that after leaving Richmond, he would go on to a senior college upstate—his brother would stake him to his degree—and that he hoped to use his experience producing performances by rock groups to go on to a career in the entertainment industry. But I learned later that, as one of the "red carpet people" in Bill's life, he would not let me know his dark side. Helen had been certain the success she had achieved would never be repeated; Bill had believed he was unworthy of what success he might achieve, and each had chosen to end the anguish. Why had Bob chosen to end his anguish? Because he too knew what lay ahead would be worse than what had gone before?

Why, I asked myself at last, was I worrying so much about people beyond my help or love? As I lay in bed staring at the ceiling, I felt the prop of having to meet the needs of others fall away, leaving me with a sense of my own unmet needs. I had been in peril the day before, and while the man who had put me in danger was dead, his death probably linked to his wish to destroy me for having failed in that aim, he had turned his wrath upon himself, I still had my own wrath to deal with. Even if I could not tell Ted what had happened, I wanted to have him with me at that moment just to be comforted by his presence. Suddenly, I felt a chill, as if Bob's hate-filled, tormented spirit were with me, and a message formed in my brain as if a ghostly voice were whispering it to me: "Your marriage is not to be." I told myself Ted was too solid a man to make a commitment and then withdraw it. But why had his voice been so tight when he spoke to me on the phone? Grief was in his voice, but was there not something else as well? Resentment against me? Would Ted, feeling he had failed to save Bob, try to punish himself by refusing the happiness we might have? The man would not be so perverse, I told myself. I tried to purge my demons, and by three o'clock I succeeded. But I awoke late Sunday morning with wisps of gloom hanging above my bed.

Gloom and a sudden rush of resentment. More than resentment – anger at Ted. He had championed Bob, had made plain to me that he would never let our love for each other come between his friendship with Bob. Ted had been the one exception to Bob's making everyone around him suffer for his pain, and now I was on the verge of fury that Ted had accepted his behavior on the grounds that "whatever sins Bob has committed he has already paid for." I should have protested his response long ago instead of meekly accepting peril to Sally, their kids, and even me as a condition of loving Ted. But even as I felt anger rising inside of me, I knew it was really directed at myself. Was I really as craven as I feared I might be? Would I give up self-respect just to have a man in my life again? David had said I would never be a princess, meaning I would never issue commands to "Buy me, do me, get me, bring me, never doubting that every item or task requested would be bought, done, gotten, or bought." Men, I had learned, might complain bitterly of such women, but they also served them faithfully. I, however, was so far from princesslike that I could not even tell my husband-to-be that his best friend had tried to rape me. And I would never be able to tell him that everyone close to Bob was better off because he was dead.

I rose, dressed for running, and completed my last long run before the Marathon. Before returning home, I stopped to buy the Star Lake Daily News. The headline blared, "Local Officer Killed in Accident." According to the account, Police Officer McNeill had accidentally shot himself at home while cleaning his gun. Present in the house at the time were his wife, Sally, and his friend, Ted Ritter, who had made statements to Bob's fellow officers when they arrived at the scene. Suddenly, I understood another possible interpretation to Ted's word, "Accident."

When I returned, Janey and Teddy were sitting in the living room watching television, not talking but sharing a friendly silence. A good sign, I thought, and then asked myself why I should be pleased by their companionable and sibling-like blankness. Well, first things first. Get them to get along and then I can work on improving them. Hah. Did I not well know by now a parent's powerlessness in this area?

I showered, dressed, and prepared a breakfast which we consumed in near silence. The kids helped me clear the table, put away the food, and place the dishes in the dishwasher; then walked like twin zombies back to the living room to resume their trance before the television set.

"Oh, no, you don't," I said. It's too beautiful a day to be indoors. We're going out."

"You're not seriously planning to take us to church," Janey responded derisively, her lip curling in a way that made me want to slap her face.

"No, I'm not seriously planning to take us to church," I replied in a voice I, with effort, kept even. "The foliage is at its peak on this splendid October day, and unless you have any other suggestions, we're going for a drive to look at it and take a walk on the bluffs."

Janey and Teddy exchanged glances reflecting shared exasperation. "Good," I thought; "I've united them against me." Ted looked at me as if he were contemplating defiance, but then, as if reminding himself that at the moment he had nowhere else to go, went to the hall closet to fetch his own and Janey's jackets and the two resentful adolescents followed me out the door.

Their sulk lasted during the drive to Granddad Bluff, but after we had walked around, surveying the blazing autumn beauty of the Mississippi Valley, exercise purged their funks as it had mine earlier. As a reward to them for their transformation into humans, I stopped for pizza in LaCrosse and then drove back to our house. The telephone was ringing when I got to the front door, and I managed to get to it before the caller disconnected.

It was Ted, of course, formally thanking me in a subdued voice for taking care of his son, and asking if he could come over and get him.

"Of course," I said, inhibited by his tone and manner from questioning him or lengthening our conversation.

"I'll be over in ten minutes," he said tersely and hung up.

When he arrived at our house, he was as distant and impersonal as he had been on the telephone. He seemed not to see me as he came into the house; he merely thanked me again for caring for his son, nodded to Ted, Junior and, without a kiss, a smile, or even a handshake for me, followed his son out the door. "Don't shut me out. Tell me what happened," I silently shouted at his back as it walked away from me. I was tempted to throw a solid, heavy object after him, but I sensed Janey reading my mood and studying my response. I could not let my daughter see me as an angry, impotent woman; I had to be cool, so I turned to her with a smile I hoped she believed was sincere, and asked her to find something good on television while I made popcorn.

CHAPTER

Somehow throughout that weekend and subsequent days, the technical and ritual arrangements for undertaking, solemnizing, mourning, and burying Bob were completed. The police report that Bob's death was a fatal accident while Bob was cleaning and loading his weapon enabled Bob's parish priest to allow him to be buried in sanctified ground, and Bob's family, in particular, his father, were able to complete the funeral arrangements with formal and respectable grief.

On Monday I called Sally, still within the bosom of her family.

"Claire, you're the person I'd most like to see right now, but my family is responding with Italian grief to the situation, meaning, because they're secretly glad Bob's dead, they're trying to outdo each other in crying and wringing their hands."

"What happened, Sally?"

There was a pause while Sally waited for whoever was with her to leave the room.

"Claire, I tried to reconcile with Bob, but it would not work. He was not going to counseling, and I know enough from my work as a nurse that these situations get worse, not better. My sister came for me on Friday evening, as if we and the kids were just going out for dinner. I called Bob after I got to my sister's house and told him that I was not coming back, but I wanted to get some of my things and the kids' things on Saturday. He said fine, he understood, he'd probably get up early and go fishing, so I could come by then. He sounded so reasonable, I did not feel I could trust him, so Saturday morning I called Ted and asked him to come with me. When we got to the house, it seemed empty. I went inside, got our stuff, came down, then Bob came in through the back door. He had his gun. And he'd been drinking. He ranted on about how I had been planning to leave him, had turned the kids against him; he turned on Ted, accusing him, his best friend, of betraying him. He talked about you, how you'd made Ted soft. Ted tried to reason with him, but Bob was so wound up, I knew he was working his rage so that he would do what he had set out to do. He pointed the gun straight at me, with his finger on the trigger. Ted grabbed his hand as he was about to shoot; Ted wrenched his arm, so that when the gun fired, the bullet went into Bob's head."

"How awful." Oh my god, I thought. Ted was responsible, ultimately, for his best friend's death. He would feel guilty for the rest of his life.

"Yes. Then Ted called the police. Claire, that was the strangest part of all."

"In what way?"

"When the police, two of Bob's co-workers, came to the house, they barely glanced at Bob, and said, 'His gun went off accidentally while he was cleaning it, right?' Like they had a script ready. I was so startled, I opened my mouth to tell them what happened, but Ted signalled me to stop. But I almost have the feeling they would have said the same thing if Bob had shot me and it was my body lying on the floor."

"How are you feeling now?"

"Oh, pretty rotten. But I'm not sorry, Claire. There was no other way. Eventually, Bob would surely have killed me; me and the children, Claire. You're smart, Claire; you know what was happening. Do you doubt for a minute that what I'm saying was true?"

"No, I don't."

"Well, then, you can understand. If it had to be Bob or me and the kids who would die, then I'm glad it was Bob. Do you understand, Claire?"

"Yes, Sally, I do."

"And Claire, I want to talk to you, just as soon as I can, after this, after the funeral."

"Yes, Sally, after I get back from New York."

"New York?"

"Yes."

"Oh, my God. That's right. You're going to run in the New York Marathon. Oh, that's wonderful."

We both began to laugh then, almost hysterically.

"Oh, I wish I could go with you. I wish I could run in the Marathon with you. What a perfect, wonderful thing to do. How long is a marathon?"

"Twenty-six point two miles. Through the five boroughs of New York City."

"Oh, that's grand. When do you leave for New York?"

"Friday afternoon. Janey's coming with me. Sally, how are your girls?"

"They're numb. Enid's still too young really to know what death means. That it's permanent. She just thinks her daddy's away, and she's not too sad about it. Daphne knows what death means, but she's not letting herself know; she seems to be letting herself be as innocent as Enid so she won't have to feel guilty that she isn't sorry he won't be coming back. You know, we're all in therapy now, but if we weren't already in therapy, we'd have to start. Claire, I have to go now. The funeral's Wednesday morning. Will you be able to come?"

"Yes. I have a class, but I'll arrange to have it covered."

"I'm glad. I'll need all the support I can get. Not to help me through my grief, but to form an alliance with me against Bob's family."

"Why should that be necessary?"

"Oh, they have not been too subtle in expressing their view that I am somehow responsible for his death. They haven't gone so far as to say I drove him to it, but Bob's brother, John, and his mother have been asking questions like, 'Didn't you know something was wrong?' and 'Couldn't you have gotten him help?' I told them that Bob had refused to stay in counseling, but they don't want to deal with that. Bob's mother went so far as to ask, 'Couldn't you have saved him?' I told her no, I couldn't, but no one could have. It all started long ago, I told her, throwing the guilt back at her. After all, Bob is much more a product of his family than his marriage. Claire, run a good race."

"I will. I'll talk with you when I get back."

I called Ted immediately.

"Sally told me what happened."

"Oh."

"Ted, I hope you don't in any way blame yourself for Bob's death. There was nothing else you could have done. He would have killed Sally."

"Knowing that doesn't stop the pain. I also know that you don't share my feelings about Bob."

"No, I don't. But I love you; I care about you. Does that still mean something to you?"

A pause.

"Yes, it still does. But I just can't talk with you now, Claire."

I wanted to ask, "Are you going to punish yourself and me by killing our marriage?" but I was afraid to hear Ted say he would.

On Tuesday evening, I went to Burkes' Funeral Home; in the room where Bob was lying, his parents, siblings, other kinfolk, his police co-workers, members of the softball team, including Ted, were grouped together on one side of the room, talking softly and carefully in small clusters. Sally was flanked by her mother and two sisters, an isolated group whose only weapon against the silent but palpable hostility of Bob's family was their defiant black clothing, including thick veiling which I had never seen anyone wear before except Jacqueline Kennedy. Those widow's weeds should stifle reproach, I thought as I walked to the bier; indeed a restraining influence might well be needed, for Bob's father and some of his police buddies were moving in a way that suggested much drinking had preceded their presence here.

I looked at Bob's well-cosmetized body only long enough to appreciate the efforts of a mortician who took his work as seriously as had my former student who made explosion victims presentable to their loved ones. No wounds were visible to my unscrutinizing eyes, and Bob had been dressed, appropriately, in his military uniform. I moved toward Bob's family and made a formal declaration of regret and sympathy, moving my eyes and nodding my head slightly, trying to include every member of Bob's family so that I would only have to make the speech once. Then I moved to the other side of the room to sit with Sally and her family. I put my arms around Sally and hugged her, feeling her veil scratch my cheek. I greet ed Sally's mother and sisters, and then turned to look toward Ted. I lifted the corners of my mouth slightly, hoping for a restrained but loving greeting in return. But Ted was looking at me blankly, perhaps with hostility.

Sally did not say anything. She sat, looking down, but member of her family were acting as extensions of her, not speaking, but occasionally placing their hands to their faces, or moving their hands out from their sides in "why-o-why" gestures. Oh, they were splendid, not extravagant, not in any way speaking or behaving in ways that would give Sally's in-laws an excuse to say, "typical Italians," but their demeanor at the wake, and subsequently at the funeral, had just enough abundance and style to evoke in Bob's clan respect bordering on envy.

I had arranged for coverage of one of my classes, and on Wednesday morning I drove to Saint Aloysius. I was surprised by the number of cars parked outside the church, including so many police cars that I wondered if any members of the force were on duty to protect our community from crime. Saint Aloysius is more grand, more Gothic, more intimidating than Broadway United Methodist. I might indeed believe in heaven and hell if I worshiped here, I thought as I walked down the long center aisle and sat on the side where Sally and her family sat. The band of mourners was half the size of Bob's clan, but I was grateful that Sally now at least had support from people outside her family: hospital co-workers and other nurses. Everyone on the wife's side was female. Most of the mourners on Bob's side were male; even the children, the offspring of Bob's siblings, were male. How Bob must have hated that his brothers and even his sisters had produced sons but he had not. Ted and his son were seated next to the faimly. Behind them were Bob's co-workers, in uniform as were most of Sally's co-workers. Cops on one side, nurses on the other; enforcers versus nurturers.

After studying architecture, then mourners' faces, I directed my eyes to the rectangle in the center of the aisle before the altar. My initial reaction of relief that he was dead had not changed, but mixed with it now was a sense of wonder at death. Just days ago, the coffin's occupant was a man, alive, threatening, a presence in a number of lives; now he was gone, no sound, no word of his would ever be heard again, nor any action felt.

I heard movement from the back of the church and knew that the priest and his attendants were advancing. I did not look back, but when they were parallel with the pew in which I sat, I looked at them from the corner of my eye, and caught the glitter of church light on the priest's satin vestments. I saw with some satisfaction that the priest was silver-haired, middle-aged advancing on old, not young like the priest who had presided at poor Helen O'Rourke's funeral and had gloated over her body. But this priest was intensely sympathetic to the person he was consigning to eternity. Indeed, Bob would have liked the homily, "And greater love," etc., and the sermon. The priest spoke of Bob as "one of the fine young men of our community who had answered his country's call, ready to lay down his life for his family, his community, his country."

"He returned to his community to take up the adult roles the war had interrupted. He became a policeman, again assuming the role of protector. He married and began a family. On the surface, his life was normal, but there were scars, great wounds that were seen but would not heal. The wounds were the results of our failures, our breaking faith with this young man who had offered so much to us all. His country failed him by not supporting him as a fighting man, by not allowing him and all his comrades to win the war they had gone to fight, and then when he and the other fine brave men came home, the nation spurned their sacrifice, out of shame perhaps at our own lack of national will, we projected that shame onto the men who had defended us in that war. As a nation, we turned our backs on them, and then, as parents, wives, as brothers and sisters, we failed them by our unwillingness to understand their ordeal, and by refusing to hear them, refusing to ease their pain, we increased that ordeal, we doubled the trebled that ordeal. Bob remained in service to his country, his family, his community, in spite of the failure of all those he served to understand his anguish. He continued to fulfill his obligations, his roles, his responsibilities well, but the burden was great. The lack of support took its toll, a secret sorrow grew large within him, and made him as careless of his life as we had been. That carelessness led to the fatal accident that was the direct cause of his death, but the larger cause began years ago, when a shining young man of this community went forward to offer the gift, the great gift of his youth, his young manhood to us. Ah, brothers and sisters, is there anything in this world finer than that? Young Bob went out to become a warrior, and suffered unseen but ultimately mortal wounds, and today we honor that sacrifice and mourn that fallen warrior."

I looked across the aisle as the priest concluded his eulogy which was a fiction but not a lie, and thought I read satisfaction on the faces of Bob's family; I interpreted the expression on Bob's father's face as stiff pride, as if he too was creating a fiction of Bob's life as the heroic son of a family, who, if they had failed to understand him, had not failed to love him well. At the conclusion of the mass, the attending priests followed the presiding priest down the aisle, wheeling Bob's coffin on its gurney to the church door, at which point the pall bearers, Bob's brothers, Ted – looking older and sadder than I could ever have imagined him being – and three of Bob's fellow police officers carried it down the steps and placed it in the hearse.

After leaving the church, the rest of us went to our automobiles, some, like Sally's co-workers, to return to work, and others to form a procession which followed the hearse and the limousines carrying the O'Neills and Sally, her children, her mother and sisters out of town and down Highway 61 to Valley of Angels Cemetery which overlooked the river. A canopy had been set up over the hillside grave site and chairs had been placed on either side. Ted joined the O'Neills who sat on one side of the grave site and I sat with Sally on her side while the priest completed the ceremony. Then the cemetery workers lowered Bob's casket – a pricy oak coffin, I noted, wondering whether Sally had paid for it or whether the O'Neills were compensating for their stinginess to Bob alive with an extravagance after death which could now only benefit the undertaker. The O'Neills and their tribe departed in clusters; Bob's fellow officers spoke briefly to Sally and then departed in a group; then Sally and her children left with her family, and I walked over to Ted. He looked at me as if I were a stranger, and I felt my stomach plunge.

"Are you angry with me?"

"No, I'm not angry with you, Claire."

"Are you ang – do you blame yourself? Because there is nothing else you could have done, you know."

"No, Claire, I do not blame myself, although I wish with all my heart I could have kept Bob alive. And I guess I'll have that wish for the rest of my life."

Ted turned away from me; the graveled path crunched under his footstep.

"Don't turn your back on me; don't walk away from me; don't treat me like an enemy," I shouted after him.

Farther down the cemetery hill, another funeral party was dispersing, and the departing mourners stared at me.

"Ted," I continued, follwoing him but lowering my voice. "I want to understand why you grieve for this man so. He was so unlike you; he abused his family. He would have killed his wife."

Ted looked at me and then stood studying the ground. His silence goaded me into saying what I had vowed to myself to keep unsaid.

"Ted, Bob assaulted me; he tried to rape me."

Ted raised his head and looked at me, disbelieving. I told him the details of the encounter. When I had finished, Ted looked at me without either warmth or hostility.

"You and Sally and everyone else, perhaps, may be glad that he can no longer hurt himself or others, but I mourn the goodness in the man, the goodness he always showed to me. He was my friend, my best friend; no one else shared the experiences we shared, and I'll always be sorry I could not help him see what I saw: a basically good man."

Ted turned from me then and walked down the path and out of the cemetery. I did not try to follow him. As I watched his retreating back, I realized that I was not important enough to Ted for him to believe the evidence I had given him of Bob's treachery. Ted would remain committed to his mythic ideal of male friendship. He had, in effect, chosen the past over the future.

I turned to look at Bob's grave. The cemetery workers had finished covering his coffin and were tamping down the soil with their shovels. I imagined Bob's dead face smiling.

CHAPTER

After I got home, Janey gave me a message to call Rebecca Swinton. I did, and was summoned to Rebecca's house for a "Marathon Send-Off Dinner."

"I can't," I told her. "This has been a hellish day."

"Look, I know this is short notice, but I'm making an offer you can't refuse, if you get my drift."

Catching her drift, I agreed to come. I changed clothes and drove to Rebecca's house where all the UMW women were waiting for me, even Martha Rosenquist and Shirley Mitchell. Even Harriet Dunkel, wearing dark glasses that did not quite hide bruises over her left eye. The women had prepared a pot-luck supper which included a cake that had an icing likeness of the Verrazano Bridge and the words, "Good Luck, Claire" underneath. They had even had a t-shirt made up with the names of all the UMW women on the front and the legend, "Star Lake, Wisconsin United Methodist Women" on the back.

Marge Harrison pointed to her name and laughed, "That's the only way I'd ever cross a marathon finish line."

"You will wear the shirt, won't you, Claire?" Gloria Hartman asked.

"Of course, I will," I vowed. "I'll be honored to wear it. Thank you so much for giving me this party. I'm so pleased that you all cared enough to celebrate my running in the New York Marathon."

"Well, it just goes to show what I've always said," Harriet said as she removed her glasses and revealed her still puffy and bruised eye, "For the important moments in life, the only ones there for women are other women."

For a moment everyone was frozen, caught between wanting to confront Harriet with her patent hypocrisy and not wanting to make her feel more awkward than each one of us would feel with a black eye.

Harriet looked at all of us and then guffawed.

"Stop trying to pretend I don't look a mess and you all can't figure out how I got this way. Fortunately, I had two good friends, Kathy and Rebecca, who helped me even when I had been ungrateful for their help in the past. When I realized the slap and tickle I had tolerated, frankly even enjoyed, for years would escalate into life-threatening violence against me and my son, I called on Kathy and Rebecca yet again and they helped me get into a safe house until I can move us into an apartment. Consider this shiner I'm sporting a sign that I have come to my senses at last. Yes, I've left my husband. For good this time."

Harriet's bold announcement aroused a host of feelings Protestant women do not like to experience, let alone examine. To cover our ambivalence and embarrassment, we began forming small conversation groups and eating too much food. I tried not to mind that Harriet had taken the attention away from me; I told myself piously that her needs were greater than mine, but failed to erase entirely the resentment that someone else had upstaged me at the only party others had ever given me in my entire thirty-five years. Still, the support from the UMW women restored my spirits. Men might abuse us, betray us, disappoint us, but women friends remained faithful. I was thankful that my relationship with Ted had been discreet—I had only mentioned him to Rebecca and Kathy, who, no doubt had told the others about him, but still I would not have to make a public announcement of our breakup.

I taught classes on Thursday, and then prepared for departure to New York: made assignments for my classes to complete during my absence on Monday, left instructions for the girl I had hired to feed the cats on Saturday and Sunday, packed my clothes, and supervised Janey's packing. On Thursday evening, as Janey and I were eating a tuna fish sandwich dinner on trays in the living room, the telephone rang. I could not stop my heart from leaping with hope, but I pretended to be calm while Janey went to the kitchen to answer it. She did not quickly push back the swinging door and say, "It's for you;" her conversation continued, but Janey did not give me clues about the identity of her caller, for her tone was neither confiding, as it would be if she were talking with a girlfriend, nor flirtatious, as it would be if the caller were a boy.

Despite my disappointment and anger with Ted, I could not stop the yearning for what might have been. But I vowed not to be lured by a doomed vision of romantic love. If Ted had transferred his guilt for Bob's death to me, marriage was impossible. I would not let myself invent, imagine, hope for a happy resolution.

When Janey had finished her conversation, she returned to the living room, carefully not telling me with whom she had been speaking. I could not resist asking. "Who was that?"

"Ted; Ted, Junior."

Janey was teasing me, but I could not keep myself from rising to her bait.

"And what did Ted, Junior have to say to you?"

"Oh, he wished me a good time in New York and said to tell you he hoped you'd come in ahead of Grete Waitz."

"He really said that?"

"Yes."

"That was nice of him."

"Yes, he was really almost neat; I mean when you consider what he was like when we first met him. I think we've already had a good influence on him."

Janey was grinning at me, her face full of satisfaction. "Already" signalled her expectation that we would together transform Teddy into an adolescent paragon, a really neat male. I felt panic begin to overtake me. What would Janey think, say, do when I could no longer avoid telling her that we would never be part of the family we had begun to think of as our own? No matter what I might say to her, she would hold me responsible for the breach, for her loss. She would think of herself as again abandoned. Her self-esteem would suffer. She might hate me. I was beginning to hate myself.

The next day, I picked Janey up after school, drove to the LaCrosse airport, parked the car, and boarded a plane for Chicago, where we changed for a flight to New York. I put aside all concern, and shared with Janey my enthusiasm for flying, for the dinner we were served – I like eating on airplanes; indeed, almost any meal for which I do not have to plan, prepare, or clean up afterward delights me – riding in an airport limousine to Grand Central, where we took the 104

Legends of Good Women

crosstown bus, which turned north at Eighth Avenue, and took us close to our hotel, the Sheraton Centre, headquarters of the New York City Road Runners Club and the New York Marathon.

We lined up with throngs of other out-of-town and out-of-country runners to register, and when we got to our room, Janey predictably turned on the television set, and asked if she could order from room service; request denied. "Get a soft drink from a machine instead," I commanded. She asked if she could call Julie, at whose apartment on East 11th Street she would spend Saturday night; request granted.

"M-U-D-L-A-P-S," Janey chanted as she dialed Julie's number, and then almost immediately, I heard her at near-shriek, "Hi, Julie, It's me, Janey. I'm at the Sheraton." Drifts of the ensuing conversation came to me while I unpacked or was in the bathroom. I heard her refuse an invitation to go immediately to Julie's apartment on the grounds she had to "spend the first night with my mom and give her moral support," adding that it was kind of neat being at the hotel. While transferring clothes from suitcase to closet, I saw her signal a request to me to invite Julie to the hotel. Request denied with a vigorous shake of the head. While I was in the bathroom, Janey lowered her voice; the muffled conversation indicated that she was giving Julie a report on Star Lake's pool of attractive male adolescents. Janey ended the conversation with a promise to see Julie the next day at noon.

Janey would have been content to watch television, but I insisted she go downstairs with me while I checked in with the Road Runners Club and got my race number; a t-shirt, courtesy of Manufacturers Trust; and shorts, courtesy of Perrier. Janey's interest was stimulated when we went into the Sheraton exhibition hall to examine the displays of athletic clothing and gear, emblems of the luxury industry that had grown with the sport; many manufacturer's wares were displayed with a larger-than-life cardboard image of the runners who endorsed and wore the products, in exchange for money that was never called a fee, but a trust or another subtle word that preserved the fiction of the athlete's amateur status.

"They're really neat," Janey exclaimed, ogling a display of chic, very expensive insulated running suits. I anticipated her next statement.

"If you'd buy me stuff like that, I'd take up running."

"No way. If you have to be bribed, you don't have the sport in your heart."

Now it was I who was restless, eager to be out of the crowded, unventilated exhibition hall, and Janey who had to be pried away. At last I persuaded her to leave with me. We passed through the throngs of runners, most of them male, gathered in groups in the hotel halls and lobbies, exchanging personal information — even here, I saw business cards passing between hands — and accounts of other races, runners and personal bests.

"There are some really neat looking men, here, Mom."

Indeed there were. The presence of so many fit, attractive men awakened me to the opportunity to search for a man to replace the one who was exiting from my life. I might, I thought, take advantage of Janey's absence on Saturday to do some serious flirting. And then I thought, who was I kidding? Most of these men were already connected to women; most of the rest were probably self-absorbed, competitive jocks, and the handful of men with whom I might feel compatible would be impossible to identify under the circumstances. Besides, I had never learned how

Legends of Good Women

to flirt, seriously or superficially, and to search for a man was not, according to my idea of myself, in character.

Janey and I walked over to Broadway and then up to Central Park West, over to Fifth Avenue, across 53rd Street back to our hotel. It was too late to go to a film, or a play; the stores, to Janey's regret, were closed.

"Except down in the Village," she reminded me.

"Don't even suggest it. You can shop until you drop with Julie tomorrow."

I found a delicatessen on West 53rd, purchased coke and potato chips for Janey, apple juice and popcorn for me, and the two of us went back to our hotel room to watch television and go to sleep. I awakened at 6:30 the following morning, showered, dressed, went down to the lobby for a New York Times, returned, woke up Janey, and asked her to get up and have breakfast with me.

"Oh, Mom, do I have to? I want to sleep late, until it's time to go down to see Julie."

And why should she not do as she wished?

"All right," I agreed. "I'll have breakfast alone and then be on my way. Let me go through this with you just once. Where are you meeting me tomorrow?"

"At the Family Reunion Area in the park," Janey responded with closed eyes.

"How will you find the Family Reunion area?"

"The signs will direct me?" Janey squinted up at me.

"Yes, there will be signs. But here's a map the Road Runners Club provided. Take it with you."

"Okay," Janey mumbled, ready to resume serious sleeping.

"And here's one final thing."

I took out my wallet; even comatose children recognize the sound of paper money being extracted from a billfold. I put fifty dollars – two twenties and a ten – on the night table. Janey was all at once awake and sitting up in bed.

"Oh, Mom, thanks."

"Have a good time."

I kissed her; she kissed and hugged me.

"You too."

She lay back; then as I opened the door, she put her head up again.

"Good luck, Mom."

"Thanks."

I went downstairs; eating in the hotel would be too difficult, so I went outside and up Seventh Avenue. I stopped in a delicatessen for a container of coffee and a bagel with cream cheese and took the bag up to Central Park. I sat on a bench, ate my breakfast and read the New York Times while Road Runners Club staff and volunteers, along with Parks Department personnel, moved about, preparing the park for the Marathon, an event which had begun so modestly years before, when the distance, 26.2 miles, had been run in five plus turns around the park. That tedious competition had endured for five years, until George Spitz, a runner and political gadfly, suggested opening the course to all the boroughs, and eventually the New York marathon became a world class event.

I walked through the park where I had trained as a runner and run in races, gone to concerts, seen Shakespeare plays, wheeled my infant daughter in a stroller, watched her in playgrounds, had avoided an assault, sat often on benches reading countless books, been happy and sad on countless occasions during the days of my marriage and as a single mother. Tomorrow, some kind of ritual, a rite of passage was to be marked here, but I was not sure, as yet, of its meaning.

I entered the Metropolitan Museum of Art as it was just opening. Weeks before I had called Jean Berns and arranged to meet her for lunch in the Museum restaurant at noon. Two hours was more time than I wanted to spend walking around the Museum looking at art. I felt obliged to call Maurice, who lived very near the Museum, and thank him for making my invitation to the Marathon possible. I hoped he would not suggest a meeting.

"Maurice, it's Claire. How are you?"

"Well, Claire, how nice. In the Big Apple for the Marathon, are you?"

"That's right."

"And who made it possible for you to be in the Marathon, Claire?"

"You did, Maurice; that is why I'm calling. To express my appreciation."

"Not necessary, not necessary at all, Claire. Just think of me kindly from time to time. Are you getting laid, Claire?"

"I'll tell if you'll tell."

"What's to tell. My schlong might fall off from lack of use. Just wither away to a brown twig, and die. No, I'm joking, of course. I couldn't handle all the action that's available to me."

"Are you seeing anyone special?"

"Am I seeing anyone special? Well, yes, at the moment, I'm seeing a fine young woman. She manages a health food restaurant. But I'm getting cautious as I enter middle age and my hair gets thinner. My hair is getting thinner, Claire. You don't have that problem, do you. You don't fear to look at your comb after you've run it through your hair. You don't have clumps of hair clogging up your bathroom drain. But I'm not combing my hair from one side over the top of my head, in that pathetic manner of balding men. I'm bravely allowing my scalp to gleam through its ever thinning cover. But to get back to your question. Yes, I'm seeing someone who might just be the one. But you've heard that all from me before. Many times. And now let's talk about you. Are you getting laid?"

"I've met someone special, yes. And sex is fantastic, yes."

"I'm glad to hear that, Claire. Are you teaching?"

"Yes, I am. It's going well. Janey and I are happy in Wisconsin. How is your work?"

"It's fine. Claire, all goes well."

Maurice had hesitated just slightly before answering my last question. His voice was too hearty. I understood he was doubtful about his future at AT & T, but I did not want to press him. I did not want to hear bad news.

"I'm glad to hear that, Maurice. Are you excited about tomorrow?"

"Not really; I've become jaded, Claire. I used to go to all those pre-Marathon events—the beer and pasta party; I used to hang out with the jocks and brag, but tonight I'll turn in early, get up, go out to Staten Island, run my little race, hope for a decent time, and have a nice dinner afterward. You must be excited, Claire. You're a Marathon virgin."

"Yes, I'm excited. But I think I'll skip the parties, too. Janey's in New York with me. She's seeing her best friend, and I'm going to see a close friend in a little while and have lunch with her. I'd like to go to a play this evening, or a concert at Lincoln Center. And, like you, I hope for a decent time tomorrow."

"I wish us both well, Claire. Maybe we'll see each other tomorrow. Good luck to you!"

"I wish us both well, too, Maurice. Goodbye."

I felt glad I had spoken to Maurice, but relieved he had not wanted to see me. I wanted to remain where he had left us: on good but distant terms.

I went to an exhibit of Viking art, revisited my favorites, the Impressionists, and inspected the new American Wing; then I returned to the museum's grand main lobby, perched on a bench and resumed reading the New York Times, which told me that Carter was pulling even with Reagan. I wanted to believe that news was a good omen. I sensed a briskly walking figure nearby and looked up to see Jean Berns, turning to her left, the direction of the cafeteria. I ran after her, caught up with her; we squealed affectionate greetings at one another and hugged and kissed. Jean must be forty now, I calculated. Her appearance had not changed since our last meeting. She was my height and slender; her brownish red hair still had no grey in it and her face, free of makeup, was still youthful but serious. The cafeteria was, of course, filled with Saturday museum goers, and as we stood in line, we asked after and confirmed the good health of each other, Jean's husband Roger, her stepson Allen, and Janey. After plucking salads and bottled mineral water from the display on the cafeteria's pipe shelves, we stood holding our trays until two other women left a table. We sat down and studied one another.

"You look well, Claire. Are you happy?"

"On a scale of one to ten, I'd say I'm, at the moment, seven and a half."

"Is that an improvement over what you used to be?"

"Oh, yes. When I left new York, when I felt I had to leave New York, I was minus two. I'm much better now, but, until recently, I had expected that I would have gone through the top of the scale."

"What has happened?" Jean asked.

"I met someone who meant, who means a great deal to me. I thought we were going to be married, but now I don't think we will be married."

"What went wrong?"

"Possibly irreconcilable differences."

Briefly I summarized my relationship with Ted and our present situation; Jean looked away from me, considering the problem.

"Has Ted broken off your engagement? Have you broken it off?"

"No, we haven't spoken since the funeral."

"But you feel you cannot marry a man who refuses to recognize that his best friend was destructive, and he therefore certainly cannot acknowledge that his blindness was a kind of complicity in his friend's violence. He cannot bear the guilt he feels for ultimately being the instrument of his friend's death and therefore has told himself that none of this would have happened if you had not come along."

"Yes, Jean that's exactly what I feel."

"I think you're correct, but knowing you are wise doesn't ease the pain, does it?"

Tears were starting in my eyes. I shook my head no.

"Jean, after my marriage ended, I was reconciled to being single. I never thought I'd be in love again, but I was. And it was wonderful. And, Jean, I had good sex—great sex—for the first time in my life. The thought that I'll never be in love again or have great sex again—that I'll be alone and celibate for the rest of my life—is anguishing."

"But you're still young, Claire. Perhaps you'll find someone else."

"Not in Star Lake, I won't. Besides, I'm reaching the age where any available men my age will be looking for women much younger and the only men interested in me will be much older men looking for caretakers. Ted and I had a common history; he was the best man available to me and I still love him."

Tears were flowing down my cheeks.

"Claire, what if Ted sees the light and realizes he's wrong to blame you. Would you reconsider?"

"I might. Yes, I probably would. But I don't see that happening, Jean, and I refuse to hope for a change of heart in Ted."

I used my napkin to wipe my eyes and blow my nose. Jean watched me sympathetically and then took my hand in hers.

"It may seem unfair to say this to you, Claire, because I have a happy marriage. But I know that I am a rarely fortunate woman. You and I both know that bad marriages or broken marriages are the norm. We both know or know of other women like Sally who have been brutalized by their husbands, or who have been betrayed in other ways. By their busbands' infidelities, or by being told after years of marriage that their husbands want to divorce them to marry other women; by losing their homes and social position; by not getting child support. The loss of love is painful, so painful, Claire, but you're not a victim. You're in charge of your life. You're not and never will be like so many of the women we know, the walking wounded."

"You're right," I agreed, smiling at her with still dewy eyes.

Jean patted my hand and after a second asked: "How is your work going?"

"It's going well at the moment. But . . ."

"Yes?"

"Hang on. I'm confronting this for the first time, so it's coming slowly. I don't think I have a future at Fontbonne. I anticipate a contraction of the funding sources, possibly of enrollment, and I shall become a soft item once more."

"I'm sorry."

"I'm not. I shall never give my heart and soul again to an institution as I did when I was at Richmond. Moreover, I have never realized until this moment how much I dislike being part of the veneer of ecumenism at Fontbonne. Which will dissolve as soon as hard times come and we relics of the spirit of Vatican Two will become expendable."

"What will you do?"

"Make a living. Not adjunct teaching. Maybe become a technical writer at one of the industries in the area. I don't know, but I own my home, free and clear, so one source of anxiety is gone. To feed us, clothe us, educate Janey, supply recreation and the occasional luxury, I'll get income from work I'll find or create. My spirit will never be broken over that issue again. Now it's your turn. How is your work? Are you head of your department, yet?"

"As a matter of fact, yes."

"I don't believe it. Did your colleagues have visitations during the night from spirits with clanking chains? What made them act with such uncharacteristic wisdom?"

"It's a small department. Everyone else had been chair. It was my turn."

"That's not the reason."

"Perhaps they recognized finally that people who maintain principled positions have more tenacity than people who have no principles. Also, they knew I'd do the work. You know the CUNY bureaucracy. There are always committees and meetings. My colleagues knew if they elected me chair, I wouldn't embarrass them. In fact, they knew I would represent their interests well. But my becoming chair of my department is not what is really interesting, Claire."

"I can tell by that mischievous grin that you are about to share some juicy CUNY gossip."

"I am about to tell you why Brooklyn Technical Community College is going to have a woman president."

"Again, I'm incredulous. But I know this is leading to another tale of corruption."

"Actually the corruption is, improbably, elsewhere. You remember that our former president, the mink rancher, was rewarded for his incompetence by being named chancellor of community colleges in a western state, and that he was replaced at BTCC by the vice president, Brownstein, who was not only not corrupt, but also competent. Brownstein did what he could, but finally he had enough and began looking elsewhere. Earlier this year, Brownstein was named president of a college in New Jersey, and another search was under way. The mandate of the search committee was to demonstrate affirmative action, preferably to find a minority person in order to placate our student population, and indeed, such a candidate was found. He was vice president of the University of Puerto Rico; very well connected and had the paper credentials necessary to silence any challenge to his academic competency. The search committee and the university administration were delighted. They were on the eve of making the announcement, when someone happened to see an obscure newspaper item and a frantic series of telephone calls ensued. It seems the man, who owed his career to his marriage to a woman from a wealthy family, had embezzled funds from his university in order to further the career of his mistress, a hopeful beauty queen. Well, he obviously could not be named president of Brooklyn Technical Community, and another search could not be made, and since a woman is always in the number two slot in any major search, this one got lucky. And she seems like a good choice. She is from Brooklyn, is, in fact, a graduate of BTCC who went on to get other degrees, including her doctorate, teach on the college level, and most recently was an administrator at a branch of the State University upstate."

"Well, I declare. And if she is any good at all as president, she will recognize your merit and place you in a position of authority."

"Perhaps. Unfortunately, it is too late."

"What do you mean?"

"I mean I can't bear to stay on at that place any longer. I don't really think Rosamund Sherman, our new president, can make a difference, no matter how good she is. The forces of darkness are too well entrenched at Brooklyn Tech. And I'm too burned out to be an effective ally. I'm job hunting."

"You are getting out of Brooklyn Tech?"

"Out of the CUNY system, in fact."

"That's wonderful. Where are you looking?"

"Everywhere. My step-son is in college, now, so I feel free to look outside New York. If something good came up in, let us say, the midwest, or New England, I might ask Roger to go with me. His skills are portable."

"I am so pleased. The best thing I could imagine would be for us to be working together again. I wouldn't want you to come to Fontbonne; the place is not good enough for you."

"Especially if they are on the verge of jettisoning people not of their own kind."

"Well, I shall certainly be looking for opportunities for us. But, of course, I'm bound to my part of the country."

"Wisconsin is a progressive state, Claire. I'd be pleased to work there."

We left the museum and walked west through the park. Jean would leave me at Central Park West to return to her apartment on 92nd Street and I would walk down and then over to Lincoln Center to get a ticket for that evening's Philharmonic Concert. I had a heavy sweater over jeans and a shirt, but the air was cold and penetrating.

"Enjoy yourself tomorrow, Claire," Jean said as she kissed me goodbye. "Although I cannot imagine a less likely source of pleasure than the one you have chosen."

After purchasing the concert ticket, I walked down Broadway, browsed in the Barnes and Noble bookstore opposite Carnegie Hall, and then returned to the Sheraton. I walked through the exhibition hall and the lobby, looking for opportunities to talk with other women runners, not the lean, mean, fast track corp sport women, but those I recognized as other members of the I'm-doing-this-for-self-esteem sisterhood. I spoke with a Michigan farm wife, a postal clerk from Virginia, and a school secretary from Oregon, all of them married, and with sixteen children among them. The women, Ana, Sharon, and Elizabeth expressed, implicitly or openly, the belief that they had stolen time away from work, chores, and children to train for the Marathon, and felt guilty about spending money to travel to New York where they were staying, not at the Sheraton, but on pull-out couches in apartments of volunteer women runners recruited by the

Road Runners Club. I would have suggested having dinner or tea with one or all of them, but I understood only too well the pinched fearfulness the prospect of spending money would have imposed on them. Unlike the cohorts of hearty, affluent jocks, these women had to scrimp by, refusing to spend money on indulgences beyond what was absolutely necessary, feeding on snacks provided by exhibitors, and eagerly looking forward to the pasta dinner provided by one of the Marathon sponsors. I understood their plight, their state of mind, having been there myself, but I was in another state now, so I withheld an invitation to have tea or come to my room, for I felt another kind of neediness that day and did not wish to share my bounty with these strangers, even strangers who were sisters. I bought a bottle of cold beer from the delicatessen and returned to watch television in my room; at six-thirty I went out, walked up to a Greek restaurant near Carnegie Hall, remembered for decent food at reasonable prices, I had eaten in years before. Abandoning all concerns but my appetite, I ordered chicken soup, spinach pie, salad with feta cheese, rice pudding and coffee, enjoying every bit of food. I walked up to Lincoln Center and heard the Philharmonic under Zubin Mehta's casual leadership perform a suite of 16th century dances on brass instruments, which I enjoyed; something by Bartok which I did not enjoy, and the Tchaikovsky Violin Concerto with Nathan Millstein as soloist, which no one could not enjoy. I walked back to the Sheraton, stopping at a newsstand, in the manner of native New Yorkers, to buy the Sunday New York Times, and returned to my room. Unable to sleep, I read sections of the paper, discarding the classified advertising, and reserving the magazine, arts, and book review sections for Sunday. I was asleep by midnight, and awake again by six. Buses were already leaving for Staten Island, but I remained in bed for another half hour. Then I got up, showered, put on my running shorts and a long-sleeved turtleneck shirt under my running suit, and went down stairs and out once more to the delicatessen to buy coffee and rye toast. I ate in my room, read the rest of the Times, then left the hotel and took the bus to Fort Wadsworth.

Most of the more than fourteen thousand runners who would start the Marathon were already there when I arrived, and I immediately joined in the common effort to keep warm, for the day was very cold and a stiff wind was blowing. Maurice had told me that it had become a custom, just before the race began, for the runners to throw the suits they wore over their running shorts onto a pile which volunteers later collected and gave away to charity; in fact, a large number of people were outside the fence which enclosed us trying to persuade some of the especially well-clothed runners to throw suits to them. But I was not going to discard my plain grey sweat pants and hood shirt of fifty percent cotton and fifty percent polyester. I would wear them until the very last minute, and leave them on the bus so I could reclaim them when I crossed the finish line. Meanwhile, I walked around, stretched, and, mindful of a comment Maurice had once made that the smell of urine became powerful when runners were struggling to cross the finish line in less than three hours, lined up for my turn at a portable bathroom.

Recorded music came over the loudspeakers; so did messages of encouragement to us, as well as to the foreign runners in French, Spanish, German, and other languages I stopped trying to recognize. Finally, there was a movement toward the bridge; the runners were lining up. I quickly ran to the bus which had brought me to Staten Island and took off my suit. Then as I walked back to the throng of runners awaiting the signal to start, I thought of Bill Schwartz, for I was dedicating the Staten Island section of my run to him.

Suddenly, people around me were moving; we were pressed so close together, we could not actually run until we were near the top of the hill of the Verazzano Bridge. At last I felt myself beginning to race; the wind was raw, but I made myself concentrate on what I was doing. I moved into a steady, comfortable pace, and planned my path through and around the runners closest to me. It seemed to me there must be ten thousand runners ahead of me, but I refused to look back to try to count how many were behind me. As we came off the bridge and onto the road which curved into Sunset Park, I heard the cheers of the spectators, and felt the lift that Maurice had promised me. Again there was music, the Rocky theme of course, but not recorded, performed by actual musicians. Now I thought of Helen, my dear dead Helen; the Brooklyn section of my run was for her. I let her stand in my imagination with Bill, her twin in a need for love which she fed with sugar while Bill's need demanded white powder inhaled through a rolled-up dollar bill and yellow liquid injected into a vein. As I ran down Fourth Avenue, I kept my eyes on the clock tower over Atlantic Avenue, but as we passed it, we turned into neighborhoods of tree-lined streets and private houses, and I could not cite a landmark. Suddenly the cheers of spectators stopped, and I was running through silent throngs of people in dark clothing. We were in Williamsburg, among the Hassidim; I found it an eerie experience, as Maurice had said I would, to hear all at once nothing but the sound of runners' feet. Yet I could see, if I could not hear, the interest the face held for the Hassidim, for clusters of hatted and scarved women and girls extended long-sleeved arms, offering cups of water to the runners, while groups of men stood together with their hands behind their backs, nudging each other with their elbows and nodding their beaver hats in the direction of attractive, nearly naked women runners.

As we crossed the Pulaski Bridge leading to Queens, I looked at Manhattan on my left, then at the digital clock on my right; it told me that, at the halfway point, I had been running for one hour, forty-two minutes, and twenty-three seconds, or less than eight minutes a mile. I was pleased with my time, but I could not count on being able to keep the pace. I felt a V-shaped cramp starting to twinge my lower abdomen, but my legs were still comfortable and I did not feel cold. In Queens, the shortest section of the race, I thought of my digital-eyed ex-mother-in-law; I was dedicating this section of the race to erasing any hostility I still felt for her. I had enough time to tell myself let bygones be bygones before crossing the Manhattan bridge, where the wind howling over the East River pushed at us and made us feel we were standing still. One of the corporate sponsors usually supplied carpeting to cushion the runners' feet against the grill over which we were running, but because of the wind, the carpet was deemed a hazard, and so there was nothing between our feet and the river but a lattice of steel. As I came down the ramp from the bridge, I could hear the cheers from people lined up on First Avenue; Maurice had told me this was one of the high points of the race, and again I found he had prophesied accurately. Since we were in Manhattan, so near Bloomingdale's, I dedicated that portion of the race to Janey, who at that moment, might very well be shopping there.

After running straight up First Avenue, we were turning again, crossing another bridge. I was in the Bronx, where my race was for my beloved Frieda, who must, if there is a red heaven, a commie paradise, now be presiding as its queen, sitting on the left hand of Marx while doomed capitalists pleaded futilely not to be sent for eternity to coal mines and assembly lines.

We crossed the Third Avenue Bridge and were back in Manhattan again – in Harlem. This part was the true high point of the race for me because the crowds were the most exuberant I had encountered yet, and music, coming from speakers in open windows or from musicians in the streets, sent our adrenalin pumping again and our feet pounding with the beat. The jolt of energy was valuable, for after going around Mount Morris Park, we turned down Fifth Avenue in the last five mile stretch of the race, which I dedicated to Jean, Penny, and all the women of my early days in New York, even the women from the "awfices" where I had temped, to the VW's and the UMW, to all the women who helped me stay sane. I needed all their support at this stage of the race, for I was feeling cold, the v-cramp was fiery, and my legs felt heavy. I wanted to stop, but I made myself go forward as we ran along the east side of the park, turned west at Fifty-ninth Street, and entered the park near Columbus Circle, and finally, finally, hurting all the way, I neared the finish line, my eyes riveted on the digital clock overhead. I knew I would not make 3:20, but so what. I had run a decent race, worthy of the grit and determination which had carried me through training and other obstacles, and would continue to see me through obstacles and setbacks to come. At last I was over; the clock said 3:29 and change as I passed under the arch and into the hands of wonderful, encouraging volunteers, like the many others in bright yellow windbreakers, too flimsy for the cold and wind, who had supplied water and encouragement all along the route. I was led into one of the roped off lanes – the "chutes" – and walked behind and in front of other runners until we came to a seated volunteer who looked at our numbers and recorded them on a sheet. When I was out of the chute, an attractive young man wrapped me in a shiny mylar wrapper, handed me a rose and kissed my cheek. "Who won?" I asked him.

"Salazar, a Mexican, and Grete Waitz, of course."

Smiling, smiling, exhausted but joyful, I made my way through the throngs of other delighted runners who had finished the race, past the first aid station where a surprising number of runners were resting under blankets on cots. I made my way to the section where the buses were parked, found the one that had taken me to Staten Island, and went in. I put on my running suit and picked up a neat little bag of goodies which had been left for me and the other runners. It held an apple, a box of raisins, some nuts and a candy bar. I ate the apple, and went out again, moving toward the Family Reunion Area; if Janey was waiting for me there as she should be, I would reward her with the candy bar.

I saw her immediately as I entered the area, waiting for me with her birthday candle smile. If Janey and I were all the family either of us ever had, we would still be a fine family. I would have to help Janey overcome her dashed expectations and bring her to an acceptance of, and pride in, who we were. Janey would no doubt face difficult choices when she began her own search for love, and the best help I could give her would be to let her know that while love was a need, an even greater need was being in charge of one's own life. And the recognition of necessity, I could hear my red angel Frieda reminding me, was the beginning of freedom.